# The Minutes of the
# Lazarus Club

Dr Tony Pollard is an internationally renowned archaeologist and
Director of the Centre for Battlefield Archaeology at Glasgow
University. He has carried out pioneering investigations of battle-
fields in South and North Africa, South America and Europe,
and as a forensic archaeologist has worked with police forces
throughout Britain.

He has written numerous papers and articles on archaeology
and history and is co-editor of the *Journal of Conflict Archaeology*.
He was the co-presenter of two series of BBC2's archaeological
documentary *Two Men in a Trench*.

*The Minutes of the Lazarus Club* is his first novel.

# The Minutes of the Lazarus Club

TONY POLLARD

MICHAEL JOSEPH
*an imprint of*
PENGUIN BOOKS

MICHAEL JOSEPH

Published by the Penguin Group
Penguin Group (Australia)
250 Camberwell Road, Camberwell, Victoria 3124, Australia
(a division of Pearson Australia Group Pty Ltd)
Penguin Group (USA) Inc.
375 Hudson Street, New York, New York 10014, USA
Penguin Group (Canada)
90 Eglinton Avenue East, Suite 700, Toronto ON M4P 2Y3, Canada
(a division of Pearson Penguin Canada Inc.)
Penguin Books Ltd
80 Strand, London WC2R 0RL, England
Penguin Ireland
25 St Stephen's Green, Dublin 2, Ireland
(a division of Penguin Books Ltd)
Penguin Books India Pvt Ltd
11 Community Centre, Panchsheel Park, New Delhi – 110 017, India
Penguin Books (NZ) Ltd,
67 Apollo Drive, Rosedale, North Shore 0632, New Zealand
(a division of Pearson New Zealand Ltd)
Penguin Books (South Africa) (Pty) Ltd
24 Sturdee Avenue, Rosebank, Johannesburg 2196, South Africa

Penguin Books Ltd, Registered Offices: 80 Strand, London, WC2R 0RL, England

First published 2008
This edition published by Penguin Group (Australia), 2008

1 3 5 7 9 10 8 6 4 2

Copyright © Tony Pollard, 2008

The moral right of the author has been asserted

Typeset by Rowland Phototypesetting Ltd, Bury St Edmunds, Suffolk
Printed and bound in Australia by McPherson's Printing Group, Maryborough, Victoria

ISBN: 978-0718-15447-9

penguin.com.au

# Prologue

The waterman whistled as he pulled on the oars, his small craft carrying him slowly but steadily downstream along Limehouse Reach. He'd set out from the mouth of the Limehouse Basin and was heading for Greenwich, across the river from the southern tip of the Isle of Dogs. It was his pitch, and it took in almost three miles of river. There were other watermen and other pitches but this was his and over the years he had come to know every eddy, backwash and mudflat and had long regarded it as home.

Pausing for a moment, he tugged down the peak of his cap against a shower of rain which for a short while turned the brown surface of the water into a sheet of hammered copper. Around his feet were collected all manner of things: pieces of timber, lengths of rope, cork fenders, bottles, various sodden items of clothing and even a small chair. He didn't care who they once belonged to; they were his now. He was employed by the bailiff to clear the river of obstacles to navigation but any stray object floating in the water within the bounds of his beat was legally his property once lifted aboard. All very official it was: you only needed to look at his smart blue uniform to see that.

He had been out since dawn and by now had covered well over half the beat – the ache in his arms and the twinge from his back told him that much. It had been an average day thus far but he was pleased with the chair: the wife could put it by the fire. The boat hugged the eastern side of the channel, where it was out of the way of the heavy traffic but also close to where most of the stuff drifting downstream would naturally be drawn by the current. At low tide much of the floating windfall would be left stranded on the flats, where it would fall prey to the gangs of mudlarks working both sides of the river. There was no such worry now, though, as the tide was at its fullest.

Moored boats were always a good place – sometimes three or

four would be tied together, side by side. These tethered flotillas served as traps for anything coming into their path and so the waterman would paddle around them and snag whatever was bobbing against the hulls or caught in the ropes. It was to such a spot that he was pulling now, just on the edge of the shipyard where Brunel's great ship was being built, side on to the river. The yard also yielded more than its share of treasures – planks of timber, paint pots and lengths of heavy rope. The boats, a skiff and a pair of barges, were moored just fifty yards or so downriver from the yard and so provided the perfect opportunity for a good haul.

Favouring one oar over the other, the waterman manœuvred the boat to the stern of the stationary vessels and with the long-poled boat hook in hand began to look for floating objects. Wedged between the barge in the middle and the skiff was a length of broken ladder, just long enough, he judged, to be of use again. After some difficulty in pulling it free he stowed it with the rest of the stuff.

It was then he heard the noise, a scuffing and scratching inter-spersed with the odd sharp croak. Using the hook against the stern of the middle vessel, he nudged the small boat a little closer into shore. That was when he saw them.

Two scabrous-looking gulls were perched on something floating in the river but seemingly fastened to the lee board of the shoreward barge. They were squabbling over whatever it was the larger of the two was jealously clutching in its beak. It took the waterman a moment or two to realize that the birds were perched on the back of a dead body, the head having become wedged between the lee board and the hull. The corpse was white as a ghost and entirely naked. With its slender limbs and long hair spread out on the water like a dark weed it could only be a woman – that or a child.

Although he found the nudity distasteful, as he did the vision of two birds fighting over a freshly plucked eyeball, coming across a body in the river caused him little upset. He had, after all, encoun-tered dozens of bodies in his time, many of them suicides who had thrown themselves off one of the bridges further upstream. Quite often they were sucked under almost immediately by the current and dragged downstream, to surface again only once they reached his beat. He had no idea how many of them remained submerged and made it all the way down the river to be expelled into the open sea beyond.

Clearing the river of dead bodies, or 'floaters', as they were known in the trade, was all part of his job as a waterman. Indeed, he was paid a small bonus for every corpse he fished from the water and delivered back to the land.

After edging the boat as far between the two barges as the gap would allow, he stood in the prow and used the boat hook to dislodge the birds, forcing them to continue their fight over the morsel elsewhere. Then he used it to lever back the board just enough to allow the corpse to slip free. As it came away the body rolled over on to its back. It was then that the stench hit him.

The black funk came straight from the charnelhouse and caused him to retch and his eyes to water. He knew from past experience that the sickly-sour smell of a human corpse is just as much a taste as it is a smell, but this was the worst he had ever experienced. This one must have been under for quite some time – retting like flax in the murky depths. When his eyes recovered he was horrified to see a further reason for the noisome stench. Where the chest had once been there was now a gaping chasm, two folds of ragged flesh lying open on either side of it like the pages of a book no one would ever care to read. Catching the hook under one of the armpits, he pulled the fleshy mass towards him, taking care to turn away when he needed to take a breath. What kind of accident could have caused that wound?

Using one of the rags in the bottom of the boat to cover his hand, he took hold of an arm slippery with corruption and pulled the corpse most of the way up the side of the boat before thinking better of it and letting it drop back into the water. There was no way he was going to have that thing on board. Instead he took one of the lengths of rope and looped it around a wrist before securing the other end to the stern.

Perhaps she had come into contact with a ship's paddle wheel or one of the new-fangled screws? They'd make a mess of you all right. At times you could barely move out on the water, what with so much traffic plying its way backward and forward from the Pool of London.

He had tried not to look too hard but now, with her so close, he couldn't help himself. There was enough of the face left to tell it was a woman and that that was no accidental injury. She'd been carved, deliberately cut open – slit from stem to stern. He'd seen murder before but nothing this bad.

Peering closer, he saw something dark glistening inside, something stirring in the cavity of her chest. Whatever it was began to thrash, sending out spurts of water. Then it sprang forth, uncoiling its sleek black body and launching itself at the waterman. He let out a yell and fell backwards, landing in the bottom of the boat alongside the dreadful thrashing form of the eel. Recovering himself, he tried to get a hold of the writhing creature, but it slipped away and wriggled between the objects in the hull. Eventually he managed to trap it in a shirt and, after wrapping it as best he could, he threw the garment and the eel as far away from the boat as possible. Within an instant the shirt had disappeared beneath the surface as the beast thrashed its way downward, for a while the best-dressed fish in the river.

Returning his attentions to the corpse, he checked his knots and, not being able to resist one last look, ascertained that there had been space for the eel in the poor woman's chest because her organs – heart, lungs, everything – were missing. Surely to God the eel hadn't eaten them? He thought he was going to be sick.

Pulling himself together, he took a seat and, after pushing away, replaced the oars in their locks. Although the yard was close he thought it better to land his gruesome catch on a quieter part of the shore and so he headed downriver awhile, the body bobbing along behind. As he sat with his face to the stern he had no option but to watch as the pale form of the woman dipped beneath the water with each stroke, only to resurface a moment later. At times the free arm flexed and it looked as though she were swimming, trying to catch up with the boat.

He rowed faster.

# I

Hard used, the cadaver was reduced to little more than a tattered shell and would last no longer than one more dissection. Apart from the brain, which I would remove tomorrow, all of the internal organs had been decanted into buckets sitting on the sawdust-covered floor. In one of them was the heart, along with the liver, kidneys and lungs, while in the other coiled entrails glistened like so many freshly caught fish.

William fetched a bowl of warm water and took away the buckets while I washed the gore from my hands. The boisterous press of students had departed with its usual rapidity, and believing myself to be alone, it came as a surprise to hear a bench creak as a weight shifted upon it. I looked up to catch sight of someone moving in the gloom of the gallery. Reaching the aisle, he walked down the steps towards me – a short man, shoulders hunched beneath a head perhaps too heavy for them to bear.

He stepped into the winter sunlight shafting down through the skylight. His face was round and pale, with eyes set back in caves of tired flesh. Whiskered jowls sank below the rim of his collar and only the well-defined lines of his lips, which were clamped tightly around the stub of a cigar, suggested good looks only recently worn away. His clothes were well cut but crumpled, as though he had given up taking care of his appearance. He stopped beside the operating table and looked for some moments into the yellow face of the cadaver. This man was clearly no medical student, but nonetheless there was something familiar about him.

'It comes to us all,' I said, wiping my instruments clean before packing them away. The stranger continued to study the cadaver, his eyes travelling down the length of the gaping torso.

'Death perhaps, but surely not this,' he said, without removing the cigar from his mouth nor his gaze from the corpse.

'I think you can rest assured of that, sir. This poor soul came from the workhouse, but may as well have come from a prison.'

He looked at me and pulled out the cigar. 'So he wasn't robbed from his grave then? I thought that was how you fellows got hold of your bodies.'

This made me smile. 'You have been reading too many Penny-bloods, my friend. That sordid trade came to a stop over twenty years ago, with the passing of the Anatomy Act. Now we get our subjects legally from the hospitals and the poorhouses – generally from among those who can't afford funerals. There is no shortage of them, I'm afraid.'

I took off my surgeon's coat and hung it on a peg before trying to extract an introduction from him. 'I don't recall seeing you here before. You're not one of my students, are you?'

The cigar had long before burnt out and he looked for a suitable receptacle in which to deposit the well-chewed stump. For a moment I feared the open trough of the cadaver's torso had been selected, but to my relief he elected to drop it into the pocket of his frock coat. 'Oh no,' he replied, eyes still fixed on the corpse. 'I think I'm a little long in the tooth to be taking up a new profession. I've only just mastered my own and think I'll stick with it, if you don't mind.' Looking up, he held out his hand. 'Dr Phillips, let me introduce myself. Brunel's the name.'

'Isambard Kingdom Brunel?' I asked, now realizing why he appeared familiar to me. The man and his engineering exploits were well known, and his portrait often accompanied articles dedicated to one or other of his creations.

His handshake displayed a strength belied by his rather unhealthy appearance. He looked back at the cadaver. 'Yes. The engineer.'

'The whole of London is talking about your ship. When will she be launched?'

'I would rather not discuss her at the moment, if you don't mind, sir,' he snapped. 'That ship has become the bane of my life.'

His sharp response should perhaps have come as no surprise, as barely a week of 1857 had gone by without the newspapers revelling in the difficulties related to the ship's construction, and now that she was finally ready to be launched they took pleasure in predicting that Brunel would never get her into the water. She was, after all, by far the largest ship ever built.

A change of tack was required. 'What brings you to St Thomas's, sir? I am not accustomed to men of such reputation as yourself sitting in on my lectures.'

Brunel's expression warmed a little. 'My apologies for being brusque with you, doctor. The past few months have been a very stressful time. And as for my presence here, they say you are one of the finest surgeons in London. I hope it was not improper of me to invite myself along?'

'You flatter me, sir, but no, not at all, I am delighted you found my little performance worth your time.'

He didn't seem to be listening, for the cadaver had once again captured his attention, and so I called for William to remove the cause of his distraction.

'I have been around machines for far too long, doctor,' he said with a touch of regret. 'I have devoted my entire life to things mechanical. I thought it was time to learn something about the machine that I am. I hope to God, though, when the boilers go out they don't break me down for scrap, not like that poor wretch.'

There was a loud crash as William slammed the trolley into the side of the door. I suspected he had been drinking spirits in the storeroom again.

'William, be careful!' I shouted, not wishing to cause my visitor any more upset over the treatment of the cadaver. As a matter of course I wouldn't give two hoots. The dead are dead and that's it. They don't care if you put them in a hole, chop them up or feed them to a fire. At St Thomas's, however, the corpse was never left to such a wasteful end. After they had been worked to the bone William would take what remained down into the cellar and boil them up in a vat, removing any last remnants of flesh. The bones were then taken to the articulator, who, after purchasing them for a small fee, which William was always careful to share with me, wired them back together and sold the skeletons on to students as anatomical specimens.

I went to put on my overcoat while Brunel pulled on a strap drawn tightly across his chest to reveal a leather satchel from behind his back. Unshackling a buckle, he exposed the tips of a dozen or so fresh smokes sitting side by side in, what had to be the biggest cigar case I had ever seen; Brunel was clearly a man who didn't do things by halves. He pulled one out and rolled it gently between his lips, moistening the end before biting it off and spitting it on to the floor. As he played a match over the rolled leaf it gave off thick clouds of smoke and a pungent aroma which even the sickly haze of preserving spirit could not mask. One puff was enough to improve Brunel's humour.

'That was the third of your lectures I have attended, doctor. I have found them fascinating, most fascinating. But one thing has been puzzling me. I have been addressing you as doctor, just as I have heard others call you, but is it not usually the case that you surgeons refer to yourselves as mister?'

'Well spotted, sir. There has long been a fashion for surgeons to be misters rather than doctors; it goes back to our medieval origins as barbers, when razors were used to cut more than beards. But in addition to my training to be a surgeon I also earned a doctorate in philosophy for my research, so people tend to use my academic title. Anyway, my patients seem happier believing they are being treated by a doctor rather than a plain old mister.'

Brunel smiled. 'Research, eh? Well, *doctor*, that brings me to my next enquiry. I was hoping that you and I could talk further on aspects of an anatomical nature.'

The prospect was an intriguing one, but this was not a good time. 'Sir, it would be a pleasure to talk further with you and share whatever knowledge I have, but I am afraid I have commitments in the hospital for the rest of the day.'

Brunel walked back to the bench on which he had been seated and picked up a tall stove-pipe hat. Pressing it on to his head, and in so doing adding at least a foot to his height, he turned back to me. 'No matter. I have an appointment with a pack of scoundrels at the yard anyway. Perhaps I could call on you at a time more convenient to both of us?'

'Very well,' I replied, pushing my hand free of my coatsleeve just in time to shake his once again.

With that he was gone, leaving behind him a cloud of cigar smoke which had still to disperse by the time I made my own departure several minutes later.

There is always something special about making the first incision in a fresh cadaver, breaking the skin which, until my intervention, has served to hold inside the wonderful mechanism which is man. But today William seemed set on taking the shine off the occasion.

'That may be the last for a while, sir,' he said, mournfully surveying the corpse he had just delivered to the table.

'What do you mean, the last? You sound like a poulterer running short of birds at Christmas.'

'There may be one or two, but it's the typhus – the city fathers 'ave suspended all supplies until it passes. They're burnin' the stiffs – I mean corpses – that would normally be comin' our way.'

Of course I was aware of the outbreak, but I had not yet considered it a threat to our supply of cadavers. Under normal conditions the hospital created not far off enough corpses to feed its own teaching needs and, as I had explained to Brunel, any shortfall was made up by sources such as the workhouses and jails, but an outbreak of typhus or cholera anywhere in the city meant that all fresh corpses were buried in quicklime or burned on communal pyres.

'Then we will have to hope for a swift end to the outbreak, won't we?'

William seemed doubtful. 'My sister says she's thinkin' of movin' back to the country.'

'I can't blame her, William. What do we expect when the Thames itself is nothing but an open sewer? From what I hear, though, the source is Newgate Prison, and not for the first time.' It was well known that the inmates were kept in such dreadfully cramped conditions that any contagion spread like wildfire and inevitably escaped into the wider population.

'Give me an escaped murderer over pestilence any day of the week,' commented William.

'We must be extra vigilant. Break out the brushes and keep scrubbing. Just how bad is the situation?'

'Pretty grim, I think. Twenty or so dead. But no sign yet on our own doorstep.'

'No, William, not the typhus, the cadavers. How many do we have left?'

'Oh, can't tell you that just now. I need to do a stocktake.'

I looked at my watch. 'Well, there's no time like the present. We still have half an hour before the students arrive. Let's go down to the cellar.'

William was apt to preside over the cellar like some goblin prince of the underworld, and he was initially a little put out by my insisting that I accompany him into its depths.

'You need to be careful,' he warned. 'It can get a little close down 'ere, what with the fumes an' all.'

In the low, vaulted chamber, the walls of which were slicked with moisture, the light was poor, what illumination there was provided by a series of vents which opened out at street level. The footsteps of pedestrians could be heard as they passed by on the pavement – they surely would quicken their pace if they had any inkling of the use to which the space beneath their feet was being put.

In one corner of the brick-floored room was a large iron cauldron perched upon an inert hearth with a flue above it. It was here that William boiled down the remains of cadavers once I had no further use for them in the theatre, removing all trace of flesh and leaving nothing but the bones. In the centre of the room was a huge wooden vat, its barrel-like staves bound tightly by iron hoops and surrounded on the outside by a timber walkway at the top of a short flight of steps. William took a long pole with a hook on the end from a rack on the wall and, once on the walkway, began to stir the dark fluid within.

'Here, give me that,' I said, eager to assess the situation for myself, but before I could take a hold of the thing the vinegar-like bite of the preserving spirit threatened to knock me off my feet and I let out a choking sound.

'You may want to tie your 'ankerchief round yer mouth, doc. Like I said, it's pretty strong stuff at this volume, and you don't want to be fallin' in there.'

I did as he suggested. 'Doesn't it get to you?'

'Not any more, sir. Guess I've been pickling myself from the inside for long enough not to be fussed.'

I laughed, only to start coughing again.

'Steady, sir. Sure you don't want me to do that?'

I shook my head and swept the pole through the fluid. It continued unhindered from one side of the vat to the other. Drawing out the hook, I changed position on the walkway before trying again. This time its passage was obstructed, and with a firmer hold on the shaft I pulled the hook towards me. First an outstretched arm and then the head and torso of a cadaver broke the surface. It was a male of indeterminate age and, like a friend of William's, his mouth was set open as though to drink in the liquid in which he floated. Pulling the corpse to the side of the vat before allowing it to sink again, I moved once more and made another sweep. Nothing.

'You were right, William. This soup is thin, far too thin.'

Our faces shrank and then expanded in the surfaces of the large glass jars lining the shelves. Suspended in the clear preserving fluid were the various members of the anatomy collection; body parts now become artefacts in this museum of life made possible only through death. There were organs, limbs, almost-entire bodies, some normal, some displaying disease, others deformed. Flesh was discoloured in preservation, everything appeared strangely unreal in this freak-show cum hall of mirrors I knew as a workplace.

Brunel peered into the jars. Moving from one to the next, he stared, fascinated. I pulled one down and placed it on the table. A heart bobbed in the unsettled fluid. We had talked for most of the afternoon, and it was by now very clear that his interest in human anatomy centred around this organ in particular. He rested a finger against the glass as the liquid stilled. The heart turned gently before coming to rest. I pointed to the various parts, rotating the jar on the table as I spoke their names and explained their various functions.

I had not proceeded far when William returned from the preparation room to inform me that my instructions had been carried out. I told him to bring the subject to us and returned to my tutorial, explaining to Brunel the role of the severed vessels protruding from the organ. My guest stifled a query as William appeared again, this time carrying a wooden board with a freshly removed heart perched upon it. He put the board on the table next to the jar and returned to his duties.

I pushed the heart, which just happened to be our last fresh specimen, around the board with the blade of a scalpel. This allowed me to clarify points of detail which may have been less than clear due to the incarceration of the previous example. After pointing out the pulmonary veins, the aorta and vena cava, I turned the heart and moved on to the ventricle and the heart bulb. Brunel asked one question after another, his incisive comments and queries forcing me to dust off an expertise which had lain almost dormant since completing a programme of detailed research some years before. It felt good to be stretched, so much so that I determined to spice up the perhaps rather stale heart and lungs lecture I regularly gave to my own students. But before then, of course, I would need to acquire fresh specimens and in the midst of the current typhus epidemic that was not going to be easy.

Once the discussion of the heart's outer appearance had been concluded to Brunel's apparent satisfaction, I began to dissect, bringing the blade down on the surface at a point just to the front of the vena cava superior. For an instant the muscle refused to give, the resilient tissue springing under the blade. Then it went, and with a snap the scalpel began its work, dividing the sinews and cleaving its way through the outer wall of the heart. I cut down and back, opening a deep incision across the ventricular and auricular margins. Rotating the heart, I continued round with a sawing motion, parting the edges with my fingers. Then it was done, and the organ fell apart, separated into two slightly unequal parts.

With the internal parts exposed we studied the chambers, the walls and the entrances and exits through which the blood passed. In order to assist my demonstration I poked a brush bristle through one opening and indicated to my student where it would reappear in another. I explained that the right side, with auricle to the top and ventricle below, was the venous side, where dark blood drained of its life-giving properties arrives first, from the upper part of the body via the vena cava superior and from the lower via the minor, into the auricle and then the ventricle, after circulating around the body. From there, I went on, it is fed through the pulmonary artery into the lungs. After being arterialized the refreshed blood then returns to the left side of the heart via the pulmonary veins, pumping into the left auricle before being drawn into the attendant left ventricle. Leaving the heart through the aorta, the blood is then recirculated into the body through the arteries.

Brunel seemed intent on fully understanding the theory of the pumping action. He was fascinated by the tricuspid and coronary valves, the position of muscle walls at various points in the process being of special interest to him. All the while he made sketches in a notebook, furiously scribbling with the stub of a well-worn pencil.

Aware of time drawing on, I took an ostentatious look at my watch. But Brunel was not a man to take a hint. Question followed question until finally I had to be rather abrupt and insist that we brought the session to an end as I was by now late for my rounds. He at last demurred but asked if he could stay behind for a while and take some measurements. I left him working under the blind gaze of a pair of eyes as they floated, one above the other, in a jar beside the door. In life they had been a startling blue but now they were a dull grey.

Now, rushing from bed to bed, I tried to concentrate on the task in hand but my thoughts constantly returned to the engineer and the ease with which he had grasped details I had always considered the domain of my own profession.

Upon returning to the collection room in the late evening, the heart was still on the table and it was obvious that Brunel had made several further incisions. Next to it lay an unsmoked cigar and a note scribbled on a page torn from his notebook:

Dr Phillips,

The day has proven most informative. My thanks to you for your kind indulgence of an engineer's whims. Another engineer, by the name of Leonardo da Vinci, once wrote: 'How could you describe the heart in words without filling a book?' Such is your eloquence on the matter that I believe you could. I look forward to renewing our association in the near future.

I. K. Brunel

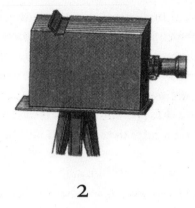

## 2

Examining a patient's stool is not the most edifying way to start the day, especially when the task is interrupted by the unmistakable voice of the hospital superintendent, Sir Benjamin Brodie, assailing one from the rear. 'Ah, Dr Phillips,' he announced, with all the satisfaction of a hunter having run his prey to ground, 'I thought we might have a word in my office at some point today.'

I turned around, only just keeping control of the contents of the bedpan, and addressed the gaunt, grey-haired man now standing before me. 'Yes, Sir Benjamin. When would suit?' I should have left it there but foolishly let my tongue run on. 'I have a relatively easy afternoon ahead of me.'

'Well, we'll see about that,' replied Sir Benjamin ominously; the old goat never missed a trick. 'Four o'clock then.' And with that he was off, stalking down the ward with Mumrill, his odious assistant, in tow.

'Shit,' I muttered under my breath, passing the pan to the nurse. She looked inside and nodded, no doubt in appreciation of my powers of observation. The stool was free of blood but discontinuous, its edges jagged and rusticated as though it had suffered violence inside its host, which was to be expected of a turd produced in a bowel so recently the subject of an operation. I smiled reassuringly at the patient, who seemed a little bemused at my interest. 'Very good,' I said. 'Nothing to worry about there.'

Having finished on the ward, I made for the sanctuary of my office, still regretting my ill-conceived comment about an easy afternoon. If there was one thing that made Sir Benjamin happy it was to see his staff kept busy. Lord knows what extra duties were about to come my way.

'What are you doing here?' I asked, somewhat irritated to find Brunel sitting behind my desk and flicking through my case notes – famous engineer or no, those records were confidential.

'Good, you're here at last,' he chimed, casually casting aside the sheet of paper in his hand. 'You have some very sick people on your hands.'

I tidied up the papers and dropped them into the drawer of a cabinet next to the desk. 'You did see the word "hospital" written over the front door as you came in?'

My ill-tempered sarcasm fell flat on his thick skin. 'Grab your hat and coat. We're leaving,' he sparked, jumping to his feet.

Surely, I thought, this was not the same morose fellow who had introduced himself in the operating theatre a couple of weeks or so before. But, despite his enthusiasm, the proposal was out of the question. 'Impossible!' I insisted. 'I'm on duty. Sir Benjamin will have my guts for garters if I leave the premises.'

The engineer cocked his head and looked at me as though I were an idiot. 'Do you or do you not want to see history being made?'

I closed the cabinet drawer. 'You're going to launch the ship?'

'Yes. Now get a move on.'

Against all better judgement I followed him out into the hall, pulling on my coat as I went but returning briefly to pick up my medical bag.

The prospect of witnessing the monumental feat of pushing the ship into the water quickly overwhelmed all sense of responsibility. I had memorized its weight of 22,000 tons from the newspapers. That made it the heaviest object ever to be moved by man – if he managed to move it, of course. According to the papers, very few people, including fellow engineers, believed that such an incredible feat was possible.

Irresistible as the attraction was, I took my Hippocratic oath seriously enough not to leave my patients at risk. I had no rounds to make and had planned to spend the rest of the day, until my evening duties, on tiresome paperwork. Nonetheless, just to make sure my absence was known to someone I reported to the senior physician and told him I had been called to attend an unexpected emergency, little realizing how prophetic this fabricated excuse would later prove.

Less anxious now, I departed with Brunel, satisfied that as long as I returned in time for our meeting there was very little chance of my absence coming to the attention of Sir Benjamin.

As we drove towards the docks I sat in the grip of an excitement that had lain dormant since the last time I played truant from school.

Brunel's carriage was like no other I had seen before and contained a folding table and bed. 'It was my office and accommodation while I worked on the Great Western Railway,' he explained as we trundled along.

'But an office built for speed,' I said, having taken note of the graceful lines and sleek four-horse team.

My comment serving as a spur, the engineer checked his watch. 'The navvies called her the flying hearse, and we might as well be on our way to a funeral for all the progress we are making. Samuel, pick up the pace,' he yelled, 'at this rate I'll miss my own ship's launch.'

The driver replied through a small hatch in the roof. 'Sorry, sir, the traffic's dreadful.'

Putting my head out of the window, I looked ahead to see an abnormal number of cabs, wagons and omnibuses – a logjam of humanity threatening to choke the road before us. The closer we got to the river, the worse the congestion became, the carriage by now moving in stomach-churning stops and starts.

Brunel's patience had run out. 'Samuel, we're going ahead on foot. Follow us when this madness clears.'

We trotted along the pavement, but by now it was almost as choked with pedestrians as the road was with vehicles. All of them were walking in the same direction, towards the river. Then the truth of the situation dawned on Brunel. 'Look at this, Phillips! I don't believe it. Those dolts from the company have broken the news about the launch. The fools have turned today into a circus!'

By now we were barging our way through the dockyard gates, and Brunel almost exploded when a man wearing a steward's armband asked him for his ticket. 'Ticket, ticket! I have a ship to launch! Now let us through and for God's sake close those gates.'

The steward, suitably admonished, waved us by, but I saw no sign of the gates closing behind us and people continued to pour through.

'I'll have somebody's head for this, mark me, Phillips,' stormed Brunel.

People were everywhere. A sea of top hats and ladies' bonnets lapped around the foot of a platform near the ship's prow. Crowds swarmed around two huge wooden drums at either end of the ship. These huge bobbins were wound with chains, the links of which were twice the size of a man's head. Having lost all that remained of his patience, Brunel ran around like a dog chasing rats in a barn, yelling and waving his arms wildly as he tried to clear the spectators away from the ship.

Chaos reigned, but it would have taken a riot of national proportion to distract me from the spectacle of the ship, the hull of which rose above the pandemonium like a cliff of riveted iron. The bow traced a graceful curve against the skyline while at the stern the suspended blades of the huge propeller threatened movement. The distance between the two extremities, I was sure, would be measurable as a respectable cab fare. Five funnels towered above the straight line of the deck, where a few tiny human silhouettes could be seen moving about.

The behemoth, which in his lighter moments Brunel referred to as his 'great babe', sat side on to the river. Her hull was supported by latticed cradles resting on a raft of rails which ran down the gentle slope of the yard and into the dark water. Halfway along the red-and-black-painted hull was a timber tower, rising up like a medieval siege engine resting against a castle wall, inside of which a set of stairs zigzagged from the ground up to the deck so high above. Alongside it the iron-framed skeleton of one of the ship's paddle wheels sat as motionless as an off-duty carnival roundabout. The noise of the crowd's excited chatter competed against the tuneless cacophony produced by a brass band much in need of practice. As if that weren't bad enough, many people, including most of the musicians, appeared to be drunk.

With the help of stewards, his assistants and a small army of yard employees Brunel eventually managed to pull the crowd back from the ship and the launching equipment. He was still angry and as I walked towards him was giving someone a piece of his mind. 'Idiots, what the hell do you think you're doing? You've turned this into a bloody sideshow. I made it clear to the board of directors last week that silence would be essential during the launch, but then you go behind my back and sell damn tickets. How are the men going to hear my orders over the racket made by a drunken, rowdy mob! My God, there will be hell to pay.'

Brunel finished his tirade and the well-dressed man sloped off with a flea, or rather a swarm of fleas, in his ear.

To my relief his anger subsided when he caught sight of me again. 'What do you think of her then?' he asked as I drew up to him.

'She's beautiful, Mr Brunel. And her size! None of her pictures does her justice. I'm surprised I couldn't see her from the hospital!'

'There are those who say she is nothing more than my ego cast in iron, but they forget there is no coal in Australia. As I am tired of saying, if she is to get there and return home without once re-coaling, then she must be big enough to carry enough fuel for the entire voyage.' He paused for a moment and took a thoughtful draw on his cigar. 'You know, Phillips, there are times when I think I have built nothing more than a glorified coal bunker.'

The gates had at last been closed, but this only prompted men and boys to climb up on them to secure a view of the proceedings. Likewise, they were using the yard wall as a grandstand, with so many sitting along its top that I feared collapse was a real possibility. Another man approached and I waited for Brunel to deal out another tongue-lashing. Luckily for him, though, he had nothing to do with the company that owned the ship but was a photographer eager to have Brunel pose for a portrait. Brunel agreed, and the grateful photographer directed us to the nearest of the chain-decked drums, which now it was clear of people would provide a suitable backdrop.

Before we reached our destination Brunel was accosted by yet another individual, this time a flustered-looking man carrying a sheaf of papers. 'Mr Brunel, sir, could I ask you for your preference for the ship's name? The ceremony is due to start within the next half-hour.'

Brunel pondered the question for the slightest of moments. Then he replied, 'You can go and call her the Tom Thumb for all I care.'

The company man referred to one of his sheets of paper. 'But Mr Brunel, that name doesn't appear to be on the list.'

Brunel let out a mocking laugh. 'Is that so!'

'Shall I remind you of the approved names, sir?'

'No, don't trouble yourself. Take your list to your superiors and tell them I don't give a damn what they call the ship.'

The camera stood on a spindly wooden tripod and was covered by a black sheet. It looked such a fragile little thing when compared with the gargantuan pieces of timber and paraphernalia surrounding it. The photographer gently manœuvred Brunel into the desired position, the drum's massive chain links behind him. 'Come on, Phillips, stand beside me and enjoy immortality.'

As I wasn't supposed to be there in the first place, the last thing I wanted was proof of my presence. And so, much I am sure to the photographer's relief, I declined the invitation and stepped behind the camera to watch the picture being made. Despite the photographer's earlier efforts to pose his subject, Mr Brunel adopted the most casual of stances, looking away from the camera with hands in trouser pockets and cigar wedged into the corner of his mouth. I wondered whether the photograph would take in his legs beneath the knee, as his trouser bottoms and shoes were spattered with mud after his frantic crowd-herding escapade – if it did, then a more fitting expression of the man's dynamism I could not imagine.

'Stand perfectly still please, Mr Brunel,' requested the photographer, his head shrouded beneath the black sheet. Removing the cap from the lens, he began to count. When he reached eight the cap was replaced and he stepped from under the shroud, thanking the engineer for his cooperation. In return Brunel asked for copies to be sent to his office.

I checked my watch. It was after one.

'When are you going to launch?' I asked. 'I have to be back at the hospital by four o'clock.'

'Don't worry, she'll be in the water long before then,' said Brunel, looking up at the hull, his tight jaw betraying a hint of self-doubt.

The prospect of being late for my appointment with Sir Benjamin or, God forbid, not arriving at all, was not one to be relished, but nevertheless my inquisitiveness again got the better of me. 'How does it work?'

'What?' he replied, clearly distracted.

'The launch, how does it work?'

He pointed towards the interlaced timber beams wedged under the curve of the keel. 'Hydraulic rams give her a push, and then steam winches pull her down the rails, via chains sheafed on barges anchored in the river.'

'Why are you launching her sideways? Don't most of them go in bow first?'

'They do, but she's nearly 700 feet long, and the river at this point isn't much wider. I set out to build a ship, Phillips, not a bridge. And this,' he went on, slapping the wooden cylinder around which the chain was wound, 'is a checking drum. There's another one near the stern. They will control the descent of the bow and stern once the ship starts to move down the rails. There are also brakes on the cradles themselves. The drum plays out the chain attached to the hull until we need to stop her. Then we press down on the levers' – he gestured towards a pair of long shafts extending from the base of the drum – 'and wait for the other end to catch up and then let her go again.'

'Checks and balances,' I remarked.

'Exactly. And all controlled by yours truly from up there.' He half turned and pointed at a precarious-looking rostrum way up above our heads. It extended from the side of the deck like an unfinished footbridge. It was positioned exactly halfway along the ship's length, providing a clear view of both drums and allowing him to judge the relative movements of bow and stern. Rather him than me, I thought.

'What if she hits the water stern or bow first?' I asked, intrigued by the great care to be taken in keeping her on a parallel course.

'If we allow one end to get too far out of kilter,' he replied, using his forearm to demonstrate the shift in movement, 'she won't get to the water. With the weight unevenly distributed like that she'll stick and we'll be lucky to get her moving again.' The prospect was a daunting one, and I couldn't help but admire his ability to operate under such extreme pressure. 'But before we can get started we've got to get the damned naming ceremony out of the way. Come on.'

We made our way to the raised platform near the bow. At the top of the steps an uncomfortable-looking Brunel was greeted by a flurry of handshakes from the men gathered there and with curtsies from the excitable females. Duty done, he introduced me to a tall, heavy-set gentleman with a red chinstrap beard. 'Dr Phillips, this is Mr John Scott Russell, my partner in this enterprise.'

'He means that I built the ship he designed – this is my yard,' said the big Scotsman, somewhat proprietorially.

'Quite an operation you have here, Mr Russell.'

'Let us hope so, doctor,' he said, before turning his attention to Brunel. 'I trust you find everything in order?' The engineer glowered. 'This,' said Russell, gesturing to the crowd in the yard, 'had nothing to do with me. You know how the company views our finances – anything to make an extra shilling or two.'

'We will discuss shillings later, Mr Russell. In the meantime, let us hope that these . . . these people don't get in the way of our task.'

Russell nodded and stepped off the platform.

The steward in charge called us to order and handed a bottle of champagne attached to a cord to a young lady, who Brunel informed me was the daughter of one of the company directors. There was a moment of hesitation before the man with the list of ship's names whispered something into her ear. She smiled and without further ado announced, 'I name this ship *Leviathan*, and God bless all who sail in her.' With that, she let go of the bottle, which span through the air and shattered against the metal hull. There was a ripple of applause as the champagne dripped down the plates of painted iron. I turned to Brunel and said quietly, 'They decided against Tom Thumb then.'

He laughed and, clearly excited by the prospect, told me he was going up to the launch podium, suggesting I find myself a good vantage point somewhere at a safe distance.

Accompanied by his assistants, Brunel climbed the steps inside the siege tower while I made my way back up the slope towards the gates, where an expectant hush had fallen over the assembled mass. It was only when I got closer that I realized stewards led by Russell himself were working their way through the crowd calling for quiet.

Along with a few other privileged sightseers I was permitted to roam fairly freely in the area between the crowd, now kept in check by a rope strung out across the yard, and the ship. Selecting a rusty circular saw mounted on a sturdy trolley as my own viewing platform, I clambered up and, careful to avoid the jagged blade, sat with my legs dangling beneath me.

The diminutive figure of Brunel appeared on the podium, his hat removed so as to prevent it blowing away in the breeze which caused the flags he held in each hand to flutter healthily. The one in his right hand was red and that in his left green. I guessed that these were to be used in the same fashion as a conductor's baton, to send signals to the teams of men who had by now mustered around the levers of the forward and aft checking drums. Other groups of labourers were positioned at the rams distributed along the length of the ship.

A shout went up: it was Brunel, who at the same time waved the red flag from side to side over his head. The cry was repeated, this time coming from somewhere in the yard, and followed by the sound of chains crashing to the ground as the ship's restraints were released.

The *Leviathan* was unbound, but as yet unmoved. Smoke belched into the air as steam winches took up the strain on the chains running through the barges anchored in the river behind her. With a flourish of the green flag the hydraulic rams on the landward side were engaged. The hull groaned and shivered, but despite the pull and push exerted by what Brunel had explained were some of the most powerful machines known to man the ship refused to yield. But then, just when I was beginning to think Brunel may as well try to move a mountain, the bow shuddered and shifted a few feet.

Almost immediately the stern began to slip away, the iron shoes on the cradle screaming as they slid over the metal rails. The ground shook and I took fright as the saw blade behind me made an involuntary half-turn in response. Unlike the bow, the stern did not come to a sudden juddering halt and continued to move at quite dramatic speed, very soon passing what I judged to be the line of the bow, in exactly the fashion that Brunel had demonstrated with the movement of his forearm.

The stern of the ship, having shifted further down the ramp than had been expected at this stage, took up more chain than had been let out from the stern checking drum, which began to spin wildly on its axle. The friction produced a cloud of smoke and, through this, the crowd and I watched in horror as the brake levers shot upwards, moving like the spokes on a spinning wheel. The drum's crew, who were at the time resting on the levers, were thrown up into the air. It was as though they had been caught in an explosion, their bodies flying this way and that, limbs flailing. Women in the crowd screamed and men shouted in panic. Brunel frantically waved both flags above his head, and all means of propulsion were instantly halted and the brakes on the cradles applied. The ship shuddered to a halt – in fact, it appeared to me to have done so as soon as the drum began to spin, almost as though she sensed what damage she had done.

I dropped off the saw bench and ran towards the scene of the accident, losing my hat somewhere on the way. 'Step back! I'm a doctor, give me room!' I yelled at the men gathering around, quickly moving from one fallen brake-man to the next, trying to gauge the extent of their injuries. Six of them lay on the ground, scattered among the lengths of timber like so much flotsam on the beach, three of them knocked unconscious. Three more men hobbled around in a state of shock, one of them clutching what I could see to be a broken arm. My medical bag was still in the carriage, which I could only hope had by now arrived at the yard.

Brunel, accompanied by his entourage of assistants and clearly out of breath after running down the stairs, stepped into the scene of carnage some minutes behind me.

One of the injured men was in a very bad way, head twisted and blood trickling from his mouth and nose. I crouched beside him and listened to his breathing, which was shallow and erratic. I took off my coat to provide him with some comfort but he was dead before I could cover him so I closed his eyes and gently pulled the coat up over his head.

Brunel was standing over me, his face ashen. 'His neck was broken,' I said, switching my attentions to one of the unconscious men.

'You can't blame this on the company,' bellowed an enraged Russell as he broke through the crowd. 'If we'd used wooden rails and iron sleeves like I'd suggested then she wouldn't have stalled like that. But no, you wouldn't have it. Iron against iron it had to be. Always the same with you, isn't it, Isambard? If there's a problem, throw iron at it. Now look where it's got you.'

Brunel made no reply and, unable to do anything for the victims other than coax the walking wounded into sitting down, he wandered away.

Following my instructions, one of Brunel's subordinates, a young chap who had distinguished himself by volunteering to assist, returned from the carriage with my bag, which I exchanged for a request for litters on which to carry away the injured. The dead man was laid out on a ladder, carried by a man at either end. Reclaiming my coat, I replaced it with a tattered old blanket, taking one last look at the man's pale and bloodied face before covering it again. Two wagons were commandeered to take the wounded to the nearest hospital at Mile End. Once everyone was boarded and made as comfortable as could be expected I told the men accompanying them to inform the hospital that they were dealing with serious concussions, multiple broken bones and some risk of internal bleeding among the most seriously injured. I watched as the dreadful convoy made its way slowly through the crowd.

Back at the scene of the accident I came across Brunel by the ship's stern, which sat much closer to the river than the bow. He was alone and seemed lost in his thoughts. At last noticing my presence he thanked me for my efforts and after ascertaining that the injured had been removed he set about preparing for a second launch attempt. I expressed my surprise at his desire to continue so soon after what had happened, but he was determined to proceed, explaining that it would be weeks before the next spring tide.

Giving fresh orders to the men, he oversaw the resetting of the equipment and then once again ascended the siege tower. The crowd of spectators was rapidly thinning, many of them having seen more than enough for one day. I was of the same opinion myself but given the chance of the accident repeating itself felt duty-bound to stay. Retracing my steps, I came across my hat, which had been crushed by someone's clumsily placed foot, before resuming my position at the saw.

A new stern-drum crew had been assembled. This time, though, they stood well clear of the dangerous device. The precaution was unnecessary, as this time the ship didn't budge an inch, and the effort was quickly abandoned. I later learned from Brunel that one of the steam winches had stripped the teeth of a gear, totally disabling it.

When I looked at my watch again it was almost four o'clock. I had missed my meeting with Sir Benjamin but consoled myself with the knowledge that, had I not been at the yard, then there was every chance that more than one man would have died, and a stiff rebuke from my superior seemed a small price to pay for that.

Brunel, looking totally dejected, accompanied me in the carriage on the trip back into town. We sat in silence for some considerable time before he said, 'Four feet.'

I was engrossed in the forlorn task of teasing my hat back into shape and didn't quite catch what he said. 'I beg your pardon?'

'Four feet,' he repeated. 'We managed to move the ship four feet.'

'Was that all? It seemed further.'

There was another long pause as he gazed out of the window. 'Four feet for one man dead and eight injured.'

'A most tragic accident,' I added, for want of anything meaningful to say.

'Never mind,' he said. 'Only another 326 feet to go before she hits the water.'

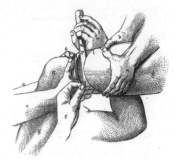

# 3

When I entered the hospital next morning the hem of my coat was still matted with blood from the dead labourer. Despite taking some satisfaction at having been able to assist after the accident, the dreadful events at the shipyard had left me unusually low of spirit. I am no stranger to suffering and death, indeed they could be said to be my stock in trade, but when confronted outside the walls of the hospital, these twin beasts seemed wild and unpredictable, rampaging beyond my influence. Of course, the knowledge that because I had missed our meeting Sir Benjamin would be after my own blood did little to lift the gloom.

But there was nothing to be gained from trying to avoid the inevitable, and so I set out to confront Sir Benjamin directly. I refused to be a fugitive in my own hospital and could only hope that he remained unaware of my temporary absence – the man, after all, had many responsibilities.

I was just about to leave my office when William appeared carrying a cylindrical parcel. 'It just arrived,' he announced, filling the room with the fumes from last night's brandy. Placing it on my desk and standing back, he watched as I cut the string and lifted the lid. Beneath a layer of crumpled paper sat a brand-new top hat of unmistakable quality. The brushed felt shimmered as I lifted it free. A note shoved into the silk hat-band read:

*A replacement for your loss while being of such valuable service. I hope it fits. Yours, I. K. Brunel*

I held it by the brim and placed it gingerly on my head. It slid perfectly into place, coming to rest just above my ears. 'Very nice,' William observed. 'A man needs a hat.'

Brunel's fine gift was much appreciated and would require a note of thanks, but first I needed to speak to Sir Benjamin. Hearing no response on knocking at his office door, I walked on a little further up the corridor, entered the anteroom next door and asked his assistant about the superintendent's whereabouts. Even Sir Benjamin seemed to have little regard for Mumrill, an unpleasant weasel of a man who would rather see a patient suffer than shift a farthing from one column of his account book to the next.

He squinted at me from behind his desk, spectacles perched on the end of his sharply whittled nose. 'Sir Benjamin is showing some important visitors around the hospital. A note was sent to all senior members of staff yesterday. Didn't you receive yours?' Then he added with barely disguised relish, 'Oh, of course you wouldn't have, would you? Sir Benjamin was most disappointed when you didn't arrive for your appointment.' All this was just the build-up to the news I did not want to hear: 'He was somewhat perturbed, to say the least, when he discovered you had left the hospital.'

'No, that's right. I had to attend an emergency,' I said, by way of explanation, the words souring in my mouth. I resented offering any excuse to the man, but needs must. I told him I hoped to see Sir Benjamin later in the day and asked if, in the meantime, he would be good enough to pass on my apologies for any inconvenience caused. As I left the office he crowed, 'I'm sure Sir Benjamin will be delighted to see you later.'

When later came, I was working with William on some modifications to the operating table. The thing was ancient and really nothing more than a heavy wooden bench, which would not have been out of place in one of Brunel's workshops. The coarsely grained surface had accumulated a veneer from years of use and despite being scrubbed down by William after every operation had turned like ebony after soaking up so much blood and visceral fluid. As we laboured together, it struck me that William was almost a product of these same processes, for a web of blood vessels covered his drinker's cheeks like the fire-cracked glaze on an antique pot; his grey teeth and yellow, straggling hair completed the picture of a man coloured by too many hard years.

As a porter William may have been less than ideal, but on this occasion I had chosen to focus my dissatisfactions on the table. I had made several requests for a replacement, but all of these had been turned down by Sir Benjamin, no doubt after seeking advice from Mumrill and his blasted ledger. I would not have minded so much if it were used only for dissecting the dead but more often than not it was occupied by a living patient. A cadaver is all well and good for getting across the principles of anatomy, but when teaching practical surgical skills there is no substitute for students witnessing a real operation.

I was sawing away at the tabletop beneath me, standing astride it. William was leaning back against the table taking a well-earned breather after his turn. Our aim was to cut a hole for a blood bucket in the table rather than simply allowing the fluid to run off in all directions, if not over me then on to the floor to be soaked up by the carpet of sawdust. I was tired of having to wade through the stuff, and more than once had narrowly avoided slipping on my backside – amusing for the students perhaps, but not so funny when I had a scalpel in my hand. Our theory was sound but the practice a different matter. The tabletop was half an inch thick and very heavy going, especially so due to a hard knot located on the very circumference of the partially cut hole. I was beginning to regret ever starting the job and was busy cursing both the wood and the saw.

'A bad workman always blames his tools,' said William.

'Thank you for that pearl of wisdom,' I gasped between draws on the saw. 'You needn't sound so smug, William – it's almost your turn again.'

'Ah well, the good news is that we're not going to want for sawdust for a while.' He was right: impressive piles of the stuff were accumulating beneath the table.

Making one last burst of effort, I looked between my legs to see an upside-down Sir Benjamin reversing into the room, pushing the double doors open with his back. The guided tour which Mumrill had mentioned was obviously in full swing, as he was delivering a spirited commentary. 'And here we have the operating theatre, where we also teach anatomy and introduce the basics of surgical technique.' He was accompanied by a man and a woman, both of whom were brought up short by the sight of a man standing astride a dissecting table attacking it with a saw. Only when he became aware that his audience's attention was fixed on something other than his speech did Sir Benjamin turn around.

Despite my obvious inabilities as a carpenter, the companionship of labour had served to lift my spirits, and my trepidation about the confrontation with my superior had almost entirely evaporated. 'Good afternoon, Sir Benjamin,' I offered, raising the saw in salutation. William, however, rightly guessed that this was no time to be seen idling and made himself scarce.

Sir Benjamin looked to be having some difficulty comprehending the scene he'd walked in on. 'Dr Phillips, may I ask what on earth you are doing up there?'

I hopped down on to the floor and brushed sawdust from my clothes as I approached them. 'Just a few modifications, Sir Benjamin. This table, as you know, is quite antediluvian in design so I thought I'd bring it into the nineteenth century. Nothing major, you understand, just the odd tweak here and there.'

After having momentarily forgotten his responsibilities to our visitors, Sir Benjamin turned back to them. 'This industrious gentleman is Dr Phillips, our senior surgeon. We are very proud of his progressive approach to surgical technique. And as you can see, there is no end to his talents.'

The woman was the first to speak up. 'I don't think I have ever seen an operation actually carried out on an operating table before.'

'Dr Phillips,' Sir Benjamin continued, 'it gives me great pleasure to introduce Miss Florence Nightingale, whose reputation obviously goes before her; also her colleague, Dr Sutherland.'

As had been the case with my introduction to Brunel in this same place I was vaguely familiar with the woman's appearance, her likeness having regularly appeared in the newspapers during her celebrated service in the Crimea. She must have been in her late thirties but still retained the handsome looks suggested by her portraits. The raven-black hair was hidden beneath her bonnet, but this also served to frame the attractive curves of her face and long neck.

'Miss Nightingale is here on behalf of the Royal Sanitary Commission,' explained Sir Benjamin, 'and will be carrying out a study of methods and practice as part of the commission's review of civil and military hospitals.'

'In truth, my report to the commission has already been submitted,' added Miss Nightingale, 'but I am keen to further my study of civil hospitals in the hope of coming up with some suggestions about improved organization and design.'

Sir Benjamin sniffed at this correction but carried on regardless. 'I must take this opportunity to congratulate Dr Phillips on his actions of yesterday. I am informed that, thanks to his intervention after an accident at Millwall docks, the lives of several men were saved.'

I saw his game immediately. He was nervous about having somebody of such high repute, and a woman to boot, examining the workings of the hospital and so was keen to cast his domain in the best possible light.

'Really,' said Miss Nightingale, breaking away from the group to take a closer look at the table.

'Does the hospital have an ambulance service?' enquired a rather bored-looking Dr Sutherland.

'Yes, we do have a limited facility,' I said, and looking to Sir Benjamin, 'but we are hoping to expand the service.' In reality, however, the issue had never been on the hospital board's agenda, nor was it likely to appear there in the near future.

'What caused the accident, Dr Phillips?' asked Miss Nightingale.

'The malfunction of a piece of equipment during the failed launch of Mr Brunel's ship. I am afraid Sir Benjamin exaggerates my abilities. I was unable to save one of the men.'

'A shame, but I am sure you did all you could. Do you think, doctor, that such tragedies are the price we have to pay for progress?'

'That may be so, Miss Nightingale, but I doubt very much whether they figure on the bill when it comes to accounting for the costs.'

The celebrated nurse looked at me thoughtfully while running a delicate hand around the edge of the cut in the tabletop. 'I am sure you are right, doctor. But you are obviously not beyond making improvements yourself, and this old table is truly in need of them.'

'It's for a blood bucket.' I said, referring to my handiwork.

'But am I right in thinking you intended to trace a circle rather than create something that looks like a jagged scar?' She looked up to see me frown, and immediately deflected it with a smile. 'I am sorry, Dr Phillips, I am teasing you, a terrible habit of mine.' She picked the saw from the table. 'I am sure you are much more accustomed to using such tools against flesh and bone rather than wood.'

'That is very true,' I admitted. 'Carpentry, as I have learned today, is not my forte.'

Sir Benjamin, no doubt feeling the two of us had monopolized the conversation for long enough, offered a third voice. 'My own feelings on amputation are well known, Miss Nightingale.'

'Oh,' she said. 'And what are they, Sir Benjamin?'

The superintendent bristled. 'Why, that in many cases, it should not be carried out if at all possible. We underestimate the body's powers of recovery and tend to use amputation as a first recourse rather than the last.'

'Most laudable, but the decision to amputate a limb must surely be taken on a case-by-case basis. In the Crimea the sanitary conditions were so bad that delaying amputation was akin to signing the wounded man's death warrant. Even a few hours' delay could give infection a foothold. Far better to apply the saw as soon as possible; only then can infection be kept at bay.'

'I cannot speak for the Crimea, Miss Nightingale, but here in a London hospital, where levels of sanitation are much higher, I have demonstrated the worth of sparing the saw.'

'I am sure you have, Sir Benjamin, and I look forward to discussing the matter with you in more depth, but now I think it is about time for lunch, don't you?'

'Of course,' Sir Benjamin responded, only too happy to have the party move on to their next destination.

Miss Nightingale withdrew to the door held open by Sir Benjamin. 'Good day, Dr Phillips. I look forward to our next meeting.'

'And good day to you, Miss Nightingale. I hope that next time you find me engaged in more medical pursuits.'

The visitors departed, their host herding them from the rear. But then, just when I thought the coast was clear, Sir Benjamin stepped back into the theatre. 'No more hiding behind a woman's skirts, Dr Phillips, you and I have unfinished business. Kindly report to my office at three o'clock.'

Left alone to ponder my fate, I too decided that it was time for lunch. Munching my way through an apple and a piece of cheese, I found some distraction in the editorial of *The Times*, which reported on the events of the previous day.

London, Wednesday, 4 November 1857

The consummate engineer must possess not only grandeur of ideas but accuracy of execution. His eye must be microscopic as well as telescopic, and as fitted to inspect a mite as to comprehend the heavens. The higher his aspirations and the more daring his plans, the firmer grasp must he have of every detail, and the surer must be his footfall at every step. If there is nothing too great for him to adventure, it is because there is nothing too little for him to care for. The case of the monster ship of which the launch was attempted yesterday at Millwall is a proof of this. The greatest and most wonderful of modern constructions is complete, and only waits for fit machinery to move it from the place where for four years it has been the admiration of the world. Yet, until cables and drums and brakes are made to do their work, it must remain stranded and unable to realize the fond hopes of its builders.

In this country we are in the midst of the movement. The most memorable scientific enterprises of late years have been the Britannia Bridge, the Submarine Telegraph, the Crystal palaces of Hyde Park and Sydenham, the Atlantic Telegraph, and the wonderful ship which was for the first time moved yesterday. All these have been carried out here, and we have learned from them to interest ourselves deeply in the progress of important works.

The Cunard line and the Collins line were content if they alternately outdid their rivals by 20 feet of length or an extra half-knot in the hour of pace. But the new ship disdained comparison. Her principle was new, she would be propelled by a union of powers never before joined, she would enter the water in a new manner, she would necessitate a new system of business to sail her at a profit, she might even be expected to call new towns into existence on the shores of harbours sufficient to shelter her.

There then followed a list of impressive dimensions which, given my first-hand experience of the vessel, I could not be bothered reacquainting myself with. The closing paragraph went on to describe the sorry events of the day before, and it came as no surprise that the article did not see fit to mention that a man had lost his life in the attempt.

'Take a seat, Dr Phillips,' said Sir Benjamin, without looking up from the notes he was writing. I settled nervously into the chair opposite him, taking time to glance around the well-filled book-shelves covering the walls of the office. After a suitably uncomfortable period of silence he looked up. 'I had hoped to see you in that chair yesterday, but then I learned you were busy saving lives in Millwall. You will, no doubt, be pleased to know I received a note from Mr Brunel this morning praising your actions.'

'That was good of him,' I replied, while wishing he had limited his praise to sending me the hat. 'But as I said earlier, my role in the affair has been exaggerated.'

'That may be true, but there is one attribute of your method we cannot overlook, as it will revolutionize medical practice.'

'I'm afraid I don't follow,' I said, unable to work out from which direction the blow was coming.

'I refer of course to your ability to forecast accidents before they happen, which allows you to be there on the scene when they do. I would be as sceptical as the next man about this uncanny talent if I didn't know for a fact that you left the hospital yesterday at eleven o'clock in the morning having reported to the duty man that you were going to attend an emergency, which, wonder of wonders, did not occur until around one o'clock in the afternoon. Incredible, is it not?'

I squirmed in the chair while Sir Benjamin surveyed the effects of his well-aimed sucker punch. His intelligence, no doubt provided by that snake in the grass Mumrill, was spot on. He had me over a barrel and there seemed little point in trying to make excuses. 'Yes, my departure from the hospital was rash, and I apologize for that. However, I cannot regret the incidental outcome of my actions. There can be little doubt that more men would have died in the absence of a doctor. Which, as fate would have it, happened to be me.'

'I am glad you are able to take comfort from that thought, Dr Phillips. I can only hope you can continue to do so after I have had your employment with the hospital terminated for gross dereliction of duty.'

'Once again, I can only offer my apologies and ask you not to take that course of action. I can assure you this will not happen again.'

'Quite right it won't happen again. You have spent far too much time over the past weeks in Mr Brunel's company. This is not the first occasion he has distracted you from your work.'

'I'm afraid that I have to argue that point, Sir Benjamin. I have never before let my conversations with Mr Brunel interrupt my duties. Yesterday was an exception.'

'That's not what my sources tell me, but never mind.' Mumrill had been at work again. 'Listen to me, Phillips. You are a first-rate surgeon and I would regret having to let you go.' He picked up his pen and wagged it aggressively. 'But I swear, if anything like this happens again, you'll be out on your ear. Do we understand one another?'

'Yes, Sir Benjamin, we understand one another.'

'Very well then, we will let the matter of yesterday's lapse in your judgement drop, but consider this a stern warning.'

'I will, sir.'

I stood to take my leave, but Sir Benjamin wasn't yet finished with me. 'One other thing,' he said, already having begun to write again.

'What is that, Sir Benjamin?'

'That infernal woman, Miss Nightingale,' he rasped without looking up.

'Oh?'

'We could well do without that . . . that nurse snooping about, but I have no choice in the matter, the board has given her free rein.' He coughed as though the words were sticking in his throat. 'Anyway, she seemed to take a shine to you this morning, Lord only knows why. I want you to keep an eye on her, help her out, that sort of thing. Just make sure she stays out of my way and goes away with a good impression of the hospital. Do I make myself clear?'

'Yes, Sir Benjamin. You can rely on me.'

'And just remember what I said about distraction from your duties. Now good day.'

Like a schoolboy having taken his punishment, I left the room feeling as though a heavy weight had been lifted from my shoulders. I noticed that Mumrill's door was open and took a glimpse inside to see him still hovering beside the dividing door between his and Sir Benjamin's office. The man had clearly spent the last ten minutes earwigging. I hadn't got far before I heard Sir Benjamin call after me. I turned to see him standing outside his office.

'Before I forget, Phillips, be good enough to warn that scoundrel William that a new table for the theatre will be delivered next week.'

'I will, sir,' I replied with a smile, before striding off down the corridor, determined at some time to thank Miss Nightingale for what had clearly been her intervention.

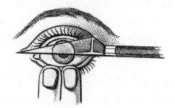

# 4

'Dr Phillips,' said William, 'there's a gentleman here to see you.'

'It's late, I was just about to leave. Is it Mr Brunel?'

'No, sir,' he replied, looking a little uncomfortable. 'It's the police. Says his name is Tarlow, Inspector Tarlow.'

'The police, eh? Well then, you'd better show him into the parlour.'

'I beg your pardon, sir?'

'A joke, William, it's just that we've had a lot of visitors of late – we'll soon be in need of somewhere to entertain our guests.'

William gave a half-hearted smile. 'Yes, sir, I see what you mean.'

'Show him to my office, will you, please?'

'He's in the yard, sir. Got a wagon with 'im. Seems pretty keen to meet you out there.'

'Really? Very well. Go and tell him I will be with him presently.'

William disappeared, and I handed over what little was left of my round to the junior doctor accompanying me. While collecting my hat and coat from the office, I wondered whether this was some sort of investigation into the accident at the launch.

There was indeed a wagon in the yard, and its driver, a uniformed policeman, was standing between the open gate and the rear of the vehicle, positioned as though to prevent anyone entering. A man in well-kempt civilian clothes and a bowler strode towards me as I stepped out of the back door and placed my hat and coat on a hook usually reserved for a horse harness. He held out a hand.

'Dr Phillips? Inspector Tarlow, Metropolitan Police.'

'What can I do for you, inspector? None of my nurses in trouble, I trust?'

'I hope not, sir,' replied the policeman gravely. He gestured towards the wagon and I followed him to the rear of the soft-covered vehicle. 'There is something I would like you to take a look at.'

'I will be happy to oblige,' I replied.

'It's a body. A woman we pulled from the Thames this morning.'

'Did she drown?'

'I don't think so. But you would know better than I.' He pointed to the flap at the back of the wagon. 'Simpkins, open her up.'

The constable hurried to do the inspector's bidding, unfastening the ties securing the flap. Tugging the canvas aside, he exposed a litter upon which lay the sheet-covered corpse. Still-damp strands of dark hair protruded from beneath the fabric at the end closest to us.

'Take a hold, Simpkins,' ordered Tarlow. 'I'll bring up the rear.'

'Wait,' I said. 'I'll get my porter to lend a hand.'

The inspector watched as the constable pulled the litter along the floor of the wagon. 'No, thank you, sir. I would like to keep this just between us, if you don't mind. I am sure you'll understand once you've taken a look.'

Tarlow took up the carrying handles, and the pair followed me through the back door into the preparation room, where the litter was set down on the table. The inspector closed and bolted the door behind us before posting the constable on the door into the theatre. Only when all was secure did he pull back just enough of the sheet to expose the face, its cheeks inflated by decay. The tightening of the skin had pulled the colourless lips back away from an incomplete set of brown teeth. But it was not just teeth that were missing. The face was scratched and scarred, as if torn by the teeth of a rodent or the talons of a bird. The eyelids were drawn back, revealing a milky globe to the left and a dark void to the right.

'She's young,' I observed, looking up to see that Tarlow now had a notebook in his hand. 'Perhaps anywhere between eighteen and twenty-two and, judging by her teeth, not from the moneyed classes. Looks as though she had a hard life.'

'And an even harder death,' said Tarlow, flipping away the remaining portion of the sheet. I was entirely unprepared for the sight he unveiled. The woman's chest was cratered, the ribcage shattered and the interior cavity exposed.

'I see what you mean about her not drowning, inspector. My God, what a mess.'

'What can you tell me about whoever did this, doctor?'

Taking a deep breath, I bent over the torso and pushed aside the cleaved end of a rib, the better to see inside. 'The heart and lungs have been removed but I'm going to need more light. Excuse me for a moment.'

With the light from a lamp reflecting a beam from the concave mirror attached to my forehead I peered once more into the cavity in the woman's chest, the opening to which had been widened by the application of a spreader clamp. 'Well, inspector, I can tell you that this wasn't the work of a surgeon. It's clumsy and amateurish – though, that said, there are a few of my students who would be put to shame by it.'

'I will remove them from my enquiries then.'

I looked up at the inspector and was relieved to see the trace of a smile. 'She's been dead for a while though.'

'How long do you think she was in the water?'

I took a doubtful look at the water-marked skin. 'It's difficult to say really. Maybe as many as three or four days, but I'm guessing that from the condition of the interior. I'm no expert on the effects of long-term water immersion.'

The inspector scribbled a note. 'That's assuming he dumped the body not long after she died.'

'A good point. The work is clumsy but not necessarily hurried, so he may have had her hidden somewhere. She hasn't been dead much longer than four or five days, that's all I can say. Was she clothed when you found her?'

'Naked, just as you see her now. How about the cause of death, doctor? Can you tell how he killed her?'

'Again, difficult to say. There don't appear to be any ligature marks around the neck so I'm guessing she wasn't strangled. Nor are there any such marks around her wrists, so she wasn't tied up. Looking at her emaciated condition, I would be tempted to suggest starvation. But I could say that of half the population of London, and that's just the ones walking around. Obviously this hole in her chest may be covering all manner of ills. He could have stabbed her in the breast six times and we wouldn't be any the wiser.'

The policeman was not to be put off so easily. 'Are you sure there's nothing more you can say?'

Just as I was about to take another look inside a small commotion broke out at the door.

'This room is out of bounds!' yelled the constable, trying to push the door closed, a task which the presence of a wedging foot protruding from the other side wasn't making any easier.

'Excuse me, inspector,' I said, with some slight embarrassment. 'It's just William, my porter. He'll be wondering what's going on. I'll tell him to go away.'

Tarlow frowned. 'If you could, doctor. I don't want word of this getting out. It will only cause a panic if the press gets wind of another murder.'

The constable stepped aside to let me through the doors. By the time I entered the theatre William was sitting on the floor rubbing his foot. 'What the 'ell's goin' on in there? I've got work to do.'

'Sorry, William, but I'm engaged in a little confidential business for the police. I am sure they will be gone soon.'

'Bloody peeler crushed my foot.'

'I'm sure your foot will be fine. Now please go and find something else to do for half an hour. Just be content with the fact that they're not here for you.' William took on a not-unfamiliar hurt expression and I watched as he made a meal of limping away before returning to the preparation room. 'You said "another murder". You mean there have been others mutilated like her?'

The inspector looked up from a jar containing a foetus which I had been using in my last demonstration. 'She's the second,' he said. 'Both of them with their hearts and lungs removed. One butchered prostitute I can put down to the rough and tumble of life in the gutter but two, two is edging uncomfortably towards a pattern.'

'A pattern? What do you mean?'

Tarlow took off his hat, set it down next to the corpse and pushed a hand through his hair. 'Well, sir, there's plain old murder. A husband bludgeons his wife because she won't let him drink his wages on a Friday night, or a man kills another in a knife fight over a woman, but then there are those who kill for the sheer pleasure of it. One type of homicide may even lead to another: a man may kill his first victim accidentally or in a fit of temper, but in doing so may find that he enjoys it and so go on to do it again and again, not being able to stop himself. It becomes a compulsion with him. In such cases it is not unknown for the killer to have particular inclinations. Invariably the victims are female, but I know of one case where the killer took to collecting ears, and another where the eyes were cut out, because the killer feared they had captured his image while in the act. But in this instance our man seems to like cutting open their chests and removing their innards.'

'And how do you know she was a prostitute?'

'You've seen her, doctor. She's not exactly Lady Muck, is she?'

'You have no idea of her identity? Someone must have reported her missing.'

Tarlow let out a cynical laugh. 'My dear doctor, do you know how many prostitutes there are in London? Thousands, many of them outsiders, peasant wretches from the country hoping to scrape a living in the big city. Some are virtually sold into slavery by their own parents. They take new names and become lost in the crowd. If they go missing, who cares? – their whoremongers and colleagues are not exactly the type of people who like talking to the police.'

I took that as a no. 'And the other one, where did you find her?'

'In the river again, floating just in Limehouse Reach about four weeks ago. Now, doctor, you were going to take another look inside.'

'Yes, forgive me. All this is rather different to my normal work.'

The inspector took another glance at the jar. 'I don't see how.'

Returning to my task, I probed the walls of the cavity with a pair of forceps. Severed blood vessels and wider tubes displayed ragged ends where a blade had been applied by an uncertain hand.

'The knife was sharp but the hand holding it not so.'

'As sharp as a surgeon's knife?'

'A scalpel? Perhaps.'

'Could we be looking for a medical man then?'

'A set of surgical instruments do not a medical man make, inspector. As I said before, this was not the work of any surgeon I would credit with the title.'

Tarlow replaced his hat. 'Thank you, doctor, you've been most helpful.' He covered the corpse with the sheet and ordered the constable to help him carry it. 'And, doctor, I hope I can rely on your discretion in this matter.'

'You can, inspector. Let me know if there is any other way I can assist.'

'Thank you again. You may be hearing from me.'

'Just one more thing, inspector.'

'Wait a moment, Simpkins. Yes, doctor, what is it?'

'The ear-collector and the eye-taker, did you catch them?'

Tarlow raised a corner of his mouth in a half-smile. 'Oh yes, I caught them all right. I dropped the trapdoor on one of them myself.'

# 5

Brunel stepped from the carriage into the cold evening and waited for me to follow. Once again, he had not seen fit to provide advance notice of our trip nor, on this occasion, to inform me of its purpose.

During our brief journey any attempt on my part to glean information was greeted with a dismissive wave of his hand or an irrelevant query relating to some or other anatomical matter.

Pushing his hat on to his head, he gave a brief instruction to the driver before the carriage pulled away. Then off he went, striding towards the public house, which from the hubbub issuing from within was replete with a full complement of revellers. To my relief, we did not add ourselves to the heaving mass of humanity in the public bar but continued along the hallway to the stairs, at the top of which we entered a spacious loft.

The place was typical of the private rooms located above public houses which for a small fee are available for hire to dining clubs or any other group of gentlemen requiring a discreet meeting place. Men were standing around a long dining table, huddled together in small groups talking quietly. The table accommodated two decanters of claret and a scattering of glasses but offered no sugges-tion that eating would play any part in the proceedings. Brunel snapped the door shut, and in doing so brought a halt to the conversation as heads turned to observe the new arrivals. For a moment the only sound in the room was that of the laughter which drifted up through the floorboards from the bar beneath our feet and with so many eyes upon us I immediately regretted not having stopped for a stiffener.

But the silence was broken by a friendly-sounding voice. 'Ah, Brunel. Here at last. Late, as usual – the big ship keeping you busy, I'll wager.'

The man moved away from his companions, who immediately returned to their conversation.

'Good to see you again, Hawes,' said Brunel. 'I would like to introduce my friend, Dr George Phillips.' And then, to me, 'Phillips, this unsavoury individual is Ben Hawes, Undersecretary of State for War.'

'Delighted to meet you,' said Hawes. 'Any friend of Brunel's is a friend of mine. Good to see a new face,' he remarked cheerily, before adding in a quieter voice, 'It can get a little stale in here at times, you know.'

'Nonsense, Ben,' replied Brunel, 'you wouldn't miss these meetings for the world. You yearn for knowledge like a butcher's dog hungers for a bone, tell me you don't!'

I had been kept in the dark long enough. 'Just what sort of meetings are these?' I asked.

'Isambard!' boomed Hawes. 'Am I to believe that you haven't told him anything about our little club?' He placed a hand on my shoulder, 'Please forgive him, Dr Phillips, he is so single-minded that he tends to overlook little things like manners. But he means nothing by it.'

Brunel was still not to be drawn on the matter. 'I want my friend here to meet our speaker. Can you bring him over?'

'I think we are about to begin,' said Hawes doubtfully, 'but give me a moment and I will see if I can extricate him.'

With Hawes departed, Brunel at last deigned to provide me with some sort of explanation. 'We engineers like to think of ourselves as individual thinkers, inventors and creators, but we cannot operate in isolation, you know, we need the encouragement, and yes, even the criticism of others; we thrive in an environment in which men of vision and imagination can benefit from one another's knowledge and experience.'

'Have you not just described the Royal Society?' I remarked, this particular institution coming to mind, as Sir Benjamin had recently been elected its president.

Brunel lowered his voice. 'Nothing more than an arena for grandstanding and backslapping. What we seek to provide here is a more casual forum, where those really concerned with the future of mankind can get away from that sort of posturing.' My raised eyebrow prompted Brunel to smile. 'Let us just say that some of our ideas are not of the most orthodox nature. They would be frowned upon in a more traditional scientific environment, perhaps even laughed at. Freedom of expression without fear of rebuke is essential to our aims.'

Before I could question him further, Hawes returned with the man I presumed to be the speaker. He was a striking-looking fellow, his well-formed head entirely bald across the top, his thick eyebrows sweeping across a wide, overhanging forehead.

Brunel extended his hand. 'Charles, delighted you could make it.'

The man let out a gruff 'Brunel.'

'Dr George Phillips, meet Charles Darwin. He is going to talk about his theory of revolution.'

'Evolution,' corrected Darwin.

'Yes, of course, forgive me – evolution. How is that book of yours coming along?'

Darwin scowled. 'Let us make a bargain, sir. You won't ask me about that damned book and I will refrain from enquiring about your ship.'

'Very well,' said Brunel with a nod. 'Let us change the subject.'

Clearly eager to do so, Darwin turned to me. 'You are a physician, Dr Phillips?'

'A surgeon at St Thomas's hospital.'

'A surgeon, eh? You know, I started out studying medicine at Edinburgh University.'

'Really? Why, so did I. But you didn't become a doctor?'

He shook his head. 'Couldn't stand it. All those dissections made me feel quite ill. Which brings me on to another matter . . . Perhaps, doctor, I could have a quiet word with you?'

Request made, he pushed a hand into the small of my back and steered me away from Brunel and Hawes. 'If you will excuse us, gentlemen.'

Backing me into a window alcove, where I became his captive audience, Darwin began to recite a litany of medical complaints. Nausea, stomach reflux, back pain – the whole gamut. While he was speaking I glanced over his shoulder and was surprised to see that Brunel and Hawes had been joined by another; surprised because the gentleman in question was none other than Sir Benjamin, and he did not look a happy man. He was talking in what looked to be heated terms to Brunel who, as usual, was in the process of lighting up a cigar. Trying my best to ignore my superior's unexpected presence, I returned my attention to Mr Darwin's catalogue of woes.

'And then there is the dizziness,' said the man, who on the basis of his own diagnosis seemed to be suffering from every ailment known to medicine.

But Sir Benjamin was not to be ignored for long. 'Gentlemen,' he announced. 'Now we are all present can we please take our seats and get started.'

Disappointed at the curtailment of his recitation, Darwin shrugged his shoulders and led the way to the table, where chair legs scraped against the floorboards as the assembled company took their places. I picked a vacant chair situated as far away from Sir Benjamin as possible. Brunel, who for some reason seemed very pleased with himself, sat opposite me, while Mr Russell, who appeared to have put his outburst at the yard behind him, settled himself next to Brunel, nodding at me solemnly as he opened a leather satchel and took out a stack of papers.

Aside from Brunel, Sir Benjamin, Russell, and now Hawes and Darwin, everyone in the room was a stranger to me. But one man in particular caught my attention, and not just because of his relative youth, for he could have been no more than twenty-five years old. I am by no means a follower of fashion, but there could be no ignoring the quality of his wardrobe, his neck wrapped in a cravat of watered silk, the bib of his waistcoat tastefully detailed with silver thread and the well-cut frock coat lined with the finest red satin. The young man also marked himself out by standing somewhat aloof from the rest of the company and was the last to be seated, hanging back while the chairs were pulled out from the table and then, like a guest unafraid of losing out in a parlour game, casually taking the last seat available.

Sir Benjamin noisily cleared his throat before bringing the assembly to order. 'Gentlemen,' he barked. 'It gives me great pleasure tonight to introduce a most illustrious guest, who I am sure will be known to most of you.'

There was a general nodding of heads. 'Mr Darwin has for many years been pioneering a most exciting new branch of natural science, and I am very pleased that, in advance of his much anticipated lecture to the Royal Society, he has agreed to provide a preview to our own, shall I say rather more select, group.'

A ripple of laughter followed this last comment, while he threw me an imperious glance. 'Before we begin, it is only proper that we reciprocate the introduction, especially as I see we have a new face at the table this evening.'

Sir Benjamin directed his attention to the man seated to his left and from there began working his way clockwise around the table.

'Among the achievements of Mr Joseph Whitworth,' he announced, 'are of course his great guns and other armaments, but we should not forget his other achievements, among which are the many machine tools without which we would have none of the mechanical wonders with which we are now familiar.'

Then, continuing his impersonation of a venerable grandfather clock, the old man moved his outstretched hand to the two o'clock position, prompting the fellow sitting there to straighten his back in anticipation of his turn. 'Samuel Perry is a representative of Blyth's shipyard, which is renowned for its products the world over.' Russell, sitting at three o'clock, was then described as perhaps the most accomplished shipbuilder working today, which raised a frown from Brunel. But his ego was quickly repaired when on reaching four o'clock Sir Benjamin described him as the most versatile engineer the world had ever known.

Five o'clock was occupied by a gentleman who appeared to be of similar age to Sir Benjamin, a man whom Brunel had greeted warmly while taking his seat. This pleasant-looking fellow turned out to be none other than Sir Robert Stephenson, who was renowned as a pioneer of the railway – or at least that was how Sir Benjamin put it.

The man sitting at the end of the table, in the six o'clock position, was of a slightly older vintage than anyone else. From his silver hair and well-lined face I would have put him somewhere in his seventies, though despite his advanced years there could be no denying he was an animated fellow, so much so that I guessed him to be of a highly nervous disposition, forever scratching his forehead and mumbling to himself. Brodie introduced him as 'Mr Charles Babbage, inventor of the difference engine'.

I was still wondering what in the blazes a difference engine might be when Old Father Time moved on to seven o'clock and gestured towards the person seated to my right. 'Mr Joseph Bazalgette, who, as Chief Engineer of the Metropolitan Board of Works, will, we hope, soon be tasked with constructing a new sewer system under the streets of London, an epic undertaking which hopefully will serve to return the River Thames to its former glory and, more importantly, have a major effect on the health of this great city's population.'

Seated between Bazalgette and myself was Goldsworthy Gurney. According to Sir Benjamin he had once been a medical doctor but then turned to inventing. Among his creations were a steam carriage and the gas jet which when played over limestone creates the bright light used to illuminate the theatrical stage. I was later to learn from Stephenson that he had adapted Gurney's gas jet as a means of propelling his now legendary steam engine, the *Rocket*.

The title of Mr Nine O'Clock fell to me, but just as Sir Benjamin began to introduce me his voice was accompanied by the sound of an accordion wheezing into life in the street below us. Before more than three notes had been played Babbage was on his feet, charging towards the window. After thrusting his head and shoulders out through the casement he bellowed at the hapless musician below: 'Cease with that infernal racket and be off, you pestilent menace!'

There was an equally colourful riposte from the busker, who, undaunted by this verbal assault, continued with the next few bars of a jaunty tune, which to my untutored ear sounded like a sea shanty.

In response, Babbage dashed back to the table and picked up a half-full decanter of wine before returning to the window and dashing the liquid down on to the head of the accordion player. The music stopped and there was further remonstration from below, where the musician sounded not a little upset to find it raining claret. 'Be thankful I do not have a chamber pot at hand!' retorted an unapologetic Babbage before closing the window and returning to his seat. 'A man cannot go anywhere in this town without having his ears assailed by some instrument of torture!'

While I was mildly horrified and not a little amused by what I'd just seen, most of my companions seemed entirely uninterested in Babbage's behaviour, acting as though it were nothing out of the ordinary – only Brunel responded, rolling his eyes and muttering, 'Here we go again.'

Babbage remained in his seat but was not to be distracted from his tirade. 'I had a full brass band outside my house the other day. They played for three solid hours and refused to disperse, even when I got the police on to them.'

'I wonder why they picked on your house?' pondered Brunel mischievously. 'It wouldn't have anything to do with the fact that you have tried to get street music banned in the metropolis, I suppose?'

'Gentlemen, gentlemen!' cried Brodie, impatiently banging his fist gavel-like against the table. 'Can we please return to the matter in hand?'

'My apologies, sir,' said Babbage, reining in his temper. 'Please continue – if you can hear yourself think over that racket, of course.'

'Thank you for closing the window,' offered a placatory Sir Benjamin. 'It has reduced the noise to a far more acceptable level. Now where was I? Ah, yes. Dr George Phillips is a fellow medical man, and one of our leading tutors at St Thomas's.'

I had no complaints with this appraisal and was grateful that, perhaps distracted by Babbage's outburst, he had passed over me as rapidly as possible. But then Brunel piped up from across the table, 'Dr Phillips is here at my invitation. He has much to teach us about his trade,' then added, as he glanced at Russell's notes, 'I also believe he may have another valuable service to offer us.'

Before Brunel could explain what this might be the irascible Sir Benjamin interjected, 'Very interesting, Mr Brunel. Now, if we could please move on. We have been delayed quite enough.'

Gesturing towards ten o'clock, he identified the well-dressed young man next to me as Mr Ockham, and then after an awkward pause, as though he were struggling to find anything more to say about him, 'who is currently serving on Mr Brunel's staff'.

Moving swiftly along, we arrived at eleven o'clock. This position was occupied by an impressively broad-backed gentleman, who from the lines on his face I guessed to be around fifty years old, though his dark beard betrayed not a trace of grey. He was almost as well dressed as Ockham but his fashion sense was far more conservative. 'Horatio, Lord Catchpole,' began Sir Benjamin, 'is perhaps best known as one of our nation's most successful industrialists, owning a number of cotton mills in the north of England. He has done much to encourage technological innovation in industry, and his factories boast the latest machines.'

'How are those new loom drivers working out?' asked a cheery Whitworth, who was either oblivious to or uncaring about Sir Benjamin's disapproving stare.

'Very well,' replied Lord Catchpole. 'Production has increased by more than 15 per cent since we had them installed. How's that money I paid you for them working out?'

'Very well, though my bank balance has been reduced by 30 per cent since I started spending it!'

Once the laughter had subsided, Sir Benjamin left the floor to Darwin and seated himself in the vacant chair at what should perhaps have been twelve o'clock but due to the presence of the speaker sat halfway between it and eleven. No doubt relieved at last to get going, Darwin pulled a sheaf of papers from his inside pocket and placed them on the table before him. 'Gentlemen, what I would like to do this evening is give you an introduction to my theory of evolution by means of natural selection, which will be the subject of a forthcoming book' – he threw a glance at Brunel, who smiled sympathetically – 'and also, as Sir Benjamin has already mentioned, the subject of a talk soon to be given to the Royal Society. If you do not mind I would like to take the opportunity of using the comments or questions you may have to iron out any shortcomings beforehand.'

The speech that followed was strong and confident, and his general bearing had little in common with the sickly individual he had earlier described to me. Only rarely did he refer to his notes. Here was a man who had spent many years pondering the great questions in life and had profited from the rehearsal of ideas inside his own head. On the few occasions that my attention slipped I looked across to see Russell scribbling frantically on his collection of papers. He was transcribing the talk, but no matter how rapidly his writing hand moved, he was finding it difficult to keep up with Darwin's words. His mouth was twisted in concentration and every now and again he shook his wrist in an attempt to wring out the cramp.

In the course of his talk Darwin put forward the hypothesis that the human race had developed – or evolved, as he put it – through a series of changes and adaptations, from the lower orders, most specifically the apes. Differences could, he explained, be thrown up by any species through the course of sexual reproduction. Some of these may be advantageous to the survival of that species and be passed on as hereditary traits through later generations while others may not be so and are therefore quickly abandoned as they die off. As a country boy I knew that Darwin was right when he told us that farmers had been exploiting this phenomenon for generations, by selectively breeding livestock displaying the profitable character-istics of greatest size and meat yield.

I had also seen examples of such differences in my own work. Indeed, the anatomy museum at the hospital contained several specimens of unfortunate mutations, the most striking of which was a newborn with two heads, one growing out of the other, their china-white faces permanently frozen into an expression of surprised injustice. Until now I had considered this and other malformations merely as unfortunate aberrations, mistakes in nature's grand scheme of things, but if Darwin was right, then these variations were all part of the process of evolution. In short, success bred success while failure was likely as not to end up in a specimen jar or, in times long ago, trapped in rock as the fossilized remains of extinct species.

The end of the talk was greeted with a warm round of applause. Darwin wiped his brow with a handkerchief, where the appearance of a few well-earned beads of perspiration would likely as not be self-diagnosed as the first symptoms of typhus.

Sir Benjamin, still clapping, rose to his feet. 'Thank you, Charles, a very thought-provoking talk. Now, with your permission, I would like to open the floor to questions.'

Darwin nodded and pocketed his dampened handkerchief.

Bazalgette was the first to speak. 'Mr Darwin, how do you see your argument that we are descended from the apes being received by the Church?'

'As heresy and blasphemy, of course,' replied Darwin with a nervous smile.

Bazalgette was about to speak again, but Whitworth beat him to it. 'And where does the Church stand on this issue of change occurring over such long periods of time?'

Darwin let out a snort of laughter. 'Well, as those of you with some knowledge of theology will know, Bishop Usher has calculated, by counting back through the generations mentioned in the Bible, that the world was created just over 4,000 years ago. This is obviously arrant nonsense. As far back as the middle of the last century naturalists such as Buffon in France came to recognize that the world must be much older than was traditionally thought, and from recent advances in our understanding of geology there seems little doubt that the world must be hundreds of thousands if not millions of years old.'

And so the questions continued. There were a few minor challenges to his thesis, but Darwin had done his work well and the response was broadly favourable. Whether the same benevolent reaction awaited him at the Royal Society remained to be seen.

Half an hour or so into the discussion Sir Benjamin made to wind things up. Standing once again, he hovered beside the table like a waiter eager to remove a finished bowl of soup. But then, just as he was about to begin his summing up, I pitched in with my own question, an act of bravado which naturally earned a disapproving frown.

'Sir, do you regard the evolution of species and most particularly the human species as an ongoing process, which may see us taking on a very different appearance many years from now?'

'A good question,' said Darwin, but as the answer required no pause for thought I guessed it was not the first time it had been asked. 'Evolution will only proceed if advantageous changes occur. I believe that, as humans, we have reached a point where we are ideally attuned to our world. Therefore I believe that further changes are surplus to requirement. If, however, an external stimulus, such as a dramatic change in our environment, were to place the species as it stands in a less advantageous position, then it is in the interest of the species to meet these new challenges through the medium of evolution.'

Interjecting before anyone else had the chance to do so, Sir Benjamin said, 'If you don't mind, Charles, with that point I think we need to draw an end to tonight's proceedings. It just remains for me to ask for a show of appreciation for such a stimulating presentation.'

There was another round of applause, coming from all but Russell, who at long last was able to put down his pencil and rub the life back into his hand. 'Splendid job,' said Brunel, collecting the papers together and stuffing them into the leather satchel.

'Never again,' said Russell, massaging his wrist. 'We really must get a secretary.'

Brunel smiled. 'Couldn't agree more, old chap,' and then, looking over to me, 'That's where our friend Phillips comes in.'

'I beg your pardon?' I asked.

Brunel fastened the strap on the satchel and stood up. 'I want you to be our permanent secretary.'

This was one assumption too far. 'You might have asked me first.'

'I just have. What do you say?'

'I am afraid,' I said, looking to Sir Benjamin, 'that I am far too busy to be taking on duties outside the hospital.'

'You mean to tell me you wouldn't like to come along to more of our meetings? I know Russell here hasn't been the best advert for the job, but it would be different for you.'

'I don't understand how.'

'Doctor, I've seen your case notes,' he said, smiling as a frown betrayed my recollection of this incident. 'Fascinating as they were, I wasn't just being nosy that day in your office. I wanted to see whether you were up to the job. They were clear and, most importantly, they left no observation unrecorded. Well, at least that was the impression they gave in my brief reading of them. It's a rare talent; you're a natural-born secretary, Phillips.'

I muttered something about giving the proposal some thought. For, when all was said and done, he was right. After this evening's introduction, I wanted to come back for more, and if the only way that could be done was by taking the minutes, then so be it.

'We can't expect more than that,' said Brunel triumphantly, as though it were a done deal, and patting the satchel under his arm. 'We must have minutes for future reference. The key to an important scientific or engineering advance may lie in a particular comment, the answer to a question, perhaps even in the question itself.'

I caught sight of the man called Ockham making for the door as I fell back into conversation with Darwin, who once again took very little time to steer the subject around to his medical complaints.

It wasn't long before topcoats and hats were being returned to their owners and farewells being said. Darwin left in the company of Sir Benjamin and Russell, who were taking him to dinner in appreciation of his efforts. Last to arrive and last to leave, Brunel and I followed Hawes and Perry down the stairs, where we found the carriage freshly returned to the same spot we had left it almost two hours previously.

'I'll give you a lift home,' said Brunel, holding open the door of the carriage. He sank into the seat opposite me and we immediately fell into discussing the evening's events, starting with Darwin's talk. But he seemed eager to move on to other matters, namely Darwin himself.

'What was he so eager to discuss with you?'

As the man was not my patient there was no confidentiality to respect and so I replied that Darwin had sought my advice on a wide range of ailments. '. . . And apparently the first thing he does every morning is vomit.'

Brunel gleefully slapped his knee. 'I knew it! Never changes, that man. A wonder to me that he's lived so long.'

'You know about his condition?'

'Of course. Nothing Darwin enjoys more than talking to doctors. Did exactly the same thing with Brodie, the first time they met.'

'Talking of Sir Benjamin, just what was he complaining about while I was talking to Darwin?'

'Nothing much.'

'Why didn't you tell me he'd be there tonight?'

'He's always there.'

'And how would I know that? Now, come on, what was it about? Was he angry that you invited me along?'

Brunel was in the midst of preparing another cigar for ignition. 'Perhaps, but it's difficult to tell with him. He's usually angry about something.'

I had to agree with him on that point.

'He seemed a little miffed that you had stolen his patient away from him. And it wouldn't surprise me if he felt the same way about me.'

'What do you mean?'

'How long have you worked in that hospital with Brodie?'

'About five years, but up until my promotion to senior surgeon I had very little to do with him.'

'Well then, let me tell you something. When Brodie meets

someone for the first time, especially someone with money and position, he first and foremost sees a prospective patient.'

'I was aware that he had a number of private patients, yourself among them.'

'Exactly, and we're a nice little source of additional income to him, as well as a passport to other things.' He took a generous puff on his cigar, smoke billowing from his mouth as he sucked the thing into life. 'How do you think he got to be president of the Royal Society?'

'Through his contributions to medical science?'

'Not quite. He lanced a boil on the backside of the previous incumbent and treated an influential member of the council for the pox. That's how.'

'I see.'

'Imagine how he felt when Darwin told him about his veritable epidemic of complaints. The man's a medicinal goldmine!'

'Ridiculous,' I countered. 'Darwin clearly has a malady of the brain; the man's a raving hypochondriac.'

'I don't think old Brodie sees it like that.'

'Well, he need not feel threatened by me. Being a personal physician, no matter how rich or famous the patient, has never been among my ambitions.'

'Of that I have no doubt, but nonetheless be warned, he is a jealous fellow.' Brunel stubbed out his cigar in the ashtray fitted into his seat and bent towards me with an air of conspiracy. 'But listen, my friend, I have greatly enjoyed my conversations with you. We engineers and you medical men have much in common; you just happen to work with flesh and bone, while my raw materials are iron and rivets. We have much to learn from one another and that's why I would like to see you as a member of the club.'

'But if what you say is true, then isn't Sir Benjamin going to be less than happy about that?'

Brunel was not to be discouraged. 'If you were also to fill the vital post of secretary, then there is really very little he could say about the matter.'

'Ah, the secretary thing again . . .'

The carriage came to a halt. We had arrived at my lodgings. I opened the door and stepped down on to the pavement.

'Sleep on it,' he said. 'And one more thing: you had better start work on your presentation on the workings of the heart.' The door slammed shut.

'Presentation!' I roared at the carriage as it drew away. 'What presentation?'

Brunel leant out of the window and bellowed back at me, 'The presentation at which we test your mettle. We don't let just anyone join the Lazarus Club, you know!'

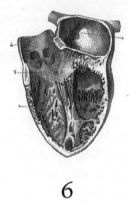

# 6

In contrast to the events of the previous evening, the day proved to be a model of normality, so much so that, for the first time I could recall, the hospital seemed a rather humdrum place to be. Even the expected showdown with Sir Benjamin, who I was certain would construe my appearance at the club as a blatant disregard of his warning against becoming distracted by Brunel, failed to materialize. Unfortunately, however, Mumrill was very much in evidence, lurking in the corridors and drifting in and out of the wards; no doubt acting as Sir Benjamin's eyes and ears while the master exiled himself in his office or outside the gates, away from the activities of Miss Nightingale.

With little else to occupy my mind, I made a full inspection of the wards and, when that was done, I took the liberty of entering William's underworld once more, this time without him as guide. Immediately thereafter I sought him out and finally encountered him in the refectory, where he was busy gossiping with another porter.

A tap on his shoulder brought the conversation to a premature end, and a flex of my finger drew him away from the table and into the corridor.

'William, how long is it now since the typhus outbreak passed?'

'Well, sir,' he replied with a scratch of his head. 'I'd say about two weeks, maybe three.'

'I would say nearer a month.' He nodded but it was clear from his expression that my question had puzzled him. 'The thing of it is, William, I have just been down into the basement.' He frowned at this. 'And before you start bleating about me going down there alone, let me tell you it wasn't by choice. You, were nowhere to be found and I didn't have all day to look for a damn chaperone. But never mind that – what I want to know is why, given the lifting of restrictions related to the recent unpleasantness, are there only two cadavers in the vat? I left strict instructions that as soon as feasible it should be fully stocked.'

William gave a nervous smile. 'Well, sir. Knowing that you prefer your specimens fresh, I've been pushin' through them that's just dead and, what with the speed you've been workin' at, I ain't had much time to build up a stock. You been goin' through hearts in particular at quite a rate of late.'

It was true: since Brunel's arrival on the scene I had indulged in a little personal research, but I couldn't see how this could impact on the ready supply of cadavers. 'But if we have another outbreak and our supplies are stopped I would rather revert to our stock of preserved cadavers than have to use the wax impressions and jarred specimens again. Why haven't my instructions been carried out?'

'You see, sir, there's also been a bit of a miss-understandin' between myself and the porters in the mortuary about our regular allotment. Been tryin' to sort it an' didn't want to worry you 'bout it. On top o' that, it's takin' a while to get things back to normal with our outside suppliers. There's a new superintendent at the work'ouse and we don't really get on. Nothin' to worry about though, sir, I'm on top of things, and that vat'll be overflowin' before long.'

'Perhaps I should go and have a word with the workhouse authorities?'

'No, sir, don't do that. I'll sort it. Leave it with me.'

'Very well, William, the matter rests in your hands. Don't let me down.'

★

With no particularly difficult case to task me I began to ruminate over the events of the night before. Brunel had said many things over the course of the evening – some of them, like his insight into Sir Benjamin's nature, had been most illuminating, while others, such as his parting cry of 'the Lazarus Club', had proved entirely the opposite.

What's in a name? There were after all dozens of clubs in London, most of them with obscure names which conjured nothing more than an image of comfort, good company and fine dining; there was White's, Arthur's, Brooks', Travellers, the Crockford, the Oriental and the Starling, to name but a few. Some of these were named after their founder, while others, such as the Reform or the Savage, reflected the interests of the members – the Reform was a den of disgruntled liberals, while members of the Savage enjoyed being rude to one another. Lazarus is not a common name these days, I grant, but I have encountered one or two of them in my time. The best-known holder of the name was obviously the man whom Christ is said to have brought back from the dead, but I saw little reason to associate him with the meeting I had attended.

But all this speculation over such a trivial matter was getting me nowhere, and it was almost a relief when, as the day drew to a close, an emergency admission in dire need of surgery on a crushed thorax required my total concentration. Unfortunately, my best efforts were in vain and the road-worker died on the table under my knife – sadly proving beyond doubt that he was no Lazarus and I no miracle-worker.

It was not how I would have chosen to end my day, but such is the surgeon's lot. After all that the thought of a cold supper in my rooms seemed an unappealing prospect and so I took a dinner of mutton chops accompanied by a nice bottle of Burgundy followed by a brandy or two at my own club, the Carlton, before finding further distraction in the arms of a young lady called Clare at Kate Hamilton's Night House, a well-respected house of ill-repute.

Next morning, feeling slightly worse for wear, I left the usual fee on the bedside table and got no further than the landing before dashing back into the room, shutting tight the door and bracing my back against it.

Clare grinned at me from across the bed, having just retrieved her stockings from beneath it. 'Can't stay away, eh?'

I could feel the colour draining from my face. 'I can't be seen here, not now.'

'What's your worry?' she asked. 'You're one of the few blokes in 'ere that ain't married. Well, you ain't, are you?'

I shook my head. 'It's not that, there are men out there who . . . who may jump to certain conclusions if I were found on the premises.'

'What kind of men?'

'Policemen.'

'What the 'ell do they want? We pay enough to be left well alone. Wouldn't mind if 'alf the force weren't bleedin' customers – the rest bein' impotent o' course.'

Clare always seemed to see the funny side of things, though I suspected this was a habit born of having to make do with less than ideal circumstances. Alas, I had a pretty good idea what the police wanted and didn't think it a laughing matter. One of the men was Tarlow, who with a pair of uniformed constables was going from door to door on the landing below and questioning the occupants. With rising panic I looked around the room and for a moment thought of exiting by the window. It wasn't so much that I feared for my reputation, as there would undoubtedly be more worthy men than myself in the building, it was the fact that Tarlow was assuming a connection between surgery and prostitutes in the murders he was investigating and here was I, the missing link between the two.

Clare saw my fear. 'Quick, under the bed!' she ordered in a stage whisper.

No sooner were the words out of her mouth than there was a rap on the door. I lay down and rolled under the bed, where my head came to rest uncomfortably close to the chamber pot. As my initial panic subsided, I began to wonder what on earth had got into me. What was I doing lying here like an adulterer hiding from a cuckolded husband? A moment more and I would have crawled out and answered the door myself. But it was too late: the door was open and, thanks to a stupid knee-jerk reaction, I was stuck there.

All I could see, alongside Clare's well-turned ankles, were a man's left foot and lower leg as he stood half in half out of the room. 'I'm Inspector Tarlow of the Metropolitan Police and I hope that you might be able to help us in our enquiries.'

'Certainly, inspector. I'll be delighted to help in any way I can,' said Clare, in her best 'sit down to tea with the duchess' voice. Her new persona was so convincing that I wasn't at all sure that the 'Bow Bells' accent she used in my earshot might not be the imitation; some of her customers probably liked the common touch. Whatever the case, the girl had clearly missed her vocation; any one of the West End's theatres would be glad of her talents, and she'd probably make a decent actress to boot.

Tarlow took another step into the room, no doubt to check whether there was anyone else in it. 'Do you recognize this woman?'

Not being able to see for more than a foot above the floor, I could only assume that Clare was being shown a photograph.

'Sorry, no. I don't recognize her,' then after a pause: 'She looks . . . is she dead?'

'We think she may have been murdered last night, perhaps the night before.'

So the inspector had a third victim on his hands. Lying there, with my eyes turned up to the bed springs, it was impossible not to conjur the image of another evisserated torso.

Clare took a step back, distancing herself from the picture. 'Why are you asking me about her?'

'We think she was a prostitute.'

'Oh I see. God rest her soul, but from the look of her she wouldn't have fitted in here.'

'I see what you mean. She doesn't look – how would you put it? – she doesn't look the right class, more likely a streetwalker. Even so, you may still be able to help. Have you had any gentlemen acting out of the ordinary, perhaps being aggressive or making strange requests?'

'Inspector, what we call ordinary would make a sailor swoon. We get all sorts of strange requests, but bad behaviour isn't tolerated, not by the girls or the management. We generally get a decent class of customer, perverted perhaps but decent, and that's why I work here. In short, inspector, I don't come cheap.'

'No . . . no, I'm sure you don't,' said Tarlow, for once sounding a little uncomfortable.

'Is there anything else I can help you with?' added Clare, as though she couldn't resist playing on his embarrassment.

'No, thank you. That will be all. You've been most helpful. I would just ask that you report anything . . . well, anything out of the ordinary, and be careful, there is a murderer at large.'

'I will, inspector, goodbye.'

With the door closed, I pulled myself from under the bed and brushed myself down.

'He must be one of the impotent ones,' I suggested, relieved that my galloping heart rate was beginning to slow.

'Don't be cruel, doctor. The copper were a gent, that's all,' said Clare, once more the Belle of Bow.

'Me, cruel? I am just glad I couldn't see his blushes from where I was lying.'

'Well, at least there ain't no blemish on your reputation.'

'Thank you, Clare, that was good of you. I'm sorry you had to see that photograph.'

She shrugged her shoulders. 'That poor slapper weren't the first dead body I've seen.' Pulling aside the curtain, she looked down into the street. 'There they go. I think you can leave now. I 'ope they find the maniac they're lookin' for.'

I picked up my hat from the washstand, looked into the mirror and grimaced at the pale face staring back at me. 'So do I.'

Tarlow's foot was unfortunately not the last of the man I was to see that day. By mid-afternoon he had tracked me down to my office.

'Not another murder, I hope.'

'I am afraid so, doctor. We pulled a body from the river early this morning.'

'And the chest?'

'The same, heart and lungs removed.'

'And you are still assuming they are prostitutes?'

Tarlow nodded. 'If they weren't, then I am sure we would have had enquiries from concerned family or friends by now. That's the third body, and not a squeak about missing people from anyone. In any case, only a prostitute would allow herself to get into a situation where a stranger could kill her unobserved.'

'And you think this killer is still out there, prowling around and looking for his next victim?'

'Something like that. We have been questioning prostitutes, hoping they may have noticed something out of the ordinary about their customers. We are working on the possibility that the murderer may be a regular customer, perhaps one who has become a little tired of the usual services on offer. Unfortunately, the prostitutes have not been hugely cooperative. But then, you would know that, wouldn't you?'

'I am not quite sure what you mean.'

Tarlow looked to the hat rack beside the door. 'I see you managed to retrieve your hat from Kate Hamilton's Night House after leaving it there this morning.'

I gave him an incredulous look.

Tarlow picked up my hat and examined it. 'A quality topper, to be sure. Distinctive, too, because of the slight kink in the band just here. You were carrying it along with your coat that first time we met. I also saw it on the washstand of one of Miss Hamilton's girls when I questioned her this morning. I am sure she will have told you of my visit. A very handsome young lady, if you don't mind me saying so.'

The kink in the hatband had been made by the card on which Brunel had written his note of thanks and to the layman's eye was all but invisible. But I was in no mood to be congratulating the inspector on his impressive powers of observation. 'I wasn't aware that my private life was under investigation by the police.'

Tarlow replaced the hat. 'I am not here to pass judgement on your personal life, doctor, just to warn you to be careful. The perpetrator of these crimes seems to have an interest in surgery and is intimate with prostitutes. You wouldn't want people to draw the wrong conclusions.'

I couldn't have agreed more.

# 7

Brunel's gift may have caused some embarrassment but it also served as a reminder of the plight of those men at the yard who had suffered such terrible injuries in his service. Thanks to intelligence from Willliam I had learned that several of them were still patients at St Clement's hospital in Mile End. Telling myself that my interest was motivated purely by a professional interest in the long-term effects of trauma, which in part it was, I decided to pay them a visit. But there was also another reason – the incident still troubled me, and I wanted to reassure myself that my intervention had been of some worth; you might say it was a case of my pride following someone else's fall.

Not wishing to incur Sir Benjamin's wrath again, this latest excursion was to be made during my off-duty hours, on one of those rare days when my time was my own.

Sporting my muffler against the winter cold, I took a cab across town. At St Clement's I asked a porter for the duty surgeon, but he was busy and so I was taken directly to the men's ward to see the patients. I could have been in my hospital, so similar was the arrangement of beds against the grey walls, only here the rooms were smaller than at St Thomas's, some of them no larger than my own parlour, but still containing half a dozen beds or more. There must have been about forty beds in the main ward, and every one of them occupied. Some patients sat up, chatting with their neighbours, while others appeared to be sleeping or unconscious. It had been weeks since the accident and only the two most badly injured victims were still bed ridden.

The porter led me to a man sat with his back cushioned against the wall by a thin pillow. I recognized him as one of those who had been knocked cold by the impact of his fall; his face had obviously been badly bruised but was now beginning to return to what I guessed to be its normal ruddy pallor.

I introduced myself and he shook my hand warmly. 'Good to see you doctor, they tell me here I'd be pushin' up daisies if it weren't for you actin' so quick. The name's Walter, Walter Turner.'

'How are you feeling Walter?'

'Not bad, sir. Should be out in a couple of days. Feel as though I've been in this bed for a lifetime. God know's when I'll be able to get back to work though, if ever. Broke hip and both legs, I did. That's on top of the nail that went through my lung. The old lady ain't too pleased, I tell you, she's goin' to have to work extra to keep us fed.'

'I'm sorry to hear that.'

'Still, not as bad as Frank over there.' He pointed to a bed on the other side of the room. 'Been slippin' in and out of it since we arrived. Not sure about Frank, they're not. Poor sod. Bash on the head, nasty, very nasty.'

I looked over at the inert form of Frank, his head was covered in bandages and he lay still as a corpse.

'But the company will see you all right?'

'Guess they'll pay us a few bob, though they won't be 'appy about it. He reached forward to rub a leg and said bitterly, 'Sometimes I think they prefer it when we're killed outright so they can forget about us.'

'Accidents happen a lot then?'

'Christ, yes – there must have been at least ten deaths and dozens of injuries since we first started work on that big bitch of a ship. You know, I've seen injured men wait for more than an hour before someone thinks to get 'em to hospital. The bloody bosses are usually more concerned about the damaged equipment and time lost than the broken men. I'm pretty sure I'd be dead now if you hadn't gotten me treated so quick, least that's what the doctor says.' He paused and looked over at Frank again. 'But as my wife says, you can't make a cake without breakin' eggs. An' I've got to 'and it to Mr Brunel, the man puts himself at as much risk as the rest of us. Got to respect 'im for that.'

'I don't recall seeing him flying through the air.' I declared, recalling how Brunel had insisted on an immediate return to the launch so soon after the tragedy.

'Oh he has, he has,' muttered Walter.

I was intrigued, but the man was clearly in need of rest and so I said goodbye, stopping briefly at the end of Frank's bed on my way out. Walter's reference to eggs and cakes brought to mind Miss Nightingale's comment about the cost of progress. Were these broken men really the price we had to pay?

My departure was delayed by the late arrival of a doctor, who was just about to commence his rounds. Once introductions were made he was happy to discuss his patients. Not surprisingly, Frank's prognosis wasn't at all good. His skull had taken the full force of the blow from the flying beam and if he pulled through at all it would be without many of his mental faculties. I was also saddened, but equally unsurprised, to hear that Walter would never be capable of manual labour again. Broken eggs, both.

While we were talking my attention was caught by someone else entering the ward. He was wearing a workman's jacket and his hobnailed boots clattered on the wooden floor as he walked between the beds before coming to a halt at the foot of Walter's. There was an exchange of words but he was too far away for me to make them out. I guessed him to be a fellow labourer come to visit his injured work-mates, and so returned to my conversation with the doctor. I was vaguely aware of the new visitor moving from Walter to Frank. As I had done, he hovered briefly before returning in our direction. As he drew closer to the door I was astonished to recognize Ockham, the well-dressed young man from the Lazarus Club, his eyes hidden beneath the peak of a shabby cap and his wiry frame now clothed in a suit, which looked to have been scavenged from a rag man's cart.

Naturally, my usual first reaction would have been to call out in greeting, but his appearance had come as too much of a surprise to permit a normal reaction and so instead I kept the doctor between myself and Ockham, hiding as best I could. Why on earth would a man of obvious means now choose to dress like a lowly labourer, and indeed mix among them?

My colleague must surely have thought my behaviour odd as, after bobbing up and down before him, I brought the conversation to an abrupt close and set off in pursuit, following the sound of Ockham's boots as they echoed along the corridor and then stamped off down the street. He walked with no apparent hurry and seemed entirely relaxed in his working man's garb, at one point stopping to purchase a bag of chestnuts. He ate them as he walked, dropping the shells on to the pavement for me to crunch underfoot as I followed in his train moments later.

We headed south through the sprawl of Limehouse, passing through West Ferry and continuing on towards the Isle of Dogs. I was now in familiar territory, having walked down this road with Brunel after abandoning his carriage before the launch. With the river flowing sluggishly along to my right, there could be little doubt that Ockham was making for the shipyard.

After two miles I was starting to flag, but if anything Ockham, his destination in sight, had picked up the pace. There was Brunel's great ship, its towering funnels cutting the skyline long before the hull hove into view. She seemed slightly closer to the river's edge than when I'd seen her last but still had a long way to go.

I was relieved to see the gates to the yard, and had to resist the temptation to stop and take much-needed refreshment at the public house strategically positioned just outside them. Ockham walked through unmolested, with me no more than thirty paces behind him, hoping I would not be stopped. I needn't have worried. The man on the gate was busy shouting at the driver of a huge wagon stopped half in and half out of the gate loaded with hydraulic rams.

'I don't give a tinker's cuss how much of an 'urry you're in, mate!' the gatekeeper roared to the driver as I used the wagon and its six horses to cover my passage through the gate. 'I need to find out where you're to unload before I can let you in. It's bloody busy in there and the last thing we need is you and your filthy big rig adding to it.'

Without the crowds of people swarming everywhere the area in front of the ship now seemed like a vast open plain, gently sloping down to the daunting iron escarpment on the horizon. In the far distance dozens of workmen ducked in and out of view among the cradles and beams along the underside of the hull. Others moved along the deck of the ship, and a small but constant stream of men passed in both directions on the stairway in the siege tower. Winches and cranes hauled payloads of all shapes and sizes up the face of the hull and on to the deck.

Closer to where I stood, at the top of the slope, a pair of heavy horses pulled on a length of chain towards the ship, its double links raising dust as it was dragged noisily down the slipway. The sound of metal hammering against metal issued from the high-roofed sheds to my left and right. Outside one of them a tenement-sized stack of wooden crates awaited opening or removal, I couldn't tell which. Just in front of me five men pulled on a rope attached to what looked like a hangman's scaffold as they lifted an iron beam on to the back of the trolley on which they would wheel it down to the ship. Three men dragged a similar empty trolley back up the hill, having delivered their load at the foot of it.

I took all of this in as I looked for Ockham, who since getting in through the gate before me had disappeared from sight. I wandered around for a while at the top of the slope and was just about to give it up as a bad job when I spotted a tell-tale fragment of chestnut shell on the ground, and then another a little further ahead. The trail led me down a roadway to the right of the gate terminating at the huge sliding door of one of the sheds. The big door was closed but cut into it was a much smaller, man-sized aperture.

Light shafted in through windows high up in the walls to illumi- nate a scene of the most intense industry. Vast pieces of machinery sat everywhere, and the entire floor was covered with steel wheels, rods and cylinders. The noise was now almost deafening, as each component was tended by a man, most of whom were beating away at their charge for all they were worth. Chains hung from girders in the roof and from these more examples of the engineer's art were suspended. I followed a path through this maze of iron, looking at each man as I strolled by, my muffler pulled up to my nose in attempted disguise.

While some men hammered others polished, rubbing metal with oily rags until it gleamed like the surface of a mirror. I turned a corner and came across three men pulling down on the long shaft of a mighty spanner, turning a nut the size of a lady's hatbox. Another chestnut shell crunched under my foot.

Ockham sat on a stool, rasping away with a file, looking for all the world like a blacksmith crouching before the hoof of a horse with a newly fitted shoe. But this was no horse. He sat beneath a many-spoked wheel, its great rim cogged with triangular teeth. The wheel hung in the air, attached to an axle set into an A-frame. He worked one tooth at a time, filing away the burr left by the casting to create crisp edges. Every now and again he stood up and, taking hold of the spokes, turned the wheel on its axis, bringing another batch of untreated teeth into reach.

Now I had found him I wasn't sure what to do next. Should I tap him on the shoulder and say hello? I wanted him to turn round and see me, to remove my freedom of action, but he was too deeply engaged in his task.

As it happened, it was I who felt a tap on the shoulder. Brunel gestured for me to follow, unwilling to raise his voice against the din.

'Couldn't stay away, eh?' he said, once we had stepped back out into the daylight.

'I just thought I'd come along and take a look at how things were going. I wanted to know whether you'd managed to get her in the water yet.'

He turned away to watch the wagon, which had by now entered the yard and was being unloaded. 'We've managed another twenty feet or so.' He seemed genuinely pleased with progress and gestured to the wagon with his cigar. 'I've ordered in just about every hydraulic ram in the country. We were under-powered, that's all.'

'You think they'll shift her?'

'They will if we can keep the chains from snapping.' He took off his hat, which prompted me to thank him again for his gift.

'Think nothing of it,' he said, 'You did a good job with the men.'

'I just did what any doctor on the spot would have done.'

'That may be, but you were on the spot.'

While he was being candid I turned the conversation towards the real reason for my visit. 'I see that Mr Ockham is employed here as a labourer. I would have thought a man of his obvious standing would occupy a position of some responsibility.'

Brunel replaced his hat and was about to speak when the sound of one of the rams crashing to the ground redirected our attentions to the wagon. 'MacKintyre!' he yelled. 'I'll have your hide if you break that ram before we have the chance to use it!' Then he turned to me. 'Forgive me, Phillips, but I'm going to have to supervise this delivery myself, things are a bit heated at the moment. Perhaps we can talk another time.

'The hat looks good on you, my friend,' he said, before returning to work, shouting orders and slapping backs. With any chance of repeating my question lost, I made my way back to the gates.

I was soon to discover that the Isle of Dogs, which, shipyards notwithstanding, is really nothing more than a fetid marsh populated by a cluster of dilapidated windmills, is not the best place to catch a cab. With no option left but to walk back to town, I set out to wear down more shoe leather. After only a few paces a carriage pulled into the side of the road ahead of me.

'Dr Phillips, isn't it?' called out the man who stepped halfway out of the vehicle. 'Can I give you a lift?'

'That is very good of you, Mr Whitworth,' I replied. 'I was not relishing the idea of tramping back into town.'

'A pleasant surprise for both of us then. Come aboard.' Whitworth grabbed a hand and pulled me up on to the step. The door closed and the carriage lurched forward. 'Tell me, doctor, what brings you to this godforsaken part of the world?'

Not quite sure of the answer myself, I told him I was on my way home after a meeting with Brunel. 'And you, sir, have you been visiting the yard yourself?'

Whitworth nodded. 'A little business with Mr Russell.'

'Didn't Sir Benjamin say you build machines?'

'That's right, everything from machine tools to cannons. In fact, I make the machines that make the cannons. I have always felt that diversification is the key to success.'

'Didn't Mr Darwin say something along those lines?'

Whitworth grinned. 'I do believe he may have done. In truth, though, I can barely remember what has been said at those damn talks from one day to the next. But I usually learn a thing or two and, in any case, the meetings provide a useful opportunity for the odd piece of business.'

Whitworth glanced out of the window, where the ship's false horizon was disappearing from view. 'I had been hoping to equip Mr Russell's yard with a new steam press, but I am not sure he is in the market for such an expensive piece of equipment at the moment.' Then he returned his attention to me. 'It sounds as though Mr Brunel has picked the right man to be our secretary. I hope that you are going to accept the position?'

'I have still to make a decision on that. I am afraid that the hospital makes considerable demands on my time.'

'Well, you have my vote anyway. We could do with some new blood.'

'Thank you,' I replied, before seizing on an opportunity while I had it. 'Mr Whitworth, could you perhaps tell me how the Lazarus Club got its name?'

'Now that I do remember,' he said with a laugh. 'Why, we have Mr Babbage to thank for that. I think it was he, along with Brunel and young Ockham who first started the thing. Then others joined. Russell and Bazalgette were early recruits, them having crossed paths at the Great Exhibition back in 'fifty-one. After that, new technology and feats of engineering became all the rage, but Brunel and Ockham, in particular, were interested in all manner of subjects, including medicine' – he nodded at me to stress this last point –

and so Sir Benjamin was invited along. The usual practice was for members to give presentations on subjects that interested them, usually relating to their own work, and then once everyone had done that, they began to invite guest speakers along, and at times encourage them to join, which is how I ended up there.

'Not long after I became a member Babbage gave a talk, in which he introduced us to the idea of the difference engine.'

'I've been wondering about that. What exactly is a difference engine?'

'My dear chap,' said Whitworth wistfully, 'we would require a journey from Edinburgh to London for me to fully explain that, and even then we'd probably need to take a detour to Brighton and back to answer your question. In any case, I think he intends to give us a talk on his latest work in the near future. Much better from the horse's mouth, as they say.' I was already regretting my interruption – we were fast approaching Limehouse and I was determined to discover why the Lazarus Club was so called before leaving the carriage.

Whitworth began again in an almost apologetic tone. 'That would be if I could remember the details about the damn thing. Complicated blighter it is, went straight over my head at the time, but I pestered him about it long enough to get the gist.

'In a nutshell, though, the difference engine does just what the name suggests; it uses mechanical means to arrange the differences between numbers and combinations of numbers.'

I was obviously looking confused.

'You have heard of logarithms?' I nodded without conviction. 'They are calculated as tables, but those calculations have up until now been carried out manually, and so they contain errors. The engine does the same calculations mechanically, through a clever system of cogs, wheels and levers. Very ingenious, but Babbage didn't stop there. More recently he's devised what he calls an analytical engine. It's capable of even greater feats of mathematics and can make any calculation you can think of, with any string of numbers.'

'And he has built these things?'

'Ah, you see, that's the thing about Babbage. He is such a perfectionist that he will set people to work at construction and then stop them because he's come up with a better idea of how such and such a part could work – quite impossible really. I offered to finance the construction of the analytical engine, but it was a disaster. I had to pull out before he lost me a packet.'

The traffic was not as heavy as I hoped it might be, and we were now making good progress through Whitechapel. 'Fascinating,' I said, 'but what about the Lazarus Club?'

'Oh yes, of course. Well, you see, the two things are related, the engine and the name. As you may have guessed from our last meeting, Babbage is a little . . .'

'Different?'

'Quite. Once he gets an idea into his head, that's it, he won't let it go until he's come up with an answer. He has many obsessions but most of these are to do with numbers, most particularly statistics, hence his machines. Now, during his first presentation to our group, for we had no name then, he talked about his investigation into miracles. You know, the type from the Bible.'

'Yes. Please go on,' I replied.

'Well, those who believe in them put miracles down to an act of God. But not Babbage, oh no. He thinks they are a reflection of the same laws that govern nature, thinks that miracles belong to a higher order of natural law. As such he believes he can calculate the statistical chances of any given miracle occurring. The example he used was of a dead man coming back to life. According to Babbage the chances of that were, one in . . . now let me think . . .'

The carriage was entering the street in which my rooms were located and still he hadn't finished his tale.

'One in . . . well, anyway, it was a mighty long shot. But the point is that this tickled Brunel pink. It struck just the right chord with him, because he saw the club as a place where no topic was out of bounds, and men of ideas were free to stray from the known world to that which may be shrouded in mystery. "That's it!" Brunel roared at the end of Babbage's talk. "We'll call ourselves the Lazarus Club!"'

It had been like delivering an awkward baby, but now it was out and I breathed a sigh of relief, just as the carriage came to a halt.

Whitworth gave a wave and the carriage clattered off down the street. Brunel had certainly been right about one thing: they didn't let just anybody into the Lazarus Club.

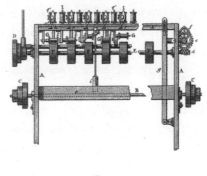

# 8

In late January 1858, after three months of pushing and pulling, without fanfare or jubilation, Brunel's great babe slipped into the river. Like the rest of London I was elsewhere when the iron mountain finally made a splash – then, as now, busy in the hospital. Through most of February that grey place, with its bed-lined wards, wood-panelled corridors and top-lit carvery served as more of a home to me than any suite of rooms. I had come to look forward to Miss Nightingale's visits, her presence in the hospital by now having extended well beyond the requirements of the inspection. Little did I know it then, but she had grand plans for St Thomas's. But perhaps most importantly, there was little in the way of outside temptation to stray from my labours, and I had not laid eyes on Brunel since that day in the yard. I could only assume that like me he was a busy man. His ship may have made it to the water but she was far from complete and from what I read in the papers he had plenty of other tasks to keep him occupied.

It was the Lazarus Club that drew me back into the engineer's orbit. Once again he had invited me along as an observer. To my relief nothing further had been said about me giving a presentation to the club, and I had no intention of raising the matter myself. On this occasion the meeting was held in the rather different surroundings of Babbage's fine home in Dorset Street, Marylebone.

On my first encounter Babbage hadn't entirely struck me as the sociable type, but his open house made more sense when I learned that his workshop was also located at the same address. As Whitworth had forecast, the reason for our visit was to attend a presentation on his analytical engine, which thanks to our conversation I had at least heard of, if not at all understood.

Babbage seemed more relaxed within the walls of his own abode, if still alert to any form of disturbance from the street. His workshop was a building in the courtyard adjacent to the property and was filled with all manner of devices, giving it more of the appearance of a cabinet of curiosities rather than a functioning manufactory. Our host was happy to explain the history and function of whichever of these objects caught our attention. These included a pair of boards with leather straps attached below which was mounted a pair of flaps, rather like the covers of a book. According to Babbage they were a very early invention of his, a pair of shoes for walking on water. 'Well, they will be of little use to Isambard,' boomed Russell. 'The man believes himself capable of that much already.' In other circumstances the comment could have been construed as an insult, especially coming from the big Scotsman's mouth, but on this occasion it elicited only laughter, particularly from Brunel himself. The truth was that we were grateful for being provided with an excuse to laugh because it would have been the obvious response to Babbage's device, and that would have been plain rude, especially in his own home.

As it happened, the idea wasn't as outlandish as it first seemed, especially when one considered that it came from the mind of the boy which Babbage had been at the time. He explained that with the shoes strapped to the feet, the flaps beneath were forced apart when the foot was brought down on the surface of the water. In principle, this would impart resistance enough to prevent the foot from sinking before the next step was made and the process repeated. Moving at a rapid pace, the water-walker would thus be able to trot across the surface. The next peal of laughter was led by Babbage himself as he explained how he had almost drowned when putting his prototypes to the test, having got no further than two steps before he was entirely swallowed up by the water. He did not try them out again.

I wish I had found the inventor's explanation of his analytical engine so easy to comprehend and was relieved that it was not down to me to take the minutes, though I was of a mind that should Brunel ask again then I would probably accept the post. It did not help that the device had yet to be constructed. Even his difference engine, an idea he had first come up with some thirty years previously, had got no further than a small prototype which Babbage used to demonstrate the function of the complete mechanism. Three columns of polished cogs sat within a framework of shafts and cranks, all of which was set into a mahogany base. Each of the cogs had numbers etched into it and it was these which provided the calculations requested of the machine by the operator. Although several members of the audience had already seen the machine in operation, Babbage was keen to show it off to those like myself who had not.

After tinkering with the device Babbage took a turn on a crank, which served to rotate various of the cogs in the columns, and after which he sometimes called it the cogwheel brain. Each motion multiplied the figures displayed on the front of the cogs by six, thus six became twelve, twelve became eighteen and so on and so forth. Impressive as this was, the calculations were somewhat basic, but after fifteen pulls on the lever had been used to produce ninety, the machine seemed to miscalculate, as the next movement produced not ninety-six but one hundred and eighty, and the next three hundred and sixty. To those who had seen the machine before this obviously came as no surprise, indeed several people, including Brunel, who did not seem to think it worthwhile to take minutes on this occasion, looked rather bored with the proceedings. It was left to Catchpole to ask what had happened with the sequence of numbers. Pleased to have elicited a response, Babbage explained that he had previously set up the machine so that it would add the figures in blocks of six and thereafter would multiply the resulting figure by two. The calculations of which the machine was capable may have been basic, but what cogs and pre-set instructions eliminated was human error, and when dealing with large numbers, as was the case when logarithmic charts were under construction, even small errors could cost lives, as the charts were used, among other things, to navigate at sea. Errors could be further compounded by mistakes in typesetting when the tables were being prepared for printing. In Babbage's finished machine these too would be eradicated as the machine would print its own tables as each calculation was made.

The analytical engine would be even more intelligent, if that is a term which can be used in reference to a machine. Not just capable of basic additions or multiplications, it would be able to execute any calculation using any sequence of numbers. The data to be fed into the device, thus providing the basis for calculation, was transferred from a series of cards with holes punched in them in a particular pattern which was then read by the machine, much like sheet music in a musical box.

Following a few perfunctory questions, we returned to the drawing room in the house for refreshments. Although I understood him to be a widower the room had a feminine quality, which I noted was entirely absent in my own residence. There were fresh flowers in vases, small ornaments and other pieces of bric-a-brac and finely worked pieces of crochet covering the backs of the chairs. As if to ensure that everything was in its place and remained so, two pairs of female eyes stood sentinel from portraits hanging side by side above the mantelpiece. I was to learn from Babbage himself that one was his wife and the other his mother. There was yet another female portrait sitting on the mantelpiece – he was certainly a man for the ladies, I thought. The image may have been much smaller than those hanging above it but the diminutive scale did little to disguise the beauty of its subject. However, before I could bring myself to enquire about her identity Babbage was called over to yet another picture, this time of a man, who from the vice-equipped bench behind him and the rack of chisels appeared to be seated in a workshop not too dissimilar to that we had recently left.

'Ah, that is Monsieur Jacquard,' said Babbage with enthusiasm as he crossed the room. 'He was the inventor of the Jacquard silk loom. You will note that you are not looking at a painting but a portrait woven from silk.'

'Good grief! So it is,' exclaimed Stephenson after making a closer examination. Taking my cue from Babbage, I joined the small crowd now gathered around the picture.

Only when my nose was almost pressed against the framing glass could I make out the different coloured threads of silk which had been woven together to make up an incredibly detailed portrait, as lifelike as any other in the room executed with paint and brush. In what was almost a continuation of his presentation, Babbage professed much admiration for the Frenchman, who had first exhibited the picture at the Great Exhibition. It had been woven on a loom which was capable of creating the most intricate patterns, as so effectively demonstrated by the portrait. The Jacquard loom, as Babbage went on to explain after pointing out that the object pictured next to the seated figure was a model of the device, operated in accordance with instructions provided by a series of punched cards which dictated the pattern of the weave. If a rod on the machine encountered a punched hole then it passed through and no action resulted. If, however, there was no hole and the passage of the rod was blocked then it engaged a hook which pulled up a particular warp thread and allowed the shuttle carrying the weft thread to pass beneath it. It was this system of information transfer which Babbage had adapted for his analytical engine, and which now, when described in the context of its original application, made much more sense to me.

Lord Catchpole put his hand against the glass. 'The effect is quite fantastic. What *incredible* detail. I had heard of the Frenchman's loom but had clearly failed to comprehend the full scope of its capabilities. Why, I must see about purchasing one for my silk mills in Macclesfield; it would both broaden our range of products and reduce manpower costs.'

'Just how many people do you have working in those mills of yours, Catchpole?' enquired Stephenson. 'If that's not an impertinent question.'

'Not at all. When last I checked with my managers there were nearly ten thousand people working in twenty-three mills scattered across the north of England.'

Stephenson let out an impressed whistle. 'No wonder they call you King Cotton! That's a veritable army of workers you have up there. Talking of which, how have your labour relations been of late, no more trouble since those riots – what did they call them?'

'They were the best part of ten years ago,' replied Catchpole, letting out a slightly nervous laugh. 'And they were the Plug riots, so-called.'

'Of course, they pulled the plugs out of the boilers in your mills, didn't they?'

'The work of a few Chartist agitators. There was a lot of rabble-rousing and some poorly coordinated attempts at halting production – the draining of boilers, damage to machinery, that sort of thing. But you would be surprised how quickly grievances melt away when they come face to face with a few horsemen with drawn sabres. Before long the workers were pleading to be allowed back to work. The yeomanry did sterling service, but don't misunderstand me, gentlemen, King Cotton I may be but a despot I am not. My workers are paid on a par with those in the employ of the most generous of my competitors, but for that I expect at least loyalty. Mark me, my friends, we cannot allow dissent, in whatever form, to interfere with the economic growth of our great nation.'

All this talk of dissent among mill workers meant little to me but I did recall a time when agricultural workers in the West Country, not far from my childhood home, rioted and smashed up new-fangled threshing machines which they feared would put them out of work. Progress, it was clear, was not regarded by everyone as a good thing.

'But enough of the past, gentlemen,' announced Catchpole. 'It is surely the future which interests us. Now, where has Babbage got to? I must ask him how I can get hold of one of these wonderful French machines.'

Babbage was now on the other side of the room, having left our company to engage in conversation with Ockham, who to my surprise had a warm smile stretched across his face. It was the first time I had seen him exhibit anything but stony detachment, let alone a smile, and there could be no doubt that it suited him. But the moment the pair became aware that attentions were being directed towards them, his new-found levity was snuffed like a candle.

Eager to pursue his latest business venture, Catchpole strode over to the pair, at which point Ockham muttered something to Babbage, nodded politely to the approaching peer and left the room.

Ockham's departure marked the end of the gathering, and people began to drift away. Among them was Brodie, with whom I had not exchanged a word all evening. Before I took my own leave I had a brief conversation with Stephenson, who like the others seemed to have enjoyed the proceedings.

'Babbage seemed much calmer than usual.'

'He always was happier in his own home. It takes me back, you know.'

'What does?' I asked.

Stephenson gestured around the room, at those of us still left. 'This, the meeting here. I remember the days when he regularly hosted little gatherings which the great names of the day would attend to discuss their latest ideas and inventions.'

'You mean like the Lazarus Club?'

'I suppose you could say he laid the foundations for the club, yes. Like Brunel, he didn't have much time for the Royal Society; in fact, he was very vocal, as he tends to be, in his criticism of it. He thought it was run by self-serving amateurs and never tired of saying so. His little soirées were in part a response to that. But things were much less formal back then – Babbage wasn't running a club, he was just being sociable.' Stephenson glanced at the portraits above the mantelpiece. 'No minutes for one thing. I think it was also a way of coping with his personal tragedies, after his wife and children died from illness. Some really interesting people, though; some of our present members were regulars but there were also artists, actors and the like – that novelist chap Charles

Dickens turned up on more than one occasion.' Stephenson lowered his voice and looked to check whether Babbage was in earshot. 'But then his work on the engines took over his life and then his mother passed away – she was the last remnant he had of a family and he was quite devoted to her. That was when his nerves started to get the better of him. There were no more meetings after that, not until he took up with Brunel, that is, and Ockham of course. He strikes me as a Babbage in the making that one, difficult to get the measure of, though.'

I could only nod in agreement. 'They seem very well disposed to one another – Babbage and Ockham.'

Stephenson nodded and I hoped for a further insight but before it could be offered Babbage approached and the moment was lost.

# 9

It had been a two-operation afternoon. First off, alas quite literally, was a little girl's arm. The poor soul had been badly mauled by a dog and from the bruising on the rest of her body it looked as though the beast had shaken her like a rag doll. If she'd been brought in immediately after the attack, then it may have been possible to save the limb. But the mutt responsible was one of her father's own fighting dogs. He ran an illegal pit in Shoreditch and so had been less than eager to reveal the dubious nature of his livelihood. The brute was in tears when he finally got around to bringing her to the hospital, and his wife couldn't bring herself to look at him. He had first entrusted his daughter to a back-street quack, whose dirty instruments merely completed the work the dog had begun. By the time she reached me, an incision halfway above the elbow was as low as I was prepared to go. Fortunately, her arm was stick-thin and after administering a minimal dose of ether I took it off in record time. As her parents made to leave the girl in the ward the mother rushed back and through sobs told me her husband had gone into the kennels that morning and cut the throats of his eight dogs. She didn't know how they were going to live now.

The second case had been less traumatic. An old woman with a bad abscess on her neck – a straightforward lancing job. The extracted pus would have filled one of William's liquor bottles.

Then Sir Benjamin appeared, looking as usual rather exercised about something. 'Dr Phillips, I trust you are fully prepared for tonight?'

I was still thinking about the little girl and so it took a few moments for his meaning to sink in.

'For tonight?'

'Yes, for your presentation at eight o'clock.'

It had been weeks since our last meeting, and Brunel's proclamation that such would be expected of me had by now entirely slipped my mind. 'You mean to the Lazarus Club?'

'I do wish Brunel would not insist on using that dreadfully melodramatic title,' exclaimed Sir Benjamin. 'I'll be frank with you, Phillips. Brunel, as you are well aware, is my patient. What you may not know is that he is in fact a very sick man and I fear that his increasing interest in . . . shall we say rather morbid matters is doing little to aid his condition. I would therefore appreciate it if you would refrain from encouraging these unhealthy interests.'

I could only assume that these morbid matters included the engineer's interest in the workings of the human body. This was after all not an unheard-of response to somebody suffering ill health but it was the first time any mention had been made of an actual condition. 'What are his symptoms?'

The abrasiveness returned. 'Never mind that. He is my patient and his symptoms are therefore none of your concern. But he has a rather obsessive nature, which I have long since refused to indulge, which is I fear why he has turned to you.'

Sir Benjamin's protective attitude was laudable but seemed a little, to use his own term, melodramatic. But I saw nothing out of the ordinary here – Brunel himself had warned me that the man would jealously guard his position of physician to the great and the good. But why he should regard me as a threat I couldn't quite understand, for there could be no doubting the high regard in which his abilities were held – why, he'd even treated royalty in his time. Perhaps his advancing years were the root cause – it couldn't be too long before he would have to step down as hospital superintendent, at which time his private patients would become a useful adjunct to his pension.

Whatever his motives, I was keen to defuse what seemed an entirely unnecessary conflict. 'Very well, Sir Benjamin, I will endeavour to steer him away from these morbid interests in future. But to get back to more immediate matters, are you certain that I am expected to give a presentation at eight o'clock tonight?'

He nodded.

'But surely I should have received something by way of a formal invitation?'

Sir Benjamin sighed but remained unmoved by my plight. 'I suspect that was deliberate. Even I learned about it only today. I suspect this is Brunel "testing your mettle", as he would put it.'

This seemed most unreasonable and I now regretted not raising the issue with Brunel at Babbage's house. 'But Sir Benjamin, I would require at least a couple of days' notice to prepare a presentation.'

Brodie seemed almost pleased by my capitulation. 'Then I am to tell the meeting you have declined the invitation?'

I pulled out my watch. 'It's five o'clock already. I have three hours.'

The mere suggestion that I might be willing to give it a try was enough to irritate him. 'Understand this, sir,' he said in his most pompous voice, 'I was less than happy to discover that Brunel had invited you along to a meeting without first seeking my opinion on the matter, and then to hear him invite you to take up the post of secretary! I trust you will be declining the offer?' At long last, here was the dressing down I had expected weeks before.

With no answer forthcoming, Sir Benjamin continued with his admonishment. 'Given what I have already said about your past association with Brunel and its ill effect on both of you, your absence tonight would probably be for the best. I shall therefore pass on your apologies and we will say nothing more about the matter, nor mention the club by name again. Are we agreed?'

'No, sir, we are not,' I replied, hotly – now convinced that he had deliberately kept the information from me. 'It would be impolite of me to decline Mr Brunel's invitation, no matter how informally given.'

Sir Benjamin bristled further at this, but I knew him well enough to turn the argument in my favour. 'And in any case,' I continued, 'would it not reflect badly on the hospital if I were to decline the invitation simply because I was not prepared? In short, sir, I think it would reflect as badly on you as it would me.'

I had him in a corner, and he knew it. 'Very well then,' he growled. 'If you insist on going ahead, I trust you will show the hospital in the best possible light.'

Sir Benjamin's departure left me very little time to enjoy what I knew might turn out to be a pyrrhic victory. I now had less than three hours to prepare a presentation to some of the nation's finest minds.

Back at my rooms, the only food I could muster was a half-plate of cold meat and for once I regretted not having engaged a house-keeper. At around seven-thirty, I set out with what few notes and diagrams I had managed to throw together.

On the tavern stairs I felt like a condemned man climbing the scaffold, throat dry and stomach bound in knots, though the latter was, I am sure, in part a result of my unsatisfactory repast. Fortu-nately, though, this anxiety passed away entirely as soon as I began my presentation.

It was Brunel's turn to take the minutes, and having begrudgingly replaced the cigar between his fingers with a pencil, he was ready for me to begin. Russell, on this occasion relieved of his responsibility as scribe, seemed much more relaxed than previously. Ockham, dressed again as dandy rather than labourer, occupied the same seat as before, while Perry, Bazalgette, Whitworth and the others distributed themselves around the flanks of the table. Sir Benjamin offered apologies on behalf of Stephenson, who was unwell, and Hawes, who had urgent government business to attend to.

My master stroke, or so it proved, was to repeat my earlier, private demonstration for Brunel, placing minimal reliance on the drawings and making constant reference to a real heart, which sat on the small cutting board before me. The next hour was something of a blur, but by the end of it the heart lay in pieces and the audience was satisfied enough to offer up a robust round of applause. Even Sir Benjamin seemed pleased with my performance, but perhaps not quite as pleased as Brunel was to put down his pencil. There were questions aplenty, not surprisingly many of them from Brunel, who had obviously given the subject some considerable thought since our early encounters.

The company began to disperse while I tidied up the detritus of my presentation, wiping down the board with a cloth and wrapping the pieces of the heart in it. Before I could return it to the bag Brunel asked if he could take it away with him, explaining that he would find it useful to examine the pieces at his leisure. Grateful to be relieved of the item, I handed over the heart, but not before removing the gore-soaked cloth and rewrapping the pieces in a clean handkerchief. 'Don't hang on to it for too long. It hasn't been preserved in liquor and so will decay rapidly.'

'Just a couple of hours will suffice,' he said, dropping the bundle nonchalantly into the pocket of his coat. 'But first things first,' he said, slapping me on the back. 'Myself and some of your fellow Lazarians would like to take you for dinner to celebrate your success this evening.'

And so it was that I came to be accepted as a fellow member of this illustrious but obscure little club, albeit in the guise of its unpaid secretary. My decision to accept the post had delighted Brunel as much as it had irritated Sir Benjamin. It was however Babbage, who in addition to inventor of calculating machines and scourge of street performers happened to be a talented cryptographer, who told me that the earliest holders of the post did just what the name suggests – they kept secrets. Little did I know then just how many secrets I would uncover while serving as secretary to the Lazarus Club.

Satisfying as it seemed at the time, not least because it must have come as something of a kick in the pants to Brodie, my induction into the Lazarus Club in fact marked the beginning of my troubles, the first inkling of which came in the form of another visit from Inspector Tarlow. Since our rather difficult second meeting another corpse had been pulled from the river, again minus heart and lungs. He had not however troubled me for a post-mortem examination on that occasion and I only learned that a fourth body had been discovered when he came to visit me just a few days after my formal acceptance into the club.

Tarlow was alone, which at first made me think he was here to deliver another warning, as I had done little to alter my personal habits since our last meeting. What he did deliver was a small wooden box, which he gestured for me to open.

'Careful, doctor, the contents are a little ripe.'

Indeed they were, for the removal of the lid liberated the unmistakable stench of rotting flesh. The contents were wrapped in hessian sacking with ice packed around it, though this was rapidly melting, so much so that I had noticed water dripping from the box even before it had been handed to me. Placing the bundle on the table, I carefully unwrapped it. The stench grew stronger as the coarse fabric was teased away from the adhesive surface of the carrion which lay within. With the gore-impressed sacking removed I took up a scalpel and poked at the grey mass of muscle sitting upon it. A little prodding and pushing was enough to separate what had at first seemed an amorphous mass into four distinct pieces and to my horror I recognized the atrophied remains of the heart I had dissected during my presentation to the Lazarus Club and then given to Brunel for his further delectation.

The quartered organ presented me with a terrible dilemma. My immediate inclination was to come clean and tell Tarlow everything; after all, no law had been broken. But to do that I would have to tell him about the club, the existence of which seemed to be a fairly well-kept secret among its members and their friends. Further, it struck me that having won the trust and respect of such an esteemed group such a confession would be regarded as nothing other than an act of betrayal.

'Well, inspector, as I am sure you are aware, what we have here are the remains of a human heart. One of the pieces has been badly mauled, looks like it has been chewed. Where did you find it?'

'The mauling was inflicted by a small terrier, the owner of which was taking it for a walk in a very respectable area of the city when it dug the thing out of a pile of rubbish. As fortune would have it a police constable was passing by as the dog-walker struggled to wrestle that piece of gristle from its mouth, causing quite a commotion into the bargain. The constable recognized the mouldering scraps for what they were and took charge of them. You have just confirmed our suspicion that they did in fact constitute a human heart.'

'You think that it came from one of the corpses pulled from the river?'

'A natural conclusion, wouldn't you say? How many human hearts can there be kicking around the city?'

'Not many, I suppose – all of our anatomical leftovers are incinerated and certainly don't end up on the rubbish heap. What about that rubbish heap? You said it was in a respectable part of the city?'

Tarlow nodded. 'In Pall Mall, awaiting collection by the dust cart.'

I tried not to sound anxious. '*Very* respectable. Can you tie it down to an address?'

'Unfortunately, no, not even to a street. The rubbish had come from several adjoining streets. I sent men back to examine it more closely but by then it had been cleared. It may not even have come from the locality, just dumped there by somebody walking by.'

The news was not as bad as it could have been. Duke Street, where Brunel lived, joined with Pall Mall, but in the circumstances it would be impossible to trace the heart back to his house at number 18. It also seemed likely that as the area was so respectable Tarlow was favouring the hypothesis that it had been dumped by a passer-by. This was enough to satisfy me that it was highly unlikely that the heart could be connected either to Brunel or myself and so I saw no reason at all to broadcast my involvement.

The inspector seemed to think I had asked enough questions.

'What can you tell you me about it, doctor? Anything special in the way it has been cut up into four pieces like that?'

I looked down at the mess on the table. 'It would allow for a thorough examination of the interior aspects, giving access to all the chambers.'

'Would you cut it up like that, perhaps to demonstrate the organ to your students?'

I was tempted to answer no, there was no way a surgeon would cut up a heart like that, but he may already have sought advice from elsewhere and already know it was an accepted dissection technique. If that was the case then he was merely testing me.

'Yes, it's not far off the sequence of incisions that I or any other surgeon would use. The technique is clearly set out in the surgical textbooks.'

'Then it needn't be the work of a surgeon?'

There he was with the surgeon thing again. 'Not really,' I replied. 'There is no great skill involved. In fact, it's almost the natural way to quarter a heart, if that's what you want to do.'

Tarlow seemed disappointed. 'So it doesn't narrow down our search.' But then, sounding a little cheerier, he announced: 'There is one other thing that may prove of assistance.'

'Oh, what's that, inspector?'

The policeman reached into his pocket and pulled out a heavily stained piece of white cloth. 'The bits of the heart appear to have been wrapped in this handkerchief.'

My own heart sank like a stone. Tarlow unfolded the handkerchief and examined one corner, where even before he showed it to me I knew the letters 'G' and 'P' were embroidered in blue silk thread. I had thought nothing of it at the time but the handkerchief in which I had wrapped the heart had been embroidered with my monograph by my sister and given to me as a present some years previously. Since the meeting I had come to regret the loss of the keepsake but nowhere near as much as I did now. How could Brunel have been so foolish as to dump the heart on his own doorstep, and still wrapped in my blessed handkerchief! If only I hadn't been so carried away with the excitement of the moment and warned him to be careful.

'There's a monograph on it,' observed the inspector as I prepared myself for the worst. 'But, unfortunately,' he continued, 'the dog also got hold of the handkerchief and chewed into the corner. Only part of a letter remains. Looks like it could have been a "C" or an "O", perhaps even a "G".' He handed me the rag. 'What do you think?'

Suppressing a sigh of relief, I looked at what remained of the letter, remembering how much care my sister had taken with the stitching. 'It could be a lower case "a", or even a "Q", I suppose.'

Tarlow took the handkerchief back, looked at it once more and nodded before stuffing it back into his pocket. 'I won't keep you any longer, doctor. My thanks for your assistance once again. Could you do me a favour and dispose of that wretched thing for me? I can't bear to carry it around any longer.'

'I will be glad to, inspector. By the way, how long ago did the last body come to light?'

'About three weeks ago. Why?'

I made a performance of wrapping the heart back up again. 'Well, if we assume that there was a timelag between removal of the heart and the dumping of the body, and then presumably further delay before it was recovered, let's say that the heart would have been removed from the fresh body perhaps four weeks ago, maybe even longer.'

'Right, go on.'

'If I understand you, this heart came to light much more recently.'

'About two days ago.'

'Then, as there is no evidence for the artificial preservation of the heart through the use of chemicals, it would seem unlikely that it comes from that body. I'll grant you, it is past its prime, but it is not as badly decayed as it should be if it was removed from a body around a month ago.'

The inspector did not seem entirely convinced. 'What about ice?'

'It's a possibility, but difficult. As you've no doubt found yourself, keeping a regular temperature with ice for that long is tricky. We use it in the mortuary sometimes but it only gives us a few days' more grace.'

'So what you are suggesting is that this heart may not be related to the last murder or indeed any murder at all?'

I nodded. 'It's a possibility.'

'Or perhaps we just haven't found the body from which this heart was removed yet.'

Tarlow reminded me of the terrier chewing on the heart: once he got hold of an idea it took a real struggle to get him to let go.

'I had better be on my way,' he said, and then, turning to leave, he put his hand in the pocket containing the handkerchief. 'I never caught your first name, Dr Phillips.'

I almost choked on my reply. 'George, the name's George Phillips.'

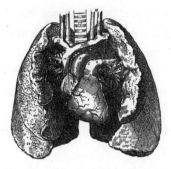

# IO

As the spring of 1858 passed into summer, so the meetings of the club became more regular and I soon fell into my new role, and truth be told I found it no chore at all, jotting down the salient points and then fleshing out my notes in longhand before surrendering them to Brunel. There were talks on all manner of subjects, from mechanical tunnelling devices to the medicinal use of exotic plants from the Amazonian rainforest. Though new speakers appeared every month the core membership of the club remained constant, and I began to feel very comfortable in the company of my fellow Lazarians, though there were times when Brunel and Russell could barely bring themselves to talk to one another, so strained was their professional relationship. If there was an occasion when Russell failed to appear at a meeting, however rarely that might be, then it was obvious to all that the cause had been a particularly unpleasant spat between the two of them – Brunel however seemed entirely unmoved by such unpleasantness and never failed to appear.

Ockham remained as aloof as ever, slinking away after every meeting without so much as a by your leave. He always kept his own counsel after presentations, never asking questions or joining in the discussion. But if a man wants to keep himself to himself, then that's his business; I had more important things on my mind.

It was the summer of the Great Stink, so-called because high temperatures turned the effluent-rich waters of the Thames into its closest impersonation yet of a vast open sewer. The stench was dreadful, assailing even my well-tempered nostrils, and on some days was only bearable from behind a scented handkerchief tied over mouth and nose. But this primitive measure was as ineffectual against disease now as it had been during the plagues of years gone past, when a pocketful of posies was carried as a preventative measure.

In a similar vein, the curtains in both Houses of Parliament were soaked in chloride of lime to reduce the foul odour, but to no avail, and in June the building was evacuated. It was a national disgrace, and *The Times* regularly carried some story or other about the dangers to public health posed by these dreadfully unsanitary conditions.

The typhus epidemic, which fortunately did not spread too far away from the neighbourhood of Newgate prison, had died down months ago but now it had been replaced by the spectre of an equally deadly disease. It was now widely held that the high temperatures and disgraceful condition of the river provided ideal conditions for a major outbreak of cholera, and I prepared my staff for the worst. London's last major outbreak had been just four years before, when hundreds had fallen victim. The celebrated Dr John Snow may have recognized the connection between contact with polluted river water and the spread of the disease, but the authorities had taken an age to authorize the grand new sewer scheme.

'Keep together, gentlemen,' insisted Bazalgette, sounding more like the master of an unruly school class than the leader of an outing of the Lazarus Club. The comparison, it must be said, held equally for his charges, who after disembarking from a small convoy of specially commissioned carriages commenced to wander willy-nilly, get in the way of workmen and generally make a nuisance of themselves. 'Gentlemen, please,' Bazalgette pleaded. 'The workings are dangerous. I would hate to lose any of you to an unfortunate accident.'

It was October 1858, and we had come down to Deptford to inspect a trial length of the new sewer. The long hot summer had finally drawn to a close and thankfully the expected outbreak of cholera had not occurred. The trip had been Brunel's idea, 'We need to get out and see more,' he had suggested after a particularly dull presentation in the stuffy environs of our hired room. A debate over which locations might be worthy of our interest ensued, with places as diverse as the Woolwich arsenal, Millwall docks, the Greenwich observatory, Pentonville prison and the British Museum nominated. Catchpole suggested that we should all get on the train to Bradford and visit one of his mills but it was unanimously agreed that the distance was too great. Diligent as ever in my duties, I noted down these potential destinations and, feeling slightly mischievous, had to pull myself up short from adding Kate Hamilton's Night House to the list.

Unlike Brunel's famous tunnel under the Thames, the southern entrance of which came to the surface not far from us, the drains were, wherever possible, not to be dug underground but from the surface, the brick vault being constructed in trenches before the reinstatement of the excavated earth. Bazalgette called the technique 'cut and cover', and it was one such section which we had come to see at Deptford. The site of the works was marked by wooden scaffolding which kept the mouth of the brick tunnel upright as work proceeded on extending it. Workmen shouldering hods full of bricks clambered down ladders while others placed them in position with a speed made possible only through long practice. Men pushed wheelbarrows along planks of wood laid across the trench and from there dumped earth on to the curved roof of the brick tunnel beneath them. Recent progress was marked by a long fresh scar of broken ground the width of a road.

'We've built the best part of half a mile in just over a month,' announced Bazalgette with fatherly pride before going on to give a brief overview of the project. The brick tunnels would transport fouled water away from the Thames and carry it to outfall points at Beckton to the north and Crossness to the south. Infiltration plants there would then facilitate the removal of solid waste from the water before it was released into the river outside the city and carried out to the sea.

'How long do you think for the entire scheme?' asked Russell.

'We will finish the main works within five years,' said Bazalgette, who seemed entirely undaunted by the immensity of the project. 'The main interceptor system will require over eighty miles of tunnels, and that doesn't include connectors, outfalls and storm drains like this one. Now, gentlemen, if you would like to take note of the mortar being used to bind the bricks.'

All eyes became focussed on the men slapping the mud-like substance on to bricks before fixing them into position in the tunnel mouth. 'That's Portland cement, and this is the first time it has been used in a public-works project of any scale. You take limestone and clay, mix the two together and then calcine them in a furnace to remove the carbonic acid. The result is a very strong bonding agent much stronger than the old Roman cement and, very importantly, it is waterproof.'

Fascinating as all this was, I was keen to see inside the tunnel and so was pleased when Bazalgette directed us to a shed some distance behind its mouth. Inside was a circular hole in the ground, from which the top of a ladder protruded. 'One at a time, please, gentlemen, some of you may find it a bit of a squeeze.'

Those of us who had turned out for the excursion had some idea of what awaited us and so we took a lamp each and waited for the man before us to step on to the ladder and disappear from view. The few absentees included Stephenson, who once again seemed to be suffering from ill health, while Babbage had insisted that it wouldn't be too long before he went underground for good and saw no need for a dress rehearsal.

Brunel, as befitting someone who had done much to secure Bazalgette's appointment as director of the project, went first, leaving his hat behind before taking to the ladder. I followed him, with Catchpole stepping on to a rung above my head just as I let go at the bottom. Brunel was looking out towards the open mouth of the tunnel, watching the workmen labouring on the scaffolding, from where they extended the arch, using the steady supply of bricks provided by the men we had seen clambering down from the surface. The engineer seemed lost in thought as he watched the work.

'Does it bring back memories?' I asked, my voice echoing more loudly than I would have liked off the brick walls.

'There were times down there when I never thought to see daylight again,' he said. 'Tunnelling in the dark is bad enough but knowing there is a river just feet above your head is something else entirely.'

I would have liked to hear more of his exploits in the Thames Tunnel. 'Those men out there have it easy then?'

'My friend, those men are the backbone of England. Their daily labours in light or dark would break any one of us.'

It was the first time I had heard him express any sympathy for the lowly workman, and his answer made my off-the-cuff remark seem a little foolish, but before I could respond Catchpole, freshly arrived behind me, added his own opinion: 'But backbones too can be broken. Isn't that right, doctor?' Although asking a question, he didn't seem interested in the answer. 'There will,' he continued, 'come a time when we will have machines do all of this. They will be more efficient and less expensive. Machines do not require payment, nor do they fall ill.'

Brunel had turned round, and the glare of his lamp revealed what looked to be an expression of distaste. 'There can be little doubt that you are right, Lord Catchpole, but what about them – what about the men who made our scientific and technological advances possible through the sweat of their brows? What part do they play in this mechanical future?'

Catchpole looked set to continue the exchange but the rest of the party had begun to arrive at the foot of the ladder.

'I will lead the way, gentlemen,' said Bazalgette, who with a wave of his lamp directed our attentions away from the open mouth to the dark part of the tunnel.

'I assume it will carry water?' said Sir Benjamin, who seemed a little surprised to find the channel beside the walkway to be dry.

'Indeed it will,' replied Bazalgette, who took the question as a cue to step off the walkway and position himself in the centre of the channel. 'The function of this section will be to carry excess run-off into the river at times of heavy rain.'

'Rainwater and not sewage?' said a voice from the back of the assembled mass, which I knew to be Perry's.

'That's right. Storm drains like this will provide a way of diverting excess water away from the main system. The system will cope with up to a quarter of an inch of rain during the six hours of heaviest sewer use. If that limit is exceeded then the storm drains will come into operation. Any sewage coming off with the rainwater will be heavily diluted and therefore provide no risk.'

'How certain are we that polluted water is the cause of cholera?' asked Russell, looking to Sir Benjamin for his answer.

'There seems little reason to doubt the studies made by Dr Snow. I am sure you have all seen the drawing in the newspapers depicting the skeletal figure of death dispensing water into the cups of young children from a street pump. It is a crude image but puts across the message. Cholera is not spread by foul air or, as some call it, a miasma but by people drinking dirty water; of that I am in no doubt and I am sure Dr Phillips agrees with me there.'

I nodded, slightly surprised that he had sought my affirmation, but there were those who did not agree. Miss Nightingale for one had her feet firmly in the miasmic camp.

'Thank you for that, Sir Benjamin,' said Bazalgette. 'Your support is much appreciated. I should add at this point, gentlemen, that the full scheme has not yet been officially sanctioned. The small stretch you are visiting today is only a trial, designed to demonstrate that the project is feasible.'

'I think you can rest assured there,' chimed Brunel. 'The scheme is essential to the well-being of the populace. It is just a matter of time.'

Bazalgette nodded appreciatively and with no more questions forthcoming he ushered us onwards. 'Now, if we take a walk down the tunnel I am sure you will appreciate the view.'

We moved in two lamp-lit columns, the first along the walkway and the second in the channel. Our journey through the dark was not a long one. The tunnel took a gentle curve to the left, and even before it began to straighten, daylight was illuminating the immaculate brickwork on the tunnel wall to our right.

The lamps soon became redundant, for beyond the tunnel mouth the day seemed to burn as bright as one of Gurney's famous theatrical limelights. We gathered on the lip of the tunnel, where it gave way to the river beyond. The water lapped against a stone ramp, down which the storm water would one day find its way into the river. Those of us at the front stepped a little way further on to the ramp to allow those behind us a view over our shoulders. I couldn't recall ever being so close to the river before, not even when Brunel was trying to get the great hulk of his boat into the water. And there she was, floating some way off downstream, like a whale at last released from a beaching. Upstream was Limehouse, its dingy tenements backing cliff-like on to the river. Directly across from us was Millwall on the Isle of Dogs, where one or two families still earned a crust by processing river-delivered corn in their ancient wind-powered mills.

Spectacular as the view was, the aroma from the river was almost unbearable and even those of us accustomed to the bouquet of the mortuary found the clawing stench uncomfortable. But there was the rub: it was the smell of the mortuary, but a mortuary in which the bodies had been lying far too long. It was Russell who from his position on our upstream flank spotted the cause of the olfactory assault. 'What the hell is that?' he asked after taking an involuntary step away from the water's edge.

Floating in the water but resting against the side of the ramp was a body, the naked back bobbing just beneath the surface of the water. The only clue to the corpse's sex was the straggling dark hair, for the torso had lost integrity and looked more like a burst sack of chalk. There was a risk of someone ending up in the water as those of us at the front tried to get away while those with no clear view shifted forward to take a look.

'Calm, gentlemen, please!' cried a stern voice that for once wasn't Bazalgette's. It came almost as a surprise to discover it was mine. 'Everyone step away from the water. Bazalgette, could you please take everyone back up the tunnel and have a message sent to the police.'

While the others were herded back into the tunnel, their excited voices echoing off the brickwork, I returned my attention to the corpse.

'What are you going to do, Phillips?' asked Sir Benjamin, who had remained behind. For once he seemed entirely disarmed by the situation.

'Get the body out,' I said, uncertain how I was going to manage it without touching the thing.

I thought he was going to stay but instead, after telling me he would fetch help, he followed the others up the tunnel.

I had hoped that our last encounter, over the affair of the abandoned heart, would be our last and yet here we were again. Tarlow was using a handkerchief against the stench, and the sight of it caused me to shiver at the recollection of that previous conversation. 'The same then?'

'It appears so, inspector,' I replied, dropping the tarpaulin back into place. 'The contents of the chest have certainly been removed.'

'How long has . . . has *she* been dead?'

'Yes, it is a she and it's very difficult to say. Maybe three weeks, perhaps less. The river corrupts.'

'Is there anything else you can say about her?'

'I'm sorry, inspector, the corpse is just too far gone.'

Tarlow made to leave the hut where the body was being kept prior to the arrival of a wagon. 'We are very fortunate to have you on hand once again to assist in this unpleasant business. Quite a change for you to be finding the corpse rather than me having to bring it to you, don't you think?'

'It was actually Mr Russell who saw the body first,' I replied, trying not to sound overly defensive.

The discovery of the corpse had cast a shadow over our excursion and, following the initial excitement, the group had fallen into a thoughtful silence, watching without comment as the policeman walked by on his way back to his carriage. 'He didn't even stop to question us,' said Whitworth later, as though he were complaining about a host's failure to offer refreshments.

Despite our grizzly find, Bazalgette's sewer scheme had looked highly promising. The only thing was, it would take years to build. Never had a population been so relieved to see the cold of winter replace the heat of summer and it was generally felt to be nothing short of a miracle that the threatened outbreak of cholera had not occurred.

Not all the news was good, though, and one day in November I received a letter which was to take me away from London to attend to a more personal medical crisis.

*My dearest George,*

*It grieves me to have to write to you under such tried circumstances but I am afraid to report that our father is gravely ill. Knowing how busy you are at the hospital, I have until now resisted the temptation to worry you. But today Dr Billings made one of his regular visits and after a thorough examination told me that his condition is not recoverable. He may have weeks or even months left but, the doctor says, the outcome is inevitable. I therefore beg of you to come home and see him while you still can, even better if you could find the time to tend him. You are a wonderful doctor, George, and I might even dream that your attentions may bring about even a temporary return of his health. I look forward to hearing from you. It has been far too long since last we saw one another and I hope that this letter may help to bring our separation to an end.*

*Your loving sister,*

*Lily*

Sir Benjamin was uncharacteristically sympathetic about my plight, but more particularly my father's. Their paths had crossed many years previously, when on first setting up practice in London my father had briefly taken Sir Benjamin under his wing. I had long before given up wondering whether their acquaintance had played any part in my appointment to my present post: I hoped it had not, and indeed had taken some comfort from Sir Benjamin's prickly attitude towards me, which pointed against it. It took him no time at all to deliberate on the matter and to grant me as much compassionate leave as I would require to tend to my ailing father. He asked me to pass on his best wishes and closed by saying, 'Off you go, and don't worry about the hospital. I am sure we will manage to rub along without you.'

## II

The great vaulted cavern of stone and iron that was Paddington station echoed to the sound of people and machines. A pair of locomotives idled, their stacks pushing dirty plumes of smoke up towards the roof, where they dispersed among the girders. I bought a copy of *The Times* from the W. H. Smith's kiosk and asked an attendant which of the trains would take me to Bath. Following his directions, I walked along the concourse and down the far platform before stepping aboard the first compartment to appear less than crowded.

I flicked open my newspaper and sought the illusion of solitude behind its densely printed pages. For once there was no reference to Brunel or his ship, but as usual there was a raft of stories about dramatic burglaries, terrible fires, coroner's reports on a clutch of suicides and melancholic accidents, the latest on the bloody mutiny in India and, last but unfortunately not least, the recovery of the mutilated body of a woman from the dirty waters of the Thames.

The latest body had come to light just the day before, some three weeks since the grizzly discovery at the sewer. There was no mention in the short column of the bodies previously fished from the river, but there was little comfort to be had from this journalistic oversight as it was obvious how my coincidental departure from town would appear to the worryingly inscrutable Tarlow, who I was now certain suspected me. This was not the sort of news to bring me comfort at the outset of the journey which every father's son dreads making.

The train lumbered through a dark canyon of brick walls and building backs, cutting its way through the ever-expanding sprawl of London. Even so, the view from the window had more appeal than the depressing contents of the newspaper. Warehouses and factories gave way to terraced houses as we approached the city's outskirts. Smoke and sparks swept by the window, but as we picked up speed this fog of locomotion lifted to reveal green fields and rolling hills.

The newspaper may have been devoid of reference to Brunel, but there was no escaping the man and his influence. This was, after all, his line. Just like the station from which my journey had originated so these rails, cuttings, bridges and tunnels had sprung from his drawing board. He had personally measured out every inch of the route we now coursed along at such impressive speed. Without his Great Western Railway, my journey would have taken on a far more arduous aspect, necessitating a long and uncomfortable coach ride along uneven roads, and for this at least I offered the engineer a silent vote of thanks.

With stops at Swindon and Chippenham behind us, the daylight was suddenly snuffed from the sky as we were dragged underground, the din of the train squeezed against walls of stone. The inside of my ears popped like a bubble under the weight of the ground above. The train raced through the dark for an age, moving for a mile or more through the not-so-solid rock. On and on we went, fixed in our seats like mice trapped in the belly of a burrowing snake. I crumpled the news in my hand and was glad to be blind to it, watching as sparks whipped past the window like fireflies in a maelstrom. We were in the Box tunnel, yet another of Brunel's creations. Once he had fixed the best route for his railway, he wasn't going to let the small matter of a hill cause any deviation, whatever the cost. Two years the job had taken, and Lord knows how many men perished hewing the rock.

As ever, there had been those eager to cast doubt on the practicality of the scheme. Brunel had barely been able to hold back the laughter when he told me about the fantastically titled Dr Dionysius Lardner. The good doctor, no doubt sponsored by the engineer's rivals, postulated that the combination of the train's speed and the confined space of the tunnel would suffocate the passengers before they cleared the other side. There had been other detractors of the Great Western Railway, of course. Among them were the Provost and Fellows of Eton College, who believed the railway would bring London's houses of ill repute within the range of their wealthy pupils.

To my relief, myself and my fellow passengers were still alive and well at the other end of the tunnel. Not long after, we arrived in Bath.

It took longer than I had hoped to find a driver willing to take me as far out of town as I required. Eventually, I managed to engage a farm cart, pulled by a skinny nag and driven by a scruffy fellow who I had no doubt would drink even old William under the table. The bone-rattling ride followed sinuous tracks and droves across the gently rolling Downs. Despite the pink glow of the evening light there was a distinct chill in the air. The only sounds to be heard, aside from the constant squeak of the cart's wheels, were the chirrup of birds in the hedges and the lowing of cows in the fields. A more dramatic contrast to the hustle and bustle of London I could not imagine.

But the peaceful surroundings did little to soothe my sense of nervous expectation. Dealing with patients suffering all manner of terrible maladies in the hospital was one thing; the prospect of confronting terminal illness in one's own father was entirely another.

My childhood home was a pretty enough little place, a stone-built two-storey house nestling into the side of a hill with a front door framed by what during the summer would have been a rose-covered trellis. Having lost all feeling in my backside, I hobbled down from the wagon and paid the driver. With bag shoulder-slung I lifted the latch on the gate, pinned to which was a small brass plaque carrying the inscription:

## Bernard Phillips MD.
### Surgery by appointment only.

It was a lie, of course, for in truth the sound of the gate swinging open and then snapping closed would count as appointment enough for any patient in need of my father's curative skills. The front door opened and a blur of white fur launched itself into the garden, followed in rapid succession by a woman wearing a floral-pattern apron. The little dog, my father's over-excitable West Highland terrier, bounced around my shins, yapping and slavering over my shoes. 'Jake, leave him alone,' cried Lily with a laugh, hitching up her skirts as she hurried along the path.

I put down the bag and greeted the dog with a perfunctory 'Hello, boy!', gently pushing it aside with my foot and holding my sister tight before stepping back so as to take a good look at her. Her dark hair was beginning to show silver strands and thin lines had appeared around the edges of her eyes and mouth. She was still as handsome as ever, though, but then doesn't every brother say that about his sister?

'Oh George, it is so good to see you,' she gushed, fighting back tears. 'I had convinced myself you would not be able to come. You are always so busy at the hospital.'

'How could I stay away from my big sister a moment longer?'

'Do not fib, George Phillips,' she retorted in good-humoured admonition. 'It must be well over a year since we saw you last.'

Almost instinctively, she touched my collar, straightening it as she had so often done in years past. Mother had died not long after I was born and much of the responsibility of looking after my father and myself had fallen to Lily. It was a task to which she had taken with an at times almost irritating capability. She made to pick up my bag but I beat her to it and gestured that she should lead the way.

'I will ask Mary to brew some tea. You must tell me all about London.'

I draped the coat over a hook in the hallway and looked sheepishly towards the stairs. 'How is he?'

She paled. Only then did I guess that many of the lines on her face were recent arrivals, etched through the strain of tending our father.

'Oh, he has his better days,' she said quietly. 'Dr Billings has been very good, driving over from Lansdown whenever he can.'

'I should go up and see him.'

She shook her head. 'He's asleep. Have your tea, then we can go up.'

The old man was obviously in a bad way and Lily was trying to delay my inevitable confirmation of the fact. I smiled and played along. 'I have brought you a catalogue. If you pick out a dress I'll have it sent when I get back to town.'

She brightened. 'Thank you. You must tell me all the gossip.'

Lily's enthusiasm for such trivia had always amused me, as she had deliberately avoided any prospect of life in the city, even to the point of turning down urban-dwelling suitors. After a protracted courtship she had finally settled for Gilbert Leyton, who was the cheerful, thick-set son of a local farmer who stood to inherit several hundred acres of grazing and a burgeoning haulage business. As yet there was no sign of children and I suspected that Lily may have worked out any maternal urge on my father and myself in the absence of our mother.

Before we retired to the drawing room I pushed open the door of the surgery, glancing at the shelves packed with a multitude of bottled powders, ointments, elixirs and pills. The light reflected from the wall of glassware as though it were a crystal chandelier, a result no doubt of each vessel having recently been wiped down and polished by Lily's restless hand.

The room's pristine appearance betrayed the fact that this was no longer a working surgery. I closed the door. 'What about the patients?'

Lily answered from the other side of the hall, holding open the door to the sitting room. 'Dr Billings has taken them on, but it means people have to travel over to Lansdown to see him. He says we need to think about the future of the practice. Father will need a replacement.'

'I told him years ago he should get a partner.'

'You know full well he always hoped you would join him in the practice. But no, you had to go off and work in a fancy hospital,' she said, somewhat sniffily.

I stepped across the hall and into the sitting room, resisting the temptation to take her to task about the reality of conditions in the hospital.

'Make yourself at home,' she said. 'I'll go and find Mary.'

I hovered for a moment in front of the fireplace, noting that the room was as immaculate as the surgery. A well-stocked bookcase sat in the corner, and between it and the fire my father's old threadbare chair sat empty, his inert pipe and unfinished book sitting on the small table beside it. I took a seat by the window and sighed as the glum atmosphere washed over me. Over the next hour I found some solace in entertaining Lily with the modest amount of salacious gossip I had carried with me, without of course telling her anything of my own recent misadventures. Mary, my father's housekeeper, kept us well supplied with tea. She was no doubt grateful for the labour, my sister having once again taken over the running of the house. My brother-in-law Gilbert, she told me, had kindly agreed to her moving back into the house for as long as was required. I could think of no one better qualified to act as a nurse, as over the years she had served as father's assistant in all but name.

Not waiting for my stories to dry up entirely, Lily suggested that we go up and see Father. I placed my cup and saucer on the tray and followed her up the stairs, bracing myself for the worst. When last I had seen him he had been a healthy, active man, gaining in years but still carrying the energy of a man in his middle life. From what Lily had told me, much had changed since then. The decline had been almost instantaneous, as though age and fatigue had finally managed to break through a door long bolted against them. On the landing she held a finger to her lips and peered into the room. A rasping cry came from the half-darkness.

'Are you going to keep my son away from me all day! George, rescue me, I have become a prisoner in my own home.' His voice was weak and wheezy but still capable of making itself heard. Lily looked back at me and rolled her eyes before disappearing into the room. I stepped into the doorway as she pulled open the curtains. The light streamed in to illuminate the large timber-framed bed on which both of us had been conceived. My father's head, propped on pillows and framed by scrolls of silver hair, protruded from an untidy bundle of blankets. Pulling a hand free from the restraint of his coverings, he took hold of the headboard and tried to pull himself into a seated position, only to be scolded by Lily.

'Father, will you keep still? I thought you were sleeping. What did Dr Billings say about getting over-excited?' She rushed over and gently lifted his head, plumping his pillows as he eased his back up the bed.

He looked at me, his eyes squinting as they accustomed themselves to the light. 'They say doctors make the worst patients, but I think daughters make the bossiest nurses.'

Pleased to see he had retained his sense of humour, I approached the bed and took his hand. His pale, paper-thin skin made his lips seem an unnatural shade of red. He squeezed my hand back as best he could. 'Good to see you, son. Too many women in the house for my liking.'

'I am sure Lily is doing a wonderful job, and you should not be so rude to your nurse. I have no intention of interfering with her regime and she's right: I don't want to see you over-excited either.'

My intention was to give him a full examination but that could wait until Lily had provided me with a report on Dr Billings' latest assessment of his condition. From what I'd already heard and seen the problem appeared to be his heart. Hard facts had to be faced. He was seventy-eight years old, and nobody lives for ever, not even doctors. All I could hope to do was take some of the strain away from Lily, help make his last days or weeks as comfortable as possible and be at his side when the time came.

'I will leave you two alone,' said Lily, passing me a chair. 'You have some catching up to do.' She bent down and kissed the patient. 'But don't talk too much, Father, you know what a strain it puts on you. Let George tell you about his times in London. I'm going down to help Mary with the dinner.' She gave me a weak smile before closing the door behind her.

I pulled the chair close to the bed and sat down. There was something I had to get off my chest.

'I am sorry not to have been back to see you both for so long. My work keeps me in the hospital much more than I would sometimes like.'

'Nonsense, my boy,' he returned cheerfully. 'You love your work and there is nothing wrong with that. But before we go any further I want to be sure we both understand the situation. You and I both know that I am dying. So let us face this like doctors, with the minimum of fuss.'

'Father –'

He raised his right hand to silence me and manœuvred himself into an even more upright position. 'George, don't interrupt. This is important. Listen to me. Your sister knows I am dying just as well as you and I. The problem is she won't yet admit it. I've had a good life. I cannot tell a lie: just like everyone else I would by choice have more of it, but I am also ready for death.' With his piece said he watched my face for a sign of understanding, just as he would do after giving me a stern dressing down for some or other childhood misdemeanour. For the first time since entering the room I became aware of the sound of his favourite carriage clock ticking on the mantelpiece.

His small boy again, I nodded.

The dying man smiled. 'Good. Now tell me what has been happening in that pestilent city of yours.'

My father's no-nonsense attitude, which was so typical of him, had gone some way to put me at my ease, and so I began to regale him with accounts of my more interesting cases. He listened intently and, belatedly heeding his daughter's advice, spoke very little, limiting his words to a question here or a comment there, though he chuckled in delight when I told him about Sir Benjamin's strained relations with Miss Nightingale. It seemed as though only a few minutes had passed before Lily popped her head around the door to let me know dinner was ready. In reality I had talked for well over an hour. But her timing was perfect, as Father was beginning to nod off and, with all my travelling and nattering, I had developed a real appetite. I pulled the blanket up to his chin and followed Lily back downstairs.

The next morning, having read the notes left behind by Dr Billings, I determined to examine the patient for myself. Another doctor's diagnosis is something to be respected but independent corroboration is always preferential. The patient, however, had no intention of letting his son examine him.

'You need not waste your time, nor mine, George. I know exactly what the problem is,' he insisted. 'I suffered an infarction of the heart and my days are numbered. What more is there to know?'

It took most of the morning to persuade him.

'What did I tell you?' he said almost triumphantly as I stepped back from the bed after listening to the sorry tale his chest had to tell me. 'No long faces now,' he went on. 'It comes to us all. Sit down, lad. Now you've got that out of the way you can make yourself useful – there are a few matters I want to settle.'

I was at first reluctant to assist my father in the settling of his affairs but, with my medical services redundant, concluded that the task would at least while away the hours. But first I had to go downstairs and report to Lily, who had been waiting on tenterhooks for my diagnosis. I sat her down and in accordance with Father's instructions explained the realities of the situation to her. When I had finished talking she sat for a while, staring out towards the window.

'Are you sure there is nothing you can do?' she finally asked, as though giving me one last chance to recall a remedy which I had for some reason overlooked.

'I'm afraid not, Lily. Time must be allowed to run its course. We should prepare ourselves for the inevitable. He certainly has.'

She stood up and, hiding her emotions, briskly announced that she was taking the dog out for a walk. I knew better than to offer to join her. Lily always went for a walk when she had something important to think about. 'The air helps me think,' she would always say. The poor dog's short legs had almost been worn down to the nub after Gilbert had asked her to marry him. I knew that by the time she returned, probably after shedding a few private tears, she would have come to terms with the situation.

With Lily out of the house I rejoined Father in the bedroom.

'You told her?' he asked.

'Yes, Father, I told her.'

'And she's taken the dog out for a walk?'

'Yes.'

'Good.'

The matter was closed and without further ado he began to issue me with orders. I was instructed to go down to his study and retrieve a wooden trunk.

The study was tidier than I had ever seen it, the desk almost devoid of its usual scattered papers and documents. Once again, I detected the hand of my sister. Like the surgery, my father's study had been strictly out of bounds when I was a child. Perhaps because of this edict the surgery in particular had always held an irresistible attraction, and when my father was out making house calls I would sometimes sneak inside and twist my tongue around the strange words written on bottle labels or ponder the use of the terrifying collection of highly polished knives and other dreadful instruments, their steel blades glinting as I reverently lifted them from the drawer of the cabinet.

My father's inner sanctum, the study, had however remained unexplored. Only as I approached adulthood had he ever invited me to enter, and it made me smile to recall the day he ushered me in to receive the obligatory lecture on the birds and the bees. He had blustered for a while, unable to find words he felt comfortable with. Eventually, red-faced and frustrated, he gave up on the task and presented me with a medical textbook, 'Go away and study this,' he had ordered. The diagrams were fascinating and from that moment on my future in medicine was assured. I remember my father's obvious pride when I told him of my desire to follow in his footsteps. Little did he know that the ambition had been born of my illicit visits to the surgery and his fumbled attempt at doing what fathers had always felt to be their duty.

I crawled under his desk and pulled out a heavy wooden trunk. It was all I could do to get up the stairs and drag it to my father's bedside.

'Well done,' he sighed, lifting himself on to his elbows. 'Behind the clock.'

I reached behind the marble casing and pulled out a key.

'Well, don't just stand there, open the box.'

After some twiddling the latch gave, the lid creaking on its hinges as I pushed it back. The musty aroma of leather and aged paper rose from the interior. My father shuffled to the edge of the bed and looked down into the open trunk. A much smaller wooden box, highly polished and with brass fittings, sat on top of a pile of documents and notebooks.

'Memories,' he said, reaching down a thin, vein-lined hand. 'But first things first.' Fearful that he would topple from the bed and guessing that he was making for the small box, I passed it up. He half twisted and placed the object on the bed behind him. 'Now, somewhere in there are the deeds to the house, and . . .' He went on with a touch of mischief in his voice, '. . . most importantly, my last will and testament.'

'Shouldn't you be doing this with your notary?' I asked.

'Don't be so squeamish, boy,' he retorted. 'The house will be split between yourself and your sister, but there are a few other things that need to be tidied up. If you can pull the paperwork together I will get Maitland to come round and make sure everything is above board.'

'Aren't these your journals?' I asked, picking up one of the thick leather-bound notebooks that filled the bottom half of the trunk like ballast in a ship. For as long as I could remember he had been in the habit of recording the day's events in his journal. And just as he had passed on the desire to become a doctor so the habit of setting down on paper the daily events of a life had also rubbed off on me.

'Oh, those old things,' he said ruefully. 'We will get to them, but first the papers. Try that envelope there.'

I put down the book, picked out a thick packet of papers and, sitting on the end of the bed, went through its contents. Due to the poor light and my father's failing eyesight it fell to me to read out the contents of every document, no matter how trivial. There were numerous receipts for medicines, pages torn from medical journals, old letters, and miscellaneous notes about patients – although most of his patient records were filed, however haphazardly, in his study. There was his medical degree from the University of Edinburgh, which some thirty years after his time there had become my own *alma mater.*

The search was frequently stalled, as my father stopped the proceedings to reminisce over any piece of paper that took his fancy. 'That is the receipt for my first set of dissection knives – you never forget the first time in the theatre, do you?' and, 'I remember the time so and so had me amputate his dog's leg after it was crushed beneath a carriage wheel.'

Failing to find the house deeds or the will, I pulled the next package from the trunk and, document by document, riffled through its contents. So we went on, late into the afternoon.

The sound of the gate opening announced Lily's return. My father's eyes may have been failing but there was clearly nothing wrong with his hearing. Just as I was about to suggest we bring proceedings to a close for the day he said, 'You had better go down and see how your sister is.'

Before going downstairs I insisted on putting the papers already removed from the trunk in some sort of order. Lastly, I picked up the small wooden box, which this time piqued my inquisitiveness. 'A surgical set?' I mused as I weighed it in my hands, but before I could snap open the latch my father stopped me. 'We'll get to that later,' he said, reaching across and taking it from me.

I left him squinting at a musty old parchment, the blankets covering his lap by now having accumulated a small mountain of crumbled fragments of sealing wax.

Lily was in the drawing room, sitting on a chair by the window. She was reading a book, I guessed by Jane Austen, who had always been her favourite. There was a time when she went all starry-eyed about a certain Mr Darcy, and it was only after some determined questioning from my father that we learned he was in fact a character in one of Miss Austen's novels. The hem of her skirt was peppered with mud from the rain-moistened footpath. The dog lay in its basket in front of the hearth, content for once to doze quietly rather than dash around the house like a mad thing.

Hearing me enter the room, Lily looked up and smiled, her eyes rimmed with the afterglow of tears. 'How is he?'

'I left him going through his trunk of papers. Goodness knows what he's got hoarded in there.'

'Best to get things sorted out now, I suppose.'

As I had hoped, her walk appeared to have done the trick.

## 12

I checked on my father's condition several times during the night. Unlike me, he slept soundly throughout. In the morning we resumed our clerical chores, delving deeper into the dark recesses of the trunk, which had come to feel more like a bottomless mineshaft. My father seemed greatly relieved when at last we untied the ribbon binding the deed to the house. 'Well, at least the family pile is safe for future generations,' he announced, waving the stiff old document before him.

I should have guessed what was coming next: 'What about future generations, my boy? What prospects are there for our modest little tribe to go marching on into the future?'

I was in no mood to discuss the prickly subject of marriage and children, never mind that it was one of my father's favourite subjects of interrogation. 'Your sister,' he continued, slapping the deed on the bed, 'has shown absolutely no interest in providing me with grandchildren, and I fear she may have left it too late. What about you? Is there a lady in your life?'

'I have hopes,' I lied, 'of attracting a certain young lady's favour.' What alternative did I have? I was certainly not going to admit to my dying father that the only women with whom I was intimate were those I paid for.

'Well, I wish you all the best with her,' he said, a little too knowingly for my liking.

Keen to move on, I asked, 'Now, what about the box?'

'Well,' he said with a grunt as he lifted the small mahogany case from the bedside table, 'I was saving these for you as a wedding present. But as I'm unlikely to see that happy day I might as well hand them over now.'

I pulled up the chair and watched as he fiddled with the latch on the box. The lid opened to reveal a pair of antique pistols, sitting in recesses lined with green baize, arranged one above the other, nestling barrel to butt. He pulled the upper pistol free and, holding it by the barrel, passed it to me. Even in my inexperienced hand the weapon felt well balanced. Growing up in the countryside, I had handled guns before, but other than a couple of half-hearted hunting excursions with an old fowling piece had only a passing acquaintance with them. 'How long have you been hoarding them?'

He picked the second pistol from the box. 'Oh, a good few years. They have quite a history, you know.'

Only then did I notice the inscription etched along the side of the barrel. I turned the pistol in my hands and, as the light cast them into relief, read the words: 'Presented by the Duke of Wellington to his good friend Dr Bernard Phillips in appreciation of long service under fire.'

Impressive as the inscription was it did not take me wholly by surprise. It was common knowledge within the family that in the years before he settled down my father had been a surgeon in Wellington's army. It was however a part of his life about which he had never spoken, at least at any length. There was a rather grimy painting of the battle of Waterloo in the house, but it languished in obscurity on a wall in the back where few people ever saw it. He had been there, at the battle, but again I had never known him to reminisce about the experience.

'War must be a terrible thing,' I said, stating the obvious, but curious to see whether I could draw him out on the matter.

'Civilians!' he barked, sounding like a cantankerous general. 'These are duelling pistols, my boy, not weapons of war. And what a story these have to tell.'

'Forgive me if I don't put the muzzle up to my ear to hear what it has to say!'

The old man smiled. 'Then I will have to speak for it.'

I set the pistol across my lap and sat back to listen.

'Well, let me see,' he began, his voice now a little stronger than it had been earlier in the day. 'It was some time after the war. I had served under Wellington in all his campaigns against the French – all the way from Salamanca to Waterloo. Then came peace. Old Boney was shipped off to St Helena and we came home. Wellington, I think somewhat to his surprise, became Prime Minister and I set up my first practice in London. This suited the Duke down to the ground. He hated doctors but had come to trust me, and so whenever he needed treatment would call on my services. He adopted me as his personal surgeon.'

I wondered with some amusement whether my father's appointment by Wellington may have inspired Sir Benjamin to ingratiate himself with the great and the good.

'He suffered from terrible gout in his later years,' Father continued. 'Everyone's heard of Napoleon's piles – some even say he lost the battle of Waterloo because of them – but only I know about Wellington's gout.

'I settled into civilian life once again and your mother and I began to walk out. But that is most definitely another story.'

The memory of those happy days caused him to drift off for a moment. But he quickly returned.

'It was 1829 and the great general was by then Prime Minister. But did that soothe his warlike manner? No, he continued to be a prickly character and to say he didn't suffer fools gladly would be something of an understatement. I've seen him reduce experienced staff officers almost to tears in the field, and that continued to be the state of affairs in Parliament.

'Then he went and franchised the Catholics. Now, Wellington was no reformer, far from it, but he was canny enough to realize that accepting if not quite embracing change was sometimes the only way to head off real trouble – so he gave the Catholics the vote.'

I snorted at this. The most civilized country in the world we may be but the Dark Ages are not so far behind us.

Never one to take religion seriously, my father nodded. 'Strange to think, isn't it? Just thirty years ago and Catholics couldn't vote. That's what comes of losing the Civil War, I suppose. But it wasn't a popular move. Some grumbled in quiet corners while others wisely held their own counsel. But not Lord Winchelsea. That buffoon made the Prime Minister look like a radical, and the fool made the grave mistake of openly criticizing him for propagating Popery. Do you know what the Iron Duke did?'

I shrugged my shoulders.

'He challenged him to a duel, that's what.'

I glanced down at the pistol in my lap. 'That's right, Wellington called him out. They tried to hush it up, of course. Duelling had been illegal for years, and for a Prime Minister to partake was unheard of. He had himself tried to ban it among his officers during the Peninsular campaign, but to no avail. A tetchy lot, your officer class.'

Although fascinated, I interrupted. 'And where exactly do you enter the story?' I asked, keen to prevent him talking for too long.

'According to the rules of the game, every duel had to be attended by a surgeon, to dress wounds or pronounce death. The old war-horse called on my services, and against my better judgement I agreed to attend – not that I had much choice in the matter: he was the Duke of Wellington, and the Prime Minister to boot, if you will allow a dying man the pun.'

He laughed at his own joke and for a moment seemed like a younger man. I handed him a glass of water, from which he took a couple of sips before going on. 'The appointed day and hour arrived and so it was that I found myself on Battersea Fields at a godforsakenly early hour of the morning. I joined the Duke, who was accompanied by his second and a third man who was introduced to me as the adjudicator. Together we waited for Winchelsea to arrive. A last-minute attempt by myself to dissuade the Duke from proceeding was met with a stiff rebuff: "You are here to provide medical assistance, Phillips, not to interfere with due process. Now kindly attend to your surgical tools."

'And so with Winchelsea's arrival I was guided out of the way by the Duke's second, who from his constant surveillance of the deserted common seemed more concerned with the affair being discovered than the outcome of the forthcoming combat. Then I watched as the pistols were taken from the box and loaded, a process witnessed and checked by both principals. The weapons were then handed over and after the exchange of a few words I could not hear the two men stood back to back. I guessed that the final chance for Winchelsea to offer an apology to his challenger had been rejected. A coin was tossed to decide who would fire first. I found it astonishing that these men were prepared to risk their lives on something as insignificant as the flip of a coin. They walked six paces apiece before turning to face one another over their carefully measured killing ground.

'I had seen men kill one another in their thousands before, but that was in wartime; this was a Thursday morning in London. Absolute madness, I thought, and shivered at the prospect of the Prime Minister dying in something as self-indulgent as a duel. And if he were injured and I failed to save him, what then? To be known forever as the doctor who let the nation's greatest hero die! It wasn't a prospect I relished. But my misgivings were an irrelevance; the duel was going ahead and I was powerless to stop it.

'Both men signalled their readiness to the adjudicator and so he gave the order for Wellington, who had won the toss, to fire at will. Accordingly, the Duke levelled his pistol at his opponent. There was a dreadful pause, but then he turned his pistol away and sent the ball well wide of his mark. In response Winchelsea lowered his pistol and buried his ball in the earth. And that was it: the duel had been fought; the honour of both men satisfied. I opened the bag at my feet and took a deep draught of the brandy I kept there for medicinal purposes.'

Fatigue was now taking its toll and he sank back into his pillow. I felt guilty at allowing him to go on for so long, but had become so enthralled. As he took his ease I picked up the pistol and held it as Winchelsea must have done, the muzzle pointing down towards the floor.

I should have let him rest but my movement roused him again. 'Wellington presented me with the pistols three days later. He must have delivered them to the engravers on his way to Parliament that same morning. No harm had been done, but nonetheless word got out that the duel had taken place and there was a hell of a stink. The scandal was a nail in the coffin of his political career, of that I have no doubt. A Prime Minister risking his own life in a duel was carelessness of the first order. He was the most arrogant, self-determined fellow I ever knew, on and off the battlefield. But for all his pig-headedness you couldn't help but admire him.'

I returned the pistol to its box. My father had now completely exhausted himself and before I stood up from my chair had fallen into a deep sleep. It was fortunate that Lily was out of the house, for she would have chastised me for allowing him to talk for so long. Perhaps, though, it takes a doctor to know that not all medicine comes in a bottle. Tucking the box under my arm, I quietly left the room.

Next morning, I took myself away from the house and spent a distracting hour or so blasting away at empty bottles with my latest acquisitions.

Days passed into a week and before I knew it three weeks had gone by. My father's condition showed little change and I began to give serious thought to returning to London, where my prolonged absence from the hospital must surely be making itself felt. To pass the time I began to see one or two of my father's old patients from the village. As I had nothing better to do it seemed only right to save people the trouble of travelling to Lansdown to see Dr Billings. The work was unchallenging but my presence in the surgery seemed to be appreciated by the populace and, more importantly, pleased Lily no end. I am sure she hoped I would see the light and choose to take over the practice permanently. Aside from a visit from Maitland, my father's notary, and a regular house call by

Dr Billings, with whom I spent a pleasant hour or so in conversation, the house remained quiet.

It did not take long to fall into a comfortable routine, in the mornings opening the surgery, while the afternoons were divided between my father, who would insist on a full report on the morning's proceedings, and the dog, who was by then ready for his daily constitutional. Two or three times a week Gilbert would join us for dinner and provide the welcome opportunity to share a glass or two of brandy. Every other night Lily returned to her own house to catch up on her domestic and matrimonial duties while I was left in sole charge of the patient. All in all it was a not unpleasant existence, and as time passed I felt my thoughts being drawn back to London less frequently than had at first been the case. Foremost in those troubled thoughts had been Inspector Tarlow. The policeman's unwarranted attentions had made Sir Benjamin's draconian management style seem quite benign.

The fact that I did have another existence was brought home by the arrival of a letter. It was from Brunel, whose company I had last shared almost two months previously. It was written in his usual spidery hand, with the head of the paper embossed with his Duke Street address. I could only surmise that he had obtained my own address from Sir Benjamin.

*Dear Phillips,*

*I hope that this short missive finds you well. Also, that the past weeks have seen an improvement in your father's condition.*

*You have missed very little by way of excitement in the city. Work on the ship progresses at a damnably slow pace but the engines at least are all but fully installed. In spite of Russell's procrastinations I am sure she will be ready for sea trials in no more than six weeks.*

*Despite the continued labours required of the ship I have found time for a new project, which though far more modest in scale is imbued with much greater ambition. There is still however much work to be done here and I suspect I will require further assistance from your good self with the matter.*

*The Lazarus Club continues to meet irregularly, although your*

*presence as secretary is sorely missed. We all look forward to your*
*return. But things are alas not what they were. I fear that our small club*
*has forgotten the thirst for knowledge that motivated its formation. Too*
*many of our members seem overly concerned with lining their own*
*pockets, and Russell I fear is the worst offender – the man should never*
*have been put in charge of the ship. But I should not be burdening you*
*with my worries. You have more important matters at hand.*

*My kindest regards,*
*I. K. Brunel*

Whether it had been his intention or not, Brunel's letter served to shatter my rural idyll, and all at once I ached to be back in the city, at the hospital and in the thick of things. But I also craved a return to the world of Brunel and his engineering marvels. Once again he had piqued my inquisitiveness – what project could be more ambitious than the great ship and what assistance could he require of me? It sounded as though his relationship with Russell had reached a new low, and I could only hope for both their sakes that the ship was soon finished once and for all.

As if in perverse compliance with Brunel's desire to renew our acquaintance my father's health took a serious downturn not two days after the arrival of the letter. This came immediately after a marked lifting of his spirits which, although providing Lily with encouragement, had caused me some private concern. How many times had I seen patients rally just before a rapid decline and death?

I was between consultancies when Lily came running down the stairs and burst into the surgery in a highly agitated state.

'He is having great difficulty breathing,' she gasped between deep breaths of her own. 'He seemed so well yesterday.'

The sound of my father's dreadful rasping gasps greeted us as we entered the room, and even before reaching the bed I could tell that the final crisis was upon him. I took his wrist and felt for the pulse, which just as I feared was now dangerously thready. His eyes were open but he seemed barely aware of our presence, a clear sign that his body had entered into its last, involuntary struggle.

He was now fighting for every breath. Lily stood at his feet, her knuckles whitening as she gripped the bedstead. I put my arm around her and guided her to the chair in which we had spent so much time over the past weeks. 'We need to prepare ourselves, Lily,' I whispered. 'We are here with him, that is the important thing now.'

Lily took hold of his right hand, and his fingers flexed in an attempt to take a grip. I do not know how long we waited, perhaps an hour, maybe two. On one occasion he seemed to stop breathing, but then exhaled and continued, only much more quietly this time. Lily, who unlike Father and myself had always been a churchgoer, began to utter a quiet prayer. I am sure that if I had known the words I would have joined her gentle incantation.

Then at last it came. His mouth opened wide and issued a last draught of air, a terrible rattle coming from deep within his throat. Lily let out a cry, and later informed me that I too called out just on the moment of losing him. There had been no last words, no final farewell, but I am sure there had been a faint glimmer in his eyes, a flicker of acknowledgement just as he expired. We stayed with him for what seemed a long time afterwards, Lily weeping quietly. Only when Mary entered the room and let out her own expression of grief did we leave him. It had been a quick and painless passing, I told Lily, but in reality what did I know? What do any of us know until our own time is upon us? I suggested fetching the undertaker, but Lily would not have it, at least until she had washed and dressed him.

The funeral was four days later, and what seemed the entire population of the village turned out to pay their last respects to their good doctor. I stayed on at the house for as long as I felt able, which was long enough to mark a very subdued Christmas with Lily, who in normal circumstances so much enjoyed this time of year. On Boxing Day I told her that I had to return to London. She asked me to stay but knew that I felt my proper place to be in the hospital. Seeing that she was fighting a losing battle, she volunteered to accompany me to the station, but I told her it would be easier for both of us if we said our goodbyes at the house. Two days later, following much hugging and mutual promises to visit in the near future, we parted company at the garden gate.

After loading my bags, which were heavier than on my arrival due to the addition of the pistols and a single volume of my father's journals, I clambered into the carriage. Fortunately, this vehicle, which had been laid on by Gilbert, seemed better disposed to movement than the wreck of a cart which had dropped me at the same spot six weeks previously.

Little more than an hour later I was standing on the platform at Bath, watching as the train to London pulled out of the station – a situation that would have been a little difficult to explain to Lily if she had come along to say her farewells. Not thirty minutes later the train to Bristol, which had started its journey in London, pulled in and I stepped aboard. Having racked my luggage I pulled Brunel's letter from my coat pocket, and then removed from the envelope the key which had come with it. Then I reread the PS to his missive:

PS Should you have time on your return to London, if it occurs within the next few weeks, I would be extremely grateful if you could take a small detour to Bristol, which I know lies in the opposite direction, but is not too far away. If you can, then please call on my old friend Mr Leonard Wilkie and collect a package from him on my behalf. I would not like to entrust it to the postal service and cannot find the time to make the trip myself. Should you require an overnight stay then please feel free to make use of rooms I retain in the town, the key to which you are now holding. Should this prove impossible then I will fully understand.

In eternal gratitude,
I.K.B.

On a tag attached to the key were a pair of addresses: the first for Mr Wilkie and the second for Brunel's lodgings. Here was the real reason for Brunel writing to me. Yet again he was after something – but I was well accustomed to his audacity by now, while he knew that his request would intrigue me. Obviously, I couldn't tell Lily that I was leaving to carry out an errand and so had made much of my need to return to the hospital. And now here I was, heading west instead of east, my destination the town they say Brunel built.

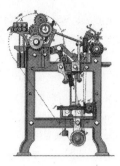

## 13

The train came to a halt at Temple Meads, the bustling western terminus of the Great Western Railway. Beneath the iron-spanned roof of the passenger shed the tracks lay five abreast, with those on the outside running alongside the pillar-lined platforms. On to one of these the train debouched its passengers, myself among them.

It was strange to see so many people after months in the peaceful surroundings of home. Even Bath had been much quieter than this. With my fellow passengers I made my way to the exit, where coloured light streamed through cathedral-like windows. Porters dragged trolleys heavily laden with boxes and trunks while others manhandled a large coach, minus its horses, up a ramp on to an open freight carriage on one of the inside tracks.

The street was no quieter; carriages and carts drew away from the station in a steady stream. A fly poster on the wall gave notice that the transatlantic packet was leaving with the tide next morning. As many of the people seemed to be carrying all their worldly possessions I assumed they would be on it, their hearts set on a new life in America. Watching the already bedraggled travellers, I was grateful that Bristol marked the end of my own journey.

People were crammed uncomfortably into every available con- veyance, and the exodus did not bode well for a rapid departure from the station but, to my surprise, it wasn't long before I was sitting in a cab. My driver waited as I pondered which address on the tag to request. Since there wouldn't be another train back to London until the next day I called out the address for Brunel's lodgings, as there would be time enough to track down Wilkie once I had secured a bed for the night.

The cab drew to a halt on a street high on a hill. It was less affluent than I had expected, not down at heel by any means, just very ordinary. Paying the cabbie, I asked him for directions to Wilkie's address, thinking it might be within walking distance. After a number of rights and lefts I would find the street in question, near the floating dock, whatever that might be.

The door gave way to a flight of stairs, at the top of which was a suite of three modest rooms, in addition to a bathroom and kitchen. Aside from the telltale signature of stale cigar smoke the place had the musty smell of a property left vacant and unaired for some time. I had known married men to keep a second address purely for the purpose of entertaining women other than their wives, but Brunel was not one of them. Work was his only mistress, of that I was sure. The apartment had the look of somewhere occupied by a man barely aware of his surroundings, with nothing in the way of decoration or embellishment. It was a bolt-hole cum office, nothing more.

A small mountain of stubbed cigar ends sat in a bowl on the desk. Alongside it lay the shrivelled and blackened husk of what had once been an apple, probably dating from the same time as the most recent of the drawings scattered across the desk, some three months before my arrival. All of the sheets appeared to relate to the same project – a bridge. Brunel had been working on the suspension bridge across the Avon Gorge for years, and like the ship it still wasn't finished. I hoped my visit would provide an opportunity to see what some said would be among his greatest achievements.

I opened a window and was disappointed to find that despite being on a hill the buildings across the street blocked any view of the town. Leaving the sash up, I checked my watch – half past three. Just enough time to track down Wilkie and collect the package, take a quick stroll around the town and find somewhere for supper. Before leaving, I took the blankets and sheets off the bed and hung them over the chair by the open window. Whether or not they were clean was not a concern, and it was obvious from the cloud of cigar ash produced by a brisk shake that they were not, but lying down in them would be a more appealing prospect once they had been exposed to a little fresh air.

Liberated of my luggage, I set out to walk into town. It was a pleasant enough afternoon, if a little cold. Indeed, as I watched the seagulls circling overhead I realized I was quite enjoying my little excursion. It was a relief to be away from the confines of the family house. Momentarily distracted by the memory of my father, I tried to recall the directions given by the cabbie.

Wilkie's address was not in a residential area, not if the ramshackle sheds and warehouses were anything to go by. I wandered along the street looking for the number on the tag, which had by now taken on a rather dog-eared appearance. Some of the buildings had numbers painted on their doors while others bore signs instead. I walked past Henry Bryant and Son – Chandlers; Thomas Etheridge – shipwright and carpenter; William Forsyth – coffin manufactory; and then over the double doors of the largest of the sheds Willard Semple – ropemaker. Although I had not as yet seen a single stretch of water, it was apparent that the dock mentioned by the cabbie could not be far away. Given the inherent risks in going to sea, even the coffin maker did not seem too much out of place in this maritime quarter.

After walking half the length of the street I came across an unassuming door with the number 16 daubed in bitumen. Returning my trusty key to my pocket, I knocked soundly – nothing. Just as I was about to give up and walk away the sound of a bolt being drawn came from inside. The door creaked open and a big man emerged from the gloom within. 'Oh, hello,' I said brightly.

Instead of replying, the man craned his thick neck forward and checked to the right and the left. Apparently satisfied that I was alone, he asked in a deep voice in keeping with his stature, 'Who are you?'

'I'm Dr Phillips,' I replied, taken aback by the man's brusqueness. 'Mr Brunel sent me to collect a package?'

'Keep your damn voice down,' the man boomed, and then in an equally resonant tone, 'Prove it.'

'I beg your pardon?' I asked, not knowing whether to be worried or amused by the chap's manner.

'If Brunel sent you, show me the key.'

Once again I pulled the object from my pocket and, stepping towards him, dropped it into the open palm of a hand almost twice the size of my own.

Reading the label appeared to provide all the proof he needed. 'All right, come in.'

The giant stepped fully into the street to allow me entry before following and bolting the door behind us.

'Sorry about that,' he said, handing back the key, which clearly had more than one way of opening a door. 'It's just that there have been a few strangers poking about of late, and you can't be too careful.'

'Quite,' I said, for want of any other response. It was only then I noticed the heavy spanner he was hefting in his right hand. Could his suspicion of strangers be great enough for him to feel in need of a weapon?

I felt a little better when he put the spanner down on a bench and took my hand in a surprisingly gentle grip. 'I am Leonard Wilkie.'

'Good, then you're the man I've come to see. I am sorry to catch you so late in the day.'

'You're still earlier than I would have liked. I'm not ready for you.'

This was not going as I had expected. 'You mean you don't have the package?'

'I haven't quite finished it yet. Mr Brunel didn't tell me when you were coming.'

'No, he wouldn't have done. My arrival was dependent on rather unpredictable circumstances.'

134

Introductions complete, I looked around the room. Machines filled almost every available space. I had seen some of these metal beasts before in the sheds at Millwall. There were lathes, drills, borers and cutting machines, along with other devices with which I was unfamiliar, all with their own cogs, gears and drive belts. In one corner a gangly young lad was filing a piece of metal held fast in a vice, his narrow back arched over his work.

'You've been building something for Brunel?' I enquired, using powers of deduction that would have made my father proud.

'Just a small job. I specialize in small jobs,' replied my host, scratching his brow as if wondering what to do with me. 'Truth be told, we've fallen behind schedule. It's not too much to look at, but a tricky little blighter it's been to get right.'

At the rear of the workshop a pair of sliding doors gave way to another room. There, the hot coals of a smith's forge sent out a flickering red light, which gave the brick-vaulted hall and the machines within something of the look of a castle dungeon complete with terrible torture devices. Now that I looked again, the drills did appear to have very narrow bits, and some of the lathes were no bigger than Lily's sewing machine. Perhaps it was all just a matter of scale: Wilkie wasn't a big man after all, just a normal-sized chap working with undersized machines. A fine theory, but then I had to look up again to talk to him.

The mention of a project of modest scale in Brunel's letter came to mind. 'When you say small jobs, you mean you make small things?'

'I'm a metalworker, just like any other. Made a bit of a speciality of one-off, high-specification jobs, that's all. I've built full-sized engines for ships and fully working models of the same thing you could sit on a dinner table.' Holding out the shovels he used for hands and looking from one to the other, he said, 'Hard to believe really, isn't it?'

'I'm a doctor, Mr Wilkie, I see all manner of strange things. But I can only thank you for your talent. Who, after all, would relish the prospect of carrying a ship's engine back to London?'

He chuckled at this. 'Indeed, no, you'd have a pretty sore lap by the time you got there.'

'But I do need to get back to London,' I said, more relaxed now that the ice had been broken. 'Mr Brunel may have to make other arrangements for the collection of his package.'

'When do you need to be back?'

'The train leaves at ten o'clock tomorrow morning.'

Wilkie glanced back towards his machines and the boy. I wondered if the lad was working on whatever it was. 'Ideally I would like another day. But if we work late tonight I can get far enough along for you to collect it in the morning. Brunel may need to do some fine-tuning at the other end, but it's caused me enough grief already. I have other work I need to concentrate on.'

'Can you tell me what it is?'

Wilkie sighed, beckoning me to follow him into a crypt-like chamber leading off the main hall. 'I wish I knew,' he said over his shoulder. 'Brunel sends me drawings with instructions to make things just so. They're parts, that's all. Some of them fit together but I haven't got a clue what they're for. He provides a specification and I meet it. If it was anyone else then I'd tell them to go elsewhere. There's little satisfaction in making objects you don't understand the purpose of.'

We climbed a short flight of rickety wooden stairs and entered a loft-like space with a small recessed window at one end. The tracery of timber beams and plastered surfaces created a less oppressive atmosphere than the heavy brick vaults beneath our feet. But Wilkie may not have seen things the same way. For up here, beneath the low-slung eaves, he was cast into a permanent stoop until he took a seat behind a large desk. The rest of the room was taken up with cabinets of papers and plans and a drawing board, but there was also a stove and an unmade cot.

'I like to stay close to my work,' said Wilkie as I took in the cramped mix of living and workspace. There was nothing new here though – was Brunel's apartment not full of plans and sketches, and were my own rooms in London not equipped with anatomy texts and even an articulated skeleton?

I positioned myself in the window recess and looked out over the back of the building at a small flotilla of ships.

'So that's the floating dock,' I remarked, almost thinking aloud.

'It keeps us busy,' said Wilkie as he began to sort through papers on his desk.

'Why is it called the floating dock?' I enquired, looking out over the wide stretch of black water. 'It looks fairly stationary to me.'

The riffling stopped and Wilkie turned in his chair. 'Have you ever heard the phrase "shipshape and Bristol fashion"?' he asked. I nodded and he went on to explain that it referred to the strong keels ships moored in the River Avon needed to survive the dramatic changes in tide which twice a day left them grounded in the mud. That was why the dock had been built early in the century. The water level in it was kept high through a series of channels and gates and it was called the floating dock simply because the ships in it stayed afloat. It was no surprise to learn that Brunel had also had a hand in the enterprise, later adding a system of sluices and channels to keep the dock free of silt. The dock, Wilkie explained, had also been the birthplace of Brunel's first two ships, the SS *Great Western* and then the *Great Britain*, both of which were depicted in paintings hanging on the wall above the big man's desk. The relationship between the two men became clearer when he told me he had worked for Brunel on both ships.

Now he was in a more conversational mood, I decided to ask about something that had been bothering me. 'What about the strangers?' I asked.

He shrugged his shoulders. 'Two of them. Nothing unusual about strangers in a port, I suppose, but I'm sure they have been watching the shop for a week or so.'

'Hence the spanner you greeted me with?'

His tone became a little more agitated. 'I'm a metalworker – what's so unusual about carrying tools in my own workshop?'

'Nothing at all,' I responded, slightly embarrassed that I might have read too much into the matter. 'But do you think there is a danger?'

'Someone tried to break in the other night, but they cleared off when they heard me coming down the stairs.' As I pondered this incident Wilkie returned to the papers and, after a moment or two, pulled a sheet clear from the pile.

Moving away from the window, I took a look at the drawing. Several components were represented, each shown in plan and elevation. It was clear from the dimensions marked in Brunel's hand that the finished pieces would be much smaller than the drawings. Although the illustrations included all the information necessary to construct the parts they provided little or no clue to the appearance or purpose of the finished machine.

Just as I was about to take my leave the big man erupted from his seat and narrowly avoided rattling his head off the roof. 'Damn it,' he yelled, making for the stairs, 'I knew we'd missed something.' I followed at a safe distance as he disappeared from view. 'Nate, did you check the screws on that hinge?' he shouted.

By the time I reached the foot of the stairs he was standing over the boy, a file in his hand. 'Fetch the tray of pieces, we're going to have to double-check those dimensions.' Quick to obey, the lad disappeared into the back room while Wilkie passed a rule over the highly polished cylinder of metal in the vice before him. Whatever the problem was, my presence had nothing to contribute to its resolution. I waited for him to finish his measurements before bidding him good evening and, as he escorted me to the door, we arranged for the collection of the package at eight in the morning.

Leaving Wilkie and his apprentice to what looked to be a long night's work, I determined to use what light was left to take a closer look at the dock before finding somewhere to eat. I walked along the street in the opposite direction of my arrival and, turning the corner, let out an involuntary whistle at the view now presented before me. To my left was the River Avon, which at low tide looked to be nothing more than a muddy trench, but ahead of me was the gorge, a massive notch cut into the horizon. Once again I was confronted with Brunel's mark on the world, for the gap was spanned by what would become his bridge, which was bounded on either side by great stone towers which seemed to grow up out of the living rock of the cliff face. The scant black line of a hawser stretched between the towers looked like the thinnest of cracks in the sky and beneath it was suspended a basket. Although empty now this would carry workmen out across the gorge as they went about their labours.

The very thought of hanging hundreds of feet above the river at the end of what looked to be nothing more than a thread was enough to make my head swim and it was a relief to turn into the docks. Low tide may have exposed the river's sticky floor but the water remained deep enough to support the dozen or so ships berthed there.

I took a stroll along the quay, where a crane lifted barrels from the dark void of a ship's hold. All the vessels were cargo carriers; the ship destined to carry hundreds of souls across the Atlantic the following morning was obviously moored elsewhere. I wondered where Brunel's ships had been built – presumably in dry docks somewhere hereabouts. It was all pleasant enough but I couldn't stop thinking about the two strangers and the attempted break-in. I kept a lookout for suspicious characters, but with everyone a stranger to me this seemed a little pointless.

It was my rumbling stomach which really put things in perspective. I had not eaten since breakfast and so curtailed my explorations to seek out a suitable hostelry.

After an agreeable meal and several glasses of wine I once again took a cab to Brunel's lodgings up on the hill. It had been a long day and I was more than ready for bed. As I replaced the blankets I gave a sympathetic thought to Wilkie, who was probably still hard at work finishing his commission for Brunel. Fatigue notwithstanding, I had an urge to partake in a little bedtime reading, having come across a large leather-bound scrapbook belonging to the engineer. Inside was page after page of age-yellowed newspaper clippings, all of them relating to the man and his endeavours. Given the day's events I plumped for a story from *The Times* dated 3 April 1838 and with my back propped against a pillow and a lamp burning on the bedside table I began to read.

The vessel got underway at 30 minutes past 5 o'clock on Saturday morning. She left the river under the most favourable prospects, the engines working as steadily and easily as the smallest Thames steam-vessel, and were as quickly halted. She stopped at Gravesend for a short time for the purpose of putting out the visitors, among whom was Mr Brunel, sen., the engineer of the Thames Tunnel, into boats, which took them ashore. The vessel again proceeded, and the patent log line was thrown out, by which her speed was ascertained to be 15 knots an hour.

Everything wore a propitious appearance; the directors and officers, who have been for several weeks engaged in superintending the fittings up, were congratulating each other on the results of their labours, when the vessel was discovered to be on fire. The smell of heated oil began to attract attention soon after the steam-ship left Gravesend, but it was not until the vessel reached the Chapman Sand, 6 miles above the Nore, that flames were discovered by Mr Maudslay, the engineer, issuing from the top of the boilers. Soon afterwards large volumes of smoke issued from the engine-room, which drove everybody on deck, and it was at least an hour before the flames were brought under control.

We are sorry to state that a melancholy accident befell Mr Brunel, jun., the engineer. He was on board and intended to proceed with the *Great Western* to Bristol. On the fire being discovered, his assistance and advice were of essential service; but in the confusion, and when the fire was at its height, he fell down the opening from the deck into the main-hold, a height of nearly 40 feet. He was soon raised, and found to be dreadfully injured. We understand that Mr Brunel is in a precarious state; his shoulder bone has been dislocated by the fall, and his leg broken. Last evening the reports on his condition were more favourable.

The fire was caused by the ignition of the patent felt with which the boilers and steam-pipe were covered to prevent a radiation of the heat and to keep the engine-room as cool as possible. The workmen had improperly used a quantity of red-lead and oil in coating the boilers and steam-pipe with the felt, particularly with that part of the boilers in contact with the chimney, and when the felt once ignited, the flames spread like wildfire, and but for the precautionary steps adopted by the Great-Western Steam-ship Company for so speedily extinguishing fire, there is no doubt their first vessel would have been sacrificed.

The story brought to mind the injured workman who had told me that Brunel had survived more than one accident himself. From what I had just read it seemed nothing less than miraculous that the man had lived so long.

Too tired to read any further I dropped the album on to the floor, turned off the lamp and settled down to sleep.

A violent rapping at the front door broke my slumber. I had no idea what time it was but the first tinges of dawn were filtering through gaps in the curtains. Lacking a gown, I jumped into my trousers and threw on a shirt before proceeding down the stairs. 'You're Wilkie's boy – Nate, isn't it?' I asked, finding the apprentice standing on the doorstep. The lad was pecking as though he had just run up the hill. Seeing his face for the first time, there could be no doubt that he was the man's son. Here was Wilkie-in-waiting, his hunched shoulders and shifting limbs reminding me of a foal still growing into its skin. 'What is it? It's still early, is it not?'

The boy was carrying a canvas duffel bag, which at my enquiry he held out in front of him. 'My father told me to bring this to you.'

I reluctantly took the bag from him. 'But I was going to come and collect it; there was no need for you to come all this way.'

'You don't under . . . understand, sir . . . there's been trouble,' stuttered the boy, now on the verge of tears.

'Won't you come in?' I asked.

'No. Father needs my help. The workshop, it's been . . .'

'What is it?'

'There's been . . . there's . . .' Giving up, he turned and pointed down the street. I stepped off the threshold and was shocked to see a pall of black smoke and an orange glow that had nothing to do with the sunrise.

'My God! A fire. A fire at the workshop?'

The boy nodded, a tear rolling down his cheek. 'The men came back. He wouldn't let them in.' I tried to guide the boy inside, but he would have none of it. 'I need to go,' he insisted, shaking my hand from his shoulder. 'Father says you are to get the bag to Mr Brunel.'

'Your father, where is he?'

'I need to find him,' he said, wiping his sleeve across his cheek.

'I'm coming with you,' I announced, but then looked at my feet. 'Wait here, Nate, I'm going up to put my shoes on.'

Still clutching the bag, I darted back up the stairs, the boy calling after me, 'Get the train. My father says you are to get on the train.'

I fell back on to the bed pulling on my shoes, and in my recently woken state tried to make what sense I could of the situation. Who were those men, and what were they after? But there was no time for these questions now. I threw on my coat and, taking the bag with me, ran back down the stairs. The boy was nowhere to be seen.

It was over half an hour later when I arrived at the docks, having had some difficulty in finding a cab this early in the morning. But despite the hour, people were milling about everywhere, and a fire tender stood outside the burnt-out shell of the workshop. I told the cabbie to wait and stepped into the mêlée. The cobbles were covered with mushy, wet ash and there was the dreadful, acrid smell of a fire that has burned much more than just timber or coal. The brick frontage was still intact but the roof had fallen inward on to a mound of rubble created by the collapse of the vault. The building next door was in no better condition.

Ignoring a shout from one of the fire attendants, I dashed through a gap that had once been the doorway and scrambled on to the mound. The bricks were still hot, many of them cracked by the force of the heat. There wasn't a chance of anyone trapped in the workshop getting out alive. I coughed at the intake of fumes from burnt engine oil. Every few feet I had to step aside to avoid being snagged on the twisted metal stumps of machinery protruding through the smouldering heap. Reaching the other side, I looked down on hoses lying criss-crossed on the dockside, their nozzles still submerged in the water. The pumps sat idle now, but they had succeeded in dowsing the fire before it had spread along the entire street.

Another knot of people had formed at the side of the dock. By the time I stepped off the bricks the soles of my shoes had partially melted away. Pushing my way into the crowd, I yelled, 'I'm a doctor, let me through, please.' The wall of people gave way and I knelt beside the water-soaked form of Wilkie. The big man was clearly dead, cold to the touch and his skin already discoloured. I looked across to Nate, who was crouched on the other side of his father, hands spread across his inert chest. 'He was in the dock,' he said, tears streaking the soot on his face.

I took a closer look at the body. Despite the soaked clothes and hair, the wound on the side of his head suggested that drowning had not caused the death of this gentle giant.

The boy was of the same mind. 'They killed him, the bastards killed him,' he spat, looking up at the people standing around him.

'I'm so sorry, Nate,' I whispered, 'but you need to come with me.' Putting aside my own sense of shock, I grabbed his shoulder once again, this time refusing to let go when he made to shrug it away. Breaking out of the ring of bystanders, I tried to establish what he knew. 'Did you see them, the men who did this?'

'It was them that's been watching us.'

Looking back at the crowd, I felt a growing sense of regret at not having taken some sort of action to help Wilkie on hearing of his troubles the night before. But what could I have done? 'Come on, Nate. I'm not sure what's happening here but you need to come with me. You need to get away from here. Do you have any other family?'

The boy glanced back towards the body. For a moment I considered sending him to Lily. The place was out of the way all right, but I couldn't put her at risk. Then I discovered the boy had plans of his own.

'America,' he said. 'I have an uncle in America.'

'He . . . he knew this was going to happen?'

'No, it was always the plan, just in case he got ill or something,' he said.

'What about money?'

'I have enough.'

'They weren't after money?'

'No,' he replied, looking forlornly at the bag hanging from my shoulder.

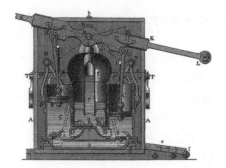

# 14

Nate watched them carry off his father's sodden corpse and then joined the thinning crowd before it melted entirely away. Other than wishing the lad well there was little more I could do. He seemed a brave young man and given his skills and a fair chance would make a good life for himself in America. But fair chances seemed thin on the ground – there was a smouldering pile of rubble and a dead man to attest to that. And no sign of the men responsible – but would I know them if I saw them?

Checking my watch, I yelled at the cabbie to hurry. There was not much time before the train left and I still had to collect my luggage from Brunel's apartment. The thought of spending another day in this woeful town was not a prospect to be savoured.

Throwing yesterday's undergarments and the package into my trunk, I checked the apartment for stray items. Satisfied that I had everything I closed the window, but then as an afterthought returned to the bedroom, lifted Brunel's scrapbook and slipped it under the leather straps on the trunk. Then, with trunk in one hand and carpet bag in the other, I tumbled down the stairs and into the street, locking the door behind me, the tag on the key by now reduced to nothing more than a tattered shred. I felt little better myself.

\*

Any doubts I had about recognizing the men responsible for Wilkie's death were immediately dispelled on my arrival at the station. The cab pulled up and while I was dragging my luggage out I saw them – just a flicker in the corner of my eye, like a crow flying past a window, but it was enough. I pushed the trunk back inside and pulled my right foot on to the step. Making as though I was tying my shoelace and trying to appear as casual as possible, I canted my head towards them, brow pricked with sweat.

Standing either side of the entrance, they were not especially imposing men and I wondered how much trouble Wilkie had given them. Their eyes were hidden beneath wide-brimmed hats, but from the regular turning of their heads it was apparent they were closely examining everyone who entered the station. There could be little doubt they were looking for me or, more precisely, the package in my bag.

I had seen enough, but unfortunately so had they. Stepping back into the vehicle, I ordered the driver to get me as far away from the station as possible. The cab had now been on hire for some time and, not having yet seen the colour of my money, the cabbie not unreasonably refused to move off until I specified a destination.

'The docks, man, to the docks,' I spluttered, horrified at the sight of the sentinels, who were now making rapid headway towards the cab.

'Back to the docks?'

'The transatlantic dock. Take me to the American packet.' The men were getting closer, and in their hurry were now pushing people out of the way. 'Go! Move, for God's sake!'

'Keep your 'air on,' replied the driver. 'First you want the train to London, now you want the ship to America. Changeable fellow, ain't yer?'

The men were almost upon me. One of them had by now lost his hat, exposing eyes narrowed in determination and dark hair slicked back over his head.

Just as I was about to leap out of the other side of the cab, the vehicle lurched forward. A well-placed flick of the crop on the horse's flank pulled us out of reach of the lead man just as he placed an outstretched hand on the rim of the wheel. I looked back to see one of them left on the edge of the kerb, but the other, the wheel-grabber, was standing in the middle of the street, having given up on a last desperate sprint for the cab as it shot away. He was bent forward, his hands on his knees and his head shaking in frustration. I allowed myself a moment of satisfaction and sat back as we sped down the street.

The cab clattered along, the driver muttering under his breath. I looked at my watch again. The train would be pulling out of the station in six minutes, and there was no chance of being on it. Even if I managed to get past the murderous sentinels it would have been no trouble for them to get aboard and then have me at their mercy. I shivered at the thought of my battered body being discovered by the trackside somewhere between here and Bath.

With the train out of the equation I would have to find another, less obvious way of leaving town. Setting sail for America seemed a little drastic but the sea at least held some prospect of escape.

The cab had travelled some distance when, to my dismay, I noticed that another appeared to be shadowing us. To check my suspicion I asked the driver to make a few superfluous turns and by now accustomed to my eccentric requests he demurred. My dismay turned once again to fear when the cab behind followed our every move. Worse still, the other cab was travelling at some speed and the distance between us closing. Realizing that urgent action was required, I called up to the driver, 'That cab, it's following us.'

He threw a look back up the street. 'Friends of yours?'

'Not really,' I replied bitterly, aware that my credit was wearing thin. With nothing else to do I pulled out my purse and emptied the coins into my hand. 'Here!' I said, reaching up and pushing a clutch of them into the driver's fist. 'And there's more once you get us away from that cab.'

The fellow smiled and tapped the brow of his hat with a forefinger. 'Whatever you say, sir.' Once again the horse was stroked with the crop and the cab shot forward, the wheel spokes blurring as it raced down a winding street. I held on to my seat as we took the next corner so fast that one of the wheels left contact with the cobbles.

I risked a quick glance behind and was perturbed to see that my pursuers must also have crossed their driver's palm with silver. People scurried out of the way as the wheel rims sent up sparks from the road. After drawing ahead far enough to put us out of sight we entered into a narrow alleyway, where we came to a sudden halt.

'Have we lost them?' I asked, feeling quite out of breath.

'They've gone clear by, sir,' said the driver as I disembarked.

'How do I get to the harbour?'

'Just round the corner,' he said, flicking his switch in the air.

I handed him his payment and offered up my thanks, then once again serving as my own porter, picked up my luggage and headed out of the alley.

I soon found myself on the packet wharf. It was a relief to join the crowd, where I became just one face among hundreds, my luggage marking me not as a desperate fugitive but just another hopeful émigré.

I wandered aimlessly for a while, uncertain how to proceed now I had made it to the water's edge. What was certain was that I was absolutely exhausted and so, fighting my way to the edge of the crowd, I threw down my trunk and, taking a perch, watched porters and sailors herding the crowd as if it were so many unruly cattle.

I pondered the idea of sneaking aboard, with the hope of getting ashore again before she left the English coast for the open sea. But the chances of getting on without a ticket seemed unlikely, particularly as prospective passengers were now being channelled between barriers from where, with their tickets checked and documents stamped, they would soon make their way up the gangplank. In any case, I didn't fancy getting stuck on board and ending up in New York. How would I explain that to Sir Benjamin?

My meditations were interrupted by the reappearance of my two new friends. It had taken them less time than I had hoped to find their way to the wharf. They had split up and were now wandering casually through the crowd, but there was no doubting their malign intent as they discreetly examined every male. By luck rather than judgement I had given myself some time by separating myself from the herd; from here I could see them, but they were too intent on the crowd to look out. But it wouldn't take long before they set eyes on me.

I made to stand up but was stopped when a hand clamped against my shoulder from behind. My blood froze. Had I for a fatal moment let one of them out of my sight?

Twisting my head and looking up, I saw Nate standing over me. His young face was drawn and pale, but his eyes burned with an animal-like intensity. His instructions were clear: 'Quickly, come with me, back here.' He picked up my trunk and I followed him through a small door in the side of a shed that backed on to the quay. Ropes and chains littered the floor and a row of huge barnacle-covered anchors lined one wall. A ripped red sail hung from a beam and a half-stitched patch drooped down like a flap of flesh on a surgical patient. Nate gently closed the door behind us and, putting down the trunk, peered through a chink in the roughly slatted wall. 'Good, they're still in the crowd. They didn't see us.'

For one so young Nate was proving to have a cool head on his shoulders, and although I felt secure in the lad's custody – this was after all his home turf – I immediately started to fret about his welfare again. 'You're getting on the boat, Nate?'

'Only if I can shake those bastards off,' he replied, without taking his face away from the crack in the wall. 'Bought a ticket, half an hour ago.' Now he turned to face me. 'I was waiting for my chance to board when you turned up.'

His tone was accusatory and I felt guilty for bringing trouble with me. 'I'm sorry, Nate. They were waiting for me at the station.'

'I thought they might be. But not to worry. Perhaps I should stay and make sure those murdering brutes get what's coming to them.'

'No, Nate, that is for the law to do. Your father would want you to go and make a new life for yourself.'

He pulled out his ticket and looked at the destination printed on it, but with uncertainty written on his face. 'All right, I'll go.'

'But before you do, answer me one thing. What is it, that thing they're after? The package I'm carrying.'

Nate shook his head. 'Haven't a clue. Just bits and pieces made up from plans sent by Mr Brunel. We don't ask questions, just do the job.'

Exactly what his father had told me. Whatever the answer, I wasn't going to find it in Bristol and I did not want to add an extra burden to his narrow shoulders. 'Enough questions then. Now, we both need to get out of this place.'

'I guess you don't want to come to America with me?'

I was pleased that the lad had determined his course but mine was yet to be decided. 'I need to get back to London, but not by train.'

The boy turned back to the peep-hole. 'I can get you out of town.'

I stepped towards him. 'How?'

He moved away from the wall and, picking up my trunk, walked past me. 'I have friends. Can get you on a coaster this morning. They'll take you out and drop you off, maybe across to Cardiff. Not exactly good for London, but better than New York.'

'And a lot safer than round here,' I added. The prospect was appealing but my conscience nipped me again. The boy had already done enough. 'I don't want you to put yourself at risk for me.'

'You only do that while you're here.' He looked down at the trunk. 'When you go, they go. They're not after me, remember.'

'I suppose you're right.'

'It will take them a while to check the crowd out there but we need to move quickly. Got to get rid of this,' he said, placing his foot on the lid of the trunk.

'Where's your luggage?' I asked.

'What luggage?'

'You're going to America on that ship and you don't even have a change of clothes?'

'The fire took everything. I can buy new clothes when I get there.'

'You can't wear the same clothes for two weeks, lad,' I told him, hurrying over to the trunk, undoing the straps and flipping open the lid, 'you're about my size, or at least you will be when you thicken out. Take these things and the trunk. There's a good suit in here and a few shirts.'

'I can't take your clothes.'

'You just said I've got to get rid of the trunk – what else am I going to do, throw them in the sea? In any case you'll look less suspicious with luggage.'

'All right, but we need to move. Where's the package?'

'In the bag.'

Brunel's album had dropped on to the floor when I undid the straps on the trunk. I opened its covers and, gripping the pages firmly, ripped them from the spine. There was no room in the small bag for the album but I didn't want to abandon the newspaper clippings. I rolled up the pages and stuffed them into the top of the bag. Then I remembered something else. I dug my hands in the trunk and from beneath my clothes, pulled out the polished mahogany box. I tried to stuff it into the bag but it wouldn't fit. With no time for repacking, I opened the box, took out the pistols and wrapped them in a shirt before putting them in the bag along with the powder flask, bag of bullets and other bits and pieces.

'Don't bury them too deep,' said Nate. 'You may need them before the day is out.'

I knew he wasn't joking, but closed them in the bag all the same.

Leaving the trunk hidden in a coil of rope, from where Nate would collect it later, I followed him to another door on the far side of the building. After checking that the coast was clear we walked out into the street, as brazenly as we dared. Keeping our eyes peeled, we walked for about ten minutes, checking every alley before crossing its mouth and looking back as much as we did forward. Eventually we stepped on to the slippery timbers of another dock. There was a smell of old fish and sea salt, but there was also something else: the acrid smell of fire-char that told me we were not far away from the torched workshop. There were no tall masters here, just the small coasters and sailing barges I had seen the previous evening. There was still a dirty streak of smoke marking the sky up ahead, but fortunately our journey came to a halt before we returned to the scene of the crime.

We stopped on the edge of the wharf alongside a single-masted barge, her well-worn but recently swabbed deck skirting a large open hold. There was no sign of life on board. 'Stigwood!' yelled Nate. 'Stigwood!'

There was a stirring within a small hatch directly below us, and a blur in the murky bowels of the boat as someone made their cumbersome progress up a ladder. Then a head appeared, followed by a stocky, sweater-covered torso. A heavily bearded face looked up at us, the man's eyes widening when he saw who had summoned him.

'Nate, my boy! My God!' exclaimed the man as he cleared the hatchway, and then, beckoning with a heavily tattooed forearm, 'Come down. Come aboard, lad.'

Nate put a foot over the edge and, turning to face me, began his descent of a series of wooden rungs set into the wall of the jetty. 'The skipper's a . . . was a friend of my father's,' he said, looking up just as he disappeared over the side.

I waited for him to step on to the deck before dropping my bag into his waiting arms. Careful to avoid the sliver of water between the boat and the dock, I stepped aboard and Nate introduced me as his friend, 'Mr Phillips', and the man to me as 'Stigwood, master of the *Rebecca*'.

We shook hands but Stigwood was understandably more concerned with Nate and the events of the last few hours. 'A terrible accident – I'm so sorry to hear about your father. He was a good man.'

'It was no accident,' insisted Nate. 'My father was murdered.'

'But the fire?' replied the now perplexed sailor.

'How do you suppose that caused him to end up in the river with his head bashed in?'

'But they said it was an explosion.'

'Did you hear an explosion?' returned Nate. 'You must have been here during the night?'

'I was here all right,' admitted Stigwood with a guilty blush, 'but with the amount I'd put away last night I'd 'ave slept through the Siege of Sebastopol.' There was a pause as the truth sank in. 'But who would want to kill your father?'

'I don't know why they did it, but I know who did it.' Nate's face hardened as his grief wrapped itself in anger. 'And they're after us now.'

Stigwood looked me up and down, wondering, no doubt, why someone in city clothes, no matter how dishevelled, should now be a hunted fugitive. 'Get below decks, both of you. We're about to cast off.'

'No,' said Nate. 'He goes, I stay. I'm taking the boat to America.'

Stigwood didn't seem surprised. 'Goin' to stay with your uncle at last, eh?'

'Aye, now I'd best be off.'

I could swear the boy was gaining years in front of my eyes. 'Nate, what about them?' I asked, looking nervously along the dock. 'Why not stay on the boat? Come with us. You can take the packet later, when it's safe.'

'The ship leaves in an hour. I know this place and they don't. They will hopefully have given up on the packet dock by now. And anyway, they're not after me, not any more.'

It crossed my mind that I had made a great mistake in leaving the rural surroundings of my father's house to return to the bustle of the city. I had gone from being harassed by the police, who appeared to think me a murderer in London, to being chased by two murderers in Bath. If I got out of this mess alive then country living would have to be given serious thought.

Maybe I should just throw the damned package overboard, or even surrender it, but before I had time to turn thought into action Nate had returned to the ladder.

'Wait!' I yelled, dropping to my knees and opening the bag.

After pulling out the clumsily rolled cylinder that had once been Brunel's scrap album, and then my underwear, I hurriedly unwrapped the pistols and placed them side by side on the deck. Then out came the powder flask and the bag of bullets. 'You ever fired a pistol, Nate?' I asked, beginning to load the first. At the shake of his head I pressed the button on the flask and dropped a measure of powder into the pan. 'Then you'll learn on the job.' In went the ball. 'You need to know how to load. The shooting's the easy part.' I pulled the rod from underneath the barrel and rammed the bullet home. Nate was standing over me and I kept my head back so as to provide him with a clear view of the process. Loading finished, I set the gun down, picked up its twin and repeated the process. 'Got that?'

'Yes,' he replied.

I drew back the hammer on the second pistol, extended my arm and pointed the pistol out towards the water. 'Then all you have to do is pull the trigger.'

Demonstration over, I gently released the hammer, picked up the other pistol and held them out to him, butt first. Nate hesitated before taking them. He weighed them in his hands just as I had done when I first held them. 'Pull the hammers back all the way, and then they're ready to go.'

He turned a pistol, studying it.

'Is this you?' he asked, reading the inscription.

'No, that was my father.'

He looked at me. 'Was?'

'He died not long ago.'

He thrust the pistols towards me. 'I can't take these.'

'They are yours now. What you do with them is up to you.'

Nate retracted his arms, cradling the pistols in his palms. Then he held out his right hand. 'All right, but I'll only need one of them; you just showed me how to reload and as long as I've got two bullets I'll be fine.'

I took the pistol from him and he tucked the other into his belt. After emptying a palmful of powder for myself I handed over the flask and half a dozen bullets, which he dropped into his pocket. 'I'll be off then. You'd better get going, skipper, they could be here any time.'

The lad raced up the ladder and, on reaching the quay, took a last glance down at us.

'Nate, I will do all I can to do the right thing by your father, see that his killers are brought to justice – that much I promise you.'

'Thank you, sir,' replied the boy, before stepping back out of sight.

'Always been a strong one,' said Stigwood.

'He'll need to be.'

Stigwood stepped towards the edge of the hold and yelled, 'Gus! Where are you? Get topside and cast off.'

Stigwood's mate was not much older than Nate, and he jumped up on to the deck with all the agility that was the blessing of his youth. 'Right oh, skipper,' he said cheerfully as he scampered up the ladder. The fore and aft hawsers were thrown down on the deck and the boat immediately began to drift away from the security of its berth. Gus hurriedly climbed halfway down the steps and then with a much-practised flourish jumped back across the widening ribbon of water on to the boat.

The skipper took the tiller while Gus unfurled the sail, pulling on ropes and tying them off. Canvas flapped and then filled as we came into the wind. I watched the dock recede in our wake. There was no sign of Nate, which was fortunate as two figures were now standing near the top of the ladder. We had pushed away just in the nick of time.

'You'd better get below,' said Stigwood, watching from the helm.

I shook my head. 'I want them to see me. It will take pressure off Nate.'

They were looking around, checking for any sign of their prey on the dock. For once eager to attract their attention, I cocked the pistol, raised it into the air and pulled the trigger. The report carried loudly across the water and both men turned to look at the boat. I picked up the bag and held it triumphantly above my head, not wanting to leave them in any doubt as to where the prize lay. My gloating had the desired effect and they began to run across the dock, following our course down the channel. Then, realizing it was hopeless, they stopped, and one of them reached into his coat, pulling out an object that I knew to be a pistol. But before he could raise it to fire his companion pushed his arm back down and the weapon was returned to its place of concealment.

Dropping the bag on to the deck, and with shaking hand leaving the pistol on top of it, I walked back to Stigwood, who was casually leaning on the tiller as though this happened every day. 'Where are we going?' I asked.

'Up the Severn to Gloucester. That do you?'

'Yes,' I replied gratefully, having only the very faintest idea of why it would. Picking up speed, we sailed past the moored steamer, its cargo of passengers milling around on the deck. I hoped Nate would soon be among them.

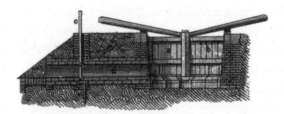

# 15

The open mouth of the dock was girded by two great stone bastions which at low tide rose up from the muddy floor of the Avon like the walls of a moated castle but now protruded just a few feet above the high water. We had made great speed through the dock, the wind pushing us from behind, but here, out on the river, the sail slapped lazily against the mast. Fortunately, though, the current provided propulsion enough and the magnificent towers of Brunel's unfinished bridge, having passed high over our heads, soon grew smaller in our wake.

Despite the excitement of my embarkation Stigwood seemed relaxed and perfectly at ease on the river, the tiller resting against his hip. In stark contrast, I skulked at the prow and looked back over the deck for any sign of movement behind us. There was still a chance of the frantic cab chase playing itself out again on the river, but after two or three miles I contented myself that no vessel had set out in pursuit. Only now we were out of harm's way did the strain of recent events show itself, my buckling knees causing me to stumble as I walked back across the deck.

Stigwood, noticing my trouble, barked at his deckhand, 'Gus, show the gentlemen below decks. He has yet to find his river-legs and looks like he could do with some shut-eye.'

The boy put down the brush with which he was daubing paint on to woodwork already thick with the stuff and led the way down a ladder before ushering me into a small cabin in the stern. There, I crawled into the confined space of the lower bunk and, without pausing to remove my heat-damaged shoes, went out like a light.

On waking, I pulled out my watch to discover I had been asleep for most of the afternoon, and by the time I reappeared on deck the sun was already sinking behind the hills to our left, or the port, as my hosts called it. Stigwood informed me that the boat was now heading north, sailing up the Severn estuary, at the head of which lay our destination. He was still at the tiller, puffing easily on his pipe. Out in the wider channel the wind had picked up and the sail billowed healthily, the taut canvas pulling us against the current.

'How long will it take us to get there?' I asked, standing beside him at the tiller.

Stigwood looked to the shore, checking our position, and then glanced up at the sail. 'If the wind stays with us we should be in Gloucester by noon tomorrow. We'll moor up for the night in a couple of hours.'

'You must know the river well,' I offered, grateful for the opportunity to strike up a normal conversation.

'You could say that,' he replied with a contented smile. 'Been on the water all my life.'

'How often do you make this trip?'

'Usually two times a week. Our other main run's across the way, over to Wales.'

'You never feel the urge to go to sea then?'

'Never had the need. She's a bit shallow in the draught for open water, built for the river, just like me.'

'It seems a pleasant way to make a living.'

'Won't make us rich, but as long as the cargoes are there we get by.' The riverman stepped forward from the tiller, relaxing his grip and pushing it slightly in my direction. 'Like to take a turn?'

I took hold of the spar, gently curved like a swan's neck and polished smooth through years of handling. 'Just keep her steady; she's almost steering herself in this breeze.'

Having cleverly pressed a second member into his crew, Stigwood went over to Gus and checked his progress with the paint job. After a few brief words he turned back to me, and with his eyes fixed on something to our stern said, 'Perhaps you're on the wrong boat?'

I glanced back over my shoulder to see the packet, which had just left the mouth of the river, turning in the estuary on her central axis like the needle on a compass. With the manœuvre completed and her stern now angled towards us she began to make remarkable speed towards the open sea. I watched as she steamed off into the distance, the funnel belching out columns of coal smoke, and wondered which one of the tiny figures on her deck was Nate.

As our journey progressed northward the estuary narrowed to something more akin to a river, giving way on either side to gently rolling hills with villages now beginning to show lights nestling in the vales between. Larger settlements crept down the slope and touched the water, where a few small boats bobbed on their moorings. The sun dipped behind the horizon and the whale-backed shadows cast out by the Welsh hills shrank back towards their source.

Stigwood returned to the helm and nudged us towards the English shore. Gus pulled on a rope and the boom swung across the deck, the sail flapping and shuddering before filling again as we came about. Once in the shallows the sail was dropped and with the anchor tipped over the side we came to rest. Although we lay close to the shore there was no attempt to leave the boat, for like true mariners our night was to be spent on board, tucked behind the walls of our wooden world.

It was a tight squeeze in the cabin, with just enough room for two to perch on the small wooden crates that doubled for chairs on either side of a small table. The stove had burned only while Gus had cooked a simple meal, but still gave out enough heat to warm the cramped space. My companions allocated themselves the makeshift seats and left me to sit back on the bunk in which I had spent a good part of the afternoon. Stigwood arranged three glasses before him and from a cupboard by his side pulled out a welcome bottle. In response, Gus produced a dog-eared pack of cards and a clutch of coins. Stigwood invited me to join in the game but, never having been a gambler, I declined, preferring instead to take advantage of the storm lamp suspended above our heads to do a little reading.

I pulled my bag from beneath the bunk where it had been stowed upon my arrival and while lifting out my father's journal checked that the package was still there, along with the pistol.

Also looking into the bag and taking account of its contents, Stigwood said, 'A bad business about Leonard Wilkie. He was a good chap. Didn't deserve that, a bloody shame it is.' It was the first time he'd mentioned the events in Bristol since we'd set out on our voyage.

After pulling out the journal I closed the bag and pushed it back under the bunk. It had crossed my mind to remove the pistol in case I should have need of it during the night but that would have been the height of bad manners.

'Don't worry about us, sir,' said Stigwood, astutely reading my concern. 'I don't know what you've got in there and I don't care. Wilkie was one of us: he lived on the river and he died on the river. The least we can do is see that you get to finish whatever business you had together. Besides, I made a promise to the boy.'

'I fully intend to pay for my passage once we reach Gloucester, Mr Stigwood.'

'Won't hear of it,' he declared, picking up a card and clasping it to his chest. 'It's not as if you've put us out of our way, is it?' Stigwood gave a wink before returning to the game. 'Now, young man, where were we? I owe you three pennies, I believe.'

'Four,' corrected Gus as he ordered the cards in his hand.

The journal lay open on my lap, my hand casually flicking over the pages without paying much heed to their contents. But then, switching my attention from the game to the book, I began to look out for one page in particular. My father's journals ran into several volumes and it had not been possible to carry them all away from the house. Forced to limit myself to a single volume I had chosen carefully, aware that within its covers should be an account of my father's experiences in one of the most momentous events to take place in his lifetime. The next hour or so was spent with my father in a derelict farmhouse on the battlefield of Waterloo, where like a spectral student looking over his shoulder I watched him cut away limb after shattered limb. He worked quickly and skilfully, entirely unflustered by the sounds of battle which all that day raged around him, but despite his successes many a man died under his knife. There had been nothing in the way of bluster or boast in his account, and now at last I understood full well why he had never spoken to me of that terrible day. Little wonder he always appeared so content with the quiet life of a country doctor.

Battle weary, I closed the book just as the card session drew to an end, Stigwood's pile of coins by now almost nonexistent. It was time to turn in, and Gus took down the lamp to guide his way to a temporary berth somewhere in the bow. Despite already having slept half the afternoon away I was grateful to lie back in my bunk. Before falling asleep once again I determined to take a leaf from my father's book and be more conscientious with my own efforts at keeping a journal, for there may come a time when I too have a son grateful to know the true story of his father's life.

# 16

Only after Stigwood had retired to the bunk above me did I finally take the precaution of removing the pistol from my bag. As it happened, though, my fear of the boat being boarded pirate-fashion during the night proved unfounded. This was just as well, because in the morning I discovered the small lead ball and most of the gunpowder in one of my shoes; I clearly had much to learn before I became a proficient *pistolero*.

Stigwood once again proved good to his word when the boat tied up at the dock in Gloucester just after midday. Only after we had said our goodbyes did it dawn on me that I had little idea about how to proceed from there.

My aim was obviously to get back to London, but finding that the next train went first to Bristol, where Wilkie's assailants might yet be residing, I decided to bide my time and take the train to Birmingham late in the afternoon. But then, when I retired to a nearby hostelry to take lunch, it became apparent that my funds were running dangerously low. This would not have been so bad if all I had to worry about was my train fare but a porter in the station had told me that there would not be a train from Birmingham to London until the following day, which meant that I would have to find overnight lodgings. The thought of spending the night huddled among mail sacks on the station platform was enough for me to constrain my appetite and despite the mouth-watering smell of steak pie and other culinary delights I settled for a bowl of soup and a mug of ale.

. While I waited for my soup the innkeeper was good enough to loan me his newspaper. Taking a stool at the bar, I examined the front page of the *Western Times* and quickly settled on a short report in the bottom corner:

### TRAGIC ACCIDENT AT BRISTOL DOCKS

A man was killed in a waterside fire in the early hours of yesterday morning. The body of Leonard Wilkie, a respected mechanical engineer, was pulled from the dock in which he is thought to have drowned while fleeing a burning building. The engineer's workshop, in which the fire broke out, was entirely destroyed, along with an adjoining property. The son of the deceased, Nathaniel Wilkie, is missing, though witnesses claim he was seen uninjured but in a distraught condition at the scene of the accident. Police are eager to learn of the young man's whereabouts. The cause of the blaze has yet to be established but is thought to have originated in the forge, where a fire burned constantly. Mr Wilkie was best known for his work on the engines of the famous ship SS *Great Britain*, the creation of Mr Isambard Kingdom Brunel, which was built locally.

Although the dispatch lacked detail it was clear that Wilkie's murder was being treated as an accident and I had to repress a face-tightening flush of anger at the thought of his killers getting away scot-free. Was the local coroner such a fool as to have overlooked the wounds on his head? Even if these had been misinterpreted as injuries sustained in a fall I could only hope that a post mortem would find his lungs clear of water and thereby provide indication enough – for a man needs to be drawing air to drown. Being in no position to offer my own professional advice, I took comfort from the fact that Nate appeared to have succeeded in a clean getaway.

The soup provided some much-needed warmth on that cold January afternoon but did little to suppress my appetite. By the time the train pulled into Birmingham station my rumbling stomach was in open competition with the noise of the engine. A place to rest my head came in the form of a rather shabby boarding house. It was all I could afford, but the landlady was good enough to provide a plate of greasy stew, which I guzzled eagerly without taking the time to study its contents too closely. My odyssey finally came to an end the following afternoon when I arrived back in London. A journey that should have taken no more than a few hours had taken the best part of four days to complete.

By now lacking enough money even for a cab, I joined the pedestrian traffic on the pavement and set out on foot for the bank.

Noise and bustle was everywhere – crowds of people in such a hurry to get about their business. Even those whom I doubted had any business to be about were eager to be elsewhere. The streets were choked with vehicles and the air heavy with a heady mix of aromas, all of them unpleasant. In addition, the place seemed so dirty, the cobbles, bricks and mortar caked in a skein of grime. I had expected to be glad to be back, but by the time I got to turning the key in my door a black humour had settled upon me – a city grime of my own mind's making.

Why had I not before considered the possibility of finding my rooms ransacked or, even worse, encountering my pursuers inside? But it was already too late; I had crossed the threshold. Even if I did choose this moment to run, escape seemed an unlikely prospect, especially when my foot slipped on the litter of post that had accumulated on the carpet beneath the letterbox. In any case, I was done with running. If they wanted the package badly enough to have killed Wilkie then, damn it, they were welcome to it. I would simply hand it over and in return would hope to be left alone.

Fortunately, though, the place was just as I had left it, untidy but not ransacked. But taking nothing for granted and with the pistol in my less than steady hand, I went from room to room, pushing the doors fully back against the walls, tugging aside drapes and even looking under the bed. I was alone. This was just as well, as in the cold light of common sense I realized that my surrender of the package was unlikely to stay the murderous hand of men such as those responsible for Wilkie's death. Then, as my nerves calmed I saw the bright side. Why should they know where I lived? Having given them the slip in Bristol I was surely home and dry, just another face in a city of hundreds of thousands.

I placed the pistol on my desk and returned to the front door to check that it was properly closed. With the bolt thrown I picked up the post and quickly sorted through it. There was last month's copy of the *Lancet*, some circulars, and in among them a couple of letters – all very boring. Apart, that is, from the envelope on which my address had been scrawled by the unmistakable hand of Brunel. I studied it more closely and, considering that calling at his offices to hand over the package was to be my next task, was rather perturbed to see that it bore a French postmark. Rushing back into the parlour, I opened it. This time, to my relief, there was no key inside.

*Calais, 28 December 1858*

*My Dear Phillips,*

*You will only be reading this letter if you have returned from your father's home. I pray that this is due to his recovery but if not then my deepest sympathies. My apologies for putting you to the trouble of a trip to Bristol (if indeed you made the trip) only to find me away from London on your return. I myself am in France, but not for long. Due to a sudden downturn in my health, and at the insistence of Brodie and my good lady wife, I have been packed away to warmer climes. I am informed that a touch of the sun will reinvigorate my constitution. I must also admit that the opportunity to get away from the infernal wrangles over the ship was not unwelcome.*

*By the time you read this I will be well on my way to our final destination – Egypt (the place was the least objectionable of those suggested by Brodie).*

With this revelation I was forced to pause and take a moment. Then, after a deep breath or two, I continued reading.

*I say OUR destination as I am accompanied not only by my family and most of the household but another member of your profession. Though coming highly recommended by Brodie, I have yet to establish to my own satisfaction that he knows his backside from his elbow, let alone my own! It would of course have been a pleasure to have you accompany me as personal physician and I am sure that you would appreciate the ancient wonders that await our arrival in the land of the Pharaohs. However, you have your own domestic concerns, and once again my commiserations on your father's perilous condition, and upon your return I am sure you will be eager to resume your important work at the hospital.*

*I look forward to finding the ship fitted out and ready for her sea trial on my own return, but with Russell at the helm in my absence I dare not hope for too much. I have yet another infuriating letter from him in front of me in which he professes to be my obedient servant, though if he were I would gladly give him a good thrashing.*

*But enough of my complaints – my 'guardians' would be disquieted to see my vexation, which as they do not tire of telling me is bad for my condition. Once again, my apologies for not being there to take delivery of the package, I look forward to doing so when I get back. I am sure when I do you will find its contents of great interest. In the meantime please take care of it for me. Should the opportunity arise I will write again to keep you appraised of our progress. I would appreciate it if you could attend the next of our gatherings and make certain that adequate minutes are kept – I fear things slipped somewhat in your absence and those fellows need someone to keep an eye on them.*

*Your obedient servant,*

*Isambard Kingdom Brunel*

I scrunched the letter in my fist and tossed it into the waste-paper basket. How typical of Brunel to leave me here with the package and all the dangers associated with it while he went sightseeing in Egypt! I fumed and fizzed, stamping about as I unpacked my bag and threw its contents hither and thither.

The pages of Brunel's scrapbook were singled out for the most brutal treatment, falling to the carpet in a flurry of old newsprint and creased foolscap after being hurled against the wall. My tantrum only abated with the removal of the last item from the bag, the scent from a pair of socks worn a day too long perhaps acting like smelling salts and bringing me round. My frenzy was replaced by a slight tinge of regret as I realized that childish petulance was going to get me nowhere. If Wilkie's fate was not to be mine then I would need to keep a level head.

The place felt damp after being abandoned for so long and it crossed my mind to light a fire. Settling for internal combustion, I poured myself a brandy and retrieved the crumpled letter from the waste basket before slumping into my favourite chair. Taking a generous slug, I unfolded the page and checked the date on which it had been written. I had clearly jumped to conclusions. The letter had been written on 28 December, while Wilkie had died just three days ago on 2 January. There was no getting away from it: Brunel had been in France at least five days, probably more, before the murder, which undermined any suggestion that he had absconded overseas at news of trouble. That was assuming of course that he had not paid the two men to do his dirty work while he created himself an alibi. But why would he go to such lengths to obtain something that was his in the first place? Immediately discounting the theory as preposterous, I drained the glass. Get a grip, man, I told myself, if you're not careful you'll turn into Tarlow and see the worst in everyone. The cruel reality was, however, that doing just that might be the only way of keeping myself alive.

Pulling the package from the duffel bag, I set to work opening it. The knot in the twine binding the oilcloth wrapping was too tight to loosen with my fingers and so I took a sharp knife to it. There was then some small pleasure to be had from shattering the wax seals which served to dissuade the curious. Released from their bonds, the folds of greasy cloth opened like heavy petals on an ugly flower.

Smoothing out the roughly cut square of fabric, I studied the object perched upon it. What appeared to be a carelessly constructed ball of paper was in turn unfolded and smoothed out like the cloth beneath it. The exposed object was about the size and shape of an ostrich egg. For a while I studied it without picking it up, noting the four voids cut into its two gently curving sides. Lifting it from its paper nest, I cradled it in my hands. There was a barely perceptible seam running around the entire surface, which from its golden sheen I guessed was made from brass or copper. Noticing a couple of tiny hinges, I realized that the seam was actually the point at which two halves joined to form the whole. A flick of a small latch and they opened out on their hinges, causing another object to fall out and clatter noisily on to the tabletop below.

Wrapped carefully in a protective shroud of cloth were four highly polished curving plates of stainless steel, shining like silver in contrast to the outer sheath of gold. Men may well have been willing to kill for silver and gold, but not for copper and steel. There could be little doubt that whatever value the object had lay in its function, but what could that be? I cupped one of the plates in my hand, the palm and fingers flexing to accommodate the outer sweep of the concavity. I noticed a couple of small rectangular notches cut into the edges, which looked as though they were designed to allow access to whatever was placed inside the chamber. Speculation was pointless; the brass egg and the four steel plates could have been parts of a musical box for all I knew about the world of engineering. What was apparent, though, even to my eyes, was the quality of the craftsmanship. Brunel had chosen well with Wilkie.

The large sheet of paper in which the thing had been wrapped was a technical drawing, and undoubtedly the same one I had seen on Wilkie's desk in Bristol. There were scale drawings of what were clearly the pieces now rendered in metal and lists of dimensions written out in Brunel's own hand. Wilkie had returned everything related to the object from its design through to its manufacture, whether this was due to instruction from Brunel or simply a desire to wash his hands of the affair I could not tell.

Puzzling the meaning of it all, I recalled that the Wilkies had told me that Brunel only commissioned them to make certain parts, without going to the bother of informing them what the ultimate purpose was. The only known fact was that, whatever it was, people were prepared to kill to get hold of it. But who were those people? Were the men I had seen in Bristol free agents operating on their own behalf or were they under instruction? If they had been commissioned for the task, then anyone could be behind the crime. Unlikely as it seemed, there was still the distinct possibility that one or more of those involved might be known to me and so, accordingly, I could trust no one.

Feeling slightly remiss at having exposed the thing, I rewrapped the plates and returned them to their housing. Instead of re-creating the paper ball I removed the sheet of drawings and, temporarily dropping it to the floor, repackaged the object in just the oilcloth. Finding a ball of string, I then retied the package good and tight. Setting it to one side, I retrieved the sheet of paper and, after properly smoothing it out, folded it into something readily concealable. With the drawing pressed within a book, which was then returned to anonymity on the shelf, the package was stuffed into the murky bottom of an elephant's foot umbrella stand in the vestibule, where it would remain until I decided what to do with it. I was quietly pleased that the ugly curiosity, which had been a gift from a grateful patient newly returned from Africa with a nasty parasite, had at last found a use, as I possessed only one umbrella and it always seemed quite happy to spend its off-duty hours suspended from a coat hook. For once, I lifted the umbrella from its hook and dropped it into the stand, where hopefully it would serve as added camouflage.

The evening was drawing out and it was time for dinner. Stuffing the pistol into my only coat with pockets big enough to accommodate it, I closed the door behind me and with my freshly stocked purse took a cab to my club. I also carried with me a couple of pages from Brunel's scrapbook, which would provide an effective buffer against conversation with fellow members.

On arriving I made directly for the dining room and was quickly seated at my usual table in a discreet corner. Placing my order without reference to the menu, I began to read the first newspaper cutting that came to hand. Yet again, albeit thirty years old, the news did not look good. The report concerned one of the engineer's first projects, the tunnel beneath the Thames at Rotherhithe.

*The Times*

14 January 1827

## ACCIDENT AT THE THAMES TUNNEL

The following letter was on Saturday laid before the Directors of the Thames Tunnel Company, which had been written by Mr Brunel, jun., when suffering great bodily pain:-

*Saturday Morning, Jan 12.*

*I had been in the frames shield with the workmen throughout the whole night, having taken my station there at 10 o'clock. During the workings, through the night, no symptoms of insecurity appeared. At six o'clock the morning shift of men came on. We began to work the ground at the west top corner of the frame. The tide had just then begun to flow, and finding the ground tolerable quiet, we proceeded, by beginning at the top, and had worked about a foot downwards, when on exposing the next six inches, the ground swelled suddenly and a large quantity burst through the opening thus made. This was followed instantly by a large body of water. The rush was so violent as to force the man on the spot where the burst took place out of the frame, on to the timber stage, behind the frames. I ordered all the men in the frames to retire. All were retiring, except the three men who were with me, and they retreated with me. I did not leave the stage until those three men were down the ladder of the frames, when they and I proceeded about 20 feet along the west arch of the tunnel; at this moment, the agitation of the air by the rush of the water was such as to extinguish the lights, and the water had gained the height of the middle of our waists. I was at that moment giving directions to the three men, to what manner they ought to proceed, in the dark, to effect their escape, when they and I were knocked down and covered by a part of the timber stage.*

At this point my dinner arrived and before long I was using a fork to tunnel through a mound of mashed potato, only to watch as a flood of thick brown gravy inundated the freshly excavated void. What was becoming very apparent, from this and my previous readings was that Brunel had experienced more close shaves than I'd had, dare I say it, hot dinners. Stemming the tide of gravy by mopping it up with succulent slices of lamb, I continued to read.

> *I struggled under water for some time, and at length extricated myself from the stage and by swimming, and being forced by the water, I gained the eastern arch, where I got a better footing, and was enabled, by laying hold of the railway rope, to pause a little, in the hope of encouraging the men who had been knocked down at the same time as myself. My knee was so injured by the timber that I could scarcely swim, or get up the stairs; but the rush of the water carried me up the shaft. The three men who had been knocked down with me were unable to extricate themselves; and I am grieved to say, they were lost; and, I believe, also, two old men and one young man in other parts of the work.*

My plate was now empty and, with dessert pending, I went on to read about an unsuccessful attempt to drag the still-flooded tunnel for bodies and to locate the offending hole in the riverbed through the use of a diving bell. The newspaper report ended on quite an unexpected note by relating an earlier incident which had occurred in the tunnel one night.

> Mr Brunel, jun., and some others engaged in superintending the work, were alarmed by a voice from the farthest part of the excavation, exclaiming, 'The water! The water! Wedges and straw here!' This was followed by a dead silence. Those in attendance were at first paralysed by an apprehension that the men who were known to be at the spot from whence the voice was heard had been overwhelmed by some disaster.

Young Mr Brunel, however, boldly pushed forward with others to ascertain what had happened, when they were overjoyed to find the men fast asleep, and all safe. They had fallen to sleep from fatigue, and one of them made the exclamation when under the influence of a dream that the water was breaking in.

Although this closing paragraph was an almost light-hearted postscript to what was otherwise a catalogue of catastrophe, there would come a time when I too would discover that Brunel's projects had a way of driving themselves into a man's dreams with all the power of the raging waters in his tunnel.

Feeling almost human again, I returned home. I was ready for bed but first sat down at my desk to dash off a letter to the coroner in Bristol. I was in no condition to create a well-crafted essay so settled for a brief sketch of the facts surrounding Wilkie's death.

If nothing else, I hoped the missive would give the authorities some pause for thought before writing his murder off as an accident. The contents of the letter would hopefully exonerate Nate from any suspected involvement but, given the circumstances, I omitted all reference to the package, its connection with Brunel and, most importantly, my own name. Satisfied that I had done the right thing by Wilkie without needlessly putting Brunel or indeed myself at risk, I sealed the envelope.

Carrying the pistol before me as though it were a warming pan, I retired to bed, and within minutes was enjoying the sleep, not of the just, but just the tired.

# 17

The omnibus overturned during the morning rush hour – crushing pedestrians beneath as passengers on the open upper deck were thrown into the street like jacks cast from a child's hand. The fatal combination of a shying horse and a badly fitted wheel was said to have been the cause. Two passers-by and one passenger were dead while six passengers had been badly injured. A terrible accident by any measure but, and God forgive me for this, I was almost grateful for it, for any anxiety I had about returning to the hospital after so long was washed away in the floodtide of victims requiring immediate attention.

The serious cases were carried in on litters but there were also dozens of walking wounded, and for a few hours the scene cannot have been too far removed from the battlefield hospital described in my father's journal. Even the injuries bore some similarity to the horrors of war, with razor-sharp shards of the vehicle's window glass cutting through flesh and muscle as effectively as any sabre. This flurry of operations, which included a trepanation to remove pressure on the brain, numerous bone settings and one leg amputation, ensured that my return went almost entirely unnoticed among the hospital staff, or at least uncommented on. And for my own part, there was no time to fret over procedures and regimes unpractised for some time, as life-and-death decisions had to be made without the luxury of contemplation.

It was well into the evening by the time the crisis passed, and by then it felt as though I had never been away.

With the emergency over I thought it best to go along and make my presence known to Brodie, who, I was sure, would be delighted to see me back. Hoping to bypass Mumrill, I made directly for his master's door but before I could knock it flew open and the corridor filled with a cloud of billowing crinoline. Miss Nightingale made to brush past me, but stopped and with nostrils flaring and dark eyes ablaze announced, 'The man is impossible, quite impossible!' Before I had time to agree with this sentiment she was off, sweeping down the corridor.

Brodie's door was still swaying on its hinges when I poked my head into his office. He was standing at the window, fists knotted behind his back. For a moment I considered coming back at a more suitable time, but my days of tiptoeing around him were gone. Announcing my presence with a cough, I stepped into the lion's den. Brodie turned around, his face still flushed red. I smiled at him and he beckoned me to take a seat while returning to his own.

'So you have decided to come back to us. I believe you acquitted yourself well today.'

His intelligence took me slightly by surprise. Whoever his source was it wasn't Mumrill; the maggot would rather have his tongue cut out than say anything good about me.

'I believe we did the best we could, Sir Benjamin.'

'Do not think for a moment, Dr Phillips, that we have not had to deal with a good number of such incidents in your absence.'

'Yes, I am sure of it.'

'And while we are on the subject of accidents I want to discuss the thorny subject of Miss Nightingale.'

'Miss Nightingale is a formidable woman.'

His fist hit the desk. 'She is a meddler and a burden!'

'I think she is accustomed to getting her own way after her time in the Crimea.'

'She has powerful friends,' replied Brodie, returning to his feet and pacing the office. 'She has talked the hospital commissioners into turning the hospital into . . .' there was a brief pause as he wrestled with the words. '. . . into a training facility for nurses.' He returned to the desk but only to slap it. 'We are to become a school for nurses, sir! What do you say to that?'

'There is a shortage of good nurses. Those few that we have are worth their weight in gold. As for the rest, well, let us just say there are times when they are more of a hindrance than a help.' It came out as more of an endorsement for the proposal than I had intended.

Brodie produced a worrying smile. 'Very well then, doctor. As you think it such a good idea and have already served as something of an intermediary between us, I am appointing you as official hospital liaison to Miss Nightingale on this matter, and I wish you better luck than I have had with her. You will report regularly to me. I want to know everything that transpires, but I do not want anything to do with that woman from this moment on.'

I had been back at the hospital for less than a day and had already been saddled with a task I could well do without. He had asked me to look after her in the past, to keep her out of his hair, but this was different: establishing a nursing school was a major undertaking; it would take months, years!

'But, sir, I am a surgeon not a go-between. Isn't that a task best taken on by . . . by Mumrill? He would be much better at dealing with such a sensitive matter.'

Brodie glowered at me. 'You and I both know that the man is a sycophant. I am not looking for a yes man here. Nor am I asking for volunteers. This job calls for a man of . . . dare I say . . . integrity? I want this situation handled properly. If we are to have a nursing school then, by God, it will be a good one. And you, doctor, have more of an idea than anyone as to what we should expect from a good nurse. You teach surgeons, don't you?' I nodded grimly. 'Well then, you should have some opinion on the teaching of nurses. And as for your other duties, I think we have already established that the hospital has managed to get along without you quite adequately these past weeks. It follows that you will manage to find time in your busy schedule to oversee this matter. Do I make myself clear?'

'Very clear,' I replied quietly. My capitulation had nothing to do with his flattery, which as ever he had applied with the toe of his boot. The truth was there was just no point in arguing with the old goat.

He shifted position in his seat, flexing his shoulders as though a weight had been lifted. 'Good,' he said. 'I will leave it to you to explain your new role to Miss Nightingale. Proceed as you see fit, but do not forget I will expect regular reports.'

'Yes, Sir Benjamin. If that's everything I'll get back to my duties?'

'Fine, I think we are finished,' he said, as usual signalling that the audience had come to an end by returning to his paperwork.

I turned to leave but then span around on my heels. 'Is it true,' I asked, 'that Mr Brunel has been sent overseas?'

Brodie replied without looking up. 'Yes, I am afraid his condition has worsened.'

'Sir, just what is his condition?'

At this he raised his head. 'You need not concern yourself with my patient's condition, Dr Phillips. The man pushes himself far too hard; that much is clear for all to see. Hopefully the change of climate will reinvigorate him. Now, if you will excuse me.'

Again, I made to leave the room, but as I opened the door Brodie spoke up behind me. 'I am sorry to hear about the passing of your father, Phillips. He was a fine doctor.'

My first day back had proven an eventful one, so much so that I had not given a moment's thought to the grim events of the past few days. Not until I put on my coat and felt the weight of the pistol did I recall that my life was at risk. But while walking to my club, where I intended to take supper on my way home, I once again reassured myself that with Brunel well out of the picture and my identity, God willing, entirely unknown to Wilkie's assailants there was little likelihood of trouble finding me here in London. Calmed by this reasoning and reinvigorated by a good meal, I turned my thoughts to affairs more befitting a surgeon.

There could be no denying that the idea of a nursing school was a good one. The present system, which provided little or no training for nurses, especially in basic medical skills, was in much need of an overhaul. And who better to oversee this revolution than Miss Nightingale? It also had to be admitted that she was a handsome woman and when all was said and done there had to be some merit to anyone capable of irritating Sir Benjamin Brodie so effectively.

'They need discipline, Dr Phillips,' insisted Miss Nightingale as she glanced disdainfully around at the undisciplined clutter of my office. Word had been sent via William that I would be pleased to have her take tea in my office. It occurred to me that the choice of venue may have been misjudged. 'My nurses in the Crimea were drunk more often than they were sober. And if that were not bad enough, I regularly had to drag them from the beds of their patients. The nurse should be the backbone of a hospital, Dr Phillips, not a prostitute with a bandage in one hand and a bottle in the other.'

'I agree entirely, Miss Nightingale,' I said, trying to conceal a smile behind my teacup. 'There are a few here I can rely on, but the others are essentially chambermaids.'

'Nursing should be a vocation and not just an alternative to the workhouse. I want to make it a profession with training and a fair wage; only then will we be able to recruit suitable women.

'What I propose will be better for both nurses and patients. Self-respect is the key to an efficient nursing service. Though I am sure that Sir Benjamin disagrees with me on that point.'

At this juncture I found myself, of all unlikely things, making excuses for my superior. 'He's a cantankerous old devil, of that there can be no doubt, but like all men of his years, he comes from another age. Nonetheless, I am certain he recognizes the benefits of the school.'

'That may be so, but it is very clear that he resents me and, I do not doubt, women in general. Is that not why you and I are talking now? Because he cannot bring himself to deal with me on a professional level? He would rather I leave the room while he takes his port and cigars than face up to the failings of his own hospital.'

'Who wouldn't feel a little aggrieved at someone coming in from the outside and criticizing their work? – because that's the way he will see it. And as for me, perhaps he just wanted to make my life difficult. I do not wish to cause offence, Miss Nightingale, but you are hardly a typical example of your sex.'

Now she smiled. 'None taken, Dr Phillips, on the contrary, I appreciate your candour. And you must forgive me if I appear a little sensitive, but as a woman in a world of men I long ago learned that I have to struggle to make my voice heard. Whatever motives may lie behind Sir Benjamin's choice of appointment I am confident he has made the right one.'

'It is good of you to say so.'

'I have seen enough to know that you are a much better surgeon than you are a carpenter.' She gave a chuckle at the recollection of our first meeting. 'You handled yesterday's crisis very well, Dr Phillips. We would have done well with more of your type in the Crimea.'

So it was she who had been singing my praises to Brodie. Draining the last of her tea, she rose to her feet. 'Well, Dr Phillips, I will keep you no longer. There is a meeting next week with the hospital commissioners to discuss new accommodations for the school. I trust I will see you there.'

'I am sure Sir Benjamin will insist on my presence,' I replied, recalling my instructions to provide regular reports, though it was probably best for all of us, especially me, if this first conference with Miss Nightingale went without minutes.

Opening the door, she took another look at my surroundings. 'We should perhaps take the opportunity to request that the new wing includes a more suitable office for you. This poky closet just will not do.'

# 18

William was hard at work scrubbing down the table after my first demonstration in seven weeks.

'It's good to have you back,' he said, rinsing the brush in reddened water and glancing up at the empty gallery. 'There were more students in today than I seen any time while you were away. You really pack 'em in, sir, like a Friday night down the Alhambra.'

'Is that so, William?'

'Those other doctors, they're fine if you're in need of fixing, but for instruction they don't hold a candle to you. The gentlemen love watchin' you work, I've heard 'em say so.'

'Thank you, William. I only wish that Sir Benjamin felt the same way.'

'Oh, he does, sir, he does.'

'And how would you know that, you sly fox?'

William grinned. 'He was often in while you were away. Pace about he would, like a cat on hot tiles, that man.'

'Indeed.'

'It gave the other surgeons the jitters, that's for sure – him here, looking on. Then after a while he'd come and seek me out. Thought at first he was checking up on me, you know.'

'Yes, William, I know only too well.'

'But it was only to ask me if I knew when you would be back.

Why he should think you would tell me before 'im I don't know. But he was very keen to 'ave you back, that much was clear.'

'Strange old bird, wouldn't you say?'

'Oh, I don't know about that, sir. He just knows which side 'is bread's buttered on, that's all. The more students there are to pay fees the bigger 'is bonus.'

'You have been away for quite some time,' said Inspector Tarlow, who seemed almost disappointed to find me at my desk.

'I have,' I replied. 'My father was ill.'

'I hope he is better now.'

'I'm afraid not; he passed away.'

Only then did the policeman remove his hat. 'I am sorry for your loss.'

'Thank you, inspector. Now, how can I be of help? Not another murder surely?'

'Yes, I'm afraid so. I thought the killer might have given up but he's back on the job. We found another body last night.'

'In the river?'

Tarlow nodded. 'Exactly the same as the others, with the contents of the chest removed. The corpse was pretty fresh; couldn't have been dead more than a couple of days.'

'And you want me to take a look?'

'No, doctor. I just have a couple of questions.'

'I see.'

'When exactly did you get back?'

'A week ago yesterday.'

'In plenty of time for the latest murder to be committed.'

'So now I am a suspect?'

'I have resisted as long as I can, doctor, but I'm afraid there are now just too many coincidences for me not to consider you as such.'

'Might I ask what they are?' As if I didn't already have a good idea.

The inspector pulled out his notebook and flicked it open. 'First and foremost, the killer has an interest in surgery.'

'But I have already told you the work is unprofessional. If merely cutting flesh is to count as surgery then every butcher's apprentice and knifeman in London should perhaps come in and do a shift in the theatre.'

'But we are not talking about your average Saturday-night sticking here, are we, doctor? The removal of organs in such a consistent fashion smacks of something much more . . . much more clinical. Now, if you would let me continue.'

I should have known better than to try to argue the point. 'Of course, inspector. Please, do go on.'

'The killer removes the heart and lungs and it just so happens that you are something of an expert on the heart.'

'At the risk of repeating myself . . .'

Tarlow glowered at me. 'The handkerchief in which a disposed-of heart was wrapped bore a monograph which could be construed as matching your own initials.'

'It had been chewed off by a dog!'

He was calmer this time. 'I grant you, it wouldn't stand up in court, but when weighed alongside the rest of the list the handkerchief has its place. Next on that list is your interest in prostitutes themselves, something which you went to rather extreme lengths to hide from me.'

'Leaving the hat behind wasn't clever,' I admitted, not for the first time feeling mortified at the recollection of the incident.

'No, it wasn't, doctor. You should have taken the hat under the bed with you.'

I knew it had been a mistake to hide! 'You mean . . . you mean to say you saw me there?'

Tarlow the terrier looked pleased with himself. 'The sole of one of your feet, to be precise. But let's move on, shall we?'

I was too mortified to reply.

'There was the corpse you discovered at the mouth of the new sewer. An unfortunate coincidence, no doubt, but I can't resist using it to make up numbers. In any case, the incident demonstrated that you were no stranger to the river from which all the bodies were recovered. Then, last but certainly not least, you disappear from the city just as another body is found. I was on the verge of putting out a warrant for your arrest, but then it came to light that your father genuinely was dying. But the real killer, if you will excuse my use of the term, is that while you were out of town there wasn't a single murder. Then, no sooner do you arrive back than we find another body.' Putting away his notebook, Tarlow took a step closer to my desk. 'You have to admit, doctor, it doesn't look at all good.'

I would be the first to agree with his last point: it did not look at all good. 'Would it help to tell you that I am not your man?'

Tarlow drew his lips in towards his teeth. 'Not for much longer, no.'

'So you're not going to arrest me now then?'

'Damning as the list may be, it is still not enough, at least to my mind. There are however others on the force who would happily hang a man on the basis of less. This case has dragged on for over a year and there are now questions being asked by superiors about my lack of progress. I could throw you to the pack just to please them and, who knows, you may be the killer. But in the absence of anything more than circumstantial evidence – and it wouldn't take much – I am not going to do that.'

'Why are you telling me this, inspector?'

'Unless I come up with something soon they're likely to take me off the case, and my replacement is unlikely to be as fair-minded. Be grateful that the newspapers haven't got wind of the fact that there has been more than one body. They will, though – someone will talk, and when they do you can bet that I will be reassigned. I am just being straight with you, doctor. I am drawing a blank and if there isn't a breakthrough soon then we're both in trouble.'

'You think I'm innocent then?'

'I didn't say that. I think you are connected in some way. The list tells me as much. But I can't work out how. If you do know anything, anything at all that might help, I strongly recommend you tell me.'

What was I to say? That Brunel had approached me and expressed an interest in the human heart not long before Tarlow made his first visit? That since our first meeting I had also become involved in a murder in Bristol?

'No, inspector, I'm sorry. I can't think of anything that might help you.'

'Very well, doctor, then let us both hope that something turns up.' Watching the inspector depart empty-handed once again, it was clear that it would now be up to me to ensure that something did indeed turn up.

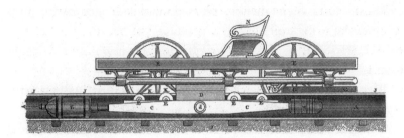

# 19

Plans for the new teaching school continued apace, and Miss Nightingale threw herself body and soul into the enterprise. She consulted with architects on ideas for the new facility; harangued potential benefactors; but on top of all that assisted in the hospital, largely so she could monitor current nursing practice and assess future requirements. Then there were meetings with the hospital commissioners, which in accordance with Brodie's instructions, I also attended. Needless to say, she was the only woman at the table otherwise occupied by a dozen bearded worthies. But I was not at all surprised to see that by the end of the meeting she had most of them wrapped around her little finger, with even those who, like Brodie, were less than comfortable dealing with a woman eventually going along with the majority.

Before long a plan for not just a new wing but an entirely new hospital was agreed, an idea which surprised me but nonetheless had my full support, despite the fact that I was there as an observer without voting powers. Medicine was advancing at an accelerated rate and it seemed doubtful that a hospital built fifty years ago would meet the needs of the next half-century. Then there was London's rapidly growing population, which was putting all of its hospitals under pressure. Even in our own it was not unusual to see patients lying on mattresses on the floor and even sleeping in the corridors.

The outcome of the meeting pleased me greatly, not just because it promised a revolutionary new hospital, but because the issue of the school was now so important that Sir Benjamin would surely feel obliged to put his anti-Nightingale feelings behind him and get involved, an outcome which would in turn see a reduction in my own commitment.

It had been a long day and tonight there would be no stopping off at the club. Doctor's orders were a good night's sleep, with at best a mug of warm milk to help me on my way. Walking was also out of the question and so I hailed a cab, but even then I could not get home fast enough.

Pushing the key into the lock caused the door to swing back on its hinges, the lock itself falling halfway out of its mounting. In that instant all the apprehensions born of my flight from Bristol came flooding back. I reached into my coat pocket to pull out the gun, but found it empty. So diminished had the threat seemed to be that some days previously I had stopped carrying my father's pistol.

I stood listening, and on hearing nothing dared to bend forward and pick up the umbrella which lay on the carpet in the hallway. With the metal tip pointing out before me I crept along and then, after a brief pause, entered the parlour, pushing the door flat to the wall.

Drawers lay on the floor, papers scattered across the table and books pulled from their shelves. Prodding the curtains with the umbrella and sidling across to the cabinet, I reached into a half-open drawer and was surprised to find the pistol still inside. Putting down the umbrella and cocking the weapon steadied my nerves a little; at least now I had a fighting chance. It was only then that the full implication of the umbrella lying on the floor in the hallway sank in. It had been sitting in the elephant's foot, at the bottom of which I had hidden the package.

I cursed myself for not finding a more secure hiding-place. The hospital would have been ideal – so many nooks and crannies that no one would ever find it there – but I had lulled myself into a false sense of security, been too confident that I had remained anonymous. The break-in and the theft were clear demonstration that my identity was indeed known to the men who had killed Wilkie.

Satisfied that my visitors had left I secured the door and went to bed, the pistol on my bedside table.

In the days after the break-in, which was quickly followed by a visit from the locksmith, I took to carrying the pistol again. There was more than the break-in behind this decision: someone was following me.

It began as a mere sensation, an almost animal instinct that I was under observation; the feeling that eyes were watching me, as I walked down the street, climbed into a cab, left my club or turned the key in the new lock on my door.

I even caught glimpses of him, or so I thought – lurking on a corner before he disappeared into the crowd, or following in my footsteps, keeping a good distance between us. Once or twice I tried to outsmart him, running around an entire block to come up from behind or nipping into an alleyway to watch as he passed by. But he was a slippery fish this shadow of mine and always managed to shake me off. Indeed, my efforts only made him more reclusive, for after a week or so of this cat-and-mouse game he disappeared entirely, or at least became more cautious in his labours.

Coming so hot on the heels of the break-in, I at first assumed that my tail was the person responsible for the theft of the package. But then I remembered Tarlow, who by now must be desperate for an arrest and so at last had concluded that dogging my footsteps was the only way to get anything further on me. It even crossed my mind that Tarlow and his police cronies were not above a little housebreaking themselves, especially if they thought they would find a nice monographed handkerchief in my underwear drawer. It was as well that Lily's boredom threshhold had not extended to more than one example of her needlework skills. But if it had been the police, then why had they bothered to take the package, an act which was surely one of straightforward theft?

My father's pistol may have had sentimental value, but it was far too cumbersome to carry all the time, and if more than one shot was expected of the old thing then powder flask and more bullets were also required. So, to save walking around with more metal on my person than a medieval knight, I invested in a revolver. Half the size of the dueller and carrying five shots to its one, it was not cheap, but priceless as far as peace of mind was concerned.

These peculiar circumstances notwithstanding, the spring of 1859 saw me fully occupied at the hospital, as with Brunel still overseas there was little in the way of outside influence to cause distraction. In contrast, the now almost constant presence of Miss Nightingale served to guarantee my enthusiasm for the work. Her famous endeavours in the Crimea had earned her the *nom de guerre* 'the lady with the lamp', and she certainly cast a fresh light across the previously drab edifice of our establishment. Even Brodie had been touched by her zeal for reform, though as she and I both knew, this change of heart was as motivated by the opportunity for self-aggrandizement as it was by a desire for improvement. Although I still served as his liaison with Miss Nightingale he had, as predicted, taken a more active role at the committee level, expressing his full support of the initiative to the board of commissioners and anyone else who would listen.

It was after one such discussion that he informed me that the Lazarus Club was to convene again in late April.

Brunel, I was sure, would be eager for me to take the minutes as usual and so it was that I determined to attend. But there was of course another, more important reason for me to be there, along with Brodie, Russell, Ockham and the others – one of them, I was sure, was involved in Wilkie's murder. I just didn't yet know which one or why.

The minutes were taken down in one of my own notebooks, as Brunel only ever provided me with loose sheets of paper. Like an attentive schoolmaster I took the register of those in attendance, studying each of them for an incriminating glance and listening for an involuntary expression of guilt.

Brodie, as usual, introduced the talk, while around the table sat Russell, Whitworth, Ockham, Perry, Catchpole, Gurney, Babbage, Stephenson and Hawes.

Following a brief interruption by Babbage, who took the opportunity to advertise the publication of his latest pamphlet, 'A Chapter on Street Nuisances', our speaker got down to business. John Stringfellow had founded the Aerial Steam Carriage Company in 1842 and since then had carried out numerous tests on flying machines, though most of these had been undertaken in secret in his silk mill in Somerset. Originally from Sheffield, the man was an expert in precision engineering and one day hoped to create a steam-powered aircraft which would carry passengers to far-distant lands in a fraction of the time taken by current modes of transport. It all seemed a little far-fetched, but then he was in good company. Despite this the talk was most interesting and his illustrations of flying devices almost convincing. One of them portrayed a carriage with windows suspended beneath a pair of wings which themselves were supported by a series of spars and wires. At the rear there was a kite-shaped tail which along with the wings gave the fabulous device the look of a fat-bellied bird.

Another of these artist's renditions showed off the pair of spinning screws attached to the rear of the wings, their function being to push the vessel through the air just as those on a ship would propel it through the water. According to Stringfellow, the location pictured in the drawing was India, but it could have been Egypt, or was at least how I imagined Egypt to look. If it were, then perhaps Brunel was somewhere in the picture, looking up at the machine and pondering how he could make it bigger. Brunel would have particularly enjoyed the aeronaut's discussion of his steam engines, which were designed to be incredibly small and lightweight, just the sort of things the unfortunate Wilkie would have taken pleasure in creating.

By the end of the evening my writing wrist was aching with the exertion of keeping pace with it all. Committed as I was to my secretarial duties, which took a great deal of concentration, it was now obvious that it would not be possible to identify the killer simply by sharing his company in this manner. Guilt, I had decided, could not always be diagnosed through mere observation; it had no obvious symptom, no shingle-like lumpy rash or measly scatter of spots – not even, as I had hoped, a tell-tale tic or a give-away twitch.

And so, as the formal part of the evening came to a close and we broke up for drinks, I made a last attempt by listening intently for a slip of the tongue – anything to give me a clue to the identity of the guilty party. Before I had a chance to circulate, however, Goldsworthy Gurney sought me out, as it happened for no other reason but to express his relief that Brodie and myself believed that cholera was carried by polluted water rather than spread by gases, because he had just designed the new ventilation system for the Houses of Parliament and had shuddered to think that he might be responsible for introducing potentially fatal vapours to the good Members.

Without a sniff of anything out of the ordinary I joined Messrs Russell, Perry, Stephenson and Lord Catchpole who, with String-fellow in their company, were discussing the big ship. 'They're calling her the *Great Eastern* now,' said Russell. 'Much more appropriate than the *Leviathan* given that her predecessors were called the *Great Britain* and the *Great Western*.'

'Always seemed a little odd,' remarked Stephenson, 'that the company chose to name her after a creature of the deep, a sea monster no less. A name like that is bad for business if you ask me. It gave the impression that the ship was a beast, dangerous and untamable by man.'

Lord Catchpole chuckled. 'A fair point, sir, and I for one wouldn't fancy playing Jonah and travelling in the belly of a great beast!'

There was some laughter but Russell didn't even raise a smile. The ship had been afloat for the best part of a year but had yet to move a foot under her own steam. 'The passenger accommodations are coming along nicely,' he said, aiming his remark at Catchpole. 'And quite luxurious they will be too. I can't say I hold with such extravagance but if it attracts well-paying customers then it will serve its purpose.'

'And how many passengers will she accommodate when fully furnished?' asked Whitworth.

'She has capacity to carry no less than 4,000 passengers using the cabins, but in times of war with the salons given over to accommodation she could carry 10,000 troops.'

'Perhaps then,' chimed Whitworth, 'there is more profit to be made from using her to invade another country than to use her as a commercial liner.'

Catchpole nudged the armourer playfully. 'And what if those troops were armed with your new rifles – not a bad business proposition by any manner of means, eh, Whitworth? But who wouldn't rather see her as a pleasure cruiser; at least then you could enjoy a whisky in the salon and admire the young ladies as they promenade on deck.'

The others laughed, but joking aside the original point was perhaps a valid one, as rumours of pending bankruptcy and shortage of funds to fit the ship out were now regularly circulated in the press.

'And what about her engines, Mr Russell, how are they coming along?'

'The port paddle engine is very well advanced and the starboard not very far behind. There is, however, much work required on the screw engine. But we are progressing at a steady rate. I would hope to see them all operable within three to four months.'

In one of his letters, Brunel had expressed the hope that sea trials were no more than six weeks away – things certainly seemed to have gone awry in his absence.

Ockham, as usual, had departed as soon as the proceedings had come to an end. On previous occasions his premature departures had seemed nothing more than a reflection of his shyness, but cast in the light of recent events such behaviour was enough to arouse my suspicions. It crossed my mind to pursue him but after my last experience on such an escapade decided against it.

To my surprise, I ended up sharing a cab with Brodie, but any thought that there may have been a humanitarian motive behind his invitation was dispelled when he asked me to report on a meeting I had had with Miss Nightingale earlier in the day. There was very little to say really, and so continuing to fish for information I turned to questioning him.

'Who exactly is Ockham?' I asked.

'I wondered how long it would take you to ask, everyone does eventually.'

'He does seem a little . . . a little unusual.'

'Eccentric, I think is the word you are looking for, Dr Phillips. Definitely eccentric.'

'His manner and attire seem greatly at odds with his situation.'

'You could say that,' said Brodie, and then added as a simple matter of fact: 'He is a viscount.'

'A viscount?'

Brodie nodded. 'You should really be calling him Lord Ockham. He holds the title in courtesy from his father the Earl of Lovelace. His grandfather was Lord Byron.'

'*The* Lord Byron?'

'The very same. The family seat is Ockham Park in Surrey.'

'Then what on earth is he doing slumming it as a labourer in a shipyard?'

'I think that is something only he, or perhaps Brunel, could tell you. As far as I understand it, Ockham turned up at his office one day and offered his services.'

'Is it true that he was instrumental in setting up the Laza – the club?'

Brodie frowned. 'Who told you that?'

'Whitworth.'

'There is some truth to that, I suppose.'

'A very unusual young man,' I observed.

'Eccentric,' he reminded me.

'Yes, eccentric,' I agreed.

'He and Brunel share a number of . . . shall we say, unusual ideas.'

'Eccentric?'

'No. Most definitely unusual.' The cab came to a halt. 'Your lodgings, I believe, doctor. There is one other thing that might be said of him. They said it of his grandfather before him, but I fear it may equally well apply.'

'What's that, Sir Benjamin?'

'That he is mad, bad and dangerous to know. Now, goodnight, doctor.'

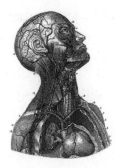

## 20

Henry Wakefield had a face made up of sharp lines, which belied his pleasant demeanour. He was one of Brunel's most trusted assistants and I was glad to find him in residence at the engineer's Duke Street office. It was my first visit and it came as no surprise to find it to be rather a grand place, much in keeping with the engineer's elevated status. The desks, drawing boards and plan chests were all in polished hardwood and along one wall was a series of box-like pigeonholes where correspondence and notes were carefully filed. There were shelves of books and journals and large paintings of Brunel's ships the *Great Western* and *Great Britain*, though not yet one of the new ship. I am sure the great engineer would have enjoyed showing off some aspect of his work, perhaps after pulling down one of the large drawings cleverly suspended from the ceiling in a series of rollers. However, in his absence I would have to make do with young Wakefield, who I hoped would be able to assist in some way in my quest to unmask Wilkie's killers.

We had met only once before, at the aborted launch of the great ship, where he had proved very helpful in the aftermath of the accident on the checking drum. The young man rose from his paperwork and greeted me warmly.

'Dr Phillips, isn't it? Very happy to meet you again, sir.'

'And you, Mr Wakefield,' I replied, accepting his offer of a chair. 'I am glad to see that Mr Brunel is keeping you busy in his absence.'

He glanced down at a long list of numbers. 'Indeed he is. I have been left in charge of the office and, as always, things are a bit hectic. The bridge at Saltash is due to open in two months and then of course there is the ship.'

'I bumped into Mr Russell last week. He seemed content with progress on the ship.'

Henry's thin lips curled into a smile. 'I am sure that Mr Russell is relieved to have Mr Brunel out of the way for a while.'

'I had guessed they don't see eye to eye on everything.'

Wakefield strode to a corner of the room, where a kettle was beginning to boil on a pot-bellied stove. 'That's one way of putting it. I guess they just have very different ways of working. The ship has been a case of too many cooks spoiling the broth from start till . . . well, up till now,' he said, pouring the water for the tea.

Carrying the teapot back to the desk, he nodded towards the column of figures. 'Mr Brunel left me with a list of economies to be made to the specification of the fitting-out. No sooner had he left than Mr Russell provided his own list with even more reductions on it. Mr Brunel will not be pleased.' He was obviously a little aggrieved at having to play pig in the middle; I knew exactly how he felt.

This was all very interesting but did not really tell me anything new. I had witnessed first-hand how one man could irritate the other, but there was nothing unusual in that; one only had to look at Brodie and myself to see that.

'I am sorry, doctor,' said Wakefield with a start. 'Is there something I can help you with?'

'I hope so. Can I assume that you are aware of the supper club that Mr Brunel sometimes attends?'

Wakefield smiled again. 'Oh yes, the Lazarus Club. He enjoys sharing new ideas, that's for sure. Did you know that he's never taken out a single patent on any of his inventions? Anyway, I hope that one day he may invite me along. From what he tells me it sounds very interesting.'

'It would be a pleasure to see you there sometime. I am a relatively new member myself. I act as a sort of secretary.'

'You mean that he talked you into taking the minutes.'

I nodded and put on my best impression of a jaundiced smile. But in truth his response pleased me: Wakefield knew more than I had thought and was making this very easy for me.

'Would you like a cup of tea?' he asked.

'Splendid, thank you.'

'He hates having to do that himself. Taking the minutes, that is. He moans the next day whenever he does. But he complains more when Russell or somebody else does it. If he asked you, doctor, take it as a compliment. He doesn't pay many, believe me.'

'I will, thank you. It was actually the minutes that brought me here. Before he left for foreign parts Mr Brunel asked if I would transcribe them into a more legible hand. He said I was to come round to the office and collect them when it was convenient.'

'Ah,' sighed Wakefield. 'I am afraid that will be a bit difficult.'

And it had all been going so well. 'Difficult?'

'They are not here,' he said.

'Oh dear.'

'Someone has beaten you to it. He came round for them a couple of days ago.'

This was not shaping up at all well, and my earlier optimism began to drain away like blood from an untended wound. 'Who?'

'I believe he is a colleague of yours? Sir Benjamin Brodie.'

Disappointment now gave way to something more serious. 'Did he say why he wanted them?' I snapped.

Wakefield was taken aback. 'Just that he wanted to take them away to read them. He is a member of the club, isn't he?'

'Quite right, Wakefield, quite right,' I said, checking my over-reaction. 'Forgive me, it is just that I saw Sir Benjamin only this morning and he could have told me and saved me some trouble.' Wakefield was right after all: why shouldn't Brodie want to see the minutes? – he had as much right to them as any of us. Perhaps he wanted to do nothing more than to check a detail for a paper he was writing for the *Lancet*, though it had been some years since he had published anything.

Whatever Brodie's motives, I could not bring myself to put him on my list of suspects, at least for now. But I did feel more strongly than ever that the minutes would provide some answers. I needed allies, that much was clear, but before I could find them I needed to know who my enemies were.

'Does Sir Benjamin call on Mr Brunel often?' I asked, keen to learn more about their doctor–patient relationship. 'Mr Brunel does not seem to be in the best of health.'

'He has his ups and downs – recently, though, more downs than ups. Sir Benjamin does his best for him, I'm sure, but he won't rest, can't leave anything alone. He hates delegating, has to oversee everything himself. It took Sir Benjamin all his powers of persuasion to get him to go overseas, which was the only way to stop him working. Eventually Mrs Brunel had to intercede and insist he follow doctor's orders.'

'I suppose you have seen him go through a lot in your time with him?'

'A fair bit, yes,' said the young man, moving his list of numbers before setting down his cup. 'Did Sir Benjamin tell you the story of the coin?'

'The coin? No, I don't believe he did.'

'That one was before my time – must have been well over ten years ago. Apparently, Mr Brunel was entertaining his children with a favourite party trick, making them believe he could swallow a half-sovereign and then pluck it from his ear. Sleight of hand I believe they call it. He'd performed the trick many times at Christmas parties and birthdays but this time it went horribly wrong. He put the coin in his mouth and then began to address his audience. My mother told me never to speak with my mouth full, and Mr Brunel could have done with heeding the same advice, because he swallowed the coin.'

'Good grief.'

'Down it went, and that was that. Thinking that nature would simply follow its course, he thought no more about it. But then after a week or so he began to suffer terrible coughing fits. It was then that he sought out Sir Benjamin, who has been his personal surgeon ever since. Well, the good doctor examined Mr Brunel and discovered that the coin was lodged in the opening to his right lung. What is the name of that bit, doctor?'

'The bronchus,' I replied.

'Yes, the bronchus, that's it. He ordered Mr Brunel to rest while he considered a suitable treatment. Mr Brunel discovered that if he bent forward the coin shifted, and then slipped back when he straightened up, bringing on a coughing fit. Thus it went on, the coin moving like a valve opening and closing the entrance to his lungs.'

I stroked my throat, imagining the discomfort that Brunel must have suffered.

'Most unpleasant indeed,' he continued, noting my reaction. 'After a few days the doctor cut a hole in Mr Brunel's windpipe and reached in with a long pair of forceps designed by his patient.'

'Did he pull out the coin?' I asked, fascinated by this incredible tale.

'No. The intervention brought on the worst bout of coughing so far and the doctor had to stop for fear of doing more harm than good. The coin had now been trapped inside him for more than a month. Enough was enough, thought Mr Brunel, and so he put his engineering skills to work again. This time he had his craftsmen build a revolving table. He was then strapped to it and the table turned so that his head was close to the floor and his feet pointing towards the ceiling. His doctor then pounded his back.'

The image made me laugh. 'You mean they beat him like an old carpet? Now that must have been a sight to see.'

'I would imagine,' laughed Wakefield. 'But it worked. The beating dislodged the coin and gravity forced it out of his mouth. Pop! On to the floor it dropped, that shiny gold coin. The good news spread across London like wildfire, "It is out! It is out!" went the cry. Mr Brunel even insisted a full account be published in the newspaper so that if anyone were to suffer the same misfortune they would know what to do!'

'The man has definitely had more than his share of close shaves,' I said, once again recalling the stories in Brunel's scrapbook.

Bidding farewell to the affable Mr Wakefield, I took a cab back to the hospital. Hearing the story of the coin and of the long-standing relationship between the engineer and the doctor had further convinced me that if I could trust Brunel then I could trust Brodie, but I wasn't yet ready to put that assumption to the test. This left me with a new problem: to get sight of the minutes without alerting their new guardian to the fact.

It was late afternoon; one more demonstration and my work for the day would be done. My thoughts were elsewhere, though, plotting how to get hold of the minutes, which according to Wakefield should now be in Brodie's office – not a place I regularly entered through choice, but by the time my students were filing out of the theatre the germ of an idea had formed, to be further refined over supper at my club. It felt good to be taking control of my own destiny.

On my return home the key at first refused to turn in the lock but with a little careful jiggling it finally clicked into place. Hanging my coat and hat in the hall, I entered the parlour, not yet decided whether to retire immediately or to have a nightcap.

I decided on the latter, but had no sooner walked into the parlour than I was lying on the floor, pushed down by someone who had been waiting for me behind the door. A foot pressed into the small of the back kept me fixed in place while the unseen assailant rifled my pockets for anything of interest. A second person was sitting in my favourite chair; that much was clear, as his well-shod feet were planted just inches from my nose. 'Good evening, Dr Phillips,' said the man in the chair, his delivery as deadpan as though I had arrived at a prearranged meeting. 'Why don't you get up and take a seat?'

The foot was removed from my back and I was pulled to my knees by a hand applied to the back of my collar. A chair was pulled from beneath the table and, seeing a pistol lying on the arm of my chair, I decided against standing and took a seat as he had suggested.

Having taken in the narrow face and well-trimmed beard of the man in my chair, I risked a glance back at the man by the open door, which he promptly closed with his foot. The door man was still wearing his hat – the height of bad manners, I thought – but its distinctive wide brim, along with his dark, shoulder-length hair helped to mark him out. There could be no doubt: they were old friends come to visit. The door man's arms were folded in such a way that I couldn't tell whether he was holding the pistol I knew him to carry. My own firearm was in my coat pocket in the hall, where alas it would have to remain. Glancing around the room, there was perhaps some small consolation to be had from the fact that this time around they had refrained from ransacking the place.

'I trust you both had a good journey from Bristol?' I asked, trying my best to sound at ease with the situation.

The seated man, who exuded natural authority, smiled. 'More straightforward than yours. We preferred to let the train take the strain, much more agreeable than a boat.'

'What can I do for you, gentlemen?' I asked, continuing to play the part of affable host. 'Did you leave something behind on your last visit?'

The seated man looked rather bemused. 'Last visit?'

'Yes, the time you kicked in my front door.'

He puzzled some more and looked over at his colleague. Then, resting his hand on the revolver as if to remind me who was in charge, said, 'Where is it?'

'You know full well where it is. You broke in here and took it, well over two weeks ago now.'

The levelling of the pistol at my chest signalled the cessation of polite conversation. Only then did I remember the drawing hidden in the book on the shelf behind him. Of course – that was it, I thought, the drawing contains some hidden detail not provided by the contraption they had already gone to such lengths to obtain.

'I'm growing a little tired of your obstructive attitude, doctor. Unless you hand it over in the next minute I will shoot you, of that you may be certain.'

Having seen the treatment my guests had meted out to Wilkie, I had no reason to doubt him. 'Very well,' I said, holding up my hands in supplication. 'I trust that you will not shoot me if I stand to get it for you.'

'Where is it?' he asked with increasing determination.

'Behind you, on the bookshelf.'

Without taking his eyes off me he tipped the muzzle of the gun upwards, in a gesture to his companion. 'Get it for him.'

Without answering, the sentinel behind me strode up to the shelves, where he paused and passed his gaze along the spines of the numerous books arrayed on them. With his arms at last unfolded I could see there was no pistol in his hands. When he spoke it was just one word. 'Where?' he asked.

'Tell him,' I was ordered.

'Third shelf from the top, the thick red book four from the left.'

He stretched out his arm and after counting along with his index finger brought his hand to rest on the book I had indicated. Pulling it from the shelf he looked at it briefly before passing it over his colleague's shoulder and returning to his original position behind me.

The seated man looked down at the book resting in his lap, which without any bidding had opened on to the pages between which the folded document was sandwiched. All of a sudden he seemed very angry. 'Where the hell is it?'

'Why, in your lap,' I said, stating what I thought was the obvious.

He cautiously pulled out the drawing, as though afraid the book would snap closed and take off his fingers. Putting down the pistol, he unfolded the sheet of paper, letting the book tumble to the floor as he did so. It was only then that he appeared to recognize what he had been given. 'Ah,' he said.

He studied the drawings for a moment or two and then looked up at me, his face pinched. 'Where are the other drawings, and more importantly where is the mechanism you carried with you from Bristol?' Once again the pistol was in his hand, a finger wrapped around the trigger.

'You know full well where the mechanism is,' I insisted. Again, the chair man seemed puzzled by the obvious. Surely there had to be someone more intelligent behind all this? – and that someone had yet to show himself. 'You and your friend here' – I stabbed a thumb over my shoulder to include the man at the door in my barely suppressed tirade – 'broke into my house, though why you had to kick the door in I don't know, given that you are obviously capable of picking locks.' He now looked more confused than ever. I deliberately slowed my speech in the hope it might make things easier for him. 'You took the mechanism. What you didn't find then was the drawing in your lap. That's why you're here again surely, to get the drawing?'

The hammer on the revolver clicked as he pulled it back, the gun now aimed at my head. 'Listen to me, doctor. I have no idea who may or may not have broken in here and taken the mechanism, but let me assure you that it was neither of us. Tell me, why should I believe this little story of yours? Think carefully, sir, you are now as close to death as you ever will be. Where is the mechanism?'

I felt the small amount of colour still left in my face drain completely away. With my guest's confusion explained it was my turn to seek clarity. 'Then who was it?' I asked, the question only just beating a pathetic plea for mercy in the race to my lips. The chair man's finger tightened around the trigger. 'It was in the hall, hidden in the bottom of the umbrella stand. I returned from the hospital to find the front door smashed in and the mechanism gone.' Seeing no relaxation in his trigger finger, I blundered on, 'Of course, given our past . . . our past association I assumed that it was you. Do you mean to tell me that it wasn't you following me around London for these past weeks?'

The chair man shook his head slowly. This is it, I thought. But instead of pulling the trigger he closed the hammer and stood up, placing the drawing on the table in front of me. Reaching beneath his coat and pushing the pistol into a leather holster suspended beneath his armpit, he ordered the door man to watch me. Perhaps he was going to let me live after all.

'Describe the mechanism to me,' he said. 'And think carefully, doctor, your fate still hangs in the balance.'

Grateful to have spent some time studying the contents of the package, I answered confidently. 'You see it in front of you, on the drawing. Those pieces, they were in the package that Wilkie gave me.'

'Pieces?'

'Yes, loose pieces, just like those in the drawing.'

He passed his open hand, palm down, over the paper. 'You are telling me that these were the only pieces Wilkie gave you? Just loose, unassembled parts?'

'Just as they are drawn. Some were of steel but there was copper as well.'

'And there were no more drawings?'

'No, that was all. The pieces were wrapped in the drawing, that is why it's so badly crumpled.'

'Shit,' said the chair man, casting a worried glance at his henchman.

Now it was clear. They had all along assumed that I was in possession of the entire mechanism, the complete device. Almost without thinking I offered an explanation. 'Wilkie told me that it was not unusual for Brunel to commission only certain parts from him. He provided the drawings and the specification, but not an explanation of their use or a description of parts to be made by others.'

'Check the umbrella stand in the hall,' said the chair man urgently, before continuing my interrogation. 'Do you know the intended purpose of the mechanism?'

'I am a surgeon, sir, not an engineer. Other than yourself, the one man who could tell me is currently overseas. Given my present position I suspect that ignorance is a rather healthier condition than too much knowledge.'

'Very wisely spoken, Dr Phillips. You may live out the night yet.'

The door man returned. 'Nothing,' he reported.

'Very well,' said the chair man as he folded up the drawing. 'I think we have finished our business here. You have been most helpful, doctor. I trust I do not have to tell you to forget this little meeting ever took place.'

I nodded and then shook my head, unsure which was the correct response. With the drawing in his pocket the chair man followed the door man out into the hall. 'Do not leave here until the morning,' he called out, just before the front door snapped shut.

It was some time before I could bring myself to leave my chair, let alone the building.

Following my encounter with Wilkie's killers, I had been forced to face up to a number of unsavoury truths. The first of these was that it was now plain that my identity was known to them, though I had thought as much for some time. The second was that another party was also keen to take possession of the mechanism, and indeed had succeeded in taking at least parts of it. Last, but not least, I was being threatened by murderers and at the same time and in the same place suspected to be a murderer myself; it was a combination of unpleasantries not to be wished on any man. That said, I had not clapped eyes on Tarlow since the encounter soon after my return from Bristol some weeks previously, which could only be put down to no further bodies having come to light, though I could also hope that his blasted investigations had taken him elsewhere – but with my current run of bad luck that seemed too much to hope. It was time however for me to set out on my own investigation and, although not one that would clear my name, it did have the prospect of shedding much-needed light on the identity of Wilkie's killers and the motive for their heinous crime.

'Dr Phillips is here to see you, sir,' said Mumrill, his head crooked around the door to Sir Benjamin's office.

'Very well, send him in,' replied Brodie gruffly.

As ever, he was engrossed in his paperwork. 'What can I do for you?' he asked, as usual without removing his eyes from the notes on his desk – which I could see were not the minutes.

I took the opportunity to take a good look around the room, stepping to the side of his desk to get an all-round view. The leather satchel was on the floor, propped against the bookshelf behind the desk. Brodie became aware of me standing over him.

'What are you doing, man? Take a seat. Not like you to go through the correct channels before coming in here. What is it?'

'A small but urgent matter, sir.' Only now did he look up. 'Miss Nightingale has asked that you write a letter to the Prime Minister requesting a special meeting relating to her proposed restructuring of the nursing service.'

Brodie rolled his eyes. 'Thank you, Dr Phillips. I will attend to the matter.' If only all our exchanges were as straightforward, I thought. 'Send Mumrill in on your way out, will you? Tell him I want him to take a letter.'

Mumrill scurried into his master's office while I was still in his adjoining office. With the door between the two standing ajar I stepped behind the desk. One of the drawers sat partially open, a set of keys hanging from the lock in its front. Clutching the loose keys in one hand to prevent them rattling, I jiggled the key from the lock and paused to cock an ear in the direction of Brodie's office. 'I hope that you will agree the scheme worthy of your support . . .'

Satisfied that his dictation was in full flow I turned my attention to the heavy mahogany cupboard attached to the wall behind the desk. Riffling through the keys, I selected the one which from its shape looked to be right and pushed it gently into the lock. The door opened to reveal row after row of keys suspended from hooks, some of them singly, some in twos and threes. Reading the labels beneath I moved along the hooks before coming to the key I was after. Pulling another from a hook which carried a pair, I dropped it on to the newly vacant hook, hoping that this would be enough to prevent Mumrill noticing a key was missing. Locking the door, I stopped to listen again. '. . . Looking forward to your reply. Your obedient servant, etc. etc.'

Returning the original key to the lock in the drawer, I bounded across the room and slipped through the door just in time to be missed by Mumrill as he returned from Brodie's office.

In the evening, I watched Brodie leave for home, and was pleased to see he was not carrying the satchel. Mumrill, as was his usual practice, was keen to be seen working longer hours, and so left some ten minutes later. Ten minutes more and I was in Brodie's office, having entered through the door in the corridor. Recent events had taught me that a lock need be no barrier to entry but having also swept up a locksmith's wood shavings I knew there was a subtler way of doing so than employing force. There was just enough light in the room to see that the satchel was no longer where I'd seen it, propped against the wall behind the desk. To my relief, however, I spotted it on a shelf. Slipping it under my jacket, I listened at the door, and satisfied that the corridor was clear stepped out, locked the door and casually returned to my office.

The satchel, with the letters IKB embossed on the flap, contained a thick sheaf of loose papers, some of them creased from being stuffed inside with no great care and others already yellowing with age. I pulled them out on to my desk and began sorting through them. Each sheet was dated at the top, beneath which was a list of those present at the meeting. Next came a heading in the form of the speaker's name and the subject of his talk. Beneath that were the notes on the talk, which could vary in length from a couple of sides of paper to four or five sheets, depending on how conscientious the minute-taker was feeling – that, and how interested he was in the subject matter. A number were written in Brunel's hand, some in Russell's and others', and just a few in my own. The report on the talk was usually followed by notes on the questions asked and answers given during the discussion. Some of the minutes, usually those by Brunel, included sketches to illustrate technical points, perhaps copied from diagrams used by the speaker to illuminate the talk.

The minutes went back over five years, almost the entire lifespan of the club, although I had learned from Brunel that they had not begun taking minutes until after a couple of meetings had been held. As Whitworth had said, the founder members appeared to be Brunel, Babbage and Ockham, with Brodie joining soon after.

There they were: talks by some of the greatest minds of our time. On 18 September 1857, some months before Brunel dragged me along to my first meeting, Henry Gray, acclaimed lecturer in anatomy at St George's, gave a presentation on the workings of the human organs. Not long after the talk, his masterpiece, *Gray's Anatomy*, was published. There was a copy on my office bookshelf, with a dedication from the author, thanking me for advice I had given him on a few points of detail. I read through the notes to find that Brunel had asked several questions on the operation of the heart, and wondered if this had in some way laid the foundation for my own invitation. My attention was caught by the title of a talk by the famous inventor Michael Faraday, 'The Romance of Modern Electricity,' but as it did not have a bearing on my search I flicked beyond it without reading any further.

There were also presentations by people entirely unknown to me, though it could be taken for granted that each and every one of them was a leading light in his field. According to the minutes, Joseph Saxton was an American gentleman responsible for the invention of a machine that cut the cogs in gear wheels for use in watches. The presentation also covered other aspects of mechanized manufacture, such as the design of lathes and gear indexing, whatever that might be. But what really caught my attention about this meeting was that Wilkie was among those present. Having seen his machine shop in Bristol, this seemed entirely fitting, but once again it also pointed to the club as the wellspring of my troubles.

There was an almost encyclopædic spectrum of subjects recorded in the minutes, and if ever they were published they would make a fascinating contribution to scientific endeavour. It would have come as no surprise if this was what Brodie had in mind when he appropriated them.

But I had little time to ponder my superior's motives, as the minutes would have to be returned to his office before his arrival in the morning. Accordingly, I concentrated on the task of leafing through the pages and studying their contents. Eventually I came to the two meetings I had missed while attending my ailing father. The first had been given by Gurney, who had spoken on 'horseless carriages and the use of steam as a means of locomotion on roads'. There seemed to be little here of relevance. The second presentation, however, immediately caught my attention, not least because it had been given by Brunel himself, just days before his departure to Egypt.

Those listed as present at the meeting were Ockham, the asterisk next to his name indicating that he had been minute-keeper on that occasion, Russell, Catchpole, Whitworth, Perry, Brodie, Babbage, Gurney, Hawes and Stephenson. A pretty full house, I thought.

The subject of Brunel's talk was not the great ship, nor his bridges, railways, tunnels, nor any of the other grand creations for which he was renowned, but something described as 'the prolongation of organ function through mechanical means'. The implication of this evaded me until I was some way advanced in my reading of Ockham's gratifyingly thorough notes. In his talk, Brunel outlined a proposal for the construction of a mechanical organ that would entirely mimic its organic counterpart. The organ selected for such revolutionary treatment was the heart, and what followed was page after page on how an artificial counterpart could be constructed from metal and other materials.

Based on information provided by our medical colleagues, including Sir Benjamin and Mr Henry Gray but most particularly Dr Phillips, it has become apparent that the double-valve construction of the human heart can be replicated mechanically. The organ is essentially a pump, a piece of machinery familiar to engineers, and as such operates in a manner known to us. I propose to use a quadruple system of interconnecting cup pistons to serve the function of the four cavities of the heart, which is to push the venous expended blood from the body into the lungs and then, once arterialized by the lungs, to push the life-giving fluid back into the body through the pulmonary artery. The prototype device operates through a clockwork system, which will allow continuous motion maintained by regular rewinding of the driving spring.

Madness, I thought, absolute madness. How on earth did he propose to link this lump of metal with the organic elements of the human body? On the basis of our current understanding of biology such a proposal was entirely unfeasible. How I wished Brunel were here so that I might set him straight. But then again perhaps this was why he had elected to unveil his device or at least his proposal for its construction at a meeting from which I would be absent?

On reading further, however, I discovered that Sir Benjamin had done just that, and had refused to be drawn into such an ill-conceived project so obviously doomed to failure. And when pressed on the issue it appeared Brunel himself had admitted that although based on sound mechanical principles his project was unachievable on the basis of present technology, though he argued that the shortfalls lay within the world of medicine rather than engineering. This did not, however, appear to have prevented him from putting his ideas into action, and although they showed little in the way of detail a couple of thumbnail sketches in the minutes left no doubt as to the intended purpose of the pieces in the package.

Some further recognition of the difficulties involved was provided by a passage scribbled on the back of the last sheet, again in Ockham's hand. I could only surmise that this was something Brunel himself had said during the presentation:

The materials at present within my command hardly appeared adequate to so arduous an undertaking, but I doubted not that I should ultimately succeed. I prepared myself for a multitude of reverses; my operations might be incessantly baffled, and at last my work be imperfect: yet when I considered the improvement which every day takes place in science and mechanics, I was encouraged to hope my present attempts would at least lay the foundations of future success.

Then, in a margin, perhaps written as a riposte to someone who came close to sharing my own view on Brunel's ideas:

I am not recording the vision of a madman.

By eleven o'clock I had transcribed almost the entire record of Brunel's presentation into my own notebook. Satisfied that there was nothing else to be gained from poring over these pages I set about returning the satchel and its contents to Brodie's office. There seemed little point in risking the return of the key to the security box, requiring as it would another exercise in distraction. In any case, it was only a spare key so it seemed unlikely that its disappearance would be discovered for a while, and when it was, there would be no reason to suspect I was responsible.

I took a very late, but well-earned, supper at my club and over a nightcap continued to mull over the results of a good night's work. In addition to understanding more fully the history of the Lazarus Club it was now clear that the contents of the package for which Wilkie had been murdered were parts of a mechanical heart. Also clear was the fact that Brunel had been working on the idea for a long while, with construction work beginning some time before his presentation on the device to the Lazarus Club. Some pieces of the jigsaw had fallen into place but I suspected that I would have to delve further back in time than the occasion of Brunel's presentation to fully understand what lay behind all of this. I called for another brandy but it was history lessons that were the order of the day.

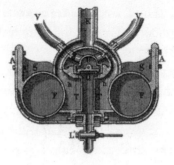

## 21

The engineer had been away for the best part of four months and still there was no word of his return. Far removed from events in London he may have been, but while on his travels Brunel carried with him not just a steamer trunk full of cigars but also the ability to shed much-needed light on my recent misadventures.

I had abandoned the idea of setting out in pursuit of the man almost as soon as it entered my head. The telegraph had yet to extend to Egypt and so there was no rapid means of communicating with him even if I had known his exact whereabouts. In fact, it seemed likely that he had been steered in the direction of Egypt for this very reason, as it would make it impossible for him to be pestered by his colleagues at home and, just as importantly, vice versa.

Recent events had shown that no less than two parties were prepared to go to drastic lengths to take possession of Brunel's creation; the prize for commitment, though, most definitely went to my friends from Bristol, who had demonstrated that they were prepared to kill for it, while their competitors had up until now extended only to common burglary. Ironically, it was the house-breakers who had thus far carried the day, though why anyone should go to such lengths to obtain a device so obviously unfit for purpose was beyond me. Having read the minutes I was now convinced, whatever their motives, that both groups included one or more members of the club, for how else could they have learned of Brunel's proposal? Despite a warning from the chair man to keep myself out of the business I had made it my mission to identify those behind the crimes and in doing so to exact vengeance for Wilkie, whose life had been so cruelly taken, and to locate Brunel's fantastical device.

With little hope of communication with the engineer it came as something of a surprise to have a letter from him fall on to my doormat not long after reading the minutes. The single page, bearing the letterhead of the Royal Alexandria hotel in Cairo, was dated 15 April 1859 – three weeks previously.

*Dear Phillips,*

*I trust this letter finds you well. Despite earlier misgivings the trip thus far has been a most interesting one and I am now almost grateful to those who insisted that I venture on it. From southern France we took a steamer to Alexandria – an ancient city port founded by the man who at the age of just 32 had conquered more lands than Napoleon could ever dream of. The crossing of the Mediterranean was a memorable experience, as our vessel fell victim to one of those unforgiving tempests the French call the Mistral. But they say everything happens for a reason, and it provided me with an ideal opportunity to assess the behaviour of our vessel in heavy seas. I positioned myself on the wheel box, where it was necessary to tie myself to the ship in order to prevent being washed overboard. From there I observed the pitch and roll of the vessel and was able to measure both the force of the wind and the size of the waves. All of this while my good doctor was confined to his bed with a bout of what for a while looked like terminal mal de mer, all most amusing!*

*From Alexandria we sailed on to Cairo, from where I write this letter. We are freshly returned from our expedition up the Nile, for which purpose I hired a local vessel known as a dahabeah, which accommodated our entire party in some comfort. Unfortunately, though, this vessel was unable to carry us to our destination, as it was incapable of navigating the various cataracts which punctuate the upper reaches of that great river. Not to be defeated I purchased a more resilient date boat and had cabins constructed on her (if only completion of the ship had been accomplished so quickly). We were able to tow and almost carry the boat through the rapids and so at last reached Luxor and spent several exhilarating days exploring the monuments there. Here we saw the most impressive sight, a great temple constructed from hundreds of vast stone columns, each of them decorated with the most fascinating designs and the ancient writing style they call hieroglyphs. On the other side of the river lies Thebes and the mountain valleys behind which they say are peppered with the tombs of the ancient kings of Egypt.*

*But the greatest wonders are here at Giza, just outside the bustling city of Cairo. The pyramids are wonders indeed to behold, each of them constructed from great blocks of stone hewn with nothing more than the most primitive of tools. It humbles an engineer of our own age to see of what great works man was capable all those many centuries ago. What labours must have been required to move all of the hundreds of thousands of tons of stones from their quarries and then to build them into those soaring man-made mountains? I have learned much and intend to study these ancient peoples more thoroughly upon my return.*

*By the by, should you be starved of worthwhile conversation until then (I jest), might I suggest you seek out Mr Ockham, who although usually quite reticent in our meetings is actually a fascinating fellow and I regret not having taken the opportunity to introduce you properly at the club. You might also give him the Bristol package, which once again I thank you for taking care of. He will know what needs to be done with it and will be grateful to take receipt.*

*Your friend,*

*Isambard Kingdom Brunel*

At last, I thought, some useful information! It was the last paragraph, apparently added as a mere afterthought, which served to guide my hand, and determined me to set out on a course of action to which I had already given some thought. I was keen to meet with Mr, or should I say, Lord Ockham, not for the purpose of idle conversation and even less so to hand over the package, if it had still been mine to give, but to get some answers from him. For since reading the minutes and his marginalia it had become impossible to think about the contraption without bringing this enigmatic character to mind – and Brunel's request that I surrender the package to him had only served to strengthen this connection between the man and the metal.

Despite Brunel's testimonial it remained to be seen whether I could remove Ockham from my list of suspects. He had also written that everything happens for a reason, and so it seemed to have been when, almost on a whim, I had, all those months ago, followed him to the shipyard – for now I needed to find him and knew where to look.

The launch attempt had been a piece of tragic theatre but the painted backdrop of the ship had long before today been cut down to reveal the river and the skyline of the south shore beyond. The stage was still there, though; the hundreds of thick wooden beams, many of them supporting the iron rails along which she made her painful, jolting journey down into the water. It had taken ninety days and most of the hydraulic jacks in England to get the ship into the river and even then she entered unwillingly, finally slipping into the water like a lazy woman nudged out of bed.

A year and more after the anti-climactic launch, debris from that desperate enterprise remained scattered across the waterfront; lengths of cable and chain, broken barrels, and stacks of timber that had once formed the scaffolding which climbed up the ship's side. The carcasses of several broken jacks also remained, the strain of pushing against the ship's dead weight having burst their lungs. Back then people had been everywhere; today the yard and the river beyond were almost entirely devoid of humanity.

Aside from the open gates the only landmarks to remain were the sheds positioned on either side of the yard, and I hoped once again to find Ockham in one of them, dressing iron or polishing steel, or whatever it was he did when he was playing at being someone else. But like the yard the sheds had been stripped of their human swarm.

One of the few men left inside was busy nailing closed a large wooden crate but was happy to answer my query about Ockham's whereabouts. He had, along with the rest of the workforce, migrated to the ship, where the assembly of the engines and all the other fixtures and fittings was nearing completion.

'Try your luck over there,' he said, pointing towards the far end of the shed, where a group of men were silhouetted in an open door, through which they were pushing a trolley carrying yet more crates.

By the time I reached the door they had made it as far as a cobbled slipway, which in turn gave way to a wooden jetty. A steam barge was moored alongside, with yet more crates stacked on its deck. The master of the vessel agreed to take me out to the ship and offload me with his cargo.

The *Great Eastern* was anchored a few hundred yards downstream from the yard. With a third of her hull submerged one would have expected the ship to look smaller in the water, but out here away from the shore the effect was entirely the opposite. While on land the ship had shared the landscape with buildings, people and all those other human points of scale, but out here on the river she occupied a world of her own and so was immeasurable, unless of course another vessel sat alongside. The five smoke stacks rose up like great cylindrical watchtowers atop an impregnable fortress. Fore and aft of the funnels and in the spaces between were the masts which when fully rigged would carry enough sail to propel the ship in the event of engine failure or increase her speed by harnessing the wind as well as steam. There were six of them, each, I was told, named after a day of the week, from Monday to Saturday, as they ran from fore to aft. When asked what happened to Sunday the crewman's stock reply was, 'There's no Sunday at sea.'

As the barge drew nearer, I saw the gantries of cranes and windlasses untangle themselves from the masts and their rigging. Down on the waterline other barges bobbed like corks alongside the hull, their cargoes in the process of being lifted up on to the big ship's deck. A great cogwheel, much like the one I had seen Ockham working on months before, was suspended about halfway up the wall of the hull, inching its way upwards on the end of two sturdy ropes. Industry on such a vast scale brought to mind the achievements of the pyramid builders described by Brunel in his letter, with the ship surely a worthy successor to those magnificent stone monuments.

The barge came alongside a platform from where several flights of wooden steps rose up to the deck, and I disembarked and began my climb up to the deck. The steps took me close to the huge blades of the paddle wheel, which had yet to turn a single revolution.

Reaching the top, I was once again astonished by the scale of things – it would have been possible to drive a pair of coaches side by side along the entire length of the deck. The funnels protruded through the roofs of low cabins which ran down the centre of the ship and which I was soon to discover were designed not to accommodate passengers but the wheelhouse, the captain's quarters, animal pens and foyers for the great stairways which led down into the ship.

The deck was a hive of activity. Gangs of men worked the cranes, at least two of which were steam-operated. One loaded crates on to the deck and another had been erected over an open hole and was busy lowering machine parts, I presumed for the engines, down into the belly of the ship. Men were painting the funnels and the masts, suspended from slings and ropes on the former or clinging to the rigging of the latter. Guessing that I would find Ockham with the engines, I set out to find a way below but did not get far along the deck before a voice called my name. I immediately recognized Russell's stubborn Scottish brogue. 'Dr Phillips. A surprise to see you aboard.'

I rolled out a smile and turned to return his greeting. 'Mr Russell, I should have expected to see you here, of course. A very fine ship you have.'

Russell was followed by a pair of harassed-looking assistants, one of whom was scratching something into a large notebook, while the other carried a roll of plans.

'And what brings you on board, doctor?' asked Russell.

I had not taken the precaution of thinking up an excuse, but Russell generously provided me with one: 'Couldn't wait for Brunel to get back and give you a guided tour, eh?'

'Something like that,' I replied with as much levity as I could muster. 'As a matter of fact he had told me that in his absence Mr Ockham would provide the service. Would you happen to know where I might find him?'

'I would normally be happy to take you to him, but on this occasion I'm afraid that would be entirely out of the question.' He smiled at my puzzled expression and added, 'But I can show you where he is. Come over here.' Russell strode over to the railings. Standing beside him, I followed his gaze down on to the water, and seeing an unusual-looking barge below us expected him to tell me that Ockham was on it.

'No,' he said, pointing to a disturbed patch of water beneath the arm of a crane mounted on the vessel's bow. The iron gantry supported a heavy cable which, like a fisherman's line, disappeared beneath the surface. Another line was suspended from a crane located on the side of the great ship, not far from where Russell and I were standing.

'You mean he's in the water?'

'Aye, he's on the end of that cable leading off the barge.' Glancing across at the crane on our ship, he went on to explain, 'The rope there snapped and the crate it was lifting fell into the water. We tried grappling hooks but couldn't get it to catch, so the intrepid Mr Ockham has gone down in a diving bell to find the crate on the riverbed and attach a new rope.'

'I have heard of such a thing,' I said, recalling a mention in Brunel's clippings. 'How exactly does it work?'

'It's just like a big church bell really. The sides are sealed but the bottom is open. When lowered into the water the difference in pressure between the inside and the outside keeps the water out and so enables men to work on the bottom for anything up to half an hour before the air starts to run out. It's ideal for recovery jobs like this. But you wouldn't get me inside it.'

'My God, how long has he been down there?'

'I'd say around half an hour.'

I couldn't take my eyes off that little patch of water, half expecting Ockham's lifeless corpse to bob to the surface. Then the engine on the barge crane hissed into life and began to reel in the lines.

'Here he comes,' announced Russell as the surface of the water began to boil. The crane pulled the rust-coloured bell clear of the river, swinging it out over the barge, where it dripped water like a wrung-out sponge. A man on the boat signalled to the crane operator, bringing the bell to a halt before the boatman hammered against its side. With the waters broken Ockham dropped like a newborn from the bottom of his metallic womb on to the deck of the barge, where he was handed a blanket by one of the crewmen. Another signal and the bell was lowered on to a timber platform. With the bell recovered the crane beside us throbbed into action, sending up a cloud of smoke and steam as the rope dangling from it went taut as a bowstring. Presently, the water broke again and a cheer went up as a sodden wooden crate appeared on the end of the rope. Within minutes it was sitting on the deck of the ship, where a pool of water quickly formed around it.

'It would have taken us weeks to replace those parts,' said Russell with a satisfied smile. 'There's your man, doctor. Forgive me if I leave you now. As ever, another very busy day.'

'Thank you, Mr Russell. I will await his return.' But even before I had finished he was gone, striding down the deck and shouting at his assistants as they struggled to keep up on either side of him. It was a relief to see him go, for I had still to strike him from the list of suspects, which with the recent removal of Ockham had become all the shorter.

The small boat moved to the platform where I had embarked and from there Ockham made his way up the flight of stairs, the blanket still draped over his shoulders.

'My congratulations on your exploits in the diving bell, Mr Ockham, a terrifying-looking machine.'

He was dressed in moleskin trousers and a heavy seaman's sweater, oil-stained and worn through at the elbows; once again, not a wardrobe one would associate with an aristocrat. When he spoke his tone was less than warm. 'I wondered how long it would take you to find me here.'

'I thought you might be able to provide me with some information.'

At this he made to walk around me, the blanket now serving as a hood. 'If you'll excuse me, I am very busy,' he said, stepping out on to the deck and heading for the nearest door.

I called after him, 'Mr Brunel sent me.'

He stopped dead in his tracks. 'But he's been away for months.'

I pulled the letter from my pocket and waved it as though it were a passport and Ockham an obstructive foreign official. 'He's in Egypt, having a wonderful trip from the sound of things. He writes in it that I should look you up and . . . well, he says that I am to give you the package from Bristol.'

On hearing this he pulled the blanket from his shoulders and, draping it over a forearm, walked back towards me. 'The package?'

'Yes, the package I brought from Bristol on Mr Brunel's behalf.'

'And you are to give it to me?'

'That's what the letter says, but there is a problem.' Before I could continue Ockham grabbed me by the shoulder and began whispering aggressively into my ear.

'What do you know of Wilkie's fate? Tell me, what do you know?'

Slapping his hand away I stepped backwards and replied angrily, 'Wilkie was killed before I took delivery of the packa –'

Ockham put a forefinger up to his lips, and hissed, 'Quietly, man. Do you want everyone to know of your involvement?'

'I was not involved,' I protested. 'I was simply collecting the package as a favour for Brunel. Wilkie's killers then chased me out of Bristol and have since held me at gunpoint. I was hoping that you may be able to answer some questions for me.'

'Then you had nothing to do with Wilkie's death?' asked Ockham, his eyes now tinged with red. 'You didn't kill him?'

The accusation angered me further. 'My God, man, what do you take me for? His son helped me escape, for pity's sake.'

Ockham stared at me for a while, still not sure whether I was telling the truth. Then at last he said, 'You had better come with me. We cannot talk safely here.'

I followed him to the door, which gave way to a flight of stairs illuminated by a skylight. We climbed down three flights before entering into a long corridor lined on both sides with doors. We stopped at a door marked 312. 'This is the third-class accommodation,' said Ockham as he pulled a key from his trouser pocket. 'They let me use a cabin while I am working on the ship. It's not much but it's better than the dusty space I had over at the yard.'

The first thing to strike me was a sickly-sweet smell, which clung to the inside of my nostrils like treacle. Familiar as I was with the drug's painkilling properties, I immediately recognized the tacky aftertaste of opium smoke.

Knowing much more about him than I had a minute earlier, I looked about the small room for more clues to the secret of this enigmatic fellow's character. A narrow bunk was set low along one wall and was hinged so that during the day it could be folded flat, though Ockham seemed to prefer using it as a couch. The opposite wall supported a small table, which could also be folded flat if required. In the corner a washstand held a metal bowl and pitcher. There was a single gaslight mounted on the wall over the table but at present the only source of light was a small glazed porthole set into a hinged brass frame. I could see no sign of the pipe which he had not long before used to stoke his habit.

The floor, what there was of it, was for the most part taken up with stacks of books. More volumes filled a shelf above the bunk, which had been knocked together from remnants of wood and looked to be a hasty modification by the occupant rather than part of the cabin's standard fixtures and fittings. Much of the remaining wall space was covered by scraps of paper. They varied from lined pages torn from notebooks to large off-cuts from previously discarded technical plans. All manner of sketched diagrams and scribbled notes were represented in Ockham's bijou gallery.

Observing my interest, Ockham proceeded to tug several sheets from the wall before stuffing them under the pillow on his bed. The first to be removed was a portrait of the young woman I took to be the object of his affections and who seemed vaguely familiar. She held a fan in her gloved hands, pale face turned outward with rosebud lips pursed invitingly, her hair resting in flaxen cones against well-defined cheekbones. Although I had given the picture only the most casual of glances it was apparently enough to ignite my host's jealousy.

With a large patch of the wall now laid bare he said, 'Take a seat,' and pulled the only chair from beneath the table, preferring himself to lean against the bulkhead next to the porthole. 'Show me the letter.'

I pulled the paper from my pocket and held it out to him. He unfolded the sheet and although less than happy to take his eyes off me began to study it.

'And the package?' was all he said after handing the letter back to me.

'It was stolen from my lodgings three weeks ago. Someone kicked in my front door, searched the place and took it.'

'I know,' said Ockham confidently.

'Well then, perhaps you could tell me who took it? All I know is that it wasn't the same men who killed Wilkie.'

Ockham stepped forward and reached beneath his bunk. 'I know that also,' he said as he rummaged around. After discarding two books and several scrunched-up sheets of paper his hand reappeared clutching a hessian sack. Clearing more books from the table in front of me, he put it down and reached inside to pull out the polished casing of Brunel's mechanical heart.

'It was you!' I yelled, jumping to my feet and struggling to pull the pistol from my coat pocket. 'You broke into my lodgings!'

With lightning speed Ockham pulled something from the wash-stand. There was a flash of steel and the dreadful sensation of something very sharp pressing against my neck.

'Ever heard of Ockham's razor?' he asked, with a new menace in his voice. Being entirely incapable of speech, I tried to nod my head without moving my neck, 'Well, this is it. And if you don't sit back down it will cut your throat.'

Pulling an empty hand free from my pocket, I regained the seat and at Ockham's insistence placed both hands on the table while he sidled around from the other side to pull out the pistol. Only then did he remove the razor from my neck.

'I took the package because I believed you had killed Wilkie.

Brunel told me he had asked you to collect the parcel, and then your arrival in Bristol coincided with Wilkie's death. What conclusion was I to draw from such a coincidence? It would appear I was wrong, and for that I apologize. Might I suggest we try and find out who was responsible?'

I rubbed my neck, and on examining my fingers was much relieved to discover no blood had been drawn.

'How did you find out about Wilkie's death? And how in God's name did you know it happened while I was in Bristol?'

'A supplier from Bristol arrived at the yard. He knew the man. The news spread quickly; Wilkie was well liked. And there was a story about a stranger there when the body was found – a doctor, he said. Who else could that be?'

'I see. Brunel left the country before Wilkie's death, and I think we can assume from this letter that he still doesn't know. Have you tried to contact him?'

'I would not know where to send the letter.' He shrugged. 'All Brunel told me was that he was going to Egypt. At least now we have an address, but who knows whether he is still there?'

Ockham suddenly seemed a little embarrassed by the gun in his hand. Gripping it by the barrel, he passed it to me. I stuffed it into my pocket as though it were a snuffed-out pipe. 'Don't know why I bought the damn thing; this is the second time it's proved useless.'

'Second time?'

'I was visited by the two men responsible for Wilkie's death. I saw them in Bristol and they managed to track me down in London, Lord knows how – but as you said, they may have been looking for a doctor. They held me at gunpoint while they questioned me about the package's whereabouts.'

'And?'

'Let's just say they were very disappointed to learn that someone had beaten them to it. Well, at least you can stop following me now. I suppose it serves me right, though: there was once a time when . . .'

'What do you mean?' asked Ockham, interrupting my confession. 'Following you? I have been doing no such thing.'

Seeing no reason to doubt him, I let the matter drop. Ockham, too, had other matters on his mind and, pondering my fresh information, he seated himself on the end of the bunk. Leaving him to think, I took a closer look at the object on the table, in part I suppose to distract myself from the thorny issue of my shadow's identity. No longer did the hinged casing hold loose parts, for the mechanism had been assembled.

'Beautiful, but alas not yet finished,' said Ockham, watching me like a protective father uncertain of a stranger's intentions towards his child.

It was indeed a thing of beauty, looking more like the work of a jeweller than an engineer. There was a danger that just looking into its sparkling surfaces would be enough to blind my rational doubts about the practicality of the device. 'I read the minutes, I know what you're trying to build here.'

'It was never meant to be a secret. But then there was Wilkie's death, and now you tell me you were held at gunpoint. Somebody obviously wants this thing very badly. So here it is: Brunel's smallest machine hidden on board his largest.'

'I would say that the underside of your bunk is about as secure as my umbrella stand, and look what happened to it there.'

'We will need to move it. But it has been so convenient to work on it here. I can even fashion parts down in the workshop. The others just assume that I'm making something for the ship.'

'You say that it is not yet finished – how much is there left to do?'

'Quite a bit: the entire valve assembly needs reworking, and I am still awaiting the delivery of some parts which are beyond my capabilities to manufacture.'

'Like those commissioned from Wilkie?'

'Yes, the same principle: a specialist up in Sheffield.'

I explained that the one thing I had learned from the chair man was that he had expected Wilkie and then me to be in possession of the entire, finished device, not just a few parts. Their initial intelligence had been flawed, and having killed Wilkie needlessly I doubted they would make the same mistake again. As long as our adversaries were under the impression that the heart was still in an unfinished condition there was a chance they would leave us alone, and only strike again when they knew their prize was ready for collection.

We were both agreed that the source of this intelligence, and indeed the mastermind behind the affair, was a member of the club, and that this was knowledge we could use to our advantage.

'Tell me, Ockham,' I said, taking another look around the small room and wondering once again about the apparently irresistible attraction of Brunel's curate's egg. 'What brings a viscount to . . . to this place?'

'I see that someone has been telling you tales about my pedigree.' He took the heart from me and sat back down on the bunk.

'Sir Benjamin told me you were the grandson of Lord Byron.'

He laughed. 'I am named after him, Byron King-Noel, Second Viscount Ockham.'

'Quite a mouthful.'

'Indeed,' said Ockham with more than a touch of bitterness, 'and along with the silver spoon, much good it has done me. I prefer to be plain old Mister.'

'You still haven't answered my question.'

Ockham looked to where his books lay. 'It is all down to dear old grandfather really. Have you ever heard of Mary Shelley?'

'The writer?'

'She was a close friend of my grandfather's. About forty years ago they were spending time together in Switzerland, at Lake Geneva, along with her husband Percy Shelley. There was a doctor also, a fellow named Polydori. Well, for want of anything better to do on a wet afternoon, my grandfather suggested they each write a story, but not just any story; it had to be a tale of the macabre, a ghost story.' Looking suspicious again, he suddenly stopped and asked, 'Are you sure you haven't heard this before? It is quite well known, you know.'

I shook my head and assured him that it was all news to me and, satisfied with my answer, he continued. 'Well, the idea for Mary's story came from a dream, or should I say a nightmare. Her story impressed the others so greatly that she later expanded it into a novel.'

'*Frankenstein!*' I announced triumphantly, at once recalling why I had recognized her name and in the same instant feeling grateful to my father for making books no stranger in my childhood home.

Ockham nodded. 'Have you read it?' I shook my head again. 'You should – you are an anatomist, after all.' He returned his attentions to the books on the floor. 'Here, take this copy. You will find it an interesting read. My mother first read it to me as a child and it has haunted me ever since. It tells the story of a doctor, much like yourself, who creates a living man from the remains of the dead, bringing life from death.'

'Hence your interest in the mechanical heart?'

'Just imagine,' he said, becoming much more animated, 'being able to bring new life or extend an old one through mechanical intervention. The heart would be just the beginning; there would come a time when we could replace every organ with an artificial counterpart.'

'Forgive my pessimism, but there is no way that this thing could work, not on the basis of our current knowledge. Why, man, it would be like walking around with a cannonball lodged in your chest.'

'Very true, but is that a reason not to be paving the way for the future, not to try and improve our knowledge about both the mechanical and medical possibilities?' He was now speaking with an almost evangelical fervour, his hands gesticulating like a preacher's in mid-sermon.

'Hence the Lazarus Club. Bringing engineers and scientists together to exchange ideas?'

Ockham nodded. 'Well, that's what Brunel used to call it, until that old stick-in-the-mud Brodie pointed out that we were in danger enough of earning the wrath of the Church without using such inflammatory titles. He was right, of course: we would only court controversy if anyone, shall we say of a less enlightened persuasion, caught wind of us trying to interfere with God's will, or even playing God ourselves.'

'Is that what you are doing – playing God?'

'Where else would a man like Brunel direct his genius after triumphing in all other spheres of engineering? But things have moved on since then. Brodie was only ever interested from an academic point of view. He thinks I'm insane, by the way.' He may have a point there, I thought. 'Well, anyway,' he continued, 'as more people were invited along, either as members or speakers, it wasn't long before the club had evolved into a talking shop for all manner of notions – fascinating, I grant you, but a much watered-down version of our original intent.'

I didn't know whether to admire Ockham's foresight or pity his derangement, but I suspected there was more to it than just his mother reading him a ghost story when he was a child.

Whatever his motives, it looked as though I had found an ally, and for that I was grateful. Thanks to his revelations it seemed for the first time in weeks that I wasn't operating on my own and entirely in the dark.

Bringing the conversation back to matters of immediate concern, we briefly discussed how we would proceed in what was now a joint effort to expose Wilkie's killers. But it was now a double game in more than one sense, as if we were to survive, it would first require us to distract them from their search for the heart. With our scheme sketched out Ockham escorted me back up to the deck.

I had one more thing to say to him before I made my way down the steps to a waiting barge. 'That the simplest explanation is always the most likely.'

'I'm sorry?' said Ockham, puzzled by my remark.

'It's the principle of Ockham's razor.'

'Of course it is,' he said with a smile. 'And let us hope that it applies to our own situation.'

I wanted to believe he was right, but from where we were standing, I somehow doubted it.

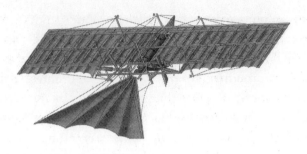

## 22

Following our experience on the last excursion of the Lazarus Club, when a close encounter with a dead body had curtailed the proceedings, and also caused me grief with Tarlow, it was a wonder that such a thing was ever tried again. But here we were, standing on a hillside in the North Downs in Kent. The object of our attentions sat above us on the summit, its nose tipped to the earth and the fan splay of its tail turned up towards the sky. Stringfellow had at last decided to move from the safe environment of his mill and the indoor tests to try to release a large-scale model into the open air. Not only that, this craft was to carry a man, or a pilot, as he described the slightly built youth who had volunteered for the task. Listening to Stringfellow talk about what he hoped to achieve with his flying machines was one thing – nobody ever got hurt looking at a picture of a machine flying over India – but this was a different basket of birds entirely.

'I notice Stringfellow's not intending to go up in that thing himself,' noted Hawes cheerily as he watched the inventor issuing instructions to the scrawny youth. 'But if these things do work,' he went on, 'they will change the world for ever.' He turned to Lord Catchpole, who was standing beside him. 'Imagine, they could even drop bombs from them. It would change the way wars were fought at a stroke.'

'You may have something there, Mr Hawes. Has the War Department sent you along to observe proceedings?'

Hawes let out a snort. 'Good grief, no. There's not a hope of that thing getting ten feet, at least not without killing the pilot in it.'

'We shall soon see,' said a dispassionate Catchpole as the pilot struggled into the machine. Stringfellow held up the lightweight, fabric-covered frame while the young man clambered beneath it and pushed his head and shoulders through an opening into which he was strapped.

'My God, he's wearing the damned thing,' said Hawes.

With his legs and feet now appearing to be part of the machine, the pilot struggled in the breeze to keep the wings level while Stringfellow and an assistant manhandled the buffeting device and its occupant into a position just behind the edge of the ridge.

At a shout from Stringfellow the pilot began to run forward, with his attendants trotting alongside, continuing to support the wing tips. By the time he cleared the edge of the ridge the pilot's feet were free of the ground and with the machine beginning to lift the handlers had no option but to let go of their charge. The pilot let out a yell – whether through exhilaration or fear it was impossible to say. The nose of the craft rose up, the tail clipping the ground before it too rose up into the air. With legs dangling the pilot was carried upwards. In the excitement Hawes took off his hat and waved it in salute.

Perhaps there was a shift in the wind or a problem with the machine itself because almost immediately it was deflected from a straight course and began to veer towards us. Whitworth was standing next to me and was the first to realize we were in danger. 'Look out, Phillips,' he barked before removing his hat and ducking down. The machine was now heading directly towards us and steadily losing altitude as it plummeted down slope. Following Whitworth's lead, I too took evasive action, and dropped to my knees. The wings were pitching from side to side, and at one point the pilot's feet made contact with the ground again, running for an instant before lifting up and pedalling for a time through empty air. There were cries of consternation from the men behind me as the bat-like shadow passed over us. I turned to see the pilot's left foot come into contact with Russell's hat and tip it from his head. Others dropped to the ground, several of them lying flat on their stomachs, their faces pressed into the grass.

Russell's hat was fortunately to be our only casualty as the craft passed overhead and then began to climb again. The pilot's fate, however, was as yet undecided and I watched as the dangling man was carried away, the device having regained its lost altitude. By the time it reached the bottom of the slope, a good few hundred yards below our position, the machine was at least twenty feet above the ground, and by then was partway through a sharp turn which brought the nose back round to face up slope. For a time it looked as though the thing was going to return back up slope but then a wingtip touched ground and the device cartwheeled to a stop, the pilot was thrown from his broken straps and landed some distance from the twisted wreckage.

While my grumbling compatriots struggled back to their feet and brushed themselves off I galloped down the slope with my bag, not at all sure whether there would be a living man to aid at the bottom of it. To my surprise the pilot had also found his feet and when I reached him he seemed as surprised as me to discover himself almost entirely uninjured. I insisted on checking him over and found only a slight twist to the ankle and a graze to the brow. The machine, however, had not fared nearly as well, one of the wings having been torn entirely away from the rest of the frame. To Stringfellow's credit he also checked on his pilot's welfare before looking over the wreckage of his craft. Hawes and Catchpole were the first of our party to reach the scene, closely followed by Ockham and Babbage. Russell was among the last to arrive and was more intent with re-forming his hat than inspecting the site of the crash.

'It flew,' said Hawes, clearly impressed. 'The damned thing flew.'

'After a fashion,' added Catchpole.

Stringfellow returned to the pilot and quizzed him about the flight, obviously keen to find the cause of what appeared to be a total loss of control. The craft may have ended up as a twisted heap of wreckage but there could be no denying that the test had been a partial success.

The original plan had been to take lunch at a local inn but, on learning of our presence in the area, Darwin, who lived close by, had sent out a messenger to invite us to his residence. The invitation was unanimously accepted and so we set off into what had turned out to be a delightfully sunny afternoon.

Down House had almost too many windows to count staring out from its bright white walls. Over time various wings and additions, including a hexagonal half-turret, had been added to what had originally been a simple Georgian house. The charm of the place was to be found in its extensive garden, where the lawns and paths were bordered by flowers and shrubs from all corners of the world, many of them, explained Darwin, brought back from his travels overseas. After coming out to greet us our host was happy to lead a tour of the grounds, during which he informed us that much of his thinking was done while walking in the garden or tending his blooms; indeed, their diverse forms had proved an inspiration while developing his theory of evolution.

Dropping a little behind the others, I fell in with Babbage, who for once seemed happy to entertain a rational conversation, and most illuminating it was too. But, as I should have perhaps expected, Darwin wasted little time in seeking me out and describing his latest symptoms. He now seemed convinced that the source of his various illnesses was an insect bite he suffered in South America. He had convinced himself of the accuracy of his self-diagnosis, but I couldn't help but conclude that his many symptoms were more likely to be the result of a highly nervous disposition. This theory seemed all the more persuasive when he went on to explain how very uncomfortable he felt about the controversy his theory had caused.

'I have barely been able to open a newspaper since my presentation at the Royal Society,' he said, as we caught up with the rest of the party. His description of the particularly unpleasant mauling meted out by members of the Church brought to mind the Spanish Inquisition. 'Very unfortunate indeed,' recalled Brodie, who, it transpired, had barely been able to keep order, despite carrying the authority of society president. I could not imagine such a thing happening at a meeting of the Lazarus Club – Babbage's occasional outbursts notwithstanding, of course. It was obvious, though, that Darwin found the garden a very calming place, and before long the conversation had turned to the role of plant extracts in medicine.

Our tour complete, we congregated beneath a glass awning attached to the side of the house, where we were served tea and sandwiches and continued to enjoy the tranquillity of the garden. Not surprisingly, our discussion turned to the test flight. Unfortunately Stringfellow was not with us to join in the debate about the future of the flying machine, as he had chosen to stay behind and oversee the packing up of his damaged prototype. There could be little doubt that the manned machine had flown, at least for a short time, but not everyone was impressed.

'If God had meant man to fly he would have given him wings,' proclaimed the reliably cantankerous Babbage, though judging from his walking-on-water shoes he wasn't above a little blasphemy himself. With that said he returned to his examination of the contents of several sandwiches, presumably in an attempt to find one suited to his sensitive palate.

'They would certainly need to be more durable than those provided by Stringfellow,' commented the ever pragmatic Gurney.

'What do you think, Darwin?' asked Brodie, who to my surprise appeared to have enjoyed his morning on the hill. 'Was man ever meant to fly?'

Darwin waited for his mouth to clear of smoked salmon before offering an answer. 'There is no evidence to suggest anything of the sort in our own evolutionary line. I think the birds we see today are most likely to have evolved from primitive lizards, and it's a view shared by my friend Mr Huxley – you must get him to give a talk to your club one day, Sir Benjamin – a little slow at first to take on board my ideas but a fascinating fellow and a very good speaker.' Brodie nodded at the suggestion. 'But that said,' Darwin continued, 'from what you tell me of Mr Stringfellow's contraption it sounds feasible that our species will one day fly, not because we will evolve wings but as a result of our own ingenuity, and that will obviously be a byproduct of our advanced evolutionary state.'

'A good point,' said Catchpole, who due to a shortage of chairs had, like me, been happy enough to stand. 'But what do we mean when we refer to "man"? Surely we cannot regard the entire human race as a single entity made up of individuals of equal status. Is it not the case that some of our species, and I include ourselves here, have advanced greatly, while the vast majority have not?'

'I don't follow your meaning, Lord Catchpole,' said Darwin, who I suspect understood his meaning only too well.

'Why, here we are, a small, elite group, discussing the finer points of human ingenuity while the vast majority of the population are concerned about little more than where their next meal is coming from.'

'That may be, but surely as an industrialist you should know that the disparity is due to economic and social factors and not a result of people existing on a lower branch of the evolutionary tree?'

If he did he didn't want to admit it. 'I very much doubt that those factors are enough to explain why one class is naturally superior to another, why one race would allow itself to be enslaved by another.'

'I take it you refer here to the African slaves who pick your cotton in America?'

'Among others, yes.'

Whitworth seemed set to say something but I interjected before him. 'Sir, with all due respect, slavery is an abomination and I find your attempts to legitimize it by using Mr Darwin's theories highly distasteful.'

I caught a momentary flash of contempt before Catchpole responded in his normal, measured tone. 'I was merely using Mr Darwin's argument to suggest that evolution is as responsible for the things men do, be it flying or taking slaves, as it is for giving feathers and wings to birds.'

Darwin scowled, his thick eyebrows curling upwards like a pair of pugilistic caterpillars. 'I have to agree with Dr Phillips when he says you are misrepresenting my ideas, Lord Catchpole, though I am sure you will not be the last to use evolutionary theory to set one race or class above another. I have opened a Pandora's box; of that much I am certain. Now, if you will excuse me, gentlemen, I am feeling a little liverish and would like to rest.'

'Well said, Phillips,' whispered Ockham as he fell in beside me and watched Catchpole stride towards our waiting carriages.

'Do you think he's our man?' I asked.

Ockham shook his head. 'He may lack compassion but that doesn't necessarily make him a murderer. If it did then most of the people we know would have been strung up at Newgate by now.'

He was right of course. 'I suppose there is little room for compassion when you're running a business empire as large as his.'

'Soft heart never won hard cash, as they say. Perhaps Darwin just needs to *evolve* a thicker skin.'

I tried to raise a laugh but couldn't get over the disappointment that we were no nearer to learning the identity of Wilkie's killer.

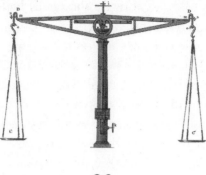

## 23

Miss Nightingale was in my office, where to my surprise she had just given me leave to address her as Florence, though she immediately threatened to withdraw the privilege when I suggested shortening it to Flo. Her edict also came with the caveat that I was to revert to the less familiar form when we were in company. 'And you shall call me George,' I told her in return.

It was no coincidence that this announcement arrived on the back of very good news.

'They want to build a new station!' Florence had announced, waving the letter from the Charing Cross Railway Company. Why this proposal should inspire such rejoicing was at first a mystery to me, but then she went on to explain that the company wanted to build the station on the site of the hospital, but only after purchasing it for a more than fair price. 'We can build a new hospital,' she said, jumping up and down in her excitement. I snatched the letter from her and read it for myself. The money would certainly go a long way to fulfilling her dream.

'Progress begets progress,' I said. 'No more going cap in hand, for a penny piece here and a penny piece there.'

Our conversation was halted by a knock at the door, followed by William's entrance. True to form, he displayed no discomfort at interrupting my meeting with Florence, who with his arrival had reverted to being Miss Nightingale, though he habitually addressed her with an almost regal 'ma'am'.

'Sir Benjamin's on the warpath; there's a key gone missin' from Mumrill's office,' he said, closing the door behind him.

'It sounds like our friend Mumrill has been a little careless with his charges,' I replied, having known full well that my failure to return the key would eventually have a consequence.

William looked at me knowingly. 'The boss is in a right old mood. You might want to stay out of his way.'

'Thank you for the warning,' said Florence, 'but I think the news we have for Sir Benjamin will put a missing key into perspective.'

'I wish you well,' said William as he made to leave, 'but I for one will be keeping out of his way for the rest of the day.'

Brodie caught up with us not long after. Mumrill was highly agitated and the hard-hearted part of me was pleased to see that he would inevitably take the blame for the missing key. As Florence had predicted, however, Brodie was most interested to hear our news, and it was agreed that a meeting should be set up between ourselves and the potential purchasers as soon as possible. With Brodie's departure Florence and I parted ways and returned to our business, mine revolving around a cadaver laid out on the dissection table.

The next formal meeting of the Lazarus Club was to be held two days later, and I had agreed with Ockham that despite drawing a blank thus far we would once again attend in the hope of picking up even the slightest hint of a clue as to the identity of Wilkie's assassins, but this time we had one further aim. Having agreed that the killers must have long been aware of the viscount's interest in the device and by now must surely have realized he had taken possession, it could therefore be only a matter of time before they made their move. Our hope therefore was to buy time by convincing our fellow Lazarians that the mechanical heart was not yet complete and in doing so to postpone a confrontation between them and us – our preference obviously being to learn their identity while we were still alive to act on the information. How this bluff was to be achieved we had not yet agreed, though we had toyed with the idea of staging a private conversation for public consumption. As it happened, though, events were to intervene before we had a chance to test our joint talents at subterfuge.

The arrival of summer had once again been accompanied by the rising stench from the river, and it could only be hoped that Bazalgette was driving his sewers through the wet London clay with all possible speed. It was the day before the meeting and I was walking to my club to take supper when a carriage drew up alongside me, the door swinging open to block my path. 'Good evening, Dr Phillips, can I offer you a lift?' called a voice from within.

Brunel was back.

I stepped into the carriage and pulled the door closed behind me. 'Where to, sir?' asked the driver, peering through a flap in the roof. Brunel looked across at me.

'I was on the way to my club in William Street for supper,' I said.

'Excellent. Did you hear that, Samuel?'

'William Street. Very good, sir.'

The engineer had changed little since last I saw him, looking less tired around the eyes perhaps but still no picture of health, and if the thick fog of smoke was anything to go by his prodigious cigar consumption remained undiminished. I had rehearsed a number of greetings for this occasion, many of them less than cordial and all of them very quickly moving on to a barrage of questions. But his appearance had taken me by surprise and it was Brunel himself who set the groundwork for my interrogation.

'Well, my friend, how have things been?'

'That is going to take a little explaining,' I said, snorting at my understatement. 'But before I do, can I ask when you got back?'

'This morning. We left Cairo two weeks ago. Did you get my letter?'

I nodded dismissively. 'Who have you spoken with since then?

'I have seen nobody yet – apart from you, of course,' he said, somewhat surprised at the urgency of my question. 'I plan to meet with Russell tomorrow morning and see what progress the scoundrel has made with the ship over the last six months. Today I just wanted to get away from the unpacking. Tell me: what news? What have I missed?'

'Wilkie is dead,' I said.

Brunel paled. 'My God, how?'

'He was murdered when I was in Bristol.'

The engineer silently mouthed the word 'murder' as he stubbed out his cigar. 'Nate – what about young Nate? My God, the poor lad.'

'The boy's in America. I saw him on to the boat.'

'Gone to stay with his uncle, no doubt. Good man, Phillips. But why? Why would anyone want to kill Wilkie?'

'That is a question I have been waiting to ask you for some time.'

Brunel was clearly shocked. 'He was a craftsman, a damn good engineer. Why would anyone wish him dead?'

This thin stew of queries was getting us nowhere, so I added more information to the pot. 'I know about the heart, Isambard.'

'The heart? I suppose Ockham told you about it? Are you telling me the heart has something to do with it?'

'Ockham didn't need to tell me – I have seen the minutes of the meeting in which you unveiled the concept.' Then, at the risk of spoiling the recipe, I threw in more ingredients. 'Wilkie was killed because he refused to surrender the components you commissioned. He gave them to Nate, who escaped to hand them on to me. Later, his killers broke into my rooms and held me at gunpoint; they were looking for the heart. But the whole of the heart, not just pieces. What the hell is going on here, Isambard?' The carriage came to a halt. 'Join me for supper,' I said. 'We have much to discuss.'

Brunel nodded and opened the roof flap. 'Samuel, leave us here. Collect me again at . . .' he pulled out his watch and flipped the lid '. . . at ten thirty. In the meantime return home and inform my wife of my intention to take supper with Dr Phillips.'

'Very well, sir. Ten thirty, it is,' came the dismembered reply.

After signing in my guest we entered the lounge, but it was busy so I asked the porter for a private room, where we could take a drink and talk without fear of being overheard.

'I know all about the Lazarus Club and I know about Ockham.'

'My congratulations,' said Brunel, a note of irritation in his voice. 'Should we not give a little thought to what you don't know?' Before I could reply a servant reappeared with our drinks and when he left Brunel continued. 'Forgive me, Dr Phillips, but I have known Wilkie for a long time. Illness, an accident, that would be another thing entirely, but murder? And as for your suggestion that the mechanical heart is the root cause of all this, I find that hard to believe.'

'It has troubled me also. Why would anyone go to such extremes to get their hands on a device with no hope of . . . well, of fulfilling the role for which it was created?'

Brunel gazed into the fire. 'You need not spare my feelings, Phillips. An optimist might call it a prototype a hundred years before its time, but you are right. Anyone else would probably dismiss it as nothing more than a piece of whimsy, a castle in the air. Why then, you ask, would anyone want to kill for it?'

'Exactly,' I said, relieved to be getting somewhere.

He dipped a splint into the flames and proceeded to light his first cigar since leaving the carriage.

He was lost in his thoughts for a moment, but then, keeping his back to me and gripping the mantelpiece with both hands, said, 'Perhaps, my friend, the device is more than just a mechanical heart.'

'How so?'

He turned to face me. 'It is an engine.' I looked at him blankly while he sat down again. 'You see, in my youth I spent many years dabbling with a design for an engine that was powered not by steam but compressed air. I called it a gaz engine. But it performed badly in tests and seemed like time and money wasted. Then along came Ockham with his dreams of mechanical organs.'

'Our mutual friend seems to come from a long line of dreamers.'

'You have been doing a little research into his family tree?'

'It wasn't difficult. He told me about his mother, about his grandfather and *Frankenstein*. But I learned more from Babbage.'

'Ah, I see. And just what did he tell you?'

'He told me about the woman in the picture on his mantelpiece, which I saw when he hosted that meeting in his house.'

'Go on.'

'A few weeks ago I was in Ockham's cabin on the ship and there was a picture of a woman on his wall, which he was keen to hide away. It took me a while to realize it, but it was the same woman as in the picture at Babbage's house. It was Ockham's mother, Ada Lovelace, Lord Byron's daughter. I spoke to Babbage while we were at Darwin's house and he told me all about her. About how she had helped him in his work on the difference and analytical engines, how they became friends. She had a peculiar talent for mathematics but being a woman did not have the opportunity to pursue these interests as she would have liked. The strain began to show, she became estranged from her husband and, despite Babbage's efforts, fell into bad company. Ada had been gambling for some time and eventually lost almost the entire family fortune on the horses. According to Babbage, she had hoped that his devices could be used to calculate odds, to predict which horse was most likely to win a given race. But then she fell ill and died of cancer. Babbage seems to have been one of the few people who treated her with any decency; she doesn't appear to have been an easy person to get along with. That's why her devoted son, who himself could be described as a difficult character, gets on well with Babbage, regarding him almost as a father figure. And to cut a long story short, that's how he ended up in your company, working at the yard and becoming a founder member of the Lazarus Club.'

'I am pleased you have learned more about him. The knowledge may help you better understand his peculiarities. Many would regard his interests as eccentric but his enthusiasm helped me to see my gaz-powered device in a new light, as did you with your surgical understanding of the workings of the human body. Over time I refined the design and created the heart, but in doing so may also have inadvertently designed a gaz engine that actually works.'

'And a new type of engine that works would be highly desirable. Much more so than a mechanical heart that does not?'

'That is so, but we will not know whether it works until it is finished and tested.'

'I suppose Ockham sees no other purpose for it, other than as a heart?'

Brunel took a contemplative draw on his cigar. 'You can rest assured that he is entirely single-minded about the issue. He set out to build a heart not an engine.'

This assessment was entirely in keeping with the impression I had gained from my shipboard conversation with the peculiar young aristocrat. 'Then who else knows about it? The engine, I mean, not the heart.'

'Any number of people. I freely discussed the idea with my colleagues.'

So much for narrowing the field, but then after a little more thought he continued, 'Most of them dismissed it as a bad idea, but there was one who showed great interest in the project.' The sense of expectation was unbearable, but then just as he was about to speak the name he shook his head. 'No, it couldn't be. Not him. Scoundrel he may be but murderer?'

The description was enough. 'Russell, you think it was Russell?'

It took Brunel the remaining lifespan of his cigar to describe how, almost four years earlier, just as a young Viscount Ockham appeared on the scene, Russell had voiced an enthusiasm for the engine and claimed to have come up with a use for it in a machine of his own design. The project, Russell had claimed, would be highly rewarding for them both, but he had refused to provide any further detail on what he had in mind. At the time, Brunel explained, their working partnership had been at an especially low ebb, though I had never known it to enjoy a buoyant high tide. Russell had just been sacked by the ship company, which not for the last time was on the verge of bankruptcy and so, not surprisingly, the last thing Brunel wanted was further collaboration with the man.

With Ockham's arrival, however, and apparently his financial backing, the design for the device went through a radical transformation, and it evolved from an engine into a heart. But this redesign only served to encourage Russell further and he made several more attempts to talk Brunel round, though he still fell short of explaining what his idea was. Then, not long after my introduction to the Lazarus Club Brunel began commissioning the manufacture of parts, including those from Wilkie. Ironically, or perhaps suspiciously, just as the gaz engine became more of a realistic proposition, so Russell's interest declined, or so it seemed.

'While I still cannot believe him capable of murder, he is the only obvious suspect, and it won't be the first time I've caught him stealing.'

'Really?'

'We had two and a half thousand tons of iron plate destined for use in the ship go missing. It turned out Russell had appropriated them for use in another of his projects. I never managed to prove it but I am certain it was him.'

'Are you just as certain this time?' I asked, concerned that Brunel was letting his emotions colour his views.

'There is one way to be sure,' he said. 'I will have it out with the man tomorrow.'

'I would strongly advise against that, Isambard. We cannot afford to make our suspicions known, not yet. If he is guilty Lord knows what powers he has under his control. Russell didn't kill Wilkie but the men who did may be in his employ. We must approach this matter with the utmost care. Firstly, we need to find out what use he had in mind for your little engine.'

'You are right, of course,' said Brunel, calmer now. 'And I know where we are most likely to get that information.'

The details were hammered out in hushed tones over supper and by the time our brandies arrived we had agreed on how to proceed.

The fight back had begun.

As fate would have it the presentation scheduled for the following evening was to be made by none other than Russell. He was to talk about the fitting out of the great ship, but Brunel's return from his travels had put an end to that and the Scotsman, who in any case was not a natural public speaker, seemed only too glad to step down and let the engineer talk in his place.

Brunel was greeted as though he were a victorious general back from the wars. Glasses were raised to his health and it seemed quite natural for him to share his Egyptian adventures with his fellow Lazarians.

He explained to us how the massive stones for the pyramids were quarried and then transported by barge along the River Nile; how the vast monoliths were moved across the land on wooden rollers and dragged up on great earthen ramps; how the dead pharaohs were preserved through a process called mummification, their bodies dried out with salts and wrapped in bandages; how these mummies were placed in wooden and stone coffins, bedecked with gold and jewels, and then sealed inside the pyramids, many of them accompanied by their freshly slaughtered wives and slaves, all of them waiting to serve in the afterlife.

With his audience captivated, Brunel placed an object wrapped in muslin on the table. The breath caught in my throat as he began to remove the protective bindings; surely it couldn't be? But to my relief, the removal of the shroud did not reveal the mechanical heart but a gently tapered cylindrical vessel with a shouldered top. The alabaster lid took the form of a falcon's head, the piercing eyes still highlighted by the layers of paint and gold leaf applied all those thousands of years ago.

'This is a canopic jar,' he said. 'Inside is the heart of a pharaoh, plucked from his chest and sealed inside the jar before the body was mummified.'

He handed the jar to Russell, who proceeded to examine it, even to the point of sniffing the wax-sealed top in expectation of detecting some aroma of the organ inside; apparently disappointed, he passed the jar to his neighbour. Whitworth repeated the process, but in addition gently shook it, perhaps hoping to hear the organ slap against the walls of the vessel. Babbage avoided any contact whatsoever by pushing himself back into his seat, thus allowing Whitworth to reach across his front and pass the object to me. Setting down my pencil, I took hold of it with both hands and first brushed my finger across the faint pattern carved into the neck of the vessel just below the falcon's head. Then I upturned the jar and, finding no maker's mark on the base, I handed it on to Stephenson; and so round it went, moving from hand to hand around the table, each recipient adding something new to the ritual of examination. By the time it reached Ockham the only thing left to do was to break it open. But he just set it down in front of him and stared at it.

Brunel continued to enlighten us as the object was doing the rounds. 'All of the major organs were removed, not by surgeons,' he explained, casting a glance at me, 'but by priests. The brain was removed through the nose, and like the heart, liver and lungs, deposited in a jar to be sealed and placed in the tomb with the mummified body. It could only be presumed, he told us, that these organs were reunited with the body on its arrival in the afterlife, where the pharaoh would enjoy immortality in the company of the gods.

'How do we know all this?' asked Whitworth.

Brunel produced a card depicting a series of symbols and motifs. 'These are hieroglyphics. The writings left by the Ancient Egyptians, carved into the columns of their temples and painted on the walls of their tombs. In these they bequeathed us descriptions of their beliefs and practices.'

I squinted at the card, trying to make out the shapes so as to complement my written notes with some rough sketches. Noticing my difficulty, Brunel passed the card to Russell, which like the jar before it began its halting journey around the table. All manner of objects were depicted: there was a feather, what I took to be a bushel of corn, an owl, a boat, a snake, a human leg and an arm.

'How on earth are we to understand their meaning?' asked Brodie.

'They have been deciphered, translated into the modern tongue. Each symbol represents a word or letter. We can now read them as though they were written in English. Or indeed French, for the work was done by a Frenchman, a gentleman called Champollion.

'It is written,' he continued, 'that before a man can pass into heaven his worth must be judged. This was achieved by weighing his heart on a set of scales. If it were heavy with sin, then it was devoured by a demon and the body passed into hell, but if the balance tipped the other way because his heart was free from sin then he passed into the afterlife.'

'Are these similar to the patterns carved into the jar?' I asked.

Brunel picked up the vessel and peered at it. 'Indeed they are. As far as I can make out they provide information on the jar's contents.'

There was a brief pause and then another question, but this time not from the audience. 'Gentlemen,' said Brunel, 'I wonder how many of us carry heavy hearts inside our chests?' He glanced around the table. 'I certainly do, but the cause is not sin but grief. Only yesterday, on my return to England, did I learn of the tragic death of Leonard Wilkie, my friend and colleague in Bristol and sometime member of the Lazarus Club. We can only hope that his brutal murder will not go unpunished.'

There was a muttering of agreement. 'His loss,' Brunel continued, 'represents a double blow, both personal and professional, and I am sure you will all wish to join me in a silent prayer to his memory.' Brunel bowed his head, and we followed suit. After a few moments I risked a glance at him. Acknowledging me with a subtle nod, his gaze finally came to rest on the crown of Russell's lowered head. Then, after a minute or so he cleared his throat. 'Thank you, gentlemen, but before we move on I have one more thing to say on this matter. With the death of Wilkie I am afraid that progress on the mechanical heart, a project I set before you some time ago, has been seriously delayed, for he was still to produce a number of essential components. I had hoped to present the finished device to you in the near future, but that will no longer be possible.'

Thanks to Brunel's splendid performance our plan had gone off better than we could have hoped. He had carried the whole thing off with a panache that Ockham and myself would have come nowhere near to achieving. The meeting closed in a subdued mood, but this was all to the good – further evidence that Brunel had succeeded in his aim.

Ockham, as was his usual custom, left the meeting on his own, while I, in keeping with my previous habit, accepted a lift in Brunel's carriage. I waited until we had turned the corner to offer my congratulations.

Brunel laughed so hard it made him cough. 'It's just as well none of them have been to Egypt!'

'I don't follow your meaning, Isambard.'

'Why, a heart in a canopic jar? What nonsense!'

He had lost me. 'How so?'

'Because the only organ the Egyptians never removed from the body was the heart; they regarded it as the home of the soul.'

'But you said the heart was weighed in heaven.'

'And indeed it was, but the task was carried out by a god, not some numbskull priest. Only a god may handle the heart.' He snatched up the jar from the seat beside him. 'Poetic licence, I know, but I thought a heart might help to draw out our man – cause him to look uncomfortable, misplace a word, anything to betray his guilt.'

I knew from experience that identifying the guilty party merely through observing their behaviour was less than straightforward. 'I didn't see anything, did you?'

'Alas no, but then he's a cold fish, isn't he?'

'Who is?'

Brunel rolled his eyes. 'Russell of course – that stony-faced shipwright is hiding something, of that there can be no doubt.'

This portrait of inscrutability did not marry with the man I had seen in a rage after the accident at the yard, but I said nothing.

The engineer tapped the falcon's beak. 'Talking of which, do you know what's really in here?'

I shook my head.

'The intestines, that's what. It says so here on the front.' He pointed at the hieroglyphs and laughed. 'Little did they know it but they were handling a jar full of guts.'

It seemed fitting that even Brunel's telltale heart had itself proved to be a liar.

Having taken my leave of a high-spirited Brunel, I wasted no time settling myself into bed with a nightcap and the book Ockham had given me while on the ship. Despite Brunel's failure to identify our foe it had been a most satisfactory evening and so a little light reading was in order.

There was an introduction to the volume, written by the author herself. In it she described the origins of *Frankenstein*, and the role played by Ockham's grandfather was again highlighted. Even here, in the introduction, her writing struck a chord:

I saw the pale student of unhallowed arts kneeling beside the thing he had put together. I saw the hideous phantasm of a man stretched out . . .

The picture she painted with these words was not an unfamiliar one; the cadaver stretched out on the table before me, my knife poised to make the first incision. '. . . and then,' she continued:

on the working of some powerful engine, show signs of life, and stir with uneasy, half-vital motion. Frightful must it be; for supremely frightful would be the effect of any human endeavour to mock the stupendous mechanism of the Creator of the world. His success would terrify the artist; he would rush away from his odious handiwork, horror-stricken. He would hope that, left to itself, the slight spark of life which he had communicated would fade; that this thing which had received such imperfect animation would subside into dead matter, and he would quench forever the transient existence of the hideous corpse which he looked upon as the cradle of life.

With Dr Frankenstein and his terrible creature for company I read on until my eyes ached, at one point leaping from the bed to retrieve the notes taken from the minutes. Several of the phrases in the book seemed familiar and my hunch proved right – Ockham had copied them into the minutes taken during Brunel's presentation on the heart. One phrase in particular stood out:

I am not recording the vision of a madman.

Casting my mind over what I had learned about Brunel over almost two years I decided to withhold my judgement.

## 24

Ockham worked against the current with a well-practised dexterity, his even strokes pulling us steadily along. With the bow of the small boat pointing upriver the monstrous hulk to our stern was swallowed up by the night. The blades cut into the water with a quiet plash, plash, the rags wrapped around the oar shafts muffling the sound of their movement in the rowlocks. We had waited until well after midnight before pushing away from the ship, by which time we could be confident of our departure going unobserved.

When we had covered enough distance to compensate for the current Ockham turned the boat into our final approach. Good early progress notwithstanding, finding our mark on the opposite shore was proving less than straightforward, as the absence of a moon, while masking our movements, also served to obscure any landmarks. We had been aiming for a point just to the west of the yard, but landed well inside the fence that ran down from the street to the water's edge. Our original plan had been to land at low tide on the bank just to the outside of the fence and then enter by paddling around it. Now, if we were to have any hope of escaping the attentions of the watchman our misjudgement would necessitate great care when disembarking and while clambering back onboard. It was just as well there were only two of us – with some difficulty I had managed to persuade Brunel that he was not up to the physical strain.

The boat buffeted against the thick wooden rails previously used to deliver the ship into the water. Taking hold of the mooring rope, I hopped from the bow, skating hazardously on the slippery surface of the timber. Finding firmer but wetter footing on the muddy gravel, I pulled the boat up into the gap between two of the rails and anchored the rope by driving the metal spike on the end of it into the gravel. With our vessel securely beached Ockham passed me the bag before joining me on shore. A flicker of light in the distance marked the watchman's hut, which like a sentry box was located next to the main gate. Even though we had landed slightly off course our arrival by boat still retained a double benefit; it negated the need to scale the wall from the street and also put us as far away from the watchman's hut as it was possible to get.

The heaps of timber and other post-launch debris still littering the foreshore provided good cover and we soon found ourselves alongside one of the two big sheds. Ockham pulled the bag from his shoulder and signalled me to grab the end of a length of timber lying at our feet. Shifting the plank to one side exposed a ladder, hidden there the day before by my partner in crime. Taking hold of an end apiece we carried it to the side of the shed and leant it up against the wall. After peeping around the corner to check there was no movement from the hut Ockham dashed back for his bag before beginning his ascent.

I then commenced my own rather unsteady climb, looking up to see Ockham crouching on the top of the wall. Like an alleycat he was studying the sloping expanse of the roof, seeking out a safe route across the fragile shingles. Unlike the huge free-standing shed on the opposite side of the yard, in which some months before I had observed Ockham at work, this was a lean-to joined to the side of the three-storey stone building that housed the yard's offices.

At last certain of his bearings, Ockham moved off his perch. Following his lead, I dragged myself on to the lip of the roof and looked up to catch a glimpse of him making rapid headway on the slope. Our forward planning was paying off.

The high stern of the ship had provided an uninterrupted view of the yard and the shed roof above it. Although the *Great Eastern* was anchored a quarter of a mile or more downstream the distance was more than compensated for by the use of a sailor's spyglass. Like a pair of surreptitious admirals we plotted a course across a roofbeam strong enough to support our weight and positioned as close as possible to the window we intended to use as a door.

With arms outstretched for balance I carefully made my way along the line of the joist. My foot slipped on to a tile, causing it to shift slightly, but no harm was done and soon I was resting my hands against the cool stone. Keeping close to the wall, Ockham shuffled the last few feet to the window, where he pulled a chisel from the bag and began to work on the base of the frame. It was vital that our visit went undetected, for even a suspicion that we were taking any form of action against our opponents might be enough to incur their wrath. Several days earlier Ockham had visited the office under a false premise and made a rapid examination of the latch on the window. Now, he slipped the thin blade of the chisel into the frame and, moving it gently from side to side, succeeded in pushing the latch aside. Then he lifted the window open without displacing a single chip of wood or breaking any glass.

Ockham pulled out the lamp and, making ready to light it, paused just long enough for me to close the shutters over the window. The ensuing darkness, although momentary, was total, so much so that the inky murkiness outside seemed like an overcast afternoon in comparison. The match flared and kissed the lamp into life, the light at first sputtering and uneven but then becoming bright and steady as the wick was adjusted. Russell's office rushed out of the dark to greet us, the stark contrast between shadows and light imbuing the furniture with a fleeting quality that for a moment could have been mistaken for animation. The corner of the desk sniffed at my groin like an inappropriately behaved dog while a stray chair was just a foot away from stumbling into Ockham.

Russell's office was smaller than Brunel's and the furnishings less accomplished examples of the cabinet-maker's art. On the pinboards on the walls were large drawings, many of them depicting heavy machinery, which I could only guess to be the ship's engines. Setting the lamp down on one of the cabinets, Ockham pulled open the top drawer of a plan chest and began to riffle through the drawings within. Every now and then he pulled a sheet part way out of the drawer and scrutinized it more closely before pushing it back in. Trusting Ockham to have at least some idea of what we were looking for, I took up position by the locked door and listened for any noise that might signal the approach of the watchman.

Finding nothing of interest, Ockham closed the first drawer and opened the one below it to start the procedure over again but only flicked through half a dozen or so drawings before pushing it closed. Instead of opening the one immediately beneath it he dropped down to the bottom of the cabinet and pulled out a drawer almost level with the floor.

'The drawings are stored in chronological order. What we're after is a couple of years old,' he said quietly, picking up the lamp and placing it on the floor beside him.

I swore under my breath as the light flooding out across the floor revealed a trail of grey slippery footprints leading away from Ockham back to the window. Another set traced my own path, terminating in a smudge of damp clay at my own feet. It had been an act of singular stupidity to enter the room without previously removing our heavily soiled shoes. Stable doors and bolting horses came to mind as I took off my shoes and instructed Ockham to do the same. Unless we cleaned up what looked to be half of the foreshore of the Thames then all of our efforts at stealth had gone for nothing.

With little choice but to abandon my post I stepped away from the door in stockinged feet and after taking Ockham's shoes from him and placing them next to my own below the window looked for something with which to wipe the floor clean. A sheet of paper only served to smear the mud across the boards. With drastic action required I took off my coat, waistcoat and shirt before replacing the two outer garments. After ripping the shirt into half a dozen strips I dropped to my knees and like a hard-pressed charlady began to work away at the incriminating stains. To my relief the fabric was much more suited to the task and gradually the footprints began to disappear. Meanwhile, Ockham continued with his search, by now having moved on to another chest of drawers. I had expended all of my cleaning rags without completing the task and needed a new source of supply. My socks lasted for little more than one footprint apiece and I was damned if I was going to sacrifice any more of my wardrobe to the task.

Before I could ask Ockham to make a contribution he called out, 'This is it, I've found it.' For the first time he had pulled a sheet entirely free from the drawer and although subdued to a half-whisper his excitement was unmistakable: 'This has to be it.'

The sock hit the floor like a soggy gauntlet and I padded over to take a look at the sheet draped across the gaping drawer. Ockham lifted the lamp and held it above his find, allowing me to study the various views, plans and elevations of what looked like a fish with the internal anatomy revealed. In truth, though, the many inked lines and curves meant very little; the object they created might as well have been one of Brunel's cryptic Egyptian symbols. 'What the hell is that?'

His answer was not all I might have hoped for. 'It looks like one of the old man's cigars,' he said with a chuckle. But there could be no denying the similarity – the cylindrical object bowed out in the middle and then tapered to a point at both ends. 'But look,' he added, finger jabbing at the paper, 'there's a screw.'

There was indeed a propeller attached to one end, but Ockham immediately put paid to my suggestion that we were looking at a ship. 'Water-borne perhaps, but far too small for a ship: look at the measurements. It's only twelve feet from end to end – no longer than our rowing boat, and a good bit leaner in the beam.'

With no time for further speculation I limited myself to just one more question. 'What makes you so sure that this . . . this propeller-driven cigar is what we're looking for?'

Bringing his finger to rest over a small patch of paper free of ink, Ockham replied confidently, 'Does that space look familiar to you? Whatever this is, it was designed to be powered by Brunel's device.'

I looked once again at the drawing. Where otherwise the thing was stuffed full of what looked like intestines and organs, there, in the belly of this strange cigar fish, was a distinctive egg-shaped void.

I patted him on the back. 'Good man. Do what you have to do. But first give me your shirt.'

'You are joking?'

'If we leave even the slightest trace of mud Russell will know we've been here.'

Ockham stripped rapidly and handed me his shirt. Despite the fraying cuffs the effort involved in tearing the garment was a sure sign of quality not apparent in my own costume. With knees scraping the floorboards I continued wiping my way towards the door. Replacing his remaining upper garments, Ockham removed a sheet of tracing paper and a pencil from his bag and, placing the drawing on the cabinet top, began to mark every last detail of it, taking care not to press so hard as to leave a detectable impression.

Engrossed in my own task it took me longer than it should have done to notice the fresh chink of light now illuminating my work. Entering the room through the narrow gap beneath the door, it was at first just a faint glimmer but grew brighter as the source drew closer.

'Someone's coming,' I hissed. My first instinct was to scramble away but, being so close to the door, there was too much risk of my movements being heard. Ockham was not constrained by the same concern and, snatching up the lamp, he scuttled for cover, kicking the rags across the floor as he went. The key turned in the lock just as the lamp was extinguished. The door swung towards me, forcing me to lean back on my haunches. With wrists touching ankles I felt like a trussed bird, which seemed apt, for if I fell backwards our goose would be well and truly cooked.

The watchman took just one step into the room but the beam of light exhibited no such caution and barged straight on in, brushing first against the closed shutters and then the desk before travelling along the floor and climbing up the side of the cabinet to settle on the drawing, where it lingered for an uncomfortably long time. The door was now brushing against my knees, aching from cleaning the floor, and only the support provided by fingertips pressed into the floor behind me kept me from tumbling backwards.

For what seemed an age the light remained fixed on the top of the cabinet but then the watchman pulled the door shut, decapitating the shaft of light and toppling the room back into darkness. Listening to the footsteps recede down the corridor, I succumbed to the overwhelming urge to settle on to my backside, my cracking knuckles and every other joint in my body screaming with relief.

'Just as well you cleaned up that mud, Phillips,' said the cheerful voice from behind the desk, 'even if it did cost the shirt off my back.' The sulphur tip of a match flashed and the lamp exploded back into life. Without waiting for the flame to settle Ockham strode confidently back to the cabinet and resumed his labours.

'Almost finished here,' he said. 'But I still have no idea what this thing is. What little text there is isn't much help either.'

I stood for a while with my ear to the door, listening out for the sound of returning footsteps. Ockham reassured me that the watchman would descend to a lower floor via the stairs at the end of the corridor rather than retrace his steps but only when I was certain that he had done so did I join him at the planning chest.

'Don't engineers ever make anything obvious?' I asked.

'Not if they want to keep their ideas to themselves.'

Ockham's pencil hung in mid-air for a while as the draughtsman assured himself that nothing was missing. Just to make certain, he lifted up one corner of the top sheet and tutted when a small detail on the original failed to show up on the copy. The sheet was pressed flat again and the error rectified with a last flourish of the pencil. 'Finished,' he announced.

'Time to get out of here.'

Ockham rolled up the copy and returned the original to the drawer while I checked the floor for any stray fragments of shirt. Only then did it dawn on me that the muddy footprints I had gone to such great lengths to wipe from the floor would also be marking our route along the rooftop. Anyone looking out of the window the following day would be sure to see the evidence of our visit. There was nothing else for it – we would have to remove as much as we could on our return trip. With the lamp snuffed out I pulled open the window shutters and scrambled, shoes in hand, back out on to the roof, which, I was delighted to discover, was at that moment being pelted by cleansing rain. Concerned that the results of his labours not be washed away with the mud I whispered back to Ockham, 'Make sure that drawing is covered.'

Following me, Ockham pulled the window down and used the chisel to flick the latch back into the locked position. Back on the ground we put our shoes on and returned the ladder to its original hiding-place. This time it was my turn to sneak a peek around the corner of the building and check that the coast was clear. The caution was merited, as the dark silhouette of the watchman was framed in the doorway of the hut, the lamp inside throwing his long shadow across the ground in front of the gate. Even though he was facing across the yard there was still a good chance of making it back to the boat without him seeing us, but I was not prepared to take the risk and so waited for him to return to the comfort of his modest abode. My patience was soon rewarded, and the sentinel turned and walked back inside, buttoning his fly as he went. Rather than brave the rain the uncouth fellow had relieved himself on his own doorstep.

The tide had turned and we found the boat fully afloat and testing the strength of its mooring. Pulling the craft to the shore, Ockham climbed aboard and sat down, taking the strain with the oars as I pushed off. The rain hitting the river sounded like a great curtain swishing backward and forward on its rail and provided a shielding counterpoint to the rhythmic slap of the oars. Rivulets of water dripped down our shirtless torsos but the discomfort was counteracted by a sense of euphoria induced by the success of our mission. Heading back to the ship with the drawing in our possession, I felt like a bandit returning to his mountain lair. I pulled a sodden mass of rags from the bag and tossed it into the river, where the knot of dirty fabric began to unravel in the current.

Back on board ship we dried off and warmed ourselves with brandy. The past few hours had taken their toll and so, with the drawing safely stowed, I was grateful to be shown to the cabin in which I would spend my first night on board Brunel's *Great Eastern*.

# 25

The last thing a doctor wants is to be a patient in his own hospital. But that was exactly what I had become by the evening of the day after our adventure in Russell's yard.

Announcing its arrival with a tingling in the throat, the chill had wasted no time in taking up residence in my chest, where it developed into a debilitating cough accompanied by a raging fever. It did not take a doctor to identify the cause of this rapid decline in my health – the drenching I had received in the boat, exacerbated by the lack of a shirt, had brought on the most dreadful bronchial inflammation. No stranger to fever, Florence recognized my symptoms immediately and, ignoring my pleas to soldier on, soon had me confined to a bed in one of the wards. Spending most of my life surrounded by sickness and remaining healthy throughout, I had come to consider myself immune to the ailments to which the general populace fall victim. My arrogance was about to receive a considerable shock to the immune system.

For thirty-six hours I slipped in and out of consciousness. Whenever I came round it was to find someone mopping my brow and pushing a cup of hydrating broth to my lips. Then, surfacing for the umpteenth time, I looked up to see Florence standing over me.

'Glad to see you are still with us, Dr Phillips' – her use of my full title indicated the presence of a third party – 'you have a visitor. I was going to send him away but he seems to have picked his time well. Your fever has broken.'

I turned to see Brunel standing on the other side of the bed, his mouth for once uncluttered by a cigar. 'They won't let me smoke in here,' he grumbled. 'I don't see why not: the cigar is surely an excellent fumigator.'

Florence plumped my pillow as I tried to pull myself up on the bed. The task left me feeling quite exhausted. 'Good to see you, too, Isambard,' I wheezed.

'You had us all very worried, but Miss Nightingale informs me that the worst is over.'

Florence placed a cool hand against my forehead and seemed satisfied that her judgement had not been premature. 'Now the fever has broken I think you will be better off recuperating at home.'

'I could not agree with you more, Miss Nightingale; a hospital is far too unhealthy a place for a man in his condition,' concurred Brunel with a laugh, and then to me, 'Perhaps next time you will dress more appropriately when boating at night.'

'How is Ockham?'

'Bright as a button and looking forward to sharing the fruits of your labours with you.'

'He must be made of sterner stuff,' I commented with an unwarranted degree of self-pity. Then, guessing that Brunel was eager to talk, I turned to Florence. 'Miss Nightingale, if you could please leave us alone for a moment.'

'Please do not detain him long, Mr Brunel, he is still a sick man.'

My visitor watched as she walked away down the ward. 'Your nurse is a formidable woman.'

'Indeed she is.'

Brunel seated himself on the edge of my bed, his hands folded across the top of the hat on his lap. 'We crossed swords more than once over the Crimean affair.'

'Yes, of course – you designed a hospital for use out there, didn't you? I imagine she had a few opinions on that.'

'You could say that.'

Unfortunately, I was in no condition to indulge in reminiscences. 'Tell me, have you seen the drawing?'

Brunel's voice softened. 'Ockham brought it over to my office this morning.'

'Don't keep me in suspense, man, what is it?'

Brunel looked around and drew closer, the better to deliver his news without fear of being overheard. 'Well now . . .' But before he could continue my body was racked by an agonizing bout of coughing. Brunel cast aside his hat and snatched a glass from the shelf by my bed. The water helped to douse the flames in my chest and the paroxysm subsided, but not before the sound of coughing had summoned Florence back to my bedside.

'Mr Brunel, I am afraid you will have to leave,' she said sternly. 'Dr Phillips must rest.'

Brunel nodded grimly and picked up the discarded hat, his pained expression betraying the fragile nature of his own health. 'I will come and see you when you are feeling better – perhaps at your lodgings? Then we can discuss our next move.'

With that he departed, and I pictured him getting no further than the front door of the hospital before lighting up his next cigar.

'It is going to be some time before you are capable of taking action of any sort,' said Florence as she rearranged blankets thrown into disarray by my fit. 'He's not the first visitor I have had to turn away.'

'Oh?'

'You are a popular man, George. An Inspector Tarlow called a couple of days ago, while you were still feverish. He said his business could wait. Now, get some sleep. I will make arrangements for you to be taken home in the morning.' She kissed her hand and touched it against my forehead before leaving me to ponder the nature of Tarlow's business.

Feeling slightly better the next morning, I walked with jellied legs to the waiting carriage. Florence promised to check on me herself or send a nurse to do so at least once a day. I spent the next two weeks in idle convalescence, taking nourishment from the regular deliveries of warming broth and using a diffuser to keep my lungs clear. Within two days I was able to leave my bed for short periods, pottering about the place with a blanket draped over my shoulders. My cough slowly improved but was to make brief visitations for some time to come.

I also took the opportunity to bring my journal up to date, always taking care to return it to its hiding-place beneath a floorboard in my bedroom once I had finished writing.

Florence called around when she could and seemed happy enough with my progress. She kept me up to date with events at the hospital, which not for the first time appeared to be getting on quite well without me. But William remembered me, and passed on his best wishes via Florence, and apparently even Brodie had asked after my health, which I found touching as it had surely taken some degree of self-sacrifice on his part to speak to Florence. She laughed when I suggested this, as he had done so through an intermediary. That go-between can only have been Mumrill and I very much doubted whether the news of my impending recovery had greatly pleased him.

Not long after one of her visits there was another knock at the door. I braced myself for a visit from Inspector Tarlow. It was a relief to find Brunel standing on the threshold.

Ockham, who could not wait to inform me that he too had come down with a chill after our escapade, followed him in. The man lied like a cheap watch, but no matter how clumsily delivered I appreciated his attempt at making me feel better.

'Delighted to see you up and about, Phillips. I am sure you have been wondering about this,' said Brunel, as he pulled a sheet of paper from a leather tube and rolled it out on the table. 'Well, in any case, you should have been: it almost cost you your life.'

The drawing was as I remembered it, showing the mechanical cigar fish from every angle, the innards visible through cutaways in what I took to be an iron hull. He was right: although I had tried to distract myself with books, the true meaning of the drawings had rarely been far from my thoughts during my convalescence.

'You know what it is then?'

Brunel beamed triumphantly. 'Oh yes, it did not take long to work that out. Come, take another look.' I edged towards the table. 'I believe that you and Ockham have christened this thing the cigar fish. Well, I could not think of a better description myself.' As if to prove the point he rolled a fresh cigar on to the drawing, where it came to rest alongside the elevation of its mechanical counterpart. 'The screw obviously means it is designed to travel through water.' He snatched up the cigar and used it as a pointer, first to indicate the propeller attached to the tapered end of the device and then moving on to the interior. 'Here is the drive shaft, the compression system, and here, most importantly of all, even if I say so myself, is the housing for the engine – my engine.' He paused for a moment to allow the last word to sink in.

'You mean the heart?' I asked.

'Although I think he originally had in mind the gaz engine he then realized that the heart may serve his purpose even better.'

'I don't quite follow.'

Brunel put a hand to his chest. 'What is it your heart does, doctor?'

'Pumps blood, of course, which in turn carries oxygen around the body.'

'And that's just what we're looking at here.' His hand travelled from his chest to sit palm down on the drawing. 'The mechanical heart will push compressed gases through a series of copper pipes after they have been released into the compression chamber here.' Brunel pointed to a chamber located some distance from where the heart would be mounted. 'Still under pressure the gas will push against the pistons, which in turn will rotate the crankshaft. Some small modification may be required but the principle is sound. The multiple heart valves will not only push the gas along but also recompress gas returned through the system. It is ideal for the purpose because, unlike a steam engine, it does not require fire or produce fumes, which means that it does not need a boiler or an exhaust, and that means it can operate in a sealed unit, without requiring the funnels common to surface vessels.'

'Then it travels underwater?'

Brunel slapped the drawing. 'There you have it in one, my friend. This is a submersible, an underwater boat. Or, if you like, a cigar fish.'

'But this thing is surely far too small to carry people.' I glanced over at Ockham, who had first pointed this out in Russell's office.

The cigar was dragged across the paper to the beast's pointed snout. 'It is not meant to. Look here. The bow is stuffed full of explosives, and there, that small button on the nose is a detonator, positioned so as to set off the charge when it strikes its target.'

'A bomb?'

'Not quite,' he countered. 'A torpedo – a device for sinking ships.'

'Then Wilkie was killed for a weapon?'

'This is more than just a weapon, this contraption has the potential to revolutionize maritime warfare.'

'How?'

'Before Russell came up with this little monster, the torpedo was nothing more than an explosive charge attached to the end of a boom, just a pole sticking out in front of a boat. The boat steams up to the ship and the torpedo is pushed against the hull, below the waterline, where it will do most damage. The charge is driven into the wooden hull using a spike and the boat sails away leaving the torpedo behind. Then it explodes and tears a hole below the waterline.'

'It all sounds very haphazard.'

'Not to say suicidal. They are more likely to kill the operator than sink the enemy ship. And how do you attach it to an iron hull? You can hardly drive a spike in. That's where this thing comes in. You launch it into the water, from a boat or even a shore battery, and it travels unseen below the surface of the water. Then bang! It hits the ship below the waterline.'

'But it can only work with your engine. That's why Russell and his cronies are so keen to get hold of it.'

Brunel slammed his fist on to the table. 'Over my dead body,' he announced. 'Don't get me wrong, gentlemen – I'm no pacifist, I've designed guns, for pity's sake – but after spending all these years building the *Great Eastern* I'll be damned if I'm going to see my device used in a machine with no other purpose than to sink ships!'

Ockham tugged the drawing towards his side of the table. 'I would imagine Russell has tried everything to replicate the design, but never having access to detailed plans he has decided to wait around for Brunel to finish with his own.'

'But we managed to get hold of his design for the torpedo – why can't he do the same thing?'

'There are no plans!' scoffed Brunel, 'just a few rough sketches, and Russell knows that.' The cigar bent close to snapping as he jabbed it against the side of his head. 'I built it up here.'

'But what about the plans you gave to Wilkie?' I asked.

'They were specific to the parts he built, and would make no sense to anyone without an overall idea of how the thing fits together. The same goes for the various other bits I commissioned. Ockham and myself have manufactured the remaining parts.'

'You certainly haven't made things easy for Russell, but what if he doesn't give up, what are you going to do then?'

Brunel looked down at the drawing for a while and then glanced up at Ockham before giving his answer. 'Nothing.'

'I don't understand. Surely we now have no option but to confront the man?'

Brunel shook his head. 'Russell is fully engaged with the fitting out of the ship. Difficult as our relationship is I cannot afford to have him distracted from the task, not now. I must see the ship through to completion. As long as we carry on as though the heart is far from finished, perhaps even abandoned altogether, then Russell will concentrate on the ship. By the time we have finished work on our little project and Russell goes to make his move I will already have taken the necessary action to forever prevent it falling into his hands.'

Fatigued, Brunel planted himself on one of the dining chairs. Plainly still a sick man, he knew that his time was short and I had little doubt that his obsession with the mechanical heart was in part driven by this sense of looming mortality.

'What do you think, doctor?' asked Ockham.

'I agree – at least I think I agree. The strategy seems to have worked thus far and as you say we would appear to have nothing to gain from confrontation. But I would like to straighten out one little detail.'

'Which one would that be?' asked Brunel.

'Just what you intend to do when Russell makes his move – what is this necessary action?'

'You will know when the time comes, my friend,' was all he said, and when he looked up his firm expression was enough to dissuade me from pushing the matter further.

'So, gentlemen, we carry on as normal,' said Ockham briskly, leaning over the table and rolling up the drawing.

I for one doubted whether anything would ever be normal again.

The next morning, feeling a little out of sorts but relieved that my illness-imposed house arrest had come to an end, I went to work. Pneumonia had come close to killing me but now I was eager to return to the fray, but only after I had thanked Florence for her ministrations. 'It was nothing,' she said. I kissed her anyway.

After my solitary confinement the operating theatre seemed livelier than ever, the bustling mass of students threatening to spill from the stands and swamp myself and the patient.

Brodie found me in my office, and I could think of only one or two previous occasions when he had gone to such trouble, both of them to admonish me for one or other oversight. This time, however, he wished only to welcome my return.

I took the opportunity to question him about Brunel's condition. There was a time when the old man would have scowled at my impudence and rebuffed me with the stock response that his patient's health was no concern of mine. But now, willing to talk, I sensed in him a desire to unburden himself of troublesome knowledge.

'If you must know,' he said, at last signalling an end to the secrecy, 'he has Bright's disease, and the news, I am afraid, is not good. His condition is well advanced, the kidneys much inflamed.'

'That would explain a lot. His face appeared swollen the last time I saw him. I assume his urine is coloured?'

Brodie nodded. 'I fear there is little more I can do for him,' he said, and then after a brief pause, 'I am sure the condition has been exacerbated by the extremes to which he has exposed his body over the years. Too much standing about in the cold and damp has done him no good at all.'

'There can be no denying he is a stubborn sort.'

'I just wish he would accept my diagnosis, but with that man nothing is straightforward – it has to be something more dramatic, something more in keeping with his epic vision of the world. He seems to be of the opinion that there is a physical connection between his creations and his health. It's almost as though he thinks they are in some way debilitating him.'

'But they are,' I said, recalling the newspaper cuttings. 'He's had so many close shaves in the past; it's a wonder they haven't killed him already. He was almost drowned in the Thames Tunnel and then narrowly escaped being burnt to death on one of his ships. I even read that he almost fell from the big bridge at Clifton. It's a wonder the man has lived so long.'

My observations seemed to be of some small comfort to Brodie, 'I can see your point,' he said. 'The man is more than a little reckless when it comes to his own safety.'

'How long do you think he has left?' I asked, bringing us back to a firmer medical footing.

'Perhaps a year or two, but only if he slows himself down. He seems set on driving himself into the grave with all possible speed.'

'With his smokestack fuming.'

Brodie smiled sadly. 'Yes, he would do well to stop with the cigars, but I have given up trying to tell him.' Perhaps this was why the old doctor had chosen to confide in me. Perhaps he felt I had some influence over Brunel, that I was in a position to offer advice that would be heeded. It was not the first time the great Sir Benjamin Brodie had been wrong.

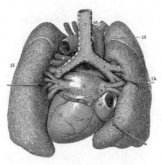

## 26

A hospital never really sleeps – there is always some poor soul crying out in the dark or an emergency intake requiring attendance – but at night the place does take on a more rested countenance. It was some time since I had been required to serve on a nightshift – one of the privileges afforded a teaching surgeon – and apart from the duty doctor the darkened wards were left to the nurses, who under Florence's watchful eye had of late had to learn to do without the benefit of their own, illicit slumbers. But I was no stranger to the place after dark, as it was the only time I could concentrate on my paperwork without fear of interruption. The twilight hours also provided the opportunity to catch up on my journal, which had come as something of a comfort of late as it allowed me to give a semblance of order to thoughts so badly confused by the incredible events that at times seemed to punctuate my days with a regularity matched only by breakfast and dinner in those of others. Nor was tonight to prove any exception, for as I was leaving my office, having spent at least two hours hunched over my desk, the sound of activity coming from the preparation room caught my attention. Aside from myself, only William and some of the other surgeons had any business being in there and given the hour there seemed little reason to think that any of them were still around.

Opening the door from the theatre just a crack, I could see

nothing in the darkened preparation room, other that is than the back door which let out on to the yard, which from the diffuse glow of gaslight from the street beyond I could see was wide open. Rather than encounter a possible intruder in the confined space of the room or the yard I retraced my steps out of the theatre and headed for the front door, though not before stopping off at my office to retrieve my revolver from the desk drawer. It did not occur to me to alert the porter in the gatehouse to my concerns; in any case he was as usual asleep in his chair with his feet propped on the stove. Outside, I turned to my left and hurried down a narrow lane which ran alongside the hospital and then, pausing at the corner, I looked cautiously down the street which led behind the building and on to which the gates of the yard opened. A horse and trap stood just outside them – the driver for the time being out of sight. But then a figure appeared, his hunched form obscured by what seemed to be a duffel bag slung over the leading shoulder. The bag was dropped unceremoniously into the trap and the man stood upright. Even from this distance and in the weak light cast by the street lamps there could be no mistaking William, who after making some adjustment at the back of the trap disappeared again through the yard gates. Relieved that this was not another visitation by my unwanted house guests of some weeks past but nonetheless puzzled by William's actions, I left the cover of the lane and strode towards the vehicle. Just as I drew alongside, William reappeared but as he was pulling the gate closed with his back to me he didn't see me until he turned around, by which time I was positioned at the rear of the trap.

His jaw almost hit the pavement. 'Dr Phillips! Good God, sir, you fair put the fear of God into me there!'

'Doing a little overtime, William?'

He risked a guilty look towards the trap as though seeking a credible answer. 'Well, sir, you see, I was just collecting some bits and pieces from the store. Been meaning to have a clear-out for a while but couldn't lay my hands on any transport.' He gestured at the trap. 'Got this for the night so thought I'd take advantage.'

'Ah yes, taking advantage. A bit of a speciality of yours, eh,

William?' He blanched and, without waiting for him to reply, I turned my attention to what would undoubtedly turn out to be contraband. Only then did I realize that what I had seen him with was not a bag but something wrapped in a canvas sheet. I unfurled a corner to encounter a pair of feet. 'What the hell –?'

'It's just . . . just part of our surplus stock, sir,' William spluttered.

By now I was disentangling the sheet from the rest of the corpse. It was the body of a middle-aged woman who had not been long dead. 'Since when,' I snapped, 'have we had more cadavers than we can use? Especially ones as fresh as this. There I am in theatre cutting them down to the very bones, only to find you shipping bodies out of the hospital at night!'

William looked nervously up and down the street, no doubt concerned that my angry words would be overheard, but I was beyond caring. 'How long have you been doing this?'

He hunched his shoulders like a small boy caught scrumping apples. 'Not sure, a while I suppose. But, doctor, there 'aven't been many, only a dozen or so.'

'A dozen! My God, man. Your pilfering is the reason we've been suffering shortages! Where are you taking her?'

'To . . . to a customer.'

'So you're in retail now, are you?'

'It's not a regular thing, sir. Just every now and again.'

I came close to hitting the old thief but settled for throwing the sheet back over the body. 'Who is this . . . this customer?'

'Don't know – just a bloke I met in a pub. We got talkin' and when he finds out what I do for a livin' he offers to take the odd stiff off my 'ands. Never seen 'im since. He lets the barkeep know when a delivery's required and I take it from there. Deliver 'em to an old fisherman's shack down at Millwall, take the money that's waiting and off I trot. No questions asked.'

'So I don't suppose you asked him why he wants them?'

William shook his head.

His response was unsatisfactory but nonetheless my rage had subsided somewhat. 'Get her back inside, for God's sake. You're shutting up shop.'

He made to lift the bundle from the trap but stopped when I gripped his arm.

'Wait. Leave her be. You're taking her along as planned and me with you.'

'But . . .'

'But nothing. Get going or I'll have you down at the police station on a charge of bodysnatching.'

Without another word he checked that his payload was secure and then climbed up on to the seat, where I joined him. A flick of the switch and we were off, trotting along through the London night like a pair of covert undertakers at the reins of our makeshift hearse.

Half an hour later and we were on the Isle of Dogs, where for a heart-stopping few minutes it looked as though we were heading for Russell's yard, but still some distance away from it, we turned off the Ferry Road and on to a rough track leading to the riverside.

'That's the hut up ahead,' said William, breaking a silence which had lasted our entire journey.

'Right then. Let me off here. Deliver the body as planned and then leave as you normally would.'

'But, sir. This is no place for you to be wandering around at night.'

I jumped down. 'Thank you for your concern, William, but it's a little late in the day for that. Now be on your way.'

William nodded and the trap continued on. I concealed myself in a nearby ditch, from where I intended to observe the proceedings. With his gruesome cargo delivered, William turned the cart around and slowly negotiated the way back along the pock-marked track.

Now alone, I remained in the ditch, where black water was already seeping into my shoes. Up on the river wall, a mill stood in cruciform silhouette, still and silent, the tattered sails straining against the breeze but frozen in place like the hands of a broken clock. Other than the wind scything through the marsh grass there was not a sound to be heard, nor any light to be seen. At night the island, which away from the yards and the road was still dominated by desolate marshland, seemed a more godforsaken place than ever.

Every now and again the wind picked up and as if it were a wounded dog let out a dreadful howl – a sound which could easily be mistaken for the ghostly bark of Edward III's abandoned greyhounds, which some said gave the place its name.

The prospect of a long vigil did little to lift my rapidly plummeting spirits, but then, just as I began to warm to the idea of abandoning my watch, a muted chink of light appeared at the base of the mill tower. It was impossible to make out details but someone had definitely slid out through the partially opened door. Clambering out of the ditch, I adopted an uncomfortable crouch in the hope of seeing better through the billowing grass.

Only when the solitary figure moved out beyond the dark mass of the mill and the wall did it become at all visible. Whoever it was they were certain of their footing for no lamp had been brought along to illuminate the short walk to the shack. A few minutes later the return trip was underway, the corpse just distinguishable as a bulk thrown, again like a duffel bag, across one shoulder. The figure disappeared at the foot of the wall and then a few moments later there was another brief emission of light as the door was opened and the figure disappeared back inside.

Keeping low, I made my way forward, pushing the grass aside with my hands. Stopping briefly at the shack, where the absence of the cadaver confirmed my observations, I groped my way to the foot of the wall, where rather than risk the stairs I scrambled up the sloping side of the clay bank. Reaching the summit, I felt the full force of the wind and fought against it to reach the side of the mill, its wooden wall clinkered like the hull of a boat. The sails rose above me, their torn fabric flapping against the ladder-like frames. Being in no mood for another climb I weighed up the options. To my left was the small wooden landing where the steps up the landward side of the river wall met with the front door, while to the right there seemed to be little other than the far side of the wall and the river beyond. The great clay bank was wide, though, and there was a footpath allowing access to the back of the tower.

The high sides of the mill seemed to be entirely unbroken by windows and so I walked around the building looking for an alternative means of access – though if all else failed I had deter-mined to enter through the front door, no matter what awaited me on the other side. To my relief I found an opening at waist-height at the back of the building, from where it would be possible to look out over the river from inside. There was no glass in the window, just a patch of canvas, and it took little effort to pull back a corner and peek inside. It was dark as pitch, which was good, as it suggested a different room to the one which had spilled light through the opening door. I ripped the canvas entirely away and feet first pushed my way through the hole, confident that the wind would mask any noise.

I stood stock still for a minute or two in what at first appeared to be absolute darkness, hoping that my eyes would accustom themselves even more so than they had outside. Cocking my head, I listened for any sound from within. Nothing. There was now some trace of light, though, coming from the opposite wall of the small room. Keeping my back against the wall, I inched my way towards it, at one point having to negotiate my way around a narrow, iron-framed bed. The light was coming through cracks in a door, which offered a very limited view into the illuminated space beyond. Whoever I had seen outside was moving around, but the cracks were not well placed and for all I knew there could be three or four people there.

The only way to get a better view was to open the door. I did not relish the prospect but surprise would be on my side and the weight of the pistol in my pocket provided an extra measure of resolve. Finding nothing by way of a handle, I applied some pressure to the door, which even with the slightest of touches began to give way. Given the mill's dilapidated condition, I doubted that the hinges had seen much oil of late. Keen to remain hidden for as long as possible, I listened out for any sound that might serve to mask the inevitable squeak when the door was pushed open. For a long time I could hear nothing, just a shuffling sound and the periodic creak of a floorboard. But then metal hit metal. It was a familiar sound and one that I knew would not last long.

With a shove the door gave, creaking open three or four inches.

The hammering stopped but there was nothing to suggest that the movement had been noticed. With pistol in hand I peered into the room. A man stood with his back to me, a long coat covering his shoulders and reaching almost to the floor. He stood next to a table, intent on the body of the woman that lay upon it. Her head lay closest to me, slightly canted back, with the chin pointing upward and mouth slightly agape. The man loomed over her, working intently on some part of the torso. The noise had come from a small hammer and chisel, tools which I had used many a time to crack open the ribcage of a cadaver. He worked quickly, trading his hammer for a blade, and very soon was lifting the inert heart from the gaping hole in the woman's chest. My gun hand began to shake as the horrific reality of the situation dawned on me. There had been no murders, no mass slaughter of prostitutes. No, the truth lay before me in the form of the miserable carcass stretched out on the table. The bodies pulled from the river had been dead long before their hearts and lungs had been cut out. Inspector Tarlow had been on a wild-goose chase all along, and yapping at my heels for most of the way. I had been suspected of committing murders of the cruellest sort simply because the lunatic now standing before me had chosen to spend his evenings carving up stolen cadavers in a draughty old windmill.

I stepped from my hiding-place and, with the removed organ delivered into a metal bowl, the miller-surgeon turned back to the table.

Ockham didn't flinch for an instant. 'Now, doctor, what brings you out on such an inclement night?'

Words did not come easily, for my mouth had dried in response to the macabre scene being played out before me. 'You can thank William for that. He gave me a lift along with . . .' I gestured with the pistol '. . . along with your patient. Are you insane? What the hell are you doing?'

'I thought that would be obvious, especially to you, doctor.'

'Don't even try to compare this . . . this butchery to my work.'

'I lack your skill, I know, doctor, but please try to be civil. We all have to start somewhere.'

'That's surely the point. We are not all surgeons, Ockham. You have no right . . . this is criminal!'

'I don't see how. This body was destined to go under the knife. Whether yours or mine, I don't see the difference.'

'You can explain that to the police. Do you know they are looking for a mass murderer who cuts the heart and lungs out of his victims?'

'I have seen them sniffing around the river. Most of the time the current takes the corpses under and they are never seen again but sometimes they resurface and get washed up. Of late I have discovered that packing the chest cavity with lead works very effectively.'

So that was why the murders appeared to have stopped.

'My God, man, how many have there been?'

'Fifteen, twenty. I lost count long ago. Your man William has provided an invaluable service, to me and to mankind.'

So much for William's claim of around a dozen. 'The police have been hounding me over this. They think I'm a killer!'

Ockham looked up, his face a picture of surprise. 'I had no idea. That is regrettable, most regrettable, and for that I apologize. Can I assume that as you are still at liberty their suspicions have not been substantiated?'

This was not the time to regale him with Tarlow's accursed list. 'For now, but this . . . whatever it is has got to stop.'

Ockham seemed to notice the gun for the first time and it caused him to raise a critical eyebrow.

'Am I going to need this?'

He shook his head.

Placing the weapon at the foot of the table, I walked round the other side. 'I trust we are alone?'

He nodded and I watched with dumbstruck fascination as he returned to the rib-lined cavity and began to work on the removal of the lungs. He was clumsy and it was all I could to stop myself from showing him how to do it properly.

'What is all this about, Ockham? What do you mean "the good of mankind"?'

'Why go to the trouble of building a heart and then not put the thing to use. A bit like building a boat and then never putting it in the water, don't you think? But you thought it was just a bauble, didn't you?'

'So you do think you can raise the dead!'

'No, not yet,' he said, his voice tinged with regret. 'We still have challenges to overcome. At present I'm working on a system for connecting the device. And you know what they say, practice makes perfect.'

'But you've only had the heart for a few months; what have you been doing with these bodies all this time?'

He looked up from his work, hands remaining wrist deep in the dead woman's chest. 'There were earlier hearts, but they were only crude prototypes, nothing like the latest design. But now we are close, very close. My thanks to you, Phillips.'

I took a step forward. 'To me?'

Ockham laughed. 'Why, doctor, you didn't think that Brunel invited you into the Lazarus Club just to take the minutes, did you? It was your expertise as a surgeon he was after. Your demonstrations and tutorials gave us new impetus, provided fresh ideas for modifications and refinements to the mechanism.'

Of course I had known that Brunel was primarily interested in my work – he'd told me so himself. Ockham however seemed to be taking me for a dupe. But now unarmed, I chose to ignore his mocking tone and leave the misconception unchallenged. 'Happy to have been of assistance,' I said. After all, it was just one misconception in a head so obviously awash with them.

As it was, however, the arrogance was short-lived. 'But not just to us,' he remarked, his voice now tempered with apprehension. 'I fear those improvements are why Russell's interest in the device was rekindled. I warned Brunel not to make that damned presentation.'

'When I was out of town?'

'I hope you weren't offended by him not waiting for your return.' Ockham didn't strike me as a man sensitive to other people's feelings. Changeable as the wind, I thought, shaking my head in reply. In truth, though, I had been. 'You see,' he continued, 'the man was under great pressure to go overseas, his health being so poor, and I suppose there was no guarantee he would make it back. Being an inveterate show-off, he just couldn't resist it before he left. And as for my work here? Well, just like him I sat in on some of your lectures, but I chose to remain anonymous.'

He returned his attentions to the cadaver but carried on talking as he worked the scalpel. 'You are a talented teacher, Dr Phillips, but there is nothing like hands-on experience – my time in the yard has taught me that. And, besides, with Brodie refusing to take any part it looked as though I would have to carry out the operation when the time came.'

Letting out a satisfied sigh, the amateur surgeon stepped back from the table with the detached lungs cradled in his open palms and placed them in the bowl, draping them over the heart as though he were building a pie.

Having now had time to take in my surroundings, it was apparent that we were standing inside a wooden machine; rising up from the centre of the floor was a heavy axle which like an architectural pillar disappeared into the dimness of space above us. The millstones to which the axle was attached occupied a space beneath our feet. From the cobwebs which spanned many a crevice and corner it was evident that the mill had last seen action some time ago, but when it was in operation the grinding stones were turned by the intermeshing of a series of giant wooden cogs which took up most of the building's interior. Elsewhere, motion would be transferred from the cogs by beams and fly-wheels, which above our heads were connected by a series of leather drive belts. These sticks and stones were of course given life by the motion of the sails outside. Although buffeted by the wind they remained stationary, but the internal workings to which they were connected creaked and vibrated, keen to be moving again.

A flight of open stairs led up to a mezzanine floor which was really nothing more than a wide landing, and from there another flight rose through a hatch in an upper floor. Standing to one side of the lowest flight of stairs was a tall oblong object covered with canvas, looking, I thought, like a cabinet or wardrobe under a protective dustsheet.

'You live here now?' I asked, recalling the bed in the small room through which I had entered.

'It's just somewhere to lay my head. When I'm not busy on the ship I'm usually working here.'

'You said "when the time comes for the operation". What operation?'

He looked up again, his brow still knotted with concentration. 'Now you are here I may as well show you.'

It was only then that I noticed the ragged hole supporting the blood bucket at the foot of the table. 'My God, man, that's my old dissecting table!'

Ockham smiled. 'Waste not want not. I was walking past the hospital one day and saw it sitting in the backyard and offered your man a fair price for it. You clearly had no further use for it.'

'I suppose he threw in a gratis cadaver to go with it?'

Ockham made no reply as he took hold of the canvas covering of the object at the foot of the stairs. With a flourish worthy of a music-hall illusionist the sheet was whipped away to reveal a glass-fronted cabinet constructed from riveted plates of iron.

There was something inside the box, apparently suspended in a murky fluid, and I took a step closer to see more clearly. What I saw, as the submerged blur hardened into a recognizable object, came as a shock even to my jaundiced surgeon's eye. One arm hung straight down along the side of the woman's body and the other was bent at the elbow and folded across the lower torso. The legs were stretched out beneath and, naked as the rest of her, were crossed one in front of the other, the feet turned downward as though with tiptoes she were trying to ground herself on the base of the tank. Strands of long red hair floated above the woman's head and left exposed a face which even in death retained a mask of rare beauty. I peered closer and satisfied myself that I had not been mistaken. There was no doubt about it. It was the body of Ada Lovelace, Ockham's long-deceased mother.

It took me a while to say anything, but when the words finally came I realized that for the first time much of what had gone before now made sense, if sense was a word that could be used in this circumstance.

'Lazarus, I presume?'

Ockham spoke with his face turned away from me, his gaze fixed on the inert form of his beloved mother. 'If it hadn't been for that damned doctor she would have recovered. It was murder, plain bloody murder.'

'But she had cancer. There was surely little hope.'

At this he turned on me, his eyes seemingly magnified through a film of moisture. 'What is done is done. Now it is up to me to make things right, to bring her back.'

I didn't know whether to feel sorry for him or fear him. I could only assume that his reasoning had been impaired by too much opium. But, whatever lay behind his bizarre behaviour, there could be little doubt that Brodie had been right to describe him as 'mad, bad and dangerous to know'.

'You think that putting the device inside her will bring her back? I am sorry for your loss, Ockham, but it's not going to work, not now, not ever.'

'And I am supposed to take the word of a doctor, a virtual colleague of the man who bled her to death?'

'There are bad doctors, I don't deny that, but you cannot blame the death of your mother on the entire medical profession.' My words were heart-felt, for, some time previously, I too had suffered at the hands of a bereaved relative; a husband who held me personally responsible for the unavoidable death of his wife.

Ockham snorted. 'Don't worry, Phillips, I don't. Cutting that murdering quack's throat was catharsis enough. Like her he bled to death, but for him there will be no coming back.'

He wasn't listening. 'Nor, I am afraid, will there be for her. How long is it now since . . . since she died?'

'Almost six years. All that time she's been waiting for me to bring her back.'

'How the hell did you get her in there? Surely there was a funeral?'

'They buried a sheep's carcass. I paid off the undertaker and had this constructed.' He stroked the front of the glass and I half expected the corpse inside to reach out for his hand. 'An apothecary provided the preserving fluid and she's been with me ever since.'

I had seen and heard enough. 'I can't be a part of this,' I blurted. 'You need to do the decent thing and bury her. Forget this fool's errand and get on with your life.'

He wasn't having any of it. 'That's just what Brodie said. But you're different, I can see that.'

'Brodie knows about this?'

'Of course, but he was too fearful of his position. He provided some anatomical advice early on, but he didn't have the stomach for this.'

'And Brunel?'

'His contribution was the device. He works with metal, not flesh.'

I had heard him say something similar. 'But he knew about this?'

'He simply lost interest, that is all. Too many jobs requiring his attention, as usual.'

'Enough Ockham, I've heard enough.' With this I turned and made for the front door.

'But you can't walk out on this now. We're in this together. Tell me you're not intrigued by the device's potential. Tell me the idea doesn't fascinate you!'

'No, Ockham, the only thing that you and I are in together is this damned windmill, and I'm just about to change that.'

I pushed open the front door to find my exit blocked, fittingly enough, by the door man. His pistol was levelled at my head.

'Back inside, please, doctor.'

'What the blazes?' exclaimed Ockham as he reached for the pistol which, in my hurry, I had left on the table.

'Leave it where it lies,' ordered the door man who, satisfied that I had backed off to a safe distance, now had his pistol trained on Ockham.

'How did you find us?' I asked.

'Been watchin' this place fer a while. We knew you'd get together sooner or later. And when yer did we'd be sure to find what we're after.'

I had expected the chair man to have appeared by now. 'Where is your boss?'

'Don't need 'im 'ere to deal with you pair. Can take the thing by mysel', thanks very much.' He pushed the door closed with the heel of his boot and advanced into the room. 'Where is it?'

'Where's what?'

'Don't start playin' games again, doctor. You were lucky when we last met. But I'm in charge now and won't be so sparin'.'

I took a backward glance at Ockham. 'You'd better give him what he's after. He obviously means business.' The man clearly fancied his chances and was taking a solo shot at glory. His superiors would no doubt have something to say about this independent action. But, whether fortunately or not, they weren't here.

He cocked the pistol. 'I won't ask again.'

Ockham pointed up to the next level. 'Up there, in the chest. I'll go and get it.'

'Not so fast,' replied the door man. 'You must be jokin' if you think I'm leavin' you to go up alone an' pull a gun out of there. An' likewise, I'm not leavin' the other down 'ere to cause similar mischief.'

'The man knows his trade,' said an unruffled Ockham.

Our visitor pulled a length of rope from his pocket and threw it to Ockham.

'Tie 'im to the chair,' he ordered.

Ockham removed his coat from the chair and when I was seated began to tie my hands behind it.

'What in God's name have you been doin' in 'ere?' asked the door man, who only now seemed to notice the contents of the room and had a thinly disguised look of horror on his face.

'That, my friend, is a long story,' I replied.

The door man didn't seem interested in hearing stories. 'Good an' tight now. Let me take a look.' He took a pull on the rope where it secured my elbows to the back of the chair and then tugged on the knot around my wrists. Satisfied, he gestured for him to climb the stairs.

As soon as his back was turned I shook loose the razor which Ockham had hidden in my sleeve and, only just managing to avoid cutting my wrist open, tried to bring the blade to bear on the cord. Meanwhile, Ockham climbed the stairs, followed at a safe distance by his escort.

I had at least expected to wait until they were both on the landing before Ockham made his move, but like the door man I was greatly surprised when something fell out of the darkness above and landed with a tremendous thud at the foot of the stairs just behind his back.

The sack of mouldy old flour had been suspended on a rope and released when Ockham pulled a pin from the landing rail just as he laid his hand on it. The door man's distraction was only momentary but it was enough to allow Ockham to turn and kick the pistol from his hand. He then launched himself down the stairs and the two men rolled on the floor punching and tearing at one another, each of them desperate to reach the pistol, which lay not far away.

At last I managed to bring the blade into contact with the rope and with great difficulty was trying to develop a cutting action while holding the blade between just the thumb and forefinger of my right hand. Both men were now on their feet, and Ockham kicked the pistol further out of reach just as the door man was about to make a grab for it. In retaliation he lunged at the viscount, pushing him with dreadful force against the wall, where the small of his back collided with a lever which on impact shifted its position. Ockham had barely recovered when the mill began to grind slowly into life. First there was a whooshing sound high up in the rafters as the sails outside started to turn in the wind. Then the cogs started to mesh against one another and the axle to revolve. The movement was not a smooth one, with the cogs stopping and starting and the axle emitting a dreadful squeal – the neglected mechanism was in desperate need of an overhaul and threatened to fall apart at any moment.

The life-and-death struggle between the two men continued, both of them apparently oblivious to the moving parts around them. The blade was biting deep now and so I pulled my wrists apart, hoping to snap the remaining few strands. As the rope dug further into my wrists I watched in disbelief as the iron tank containing Ockham's mother began to shudder and shake. The fluid inside looked to be boiling and to my amazement the body floating within had begun to move, the arms now flexing away from the torso and the feet gently kicking against the glass panel. My God, I thought, she's coming to life. Ockham had somehow managed to harness the movement of the windmill to give her life!

Then the real reason for the agitation of the tank became apparent. The canvas which Ockham had pulled from the front of the tank had been tossed carelessly aside and landed on the teeth of one of the cogs. The turning of the gear was now pulling the canvas into the machine and as the tank was standing on part of that same sheet, probably after being carried into the mill entirely wrapped in it, so its movement was causing it to shiver and shake. As more canvas was eaten up so the tank began to rock, tipping backward and forward and now threatening to topple over.

I gave up trying to snap the cord and returned to cutting. For a moment I closed my eyes in concentration, and opened them again just in time to see the iron casket rock one last time and then tip irretrievably forward. 'The tank!' I cried, but Ockham was in no position to do anything, as he was still grappling with his foe.

There was a terrifying crash as the front of the tank impacted against the corner of the table, the glass shattering and the fluid gushing out to cover the floor and soak the bodies of the two men who writhed upon it.

'No!' cried Ockham, on seeing what had happened. Thrown into a rage by the sight of his mother's shattered sarcophagus, he found new strength and for the last time pushed his adversary to the ground. Ockham let go of the door man, who slipped in the fluid as he tried to regain his feet, and before he could make another attempt his opponent was upon him, wading into him with a heavy piece of timber.

Still bound to the chair, I was powerless to intervene. 'No, Ockham! Don't kill him! We need him alive! He has to talk!'

But Ockham was in a frenzy. 'Look what you've done!' he snarled as he continued to hit the prostrate man.

At last my bonds gave way and I lurched forward from the chair, sliding across the room as I stepped into the foul-smelling pool of alcohol. 'Stop it, Ockham! Stop!'

I grabbed hold of his arm as he reached up to deliver another blow, but it was too late. The man was clearly dead, his mashed brains by now exposed through the side of his skull.

With my hand still holding his wrist, Ockham turned on me, his eyes ablaze with animal-like rage. I feared a fight but the humanity slowly returned and, once calmed, he dropped the club and lurched towards the tank, which was now propped at an angle against the table. The glass had not entirely shattered, but a large portion had broken away where it had been pierced by the sharp corner of the table. A limp arm hung from the tank, the fingers just brushing the wet floor beneath. Even as I watched, the flesh, which at first had been ivory-white, began to turn black as necrosis took hold. The long-delayed stench of decay mixed with the alcohol fumes and created a nauseating miasma, which if we didn't leave the building would soon overcome the pair of us.

'The tank, we've got to mend the tank!' blubbered Ockham as he reached down to lift his mother's arm back inside.

'It's no use. She's gone, Ockham. Your mother's dead,' I said, as though it had been the breaking of the tank which had killed her. I took a hold of his shivering shoulder and made to pull him away. 'Leave her, man, we've got to get out of here.'

All of a sudden he seemed to need no encouragement and staggered back into me. 'She's rotten! My God, Phillips, she's rotten!'

At last the truth had dawned. 'I know,' I said. 'You need to bury your dead, to let your mother rest in peace.'

Ockham looked lost, a small boy again. 'She was beautiful, Phillips, you saw that, didn't you?'

I tried not to look at the blackened mass of flesh which hung from the shattered sarcophagus. A damp cushion of red hair was all that remained of her. 'She was very beautiful. That's how you will always remember her.'

'All I wanted to do was bring her back. She meant the world to me, Phillips.' He looked not at his mother but at the badly dissected cadaver. 'She may have been somebody's mother too. I wouldn't have wished her any harm, doctor, not in life.'

'I lost my mother too, Ockham, and recently my father. I know how hard it can be,' I said, desperate to calm him and get us both away from this dreadful place. Ockham's opium habit had done nothing but feed his insane delusions, but had it been available I would gladly have administered it there and then as a sedative. I had learned from Babbage that Ada had been prescribed a similar treatment and as a result became a slave to the fuddling powers of laudanum. The diagnosis was clear: the man was as dependent on the physical presence of his mother as he was on any drug and severing the connection between them would require as much skill as any surgical operation. Just minutes ago I had been determined to hand him over to the police, explain all and clear my name, but now, in the cold light of death and destruction, things seemed more complicated. Surrendering the pitiful creature he had become to Tarlow would do nothing to help his dangerous condition and the ensuing investigation would inevitably drag Brunel and the others into the affair. Just as importantly, the scandal might create a smokescreen behind which Wilkie's killers could escape justice. There had to be another way.

Ockham wiped a sleeve over his eyes and, lifting a storm lamp from a hook on the wall, made to light it. 'Leave her to me.'

My mind made up, I took the door man's body by the shoulders and began to drag him towards the door.

'What are you doing?' enquired Ockham, who to my relief seemed more composed and indeed was looking at me as though I were the madman.

'We need him. Help me, I will explain later.'

Ockham put down the lamp and helped me drag the body outside, where we dropped it on to the ground from the top of the wall. He went to re-enter the mill and I shouted after him, 'Get me some of your clothes, a full set. Old clothes, nothing fancy.'

After no more than a minute Ockham was back outside, a bundle under his arm. With him steering our course we hurried through the long grass towards the yard, half carrying and half dragging the corpse. Behind us the windmill began to glow as the lamp ignited the spilt alcohol. Within moments the old building was engulfed in fire. Smoke billowed skyward and beneath it the orange flames consumed the wooden tower which had become Ada Lovelace's funeral pyre; a beacon warning of dangers to come.

*The Times* June 18 1858

On the night of 16 June, a woman, believed to be a prostitute, was attacked by a man wielding a razor in the Limehouse area of the city. The victim put up a spirited resistance in the face of a frenzied assault, and in the struggle her assailant lost his footing and fell to his death down a steep flight of steps. Inspector Tarlow of the Metropolitan Police has told this newspaper that he believes the dead maniac to have been responsible for the brutal murders of no fewer than eight women in the city over the past twelve months or more. The razor recovered from the scene appears to have been the same weapon used to commit an undisclosed series of disfigurements prior to the disposal of the bodies in the Thames. It would appear that despite several slashes being inflicted against the woman's torso the stays of her corset prevented the blade from penetrating her flesh. The Inspector expressed his satisfaction that the case was now closed. He refused to release the identity of the woman or attacker, and it would appear that the latter remains unknown even to the police.

Clare had been a real sport, especially when it came to attracting the attention of the police; not something she would normally choose to do. After leaving the windmill I had waited in the long grass with the corpse while Ockham laid his hands on a covered wagon and a bucket of water at the yard, where the burning mill was beginning to attract attention. While driving us into town he managed to raise a smile when he told me that the watchmen

283

thought he intended to fight the inferno with the bucket of water, but otherwise there was no disguising his anguish over the incident with his mother. I remained in the back, stripping off alcohol-soaked clothes and washing dead flesh. Only when I was satisfied that any trace of the pungent fluid had been removed was the door man's corpse attired in the funeral suit provided by Ockham.

We arrived at Kate Hamilton's place just in time to prevent Clare from entering into an assignation with a nervous-looking gentleman who, I suggested, would be much happier at home with his wife and children. Hurrying her from the premises, I told her only that the dead man in the back of the wagon had been no good in life and that she could help me get out of some serious trouble. The information was enough to enlist the dear girl's assistance, though on the condition that I pay over the odds for her lost earnings. At my instruction Ockham tipped the still-limp body over a set of steps near the embankment. After a quick inspection, during which I rearranged an awkwardly twisted leg, I was pleased to report that the fatal injuries inflicted at the mill would appear to the police to have resulted from this fall. It was Clare's idea to slash the bodice of her dress for added realism, after which we left the razor on the ground for the police to find. It was a masterstroke, and the cost of a new dress would be a cheap price to pay for explaining away the door man's death while at the same time putting an end to Tarlow's search for a murderer who didn't exist, a search which had come dangerously close to my own front door. With the scene set I kissed my sometime concubine goodnight and promised to see her soon. Ockham and I had no sooner rounded the corner when she let out a bloodcurdling scream. The girl was a born actress, of that there could be no doubt.

Tarlow appeared at the hospital the next day, his face displaying all the signs of having been up for most of the night. After I had provided him with a seat in my office he proceeded to tell me about the attack on the prostitute, during which the maniac had told her he was going to cut out her heart. The inspector guessed that the woman was healthier and stronger than his previous victims and so had put up a vigorous fight which ended with him crashing down the stone steps to his death.

'Congratulations, inspector, it would appear that you have your man. I trust that this brings an end to your investigation?'

'Not quite, doctor, there is something which doesn't quite fit.'

'What is that?'

'The prostitute involved in the attack – she was one of the women I questioned at Kate Hamilton's establishment.'

The terrier had smelled a rat. 'Is there a problem with that, inspector?'

'You were hiding under her bed when I questioned her.'

Dashing to the door, I picked up my hat and coat as if to leave. 'Clare! My God! You're sure she's all right? I must see her.'

Tarlow leant back in his chair and stopped me with an out-stretched arm. 'She's fine, doctor, and as I said, a very strong young woman. Now, sit down, please, we are not yet finished.'

Somewhat begrudgingly I returned to my seat, draping the coat across my knees.

'Now, doctor,' continued Tarlow, once again pulling out his dreaded notebook. 'Does it not strike you as a little strange that the woman who manages to despatch the man apparently responsible for a series of murders for which you were – and let us not mix words here – for which you were a suspect, just happens to share an intimate relationship with you, however professional that might be?'

I took a few moments to ponder the implications of this, my face a picture of puzzlement and confusion. 'I suppose it does seem a little bit of a coincidence.' And one that occurred to me only after the performance with Clare had been played out. 'Are you suggesting that I had a hand to play in this? That I somehow staged the attack? That's preposterous!'

'I am sure my superiors will think so too – unless of course I can gather enough evidence to convince them otherwise.'

'Who is the dead man? Surely if you know that you must be able to draw some sort of firm conclusion. Am I to be hounded for ever over this matter?'

'Unfortunately, we have not been able to identify the gentleman. I was wondering whether you may be able to assist us there.'

'You want me to examine his body? Am I to be trusted with such a task?'

'I have always found your assistance most helpful, doctor.'

'I am sure you have,' I replied bitterly. 'Now, where is this body?'

Tarlow stood up. 'It's in the backyard. Shall we?'

The inspector instructed the constable waiting by the wagon to open up the rear flap.

'If you wouldn't mind, doctor,' he said, gesturing for me to step forward and take a look.

Lifting the sheet, I peered for some moments into the face of the man who not long before had been bludgeoned to death just feet away from me. Grasping the chin, I turned the face towards me. 'This man is familiar. I know this man, inspector!' I turned and looked aghast at the policeman. 'His name is Edward Fisher. His wife was a patient of mine. She had cancer and died on the operating table, under my knife. It wasn't my fault, she was beyond help.'

'How long ago was this?'

'About two years. I may still have the records in my office. He went berserk, blamed me for her death and attacked me in my own office. I only managed to fight him off with help from my assistant, William. Then he swore he would make me suffer, to wish I had never been born. That was the last I saw of him. Grief affects people in all sorts of ways, I suppose.'

'That would certainly explain his attack on your lady friend. He may have regarded her, if you don't mind me saying, as the equivalent of your wife. An eye for an eye and all that.'

'But what about the other murders? Were they part of his . . . his revenge?'

'Looks like he was trying to put you in the frame, doesn't it? The man was obviously insane. Perhaps he was just living out some sort of dreadful fantasy. We'll never know.'

'So you think it was him?'

Tarlow pulled the sheet back across the man's face. 'Time will tell, won't it, doctor? If there are no more murders, then yes, it looks like we have our man.'

'What about William, do you want to question him? And the records? I could see if I could find them.' And indeed I could have done, for it was all true. Ockham was not the only man to have blamed a loved one's death on her doctor. I had put the incident behind me, but not surprisingly the memory had resurfaced with the viscount's confession. Unpleasant as it had been, however, there were certain factors about the case which I now hoped would operate in my favour. After his wife's death and his attack on me Edward Fisher had moved out of town to make a new life. So desperate had he been to make a fresh start that he even took another name, but his demons still found him and – as I later learned from a colleague – he ended up hanging himself.

The inspector smiled, his expression lightened by a shared relief as the dangerous game we had played for so long drew to an end. 'No, doctor, that won't be necessary. I just don't like loose ends, that's all, and you have tied them up very nicely.'

Only then did I recall that he had visited the hospital while I had been ill. 'What did you want to see me about?' I asked after reminding him of the fact.

'Oh, just the usual – we had pulled another body from the river. Very fresh this time, couldn't have been dead for more than a couple of days at most. I arrived to discover you had been in bed with a high fever for more than a week.'

The penny dropped. 'And you realized it couldn't have been me.'

'I crossed you off my list that very day.'

'So I've been in the clear for weeks?' I said, trying hard not to sound crestfallen on learning that my risky charade had been entirely unnecessary.

Tarlow nodded and gave what I suspected to be a knowing smile. 'My apologies for all the discomfort my investigation has caused you. Just be careful who you kill on the operating table next time.'

'I'm afraid it's one of the perils of the job, inspector.'

## 27

Whether he had been convinced by my story about the door man's body or not, the knowledge that Tarlow was no longer on my back did much to renew flagging spirits, but the same could not be said of Brunel. When I next caught up with him, sometime towards the end of July, he looked to have aged radically. His shoulders were hunched and the hair had all but disappeared from his head, while yellowing jowls hung heavily at the sides of his face.

'That ship is sucking the life from you, Isambard.'

He peered at me with his heavy-lidded eyes and growled, 'If Russell did things as I asked then I would not need to spend nearly so long with the task.'

I was sitting in his office, having been summoned there by the customary note. Ockham was late but arrived with fresh news. 'The chief engineer has just tested the paddle engines. All seems to be well.'

Expecting this information to please our host, it was a shock to see him explode with rage. 'What? Russell has run those engines without me on board! I left specific instructions that I was to be there to witness their first run. My God, I'll have that Glaswegian bastard's hide for this!'

Ockham tried to calm the situation. 'I believe it was Dickson who gave the order.'

For a moment I thought Brunel was going to turn his anger

on Ockham, the man who for several years had been a strange combination of apprentice and patron. But there was to be no distracting him from pouring scorn on the man he now clearly regarded as his nemesis. 'And who is Dickson's employer?' he raged. 'Answer me that? Who pulls his strings?' There was silence. 'Russell, that's who. He's behind this . . . this mutiny!'

'So has the ship sailed?' I asked, looking to Ockham for an answer.

He shook his head. 'Dickson just turned the engines over to check everything was operating smoothly. She didn't move an inch; the drive to the paddle wheels was disconnected.'

This all seemed like a bit of a storm in a teacup. Like Ockham, my main concern was to calm the situation, as Brunel could ill afford this kind of strain. But the engineer was not to be reasoned with. 'I'm going to call my carriage and get down there. I'll show Russell who's boss. I've had him dismissed before now and I will do it again.'

Ockham was by now clearly wishing he had kept his mouth shut. 'Isambard, you know you need him to finish the job; we agreed that. And anyway, he's not there.'

'Not there?' said Brunel, dropping back into his seat.

'He isn't there now and, before you blow a gasket, he wasn't there when it happened. It was just Dickson. He had been working on the valves all day. On the improvements you suggested. He wanted to check them out, that's all. He was pleased with the result and said I was to pass on his thanks to you.'

'Really?' said Brunel, biting off the end of a fresh cigar and spitting the tip on to the floor beside him. As I had expected, an earlier attempt to persuade him to cut down on his intake had fallen on deaf ears. But he was calmer now. 'I should have designed those damned engines from the very start.'

The fire of Brunel's rage had been extinguished but Ockham continued to pour water on the smoking embers. 'Which brings me to this,' he said, placing a polished box on the desk. 'I put the finishing touches to it last night, just as you asked.'

Brunel brightened. He dragged the box towards him and patted the lid before pushing it open and lifting out its contents. The weighty mass of the heart sat in his cupped hands, the combination of polished metals giving it more than ever the appearance of a splendid jewel. He looked up at me. 'And what do you think of this, doctor?'

Beautiful as it was, my layman's interest in the mechanics of the thing outweighed my appreciation of its aesthetic appeal. 'Can I take a closer look?'

Brunel rose to his feet and walked around to join us at the front of the desk, carrying the heart before him. He nodded towards the stove in the corner. 'Fetch that cloth over.'

Ockham spread the rag out on the desk and stepped back as Brunel set the object gently down on the makeshift cushion. The outer casing was adorned with a series of copper outlets and valves, which stood in for the main arterial connections of the vena cava, aorta and pulmonary artery. Brunel flicked a small catch and the casing opened to reveal the chambers inside, formed from the stainless-steel plates which had been created by Wilkie's skilful hands. I could not resist brushing my fingertips along the polished surface. To my surprise the cold metal gave ever so slightly under my touch. Afraid that I might have broken something, I snatched my hand away.

'Don't worry,' said Brunel. 'It won't bite you. Watch this.' He snapped the two halves together again, locking them into place with the latch. Turning the device on the rag, he used a forefinger to brush the edge of a wheel where it protruded through a slot in the outer casing. As the fly-wheel turned so the outer surfaces of the steel plates, where they were exposed by the oval-shaped voids cut into the casing, began to move up and down and in and out. The movement created a sucking sound and Brunel placed the palm of his hand over one of the copper outlets. 'What you would call the chambers of the heart are operating like pistons in an engine, creating a vacuum powerful enough to transfer pressure along these pipes.' There was a popping sound as his hand pulled free from the mouth of the pipe and he watched as the small red ring on his skin slowly disappeared.

I confessed to not understanding how the thing would operate as an engine, given that the function of the heart in the body was not to animate the body but to feed blood to and from the lungs.

'This is really only a part of the engine, just like the heart is only a part of the body. That is where Russell has been so clever with the design of his torpedo. His drawings show that the device would serve to distribute pressurized gases and liquids around the machine, just as the heart pushes blood around the body. Other components will serve to convert that pressure into movement, ultimately causing the screw to turn. But don't get me wrong: this little trinket is the key to Russell's machine; it is the component which will allow the torpedo to operate underwater as a self-contained unit.'

'You are sure it will work?' I asked, bending down to study it at eye level. 'Can Russell be certain that this will work in his infernal machine?'

'Of course not,' pronounced Brunel, shaking out the flame on his match after at last lighting the cigar. 'He would have to test it. The thing may require modification before he gets it to work in his own device. But I think it will run like a charm.'

'Whether it works or not the implication is clear. Now that it is finished Russell and his cronies are going to want to take delivery.'

'Very true, but how is he to know we have reached this stage?'

'Surely that ruse is wearing a little thin by now. At some point he is going to realize we are bluffing and make another attempt to get hold of it. God alone knows what the end result of that little shopping trip might be.'

Brunel, apparently unshaken by the prospect, luxuriated in the slow exhalation of a lungful of smoke. 'Well, in that case, we had better make the first move.' He winked knowingly at Ockham. 'Show him.'

Florence and I were enjoying ourselves, leaning over the rail like children tossing sticks from a bridge. We watched as far below our fellow guests disgorged themselves from small boats. It was August and half an hour before I had stepped aboard Brunel's great babe for the first time since my almost-fatal visit to Russell's office. This time however I had taken great care with my wardrobe, brushing off my evening suit and investing in a new collar for the shirt I had no intention of removing before my return home. All of this was topped off by the first-class hat gifted by Brunel as replacement for my loss at the attempted launch. Florence too had pushed the boat out and stood resplendent in an emerald-green gown, a burgundy shawl draped low over her shoulders. For once, her hair was not hidden beneath a bonnet and, as if in competition with a gleaming ribbon of watered silk, reflected light like burnished ebony.

The flotilla of boats carried some of the most influential and best-dressed people in the city. They were gathered to mark the completion of the ship's fitting out. Months of work had finally come to an end, at least officially – I did notice the odd labourer dash across the deck armed with tins of paint: no doubt they were still beavering away with last-minute jobs behind the scenes.

Brunel had handed me the invitation at our last meeting, and seeing his condition it came as no surprise that he would be too ill to attend himself. 'Dr Phillips and companion,' it said on the gold-embossed card. Of course, most respectable women would have baulked at the prospect of accompanying a confirmed bachelor unchaperoned. But Florence hadn't given it a second thought. 'Let them wag their fat tongues,' she had laughed. 'We are doctor and nurse – what more natural pairing could there be? And in any case, we shall be the most handsome couple there.'

We could barely contain our mirth as we watched our fellow guests struggle to negotiate the gap between their small boats and the boarding steps – cruel of us, I know, but it was not every day we got to see the movers and shakers stumbling about like hapless drunkards trying to step from a moving cab.

'Come on, Florence. If one of them falls in we will only have to attend once they're fished out. Why don't we take a look inside?'

'George, you could at least pretend to be a gentleman,' she cried, before picking up her skirts and hurrying to catch up. She took hold of my arm just in time to walk through a door held open by a white-gloved porter, who raised an eyebrow at our high-spirited behaviour. Florence had also noticed his reaction. 'We must behave, George,' she said sternly as we made our way down the carpeted staircase. 'Remember, I am keen to find more patrons tonight.'

How could I forget? She had talked of little else since I had first asked her to accompany me. The canny Miss Nightingale knew a golden opportunity when it landed in her lap. The new hospital still required political support, and as members from both Houses of Parliament would be present tonight she had made it her mission to charm as many as possible into supporting her enterprise. I also had an ulterior motive for coming along, as tonight Ockham and myself were to put into action the plan we had agreed with Brunel.

Descending two flights of stairs, we arrived at a set of double doors. The master of ceremonies carried a long stick, the silver head of which traced wide circles in the air as he approached us with the swagger of a dandy from a bygone age.

A silver tray flashed as he pulled it like a concealed knife from behind his back. 'Your invitation, please, sir.'

I dropped the card on to the tray. 'Good evening, Dr Phillips,' he said after reading it.

'And to you,' I replied. 'This is . . .'

'It is very good to see you, Miss Nightingale,' interrupted the man, rounding off his enthusiastic greeting with a bow. Florence smiled at me, looking a little embarrassed at her own celebrity.

After taking my coat the man turned on his heels and swaggered through the door, where at the top of a short flight of stairs he tapped the floor three times with his stick. 'Dr George Phillips and Miss Florence Nightingale,' he announced to the room, which did not yet appear to contain many people.

'I think we are unfashionably early,' quipped Florence as she hooked her arm around mine and marched us in. The great saloon was a vast hall, bedecked with rows of cast-iron pillars, and chandeliers suspended from the high ceiling. The sense of space was enhanced by polished mirrors set into a pair of centrally positioned octagonal booths located at opposing ends of the long room. I first took them to be stairwells but later learned they were the housings for two of the tower-like funnels as they passed up from the bowels of the ship to the deck above us.

'Oh, George!' exclaimed Florence. 'Are we on a ship or in a palace?'

Walking into one of the arcades running down the side of the hall, we looked up to see a balcony running its entire length. A series of skylights opened up on to the deck, the ceiling here being at least twice as high as that under which we had entered. The opulence was almost overwhelming, with every exposure of metal either gilded or painted blue and red, the walls covered with gold cloth and crimson drapes. It was hard to believe that this was just one of five saloons on the ship. This was no mere palace, I thought, it was a floating city.

Still few in number, our fellow guests stood chatting in small clusters or had taken seats on the lushly upholstered settees and chairs distributed throughout the saloon. But the master of ceremonies' announcements were now coming thick and fast as people began to arrive in a steady stream. 'Lord and Lady Wilmot,' and then a moment or so later, 'The Right Honourable William Llewellyn,' and so it went on as the great and the good continued to gather.

I stopped a waiter and picked a couple of glasses of champagne from his tray, handing one of them to Florence. 'We may as well have that long-overdue drink.'

'To the new hospital,' said Florence, raising her glass and clinking it gently against mine.

'To the new hospital,' I happily repeated.

We stood for a while and sipped champagne, continuing to admire our surroundings. All of a sudden Florence's face pinched as though the champagne had turned to vinegar in her mouth. 'What's wrong?' I asked.

'Oh, nothing,' she shrugged. 'Just the last name to be called.'

'Sorry, I wasn't paying attention. What was it?'

'Benjamin Hawes.'

'You know him?' I asked, intrigued by her reaction.

'He was in the Cabinet when I was in the Crimea,' she said, her voice as bitter as her expression. 'An old friend of Mr Brunel's, I believe.'

'Not your favourite person?'

'That man did everything he could to have me discredited. He could not bring himself to deal with a woman as an equal and so blocked every request I made to the War Department, be it for improved hospitals, more food for patients or even warm clothes.'

'I would never have thought him capable of such behaviour. He has never been anything but friendly to me.'

Florence's eyes hardened, as though for a moment turned to the same crystal she held in her hand. 'He would be, wouldn't he? You're a man.' When I offered no comment on the accuracy of this observation she continued with her character assassination. 'The man was a dictator, an autocrat, irresponsible to Parliament and definitely not to be trusted! After months of ignoring my pleas he finally commissioned Mr Brunel to design a new field hospital but deliberately kept me away from the project.'

'You mean he *tried* to keep you away from the project,' I said, recalling what Brunel had told me.

To my relief her mouth relaxed into a smile. 'I did have a few suggestions to make on the matter and so went to Mr Brunel directly.'

'I assume then, that you won't be seeking support for the new hospital from that quarter?'

'I would rather set up a nursing school in the engine room of this ship than speak another word to that man.'

Another name was announced. 'Who is Viscount Ockham?' she asked as I turned towards the door.

'A friend, only he doesn't usually go to the trouble of using his full name.' To call him a friend was perhaps an exaggeration but since that dreadful night at the windmill we had fallen into an uneasy alliance, which tonight would be put to the test as we tried to free ourselves once and for all from the attentions of those who, whatever the cost, sought to possess the mechanical heart.

It did not take him long to find us. He looked every inch the aristocrat, dressed in full evening attire and without a speck of oil to be seen anywhere on his face or hands. But he was clearly ill at ease. 'I'd rather be down below eating with the rest of the lads,' he grumbled when the dinner bell finally rang.

We were ushered towards the stairs and climbed to the upper saloon, where people were being seated at two long tables. The mezzanine, though much narrower, was very similar in appearance to the main saloon, with the funnels once again shielded behind mirror-clad cabinets. Although there seemed to be some pre-arrangement of places towards the head of our table the remaining seats were allocated on a first-come-first-served basis, which was convenient as it allowed the three of us to sit together.

The food was adequate but not quite up to the high standard set by our surroundings, an unavoidable result, no doubt, of having to cater for so many people at the same time. I made small talk with the gentleman next to me, who was, he informed me, the Member of Parliament for Stratford. Florence talked cheerfully to people seated on both sides of the table. She played them skilfully, entertaining with anecdotes about her experiences in the Crimea before bringing the conversation round to the urgent need for a teaching hospital. Ockham, seated opposite me, kept his head down and got on with the business of eating.

Whitworth was sitting just half a dozen people away from me, and as we were waiting to be seated I had spotted Perry taking his place on the far table. Then, over the top of my glass I noticed Brodie on the same table as him. Ockham had referred to my superior during our confrontation in the windmill and when I later asked him about his involvement in the affair he explained that he and Brunel had invited the surgeon to collaborate in their work on the mechanical heart, especially with regard to its practical application. He had refused point blank to have anything to do with the project, dismissing it as a fool's errand which would destroy his reputation. To Ockham's dismay Brunel himself had decided not to proceed with any form of experimentation, though he had been happy to go ahead and build the device. 'It was nothing more than a diversion for him,' he said bitterly. The engineer, it transpired, had been entirely ignorant of Ockham's desire to resurrect his mother and so knew nothing of his nocturnal activities in the windmill. Our conversation, which had taken place after leaving the door man's body in Clare's capable hands, had shed light on various matters but perhaps most importantly had explained why Brodie had been so keen to keep me away from Brunel, and by association also Ockham. It now appeared that the old man was not merely jealous of his clients, as Brunel had suggested, but concerned about my reputation and well-being should I become embroiled in the scheme. After all, had he not made a promise to my father to look after me?

Ockham had also seen fit to elucidate one further aspect of his role in the affair of the heart. Not long after Mary Shelley's celebrated book was published an event took place that was to go on and have an equally strong influence on the young man. In late 1813, immediately following his execution for murder, the lifeless corpse of a man called Matthew Clydesdale was deposited on the table of the anatomist Dr Andrew Ure in the dissection theatre of Glasgow University. Nothing unusual there, I thought, having dissected numerous executed criminals myself. What was different, however, was that Ure did not intend to dissect the corpse but to bring it back to life! The experiment, according to Ockham, had involved passing electricity, via rods attached to the man's heels and the spine, through the dead tissue in an attempt to reanimate the body, or 'galvanize it back into life' as he put it.

Long after the event, one witness claimed that the corpse had indeed returned to life, and then, apparently eager to avenge the recent snuffing of its existence, proceeded to put its hands around the throat of the good doctor; an ungrateful Lazarus indeed. Ure's neck was only released when one of his quick-thinking assistants took up a scalpel and cut Clydesdale's throat, killing him for the second time that day.

Surely, I had insisted, Ockham did not believe this. Almost to my surprise he shook his head. No, he told me, he had spoken to others who had been there, and although it seemed that the shock of electricity had caused the body to flinch and limbs to extend violently, so much so that at least one member of the audience fainted at the fright of it, at no point did life return to the corpse.

Far from dissuading him from pursuing his ambitions, the failure of electricity had only served to stoke Ockham's confidence in the use of mechanical means, though for a time he had considered inviting Michael Faraday, the celebrated advocate of electricity (and, as I recalled from the minutes, one-time guest of the Lazarus Club) to repeat the experiments.

What Brodie might have thought of Ure's experiment was uncertain but there could be little doubt that he was currently being bored to tears by the woman sitting next to him, who was talking incessantly while he tried to concentrate on his meal. Her monologue was interrupted by the sound of a knife being repeatedly tapped against a glass after which a man near the head of our table rose to his feet. It was Russell.

'Ladies and gentlemen,' he boomed. 'It gives me great pleasure to see you here tonight in the spectacular grand saloon of the *Great Eastern*. Before I go any further I would like to invite the chairman of the Great Steam Ship Company to say a few words.'

Russell sat down and was replaced by the man sitting opposite him. What followed was a vote of thanks to Russell for the hard work he had put into the construction of the ship. 'Other than Mr Russell, no other man in the kingdom could have fitted the vessel out in the same time and there were not a few who believed the task too much even for his energies.'

There was not a single mention of Brunel and his contribution to the work. An outburst of enthusiastic applause accompanied the chairman's return to his seat, at which point Russell stood up again. After the praise heaped upon him the tall Scotsman, to his credit, took it upon himself to redirect some of it towards his absent partner in the project.

'It is a source of great regret that Mr Brunel cannot be with us tonight and I am sure you will all join with me in wishing him a speedy recovery from his present illness. It obviously goes without saying that without his genius none of us would be sitting here tonight and so I would like you all to raise your glasses to the great engineer.' Russell picked up his glass and everyone followed suit. 'To Mr Brunel,' he chimed, the toast instantly returned by nearly two hundred voices.

Once dinner was finished, rather than have the ladies retire and leave the gentlemen to enjoy their port and cigars it was the gentlemen who left, going back downstairs while the women remained at table. Taking their leave, the men dropped their napkins and made their way along the balcony to the stairs. Conversations commenced over dinner were continued in transit, but in the saloon many people took the opportunity to seek out fresh company. Ockham and I stood at the foot of the stairs for a while and watched as the crowd shook itself out into smaller groups. After a minute or two he tapped me on the shoulder and pointed towards the funnel cabinet closest to the entrance.

'There,' he said. 'Babbage and Hawes.'

'And there is Sir Benjamin,' I observed, seeing Brodie standing alone. 'Come on, we'll collect him on the way.'

'We need Russell,' noted Ockham as we made our way towards Brodie.

'Don't worry, he'll come to us.'

'I hope so.'

'Sir Benjamin, good evening. I trust you enjoyed your dinner?'

Brodie looked quite drained. 'I did not, sir. The woman next to me did not let up with her chatter even when her mouth was full of food. I made the mistake of telling her I was a doctor, after which she spent the next hour regaling me with her various ailments. I was very close to prescribing hemlock, let me tell you.'

It was difficult not to feel some sympathy for him, especially as I had more than once suffered a similar fate with Darwin. 'I am sorry to hear that. Won't you join us? We spotted a couple of our old friends over there.'

'Lead on, gentlemen.'

There was a flurry of handshaking as our little group came together. The conversation was free and easy but Ockham and I kept a wary eye out for any other members of our circle, and for Russell in particular. 'Here comes Bazalgette,' said Ockham. With his arrival the conversation immediately turned to the new sewer system, which according to our burrowing colleague was going very well.

Everyone seemed to be in high spirits, the general mood of excitement no doubt inspired by our unusual surroundings. But then I noticed that Brodie, who had previously seemed to be recovering from his trial by dinner, had dropped his jaw in an unmistakable expression of horror.

'Good evening, gentlemen,' said Florence, who had refused to be left behind with the other members of her sex. Her disregard for convention did not worry me one iota, but I did feel a little awkward at her finding me in the company of the man for whom she had earlier expressed open contempt. Florence's eyes narrowed when she realized Hawes was among us, and I am sure that if she had not felt it would be construed as a sign of weakness she would gladly have walked away without saying another word.

However, it was Hawes himself who denied any chance of escape, as the movement of his jaw served to hold her as effectively as any gin trap. 'Miss Nightingale,' he said. 'It must be four, no, more like five years since our paths last crossed.' There was no warmth in his voice; the man was simply making a statement of fact.

'We were at war then,' replied Florence coldly.

'Yes, Russia gave us a real run for our money.'

'No, not Russia, I was referring to you and me.'

Hawes laughed nervously. 'Ah yes, our little spat. There was no love lost between us then.'

'Nor I suspect now,' returned Florence.

'What do you think to the ship, Miss Nightingale?' interjected Bazalgette, cheerfully stepping into the crossfire.

'They say that in times of war she will be capable of carrying ten thousand troops,' said Hawes, his words sewn together with a steely thread of antagonism. 'Imagine that: enough patients to keep even the great Florence Nightingale happy for the rest of her days.'

'If anyone thrives on conflict, Mr Hawes, it is you,' snapped

Florence. 'How many men did you send to their deaths in the Crimea?'

'We won, didn't we? And in any case, war is an unavoidable fact of life, Miss Nightingale.'

Ignoring this comment, she turned to Bazalgette. 'The ship is a thing of wonder, sir. But tonight she brings to mind not a troopship but that first great vessel, Noah's ark. The only difference is that this ark appears to be carrying one ass too many. Now if you will excuse me I have business elsewhere.' She finished with a smile. 'Goodnight, gentlemen.'

'*Touché*,' remarked Hawes almost admiringly as Florence calmly walked away. 'You know, gentlemen, one day they will all be like that.'

'God help us,' said Brodie.

'What on earth was all that about?' asked a bemused Bazalgette.

Hawes, his dander still up, was happy to provide an answer. 'Everyone thinks she is a saint, but let me tell you, that woman is a menace, an egotistical empire-builder of the first order.'

The man had gone too far but, sensing I was about to make the mistake of entering the fray, Ockham called me off with a shake of his head. He was right: the last thing we needed now was a personal squabble.

With Florence's departure I repositioned myself so that I could see the hall as a reflection in the mirror alongside which we had gathered. For a while I followed Florence's progress as she worked the room with the same skill she had deployed over dinner. Then I spied Russell, his red-topped head standing out above the shorter men gathered around him. Eventually, though, he broke out and with Perry and Whitworth in tow strode towards us, at which point they were joined by Lord Catchpole. Ockham had seen them too and after nervously clutching the hem of his jacket shuffled slightly so as to give himself enough room in which to manoeuvre when the moment came.

Russell's arrival prompted a unanimous expression of congratulation on his work and a comment from myself about the ship being a much more suitable venue for future meetings of the club.

Ockham attracted the attention of the closest waiter, who seemed only too happy to lighten his load by distributing his entire cargo of brandy amongst us. 'Cigars,' I said to the waiter. 'Could you please bring us some cigars?'

The young man pulled two from his waistcoat pocket and handed them to me. 'I shall get some more, sir. I will be right back.'

Russell, who was obviously enjoying being the centre of attention, took a healthy swig from his glass. 'If Brunel were here he could supply the entire room from that satchel of his.'

'Hang on,' said Ockham, as if hit by a flash of inspiration. 'I have some cigars.' With this he reached into his pocket and fiddled for an uncomfortably long time before pulling out three more cigars. At the same instant there was a metallic crash and all eyes fell to the floor at Ockham's feet.

'What the devil?' said Perry at the sight of the polished pieces of steel.

'Blast!' cursed Ockham, flicking open his jacket to reveal a gash in the lining of his pocket.

Perry handed his glass to Whitworth and, dropping to his knees, scooped up the pieces of metal.

'Sorry, gentlemen,' said Ockham. 'The damn things wore their way through the fabric. I should have known better than to bring them with me.'

'What strange things to be carrying in your pocket,' observed Brodie as if on cue.

'Yes, very foolish of me. I had thought to hand them over to Mr Brunel, only to find that he is not here tonight.'

Perry held the pieces in his open palms, where they rested like exotic seashells.

'What on earth are they?' asked Whitworth.

'If I am not mistaken,' began Russell, 'they are pieces from Brunel's mechanical heart.'

'A foolish idea and a waste of time,' snapped Brodie. 'I don't see why he can't be satisfied with his achievable projects.'

'Alas, this one does not appear to be going anywhere,' admitted Ockham. 'I have been tinkering with the bits and pieces on and off for weeks, but as you can see we have not got very far with the thing. I think Mr Brunel has given up on the idea altogether. I just wanted to return these parts to him.'

'You had better take them back then,' said Perry, pushing his hands towards Ockham.

'They will make ideal ashtrays,' said Whitworth.

'Not like Brunel to give up on an idea so quickly,' noted Russell thoughtfully.

I thought it was time to play doctor. 'Given his failing health I don't think he has much choice in the matter.'

'Quite,' said Brodie.

Ockham shrugged and took the pieces from Perry before making his exit. 'Gentlemen, if you will please excuse me, I had better take these away. I can return them to Mr Brunel another time.'

We watched him leave, but Russell kept his eyes fixed on the man for a little longer than the rest of us. 'A strange character,' was his assessment as Ockham left the hall.


The party broke up an hour or so after Ockham's departure, the crowd gradually returning to the flotilla of boats moored against the ship's hull. I took the opportunity to slip away and pay Ockham a brief visit in his cabin. 'Bravo! A wonderful performance. Just the right balance of eccentricity and disinterest.'

'I thought Russell may have been on to us.'

I looked behind him to his part-prepared opium pipe lying on the bed. 'No, not at all.'

'So you think our little charade did the trick then?'

'Sure of it. You did a masterful job with those replicas. I think we can safely say that, as far as the Lazarus Club is concerned, Brunel's plan for a mechanical heart is dead and buried.'

'For a while there, I was worried that the damned pocket wasn't going to give. It took far too long to release the pieces. And do you think they were up to scratch? My hand is nowhere near as good as Wilkie's.'

'They were fine, and no one's going to come and look for a thing that doesn't exist, are they? But now we need to find out what it is that Brunel has in mind to do next.'

With nothing more to be said I wished Ockham goodnight and joined the stragglers disembarking the ship, many of whom were clustered around Florence, who continued on her quest right until the very end. I looked down to the few boats still waiting, just in time to see a skiff carrying Russell and several of the others into the darkness.

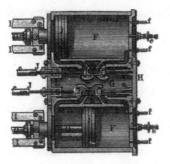

# 28

Brunel advanced up the stairs ahead of me, the stick he carried a clear sign of his increasing infirmity. My suggestion that he would be wise to remain at home had been ignored and so here he was, visiting the ship to make one last inspection before her sea trial. He had been adamant that I accompany him, a proposal to which I consented so as to keep a physician's eye on him. Most of the journey had been spent mulling over the events of the previous evening, my report on Ockham's theatrical debut eliciting a satisfied chuckle from the impresario behind it. But there was one issue we had not discussed. Despite our apparent success at convincing the others that the mechanical heart had been abandoned I was still not fully persuaded that Russell was our man.

'What about Hawes?' I asked, unable to hold my tongue on the matter any longer.

'What about him?' threw back Brunel.

'Just that it occurred to me that given his position in the War Office he may have more reason than most to take an interest in the engine.'

Brunel paused on the stairway and turned, yellow teeth pinching his cigar almost to the point of bisection. 'Are you suggesting that he is behind all of this? Am I to believe that my brother-in-law would sanction murder?'

I took a step back. 'Your brother-in-law? Why, I had no idea.'

The lacerated cigar was tossed over the side and Brunel took on the countenance of a Latin master chastising his pupil for poor translation. 'The man's married to my sister, for God's sake. I presume this groundless accusation is based on information provided by Miss Nightingale?'

I gave no reply.

'Pah,' he spat. 'The woman has never forgiven him for the position he took against her during the war.'

'I think we should leave Miss Nightingale out of this. She said nothing to single out Hawes other than to remind me that he was attached to the War Office. Her casual remark simply prompted me to reconsider the man in relation to your engine, that's all. She bears the man no warmth but . . .'

'But she does for you, my friend.'

'I beg your pardon?'

Brunel smiled and resumed his climb. 'I saw the care she lavished on you when you were ill. She barely left your bedside while you were in the hospital.'

He stopped again, turned to the rail and looked out over the river, his expression now as murky as the water below. 'Believe it or not, I do not share Hawes' low opinion of her. She is not afraid to make her opinions known and I respect that in men and women alike. When he commissioned me to design the hospitals for the Crimea I found her knowledge invaluable. Yes, I had some disagreements with her over the matter but what Hawes doesn't know is that in the end they were essentially built to her specification. But, as you say, let us leave her out of this. The real question is why Hawes should go to such drastic and underhand lengths to secure the device.'

'Perhaps because you wouldn't hand it over when he asked for it?'

'What makes you think he asked me?'

'If your invention is as revolutionary as you say then surely the British government would want to add it to its arsenal?'

Brunel shook his head. 'You overestimate the foresight of the War Office. I have offered a number of ideas to Her Majesty's Government only to have them rejected due to a blind inability to see a good idea when it falls into their lap. Why should the engine be any different? In any case, it was Russell who designed the torpedo. Even if the War Office were involved he is the guilty party in all of this, I am sure of it.'

'Then what about Whitworth? Doesn't he have an interest in building weapons? What about those guns of his?'

'Any engineer worth his salt has an interest in weapons, myself included. There was my floating battery and the screw-driven warship, both of which were rejected out of hand by the Admiralty and the War Office.' He let out a laugh. 'And as for Whitworth's guns, why, he stole the idea for those rifled barrels of his from me!'

'Well, there you go. He's stolen from you once – why shouldn't he do it again?'

Brunel stopped climbing once more. 'He only did so because he knew I wouldn't mind. If I had given two hoots I would have patented the design, but patents are for the greedy and feeble-minded. Now before we go on, are you sure there is no one else you would like to accuse?'

I shook my head and we continued on our way. On the deck we were greeted by a bespectacled gentleman introduced to me as Dickson, the builder of the engines and the man whose actions had sent Brunel into a paroxysm of rage sometime previously. Today, however, Brunel's manner was almost jovial as he questioned his fellow engineer about the status of the engines.

After a brief conversation he turned to me. 'Come, let us take a look,' and then to Dickson: 'If there is enough steam I may get them to turn them over.'

Although no stranger to the ship I had never had the privilege of seeing its engines. Leaving the open air behind us, we entered a hatchway and stepped on to a set of iron stairs. Down and down we climbed, making our way along walkways and through narrow passages. Eventually we passed beneath the waterline, where the river made strange gurgling noises as it stroked the hull in a liquid caress. After negotiating yet another set of stairs we stepped on to a platform, its edges bounded by a balustrade, which even down here had been decorated with an interlace of wrought iron.

There we stood for a while, eyes roving over the spectacular sight before us.

The chamber was criss-crossed by a series of interconnected iron beams, some straight, some curved, behind which a cylindrical shaft the thickness of a tree trunk rose up from a vat-like drum, the outside lined with timber staves and the top capped with a polished metal lid that would not have looked out of place on the roof of Brighton Pavilion. The other end of the shaft was connected to a great disc of burnished metal, which on closer inspection also appeared to be joined to the beams at the front.

That seemed to be the way of it: everything connected to everything else. An identical drum rose up at an opposing but equal angle to the first. But instead of a piston rising from its fluted cupola this drum sprouted a horseshoe-shaped bracket. This joined with the head of the piston where it was attached to the great disc, which seemed to be suspended by a heavy pivot secured to the top of one of the beams. All of this sat within an avenue of iron pillars supporting great vaulted arches; a cloister forged by Vulcan.

The only suggestion that this great beast was to operate at the behest of man was a series of levers set into the floor.

Clearly gratified by my awestruck expression, Brunel gestured over my shoulder. There, behind the stairs, was a mirror image of what I had just seen. But here mechanics were tightening nuts with giant spanners, lubricating joints and checking dials. The engines dwarfed any railway locomotive I had ever seen. It was more than I could do to imagine what power might be harnessed here.

Brunel ordered me to stay put and with Dickson climbed down to move among the men and their mechanical charges. They walked across the iron floor below me, towards a man studying a large drawing draped across his raised knee. Brunel pointed to the drawing and then to the engine, his voice inaudible from my position on the platform due to the clamour of men and metal. His instructions delivered, Brunel returned to my side. The gang of mechanics made their way down the cloister and disappeared up another flight of stairs.

Brunel explained that the boilers were in another hall somewhere behind us, and that these were currently being stoked with coal. Dickson, now standing beside the levers, studied his watch, and then, looking up, nodded at Brunel, who in return dropped his hand. The signal given, Dickson pulled back the lever. Like a waking dragon, the engine expressed a jet of steam before slowly rolling into life, the pistons and beams moving through the cloud of white vapour.

The polished parts bobbed and turned without giving any impression of effort. Once again, Dickson looked up, and at another gesture from Brunel pushed again at the lever. In response, the engine began to pick up speed, individual elements now thrashing into a blur of steam and steel. As the speed of motion increased so did the noise – the great cracks of thunder forcing me to push my hands against my ears.

The heat broke over us like a wave, engulfing our bodies and drying our mouths. Brunel's eyes were fixed on the engine, as though he were hypnotized by the whirling mass of metal. Then, snapping out of his trance, he took hold of my wrist and, pulling my hand away from my ear, pressed it against his chest. His weak heart was palpitating at an alarming rate, beating a rhythm faster than any tattoo.

The drum in his chest beat harder as the machine chewed on more steam, giving a final scream as it approached full speed. Brunel's face was set like iron and he tightened the grip on my wrist. No heart could take this pressure and at any moment I expected it to break into a thousand pieces.

But then at last Brunel waved his free arm in the air, signalling again to Dickson, who promptly pulled the lever back. Gradually the machine slowed to a lope, and then to a stop, and as it did so the palpitations of Brunel's heart calmed, its movement now almost imperceptible to my touch.

Letting go of my hand, and without saying a word, Brunel led the way back up through the hull, out into the daylight. I drank in the cool air, letting the gentle breeze soothe the back of my scorched throat. At first, all I could think of was getting back to the shore, but then my physician's composure began to return.

My first instinct was to get him into a cabin where I could examine him after what must surely have been a heart attack, but just as I was about to insist on this we were accosted by a vaguely familiar figure. Brunel, who by some miracle was still on his feet, spoke with the man, who from his equipment I recognized to be the photographer from the attempted launch. To my amazement the engineer agreed to stand once again in front of the three-legged camera. Behind him one of the ship's smokestacks rose up from the deck, its cold, riveted surface providing the backdrop to what I was now certain would be Brunel's last portrait.

Watching him stand there, shoulders slumped and chin sinking below his collar, looking for all the world like a ghost in waiting, I recalled the conversation with Brodie, in which we had discussed Brunel's medical condition. Could there be something to what he had told me, that Brunel and his machines were physically related in some way? Down in the engine room his heart had appeared to race in tandem with the machine, speeding up when it did and slowing down alongside it. But despite this I told myself the man was simply working himself to death.

Putting these morbid thoughts behind me, I looked on as Brunel took off his hat and held it down by his side. The photographer disappeared beneath his black hood and, removing the lens cap, counted to eight, fixing Brunel's image on the glass plate. 'Thank you, Mr Brunel,' he called out as he shook his head free of the hood.

The engineer made to put on his hat, but it slipped from his grasp and tumbled to the deck, where it rolled a half-circle and, before coming to rest, was joined by its owner, who collapsed on top of it. Dashing forward, I knelt at his side, releasing his cravat and loosening the collar.

Brunel regained consciousness but his condition was serious. In keeping with his role as personal physician, Brodie insisted that he treat him at his home in Duke Street rather than at the hospital. For the first time since my father's illness I felt the closest of bonds with a patient, and was glad not to be left entirely responsible for his care. Although Brunel had obviously not been in the best of health, his seizure had come as a dreadful shock, all the more so because of the bizarre circumstances under which it had occurred. It was as though he had wanted me to be there at the end, but then somehow managed to pull away from the grip which the engine seemed to have on his heart. As ever, though, there was little time for reflection as Brodie had begun to castigate his patient for requesting a cigar through the part of his mouth unaffected by the rictus which had immobilized the left side of his body. While Brodie berated him for bringing all this down upon himself I tried to offer some comfort to Mary, the patient's long-suffering wife,

I had not met Mrs Brunel before, but judged her strong enough to bear the truth, though I told her nothing about the incident in the engine room. She faced up to the situation with an air of weary inevitability, having no doubt seen her husband work himself close to death on more than one occasion.

Brodie beckoned me over to the bedside. Brunel was asking for me.

'I want . . .' croaked the engineer, his voice slurred by his twisted mouth '. . . I want you to be on the ship when she sails on her trial.' He paused to catch his breath: '. . . to keep an eye on things.'

'But Isambard, I am a surgeon not an engineer.'

'You know men, Phillips, you know what makes them tick. I want you to keep an eye on our friend Russell.'

I glanced at Brodie, on the other side of the bed. 'But Isambard, I have duties in the hospital.'

Brunel shifted his gaze to his doctor, his eyes flickering like fires burning in snow. 'I am sure an arrangement can be made.'

Brodie nodded without speaking.

'Very well. I will be there on your great babe.'

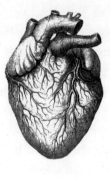

## 29

The day after Brunel's stroke I was back on the deck of the *Great Eastern* as she steamed downriver towards the North Sea and the English Channel beyond. When last I had heard from Brodie, his condition was stable but showed little sign of improvement. He feared that even if he were to pull through, the paralysis would be permanent.

Once again scenting money, the ship's owners had taken on board hundreds of passengers, all of whom had paid handsomely for the privilege of sailing on the maiden voyage. But it was a voyage without a destination. The ship was to sail out into the Channel where she would be put through various trials before returning to the river of her difficult birth. It seemed a cruel twist of fate that after devoting so much time and effort to the project, illness prevented Brunel from joining with his ship on her maiden voyage.

I was still a little uncertain why he had insisted on sending me on this mission, as since our subterfuge there had been no suggestion of interest in the mechanical heart from any quarter and I still found it hard to see Russell as the guilty party. His reaction to Brunel's seizure did nothing to settle these misgivings. After welcoming me aboard he expressed grave concern for his colleague's condition and seemed determined to go and visit him as soon as possible.

Nonetheless, I had agreed to do Brunel's bidding and place his partner under scrutiny, but it proved to be no easy task, as Russell was always on the move, striding from one part of the ship to another. Armed with a notebook and accompanied by a coterie of assistants, he battled his way through the crowds of promenading passengers on a constant round of inspections. One minute he was on the paddle box, checking on the wheel, the next he was at the binnacle inspecting the compass, which had been set high up on a mast where it could operate without being thrown off by the iron hull. Whenever possible I joined the party but refrained from imposing myself on his inspections below decks, where he spent much time with the engines. As we reached Purfleet, our first anchorage, Russell seemed entirely satisfied with the ship's performance and invited me to join him for dinner.

We sat some distance away from where the captain entertained a host of well-to-do-looking guests at the top table. Thinking that Russell might prefer this grander company, I pointed out that I would be happy to eat alone. 'Nonsense, my good doctor, I am grateful to have an excuse to be away from them. Damn passengers – it's a wonder we can get anything done with them stamping about like a herd of sheep. My God, Brunel would have had them cut loose in the small boats by now. No, I am quite happy to let the captain entertain them.'

Over dinner, Russell spoke of his regret at Brunel's condition. 'What are his chances of recovery?' he asked as our empty soup bowls were taken away by a white-gloved waiter.

'I don't know,' was my honest answer. 'He may pull through, but I am sorry to say that he will never be the same again.'

'What is it they say? The candle that burns brightest burns the shortest?'

'So I believe, but he is not dead yet, Mr Russell.'

'But you think the paralysis will be permanent, even if he does pull through?'

'Alas, it seems likely.'

'Then he is as good as dead,' said Russell with grim confidence. 'You know him as well as anyone, Phillips – can you imagine him wanting to go on living in that condition?'

I shook my head in sad agreement before he continued: 'There comes a time when an engine is beyond repair, and then it's just as well to douse the boilers and let it slow to a stop.'

My thoughts returned to the engine room. 'It's a shame he never got around to finishing his mechanical heart,' I said, almost without realizing it.

Russell's face tensed at my mention of the device. 'You don't mean to tell me that you believe that infernal thing could work?'

'Who can say what we may be capable of a hundred years from now? Perhaps by then we will be able to replace broken organs just like the parts in one of your engines.'

'Even if that were so, what gives us the right to play God? It is better that we forget the matter of his device. If Brunel had spent more time attending to things that mattered, like this damned ship, and not allowing his head to be filled with pipe dreams then . . .'

'Then what, sir?'

'Then perhaps he would not be in such a sorry state today.'

Once again his sentiment seemed genuine, and I thought it diplomatic to move on. 'What of your ship? I assume you are pleased with her performance?'

'Wait until we get out into the Channel tomorrow. Then we will really put her through her paces.'

Such optimism may have been a little premature, for at that moment a worried-looking young man, whom I recognized as one of his engineering assistants, came rushing up to the table. 'Bostock, what is it, man?' demanded Russell.

'Mr Russell. We . . . we have a problem, sir. There is . . .'

Russell threw down his napkin and stood to leave. 'I hope you will excuse me, Dr Phillips. Teething troubles – you know how it is.'

'The same with babes great and small, I am sure.'

Before retiring to my cabin I decided to take a turn around the deck, in the hope that the night air might clear my head for sleep. The place had the feel of Brighton seafront on a summer's night: all that was missing were the cabs and hawkers – and perhaps the warmth, for the breeze, which was blowing unchecked across the water from the east, had a distinct chill to it. The deck was illuminated by a series of lamps fuelled by gas produced by the ship. The shore lay some distance away in the dark, its presence only evident through the constellation of lights showing from scattered settlements.

A notice informed me that three revolutions of the deck was almost the equivalent of a mile and so, buttoning my coat against the cold, I set out on my walk.

Moving in a clockwise direction around the ship, which for now at least put the wind behind my back, I strolled towards the stern. The walk helped me to order my thoughts, most of which concerned Russell and my niggling doubts about his guilt. But then my reverie was interrupted by a flurry of activity. I watched as two uniformed crewmen clambered into a lifeboat hanging from davits over the side of the ship, one holding a lantern. Moments later they dropped back down on to the deck and moved on to the next boat, where they repeated the process.

There seemed little reason to doubt that whatever bad news Russell's assistant had brought with him to the dining room and the search I was now witnessing were related. And the search wasn't just confined to the lifeboats, for as I rounded the stern and began my walk to the bow, the wind now in my face, I spotted another pair of crewmen on the look-out for something or someone, peering into hatchways, sticking their arms down air ducts and opening lockers. Further along the deck another pair were duplicating the search of the lifeboats I had observed on the opposite site of the ship.

Then I saw Russell, talking heatedly to an officer before sending him off in the direction of the nearest stairwell. He looked set to follow the man but on seeing me he paused.

'What's going on?' I asked, glancing towards the two men in the lifeboat.

He thought for a moment, perhaps uncertain how much he should tell me. 'We may have a stowaway.'

'Do stowaways always generate such excitement?' I asked, in the naïve belief that such things were almost a tradition aboard ships.

'We have to consider the possibility of sabotage,' said Russell.

'Sabotage? But why?'

Russell watched the progress of the search. 'There could be any number of reasons. She's going to put a lot of smaller vessels out of business. Now, if you will excuse me, doctor, I must return below decks. And please, not a word of this to any of the passengers. We do not want a panic on our hands.'

'Of course,' I replied.

Russell entered a stairwell and I waited for a few moments before following him. Two flights down I caught a glimpse of him disappearing through a door on the landing, the threshold of which took me from a wide, carpeted stairway into a small chamber, where both the floor and the walls were of bare, unpainted metal. Even the air had a different feel to it, a viscous quality redolent with the taste of oil. This place could not be far away from the engine room. Pausing at the top of a spiral staircase, I listened to the sound of voices below me, one of them belonging to the big Scotsman. As they grew fainter I set foot on the first of the steps and cautiously began to make my way down.

After reaching the very bottom of the ship's hull, I lingered beside an oval hatchway in the bulkhead at the foot of the stairs. The voices were still audible but coming from quite some distance away. Stooping down, I stepped into a long hall with a high ceiling, suspended from which were all manner of pipes and tubes. A series of huge iron furnaces ran the entire length of one of the walls – inside each glowed the embers of coal fires run down for the night. Against the opposite wall were bays filled with coal.

Sitting above the furnaces were the boilers, the great tanks where water was transformed into life-giving steam and carried along to the engines by an arterial system of pipes. Rising between them was the base of a funnel, which above my head pierced no fewer than four interior decks before sprouting through the upper deck and pushing on into the sky for another thirty feet. Up ahead, beyond the boilers and their furnaces, the next bulkhead was punctured like the one behind me by an oval hatchway, which I guessed would give way to a replica of the room in which I was standing; Brunel had explained to me that there were no less than five such rooms, one for each funnel.

Satisfied that Russell and his party had passed through the hatchway before me, I began to approach it. The next instant I was lying flat on my back and listening to someone running back towards the hatchway through which I had entered. By the time I could lift myself sufficiently enough to look back there was no sign of the man who had appeared from nowhere to barge violently into my shoulder.

Regaining my feet and brushing the coal dust from my clothes, I was about to run forward and find Russell when a head, followed by a heavy, naked torso appeared through the hatchway. Once free of the hole this second man charged towards me, his bald head thrust forward like a cannonball in flight. He clearly had no intention of stopping and, having no desire to suffer another impact, I stepped to the side, only to catch my foot on a lump of coal which sent me tumbling once again to the floor. The human cannonball, who from his partial state of dress and coal-stained skin I assumed to be a fireman, stood over me, one of his great leaden feet pinning me to the floor by the wrist. There was a commotion behind him as others disgorged themselves from the hatchway.

'Got 'im, sir! Got the bastard under me foot!' shouted my captor over his shoulder.

'Good work!' said Russell, appearing at the man's side.

A third man moved behind my head and dropped a lantern so low that I could feel my eyebrows singeing.

'Phillips!' exclaimed Russell. 'What in God's name are you doing down here?'

'I was loo – looking for you,' I spluttered, the coal dust now beginning to line my throat. 'Get this – this great ape off me. He's breaking my wrist.'

'Shall I 'it 'im, sir?' enquired the cannonball enthusiastically.

'No, no,' ordered a perplexed Russell. 'Get off him, get him to his feet.'

Quick to comply, the fireman replaced his foot with a hand and, grabbing hold of my aching wrist, dragged me off the floor.

Russell wiped the sweat from his brow with a handkerchief. 'My apologies for that, but you really shouldn't be down here, Phillips. Now, what were you saying?'

'I might be able to help.'

'With all due respect, doctor, as a passenger, this is no business of yours. This area is closed to non-crew members.'

'That may be, but the man you were looking for was here.'

'What?'

'I was following you when someone came dashing out of the dark and pushed me over. They went running back through the hatch up there.'

'When was this?'

'Just before this great clunk landed on me.'

'Would you recognize him again?'

'I didn't even see him. He came in from the side, knocked me over and was gone. I guess he must have been hiding behind one of the coal piles. You must have missed him on your way through.'

Russell turned to the fireman. 'Damn it, Simms! I told you to stay back and watch this compartment. Now whoever it is has got clean away and is causing Lord only knows what mischief.'

'Sorry, sir, I just popped through to check on boiler three. I was worried about her goin' right out. I came straight back.'

Despite his heavy-footed approach I felt a little sorry for the big man, who was clearly not the sharpest knife in the drawer. 'A slippery fish all right,' I offered by way of commiseration. 'The fellow may have been on his way out when I arrived and got in his way. He must have fancied his chances better against me than . . . than with Simms here.'

'It sounds likely,' admitted Russell as he took the lamp from the third man. 'Bostock, escort Dr Phillips back to his stateroom, I'm going to have a good look around in here. Now, goodnight, doctor.'

The sound of a chain, clunking link by massive link through the bow of the ship, dragged me from a deep sleep as it pulled the anchor from the riverbed. The water in the glass beside my bunk boiled like a miniature sea as vibrations from the engines worked their way up through the vessel's superstructure. Not yet fully awake but eager to be on deck before the ship pulled away, I dressed quickly, postponing my shave until later in the day. My wrist still ached but no serious damage had been done. A peek through the porthole suggested a fine day in the making, the sky dotted with just a few clouds and the sea clear of the white tips of the day before.

On the deck a crowd was already pressed against the railings and, eager to share the view, I eased myself into a narrow gap between two fellow passengers. Out on the water small boats had gathered, their decks lined with sightseers returning our gaze. Some people had clambered up the great arch of the wheel box, and from up there enjoyed the best vantage point on the ship – if you discounted the tops of the masts of course. Those unable to fit on the box platforms but still eager for a grandstand view lined the footbridge which spanned the width of the deck between the two wheel boxes.

The tops of the paddle wheels were entirely shrouded by the boxes but if you stood far enough away and looked down over the side it was possible to see the blades as they disappeared below the surface of the water. A loud cheer went up as the wheels began to turn, thrashing through the water and adding their propulsion to that provided by the huge screw at the stern. I didn't hold out much hope for any of the smaller vessels fool-hardy enough to steer a course into the maelstrom that was our wake.

We passed the Nore light and the mouth of the estuary widened into the open expanse of the North Sea, where our course veered south towards the Channel. The ship stayed close enough to the shore for us to be able to see the thousands of well-wishers who had come down to the water to watch her steam by. I had just decided to go down for breakfast, when someone tapped me on the shoulder. I turned to find Russell, the black bags under his eyes a legacy of the unsettling events of the night before.

'My apologies for last night's unfortunate incident, Dr Phillips. I trust your wrist is recovered?'

'My wrist is fine,' I said, shaking my hand just to prove the point. 'And there is no need to apologize. Your man was only doing what he thought was right. As you said, I should not have been down there in the first place, especially as I knew that something was amiss. Did you find the man?'

'No, I am afraid not. We searched the boiler room thoroughly but found nothing out of the ordinary. Had it not been for your close encounter I would have been happy to write the entire thing off as a false alarm. You will, I am sure, understand my caution, given the importance of this voyage?'

'Of course.'

'Then I will bid you good morning. I must discuss today's tests with Captain Harrison.'

I was certain that Russell knew more than he was letting on, but I wasn't going to let that get in the way of breakfast.

After finishing my meal I returned to my cabin, where I spent some time catching up with my journal, or at least jotting down notes which would be expanded into a full entry upon my return home. After an hour or so I returned to the deck to check on our progress. The ship was still hugging the shore but our speed had suddenly increased. The cause of this acceleration became clear when I heard the mast behind me straining under the load it now carried. White sails billowed from every mast, the entire length of the vessel now overshadowed by what almost looked to be an unbroken wall of canvas.

A small town, which I learned from another passenger was Hastings, was coming into view. It looked a pleasant enough place, with a castle on the clifftop and a long breakwater stretching out towards us. Fishermen's huts were clustered on the beach and yet again people were crowded along the shore. Fishing boats, showing sails that looked like mere handkerchiefs in comparison with our own, carried people out to take a closer look and the ship's whistle began to sound in greeting. In the hope of gaining a better view of our own sails, I set out for the bow, from where I could look back down the length of the ship.

But no sooner had I arrived at the forward capstan than the ship gave a terrible shudder and a tremor rippled like a wave through the deck beneath my feet. An instant later there was a deafening roar and the sky was rent by a blinding flash of white light. The blast erupted through the deck, carrying with it one of the funnels and whatever else stood between this uncontainable force and the heavens. The funnel clanged like a broken bell as it tumbled back down on to the deck, its iron jacket torn and tattered. Pieces of timber and shards of metal and glass, even chairs from the saloon below, fell like rain, sending people previously frozen in shock running in all directions.

Steam hissed through the jagged hole now gaping in the deck and shrouded the bow in a cloud of white vapour. The cries of men and women joined with the deafening whine emitted by the wounded ship and the sound of the deck splintering under the shower of debris. I approached the scene of devastation, which was slowly revealed as the cloud began to dissipate. The sail on the forward mast was reduced to a tattered rag, its edges smouldering, while still-burning fragments fluttered through the air like leaves. People wandered aimlessly among the scrap iron and lumber littering the deck; some of them were bleeding but, miraculously, no one appeared to be seriously injured.

Glass crunched under my feet, most of it from the skylights set into the deck, but those slivers framing my reflection were from the mirrors in the saloon on the deck below. Any doubt that the level of destruction below decks was greater than that above was dispelled when a screaming man bolted on to the deck through a hatchway adjacent to the crater. His clothes had been ripped away by the force of the blast, his skin bleached white by the scalding effect of the steam, and his broiled scalp hung down from the back of his head as though it were a toupee blown loose in a high wind. So acute was his agony that he could perceive only one source of release. Before anyone could stop him, he vaulted over the side of the ship. By the time I reached the railing the man was clinging on to a spar attached to the forward part of the paddle box, his legs and torso submerged beneath the cooling water. But any sense of relief can only have been fleeting as, with his strength drained,

he let go of the spar and was devoured by the wheel as it relent-
lessly drove the ship forward. The poor soul was beyond help, his
mangled body never to be seen again – and there was more horror
to follow.

'No! Don't touch him,' I yelled at a passenger as he reached into
the hatchway to assist another badly scalded victim in his escape
from the bowels of the ship. But it was too late, and the good
Samaritan reeled backwards as the hand he held shed its skin like a
lady's glove, all the way up to the elbow, the flesh having cooked
to the bone.

Taking charge of the situation, I directed an officer to keep
people away as more victims staggered on to the deck. 'Bring
water-soaked blankets, plenty of them,' I called as he ushered people
away and shouted orders to the crew.

The most severely injured collapsed on to the deck, unable to
walk another step, while those more fortunate stood with their
faces to the wind, taking what solace they could from its cooling
quality. One man had lost his ears while the skin of his face had
taken on a peculiar sheen which would later transmute into the
most dreadful blistered mass. Sitting him down and instructing
him to keep his hands away from his face, I turned to a man in
even worse condition. The big fellow lay on his back, teeth and
parched gums exposed through the burning away of his lips. He
was fighting for breath and I feared that even his insides had
been cooked in the heat. The smell of burnt flesh was awful, like
something from hell's kitchen. The man was barely recognizable
as Simms, the giant who had pinned me to the floor with his boot,
and there appeared to be regret in his eyes just before they closed
for the last time.

The blankets arrived, along with a gentleman who hurriedly
introduced himself as the ship's medical officer. He set to work
alongside me, covering the men with the sodden blankets in the
hope that they would reduce their temperatures and soothe the
blisters. Other than that there was little more we could do.

Russell was the next to appear, accompanied by Captain Harrison. No less than fifteen injured men were now in the care of

myself and the medical officer, and with two already gone there could be little doubt that the death toll would increase. When I assured a quite distraught Russell that there was nothing he could do, both he and the captain disappeared below decks to inspect the damage and perhaps establish its cause, though in the light of previous events there could be little doubt that this was the work of the spectral saboteur.

We needed to get the men off the deck and so, leaving my colleague in charge, I went off and sought out a space which would lend itself to use as a temporary hospital. The main saloon was out of the question, as both the floor and ceiling were perforated by gaping holes. The once-luxurious hall was almost unrecognizable and it was a miracle that nearly all the passengers had been on deck because anyone in this room at the time of the explosion would surely have been killed. Pieces of furniture were reduced to match-wood and wall hangings to tatters. Several of the delicately wrought cast-iron pillars lay shattered as if made from glass and those mirrors that had not been smashed to smithereens had suffered the loss of the silvering that gave them the magical ability to capture reflection. Standing as close to the edge of the stateroom-sized hole in the floor as my frayed nerves would permit, I looked up to see the sky and then down to peer through a receding series of jagged rips in the floors of the decks below. If I were to lose my footing I would tumble clear through to the shattered boiler room in the bottom of the ship.

Although some parts of the vessel had obviously suffered terribly, destruction was limited to the immediate surroundings of the blast crater, and very soon a smaller saloon was accommodating the wounded, where we tended them as best we could. It was a great stroke of fortune and perhaps even more so vindication of Brunel as designer that the operation of the engines was unaffected by the blast, despite, as I was later to learn from Russell, the destruction of several boilers. And so, at a much reduced speed, the ship made for Weymouth, where she would put in and offload the wounded before having her own terrible injuries tended.

★

When I finally tracked Russell down to his office he looked to be swimming in a sea of scattered plans and drawings, each of which illustrated some or other aspect of the ship's workings. He turned and looked blankly at me. A half-empty bottle of whisky sat beside him.

'Any more news about the men?' he asked with a hollow voice as he pulled himself upright.

'I am afraid we lost two more this afternoon – that brings the toll up to four – and I have doubts about at least one more.'

He winced and gestured to the papers on the floor. 'I have been studying the cause of the accident . . . I mean, the incident.'

'Then it was sabotage?' I asked, working my way around the scatter of papers to sit on a leather couch.

'Undeniably.'

'A bomb?'

'No, we would have found a bomb in our search. He didn't need a bomb.'

'What then?'

'He closed a valve on one of the water-cooling jackets, as simple as that. Pressure built up until eventually the entire system exploded. He turned the ship into a bomb.' He picked up a drawing lying at his feet and glared at it.

'So we're talking about someone who knows their way around a boiler room, perhaps even knows this ship intimately?'

'Possible. He knew their business, that much is certain. It was so subtle that if he hadn't been spotted where he shouldn't have been, then the entire thing could have been written off as an unfortunate accident.'

'And that would have suited you better?'

'What do you mean?'

'Stop the charade,' I snapped, my patience by now wearing very thin. 'You know more about this than you're letting on. I think you know full well who's responsible, and you're going to tell me.'

He made no response.

'I know about the torpedo, and the part that you intended Brunel's device to play in it. He thinks you were behind Wilkie's death, but I've always given you the benefit of the doubt. After today I'm beginning to change my mind.'

The drawing slipped to the floor and Russell refilled another glass. 'The whole thing got out of hand. You have to believe that. I didn't intend for any of this to happen.'

'Go on.'

'Damn it! If only Brunel had been willing to part with his precious device. It seemed strange at first. I had never known him to be so protective about anything. You know he's never taken out a patent in his life?' I nodded. 'But then I discovered that at the same time he was doing everything in his power to get me sacked.' He paused to take a swig from the glass. 'Saying no was just another way of getting to me, that's all.'

'But why did he want you sacked? Surely the project could not proceed without you. The ship was being built in your yard.'

'There were shortfalls in the accounts, errors were made, estimates for the costs were too low.'

'Estimates made by you?'

'Yes, by me! We . . . I . . . I went bankrupt because of Brunel's ridiculous specifications. He wouldn't listen to sense. Everything had to be just the way he wanted it, no expense spared.'

'But you tendered deliberately low to secure the job. You knew there was no way you could build the ship for the amount you quoted.'

'I see Brunel's been tutoring you in the finer points of the shipbuilding business. Yes, I may have been overly competitive at the tendering stage. But I was certain we could make up the shortfall, especially when he came up with the gaz engine and then the heart. It would have solved all our financial problems at the drop of a hat. Useless, of course, for the purpose he intended, but I recognized its worth immediately. It was the missing piece of a machine I had been working on for a number of years.'

'The torpedo.'

He nodded. 'It was revolutionary – a self-propelled projectile capable of moving unseen beneath the surface of the water and guaranteed to sink any ship it hit. The only problem was the propulsion system needed to be small and operate without an exhaust. Brunel's device fitted the bill perfectly.'

'Why didn't you tell Brunel what you intended to use it for? He might have been more open to cooperation if you had been honest with him.'

'The clients wouldn't let me. They said if I told anyone else about the torpedo then . . . then the deal was off.'

'The clients? You sold the idea?'

Russell took another tug of whisky. 'That's where the trouble lies. I offered the torpedo to a certain party and they were prepared to pay a lot of money, enough to get us out of the financial difficulties we were in, but without Brunel's device the thing was just another white elephant, a worthless pile of junk.'

'So you went back on the deal.'

'I did nothing wrong. When it became clear that Brunel wanted no part in the project I went to the client and returned the down payment.'

Now we were getting to the nub of the matter. 'Let me guess. They didn't want to know? They took it into their own hands to get the device?'

'Yes, that was when they killed Wilkie.'

'And what about today?'

'They told me that unless I put things right and got hold of the device they would do something to the ship and ruin me again. The explosion was the result.'

'But even then you made no further attempt to persuade Brunel or get hold of the device?'

'Where would be the point in that? Brunel can barely bring himself to speak to me and he's given up on the device anyway. I was even pleased to hear that he had. It seemed like an end to the matter.'

'But they didn't see it that way.'

'My client has made promises to their client and they won't take no for an answer.'

'This is getting a little complicated. Just who are we dealing with here? Who's behind this if not you?'

Russell pondered the matter for a while. 'Is it Hawes?' I asked.

Russell shook his head and then, resigned to his fate, he spat out the name.

'Perry, it was Perry.'

'The shipbuilder.'

'Shipbuilder? Pah! The man couldn't build a snowman.'

Perry had been on my list, but then so had every other member of the Lazarus Club. 'Why him?' I asked, keeping up the pressure.

'He's an agent for a firm in Limehouse called Blyth's. Among other things, they build warships for foreign clients and procure weapons for overseas service.'

'You mean they're arms dealers. So who wanted the torpedo?'

'I don't know.'

'He told you nothing?'

Russell shook his head. 'It's how Blyth's operate – you know only what and who you need to know. Perry has a client but I don't know who it is. I swear.'

I believed him. 'But whoever they are they are putting pressure on Blyth's to make sure you deliver. What a bloody mess. You've got yourself caught up in all this just because you under-budgeted the cost of building this ship. What do you think their next move will be?'

'Probably to kill me.'

'Why don't you go to the police or even the government? Surely they would be interested in stopping a foreign power from getting hold of a British weapon.'

'I couldn't do that. In any case, the government would probably be happy to let them test the weapon in battle conditions and then decide whether or not it was worth buying themselves. You see, Phillips, it's all about money. All of it.'

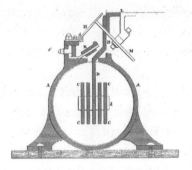

## 30

Badly wounded, the ship arrived off Weymouth, a full day after the explosion, the hole in her deck bandaged with canvas and the broken funnel strapped down under a web of ropes. Our arrival had been unscheduled, but nonetheless a huge crowd awaited the ship as she berthed in the unfinished harbour at Portland. The passengers were the first to disembark, though not before some of them had scoured the decks for small pieces of glass, wood or other debris to take as souvenirs of their lucky escape. They would now have to get home under their own steam, as Russell was determined that the ship would not put to sea again until fully repaired. With the ship returned to shore her builder appeared to have regained his composure and was even boasting that the repairs, which he intended to supervise personally, would take no more than three weeks to complete.

Only once all of the passengers had disembarked did I set about supervising the careful removal of the injured, all of them firemen who had been stoking the boilers when the blast occurred. Three men were carried off the ship on litters and loaded into waiting wagons, while the remaining four were able to walk with some assistance.

Returning to the ship to collect my luggage, I encountered Russell, who was overseeing the removal of the canvas cover.

'You have done a wonderful job with the men – my thanks for that,' he said, by way of farewell.

'Your medical officer did just as much,' I returned a little coldly.

'I know how you feel about me, Phillips, but rest assured I will see that these men are looked after, financially that is. They will want for nothing.'

I thought of adding, 'Apart from skin,' but held my tongue.

'I am the only one they will want to hurt now,' said Russell. 'But they may feel they have already done enough.'

'I hope so, Russell,' I said, feeling some small amount of sympathy for a man who had been swallowed up by events he had inadvertently set in motion.

'Please pass on my best wishes to Brunel, when you see him.'

Agreeing to do so and accepting his offer of a handshake, I took leave of him and the ship and joined the small convoy of carriages on its way to the hospital.

My intention had been to set out for London but after seeing how much trouble the influx of patients was causing at the local hospital I decided to stay on for a day or two and take charge of their treatment.

Travelling once again on Brunel's railway, I returned to London on 13 September. No more of the men in my care had died, and I was hopeful that they would all pull through. Unfortunately, Brunel did not seem to be faring so well, and when I arrived at Duke Street on the morning after my return, Brodie feared the end was very near.

'I tried to keep the bad news away from him, but he got hold of a copy of *The Times*,' he whispered anxiously, just before I entered the bedroom. 'I think one of his servants smuggled it in for him. He was naturally eager for news of the ship's voyage.'

'And he learned about the explosion – was that what caused the relapse?'

'He had another heart attack. He won't live much longer, I'm afraid. There is nothing more I can do, Phillips.'

With that Brodie opened the door and I quietly approached the bed. Brunel's head lay half buried in the pillow, where strands of his hair criss-crossed like the filaments of a broken spider's web.

His arms were motionless by his side, the only movement provided by the rise and fall of his chest. At first I thought he was sleeping but on hearing me approach the red lids of his eyes fluttered open. 'Phillips', he rasped. 'Hear you did a splendid job with the men on the ship. The second time you have been there to help when it was needed most . . .'

'I did what I could,' I said, pulling up a chair to sit beside him.

The dying man's lips moved once again, his voice so frail that it was difficult to make out what he was saying. I moved closer, my head cocked to the side and almost resting on the pillow beside his. 'The ship, how . . .' he whispered, each word accompanied by a dreadful wheezing sound as it dragged itself out of his throat. 'How did she fare?'

'She moves like a dream, Mr Brunel, and I know that the explosion had nothing to do with her design. There were other factors involved.'

'Other factors? You mean Russell?'

There seemed little point in trying to explain all I had learned and so I simply nodded. Brunel seemed satisfied.

'There is one last service I want to ask of you.'

'Anything,' I replied.

'First, have Brodie leave the room.'

I turned to the doctor, who was standing at the end of the bed. 'Sir Benjamin, he asks if you could please step out of the room for a moment.'

There was a time when such a request would have been regarded as an affront to his position, but without a word Brodie turned and left, closing the door quietly behind him.

'He's gone,' I said, uncertain as to how aware he was of his surroundings. Reaching for my handkerchief, I wiped a string of spittle from where it had formed on the twisted corner of his mouth.

He put his hand on my shoulder and drew me closer still. 'The heart. I want you to place it inside my chest.'

At first I wasn't certain I had heard him correctly. 'In your chest?'

I asked, looking across at the agitated blanket. 'You mean cut you open and put it inside you?'

He tried to nod, but the pillow pressing into the side of his face stopped him. 'Take out the old and put in the new.'

It crossed my mind that he seriously expected the heart to improve his condition, to bring him back to life, but then it dawned on me: that wasn't it at all. This was how he planned to dispose of the heart, to remove it from circulation and keep it out of Russell's grasp. 'But when?' I asked, seeking reassurance that I was right.

'Preferably not while I'm still breathing,' he replied, his mouth trying its hardest to form a smile. 'I have made arrangements. You will be allowed access to me . . . to my body before they put me in the ground.'

When I said nothing, he pressed the issue further. 'Promise me, Phillips, promise you will carry out this old engineer's last wish, as a friend.' His eyes gave up what must surely be their last flicker of passion. 'Promise!'

I touched his cold hand. 'I promise.'

Brunel turned his head until he was once again looking up towards the ceiling. 'Then all is well. Thank you, my friend.'

Our business concluded, I readmitted Brodie to the room. I asked him whether he would be returning to the hospital. 'Not until I am finished here,' he replied, now sounding more like an undertaker than a doctor. I offered to take his place but he would not have it, and so, feeling very low, I took my leave.

'Goodnight, Isambard.'

'Farewell, Phillips,' returned Brunel, his eyes now closed.

Brunel and my father appeared side by side in my dreams that night, but then their faces merged and melded, as each of them tried to tell me something I could not hear.

The next morning, on his return to the hospital, Brodie delivered the anticipated news of Brunel's death. The great engineer had passed away just hours after my departure. Sir Benjamin's constant attendance had also taken its toll, and he looked terribly tired and drawn, and took me at my word when I offered to take charge of things so he could rest.

To my disappointment I discovered that Florence was away recruiting for her nursing school. There had been several occasions on the ship and in the hospital at Weymouth when I had wished her present, and not just because of her expertise in dealing with cases of mass injury.

Once again, the hospital seemed dull in comparison with my recent adventures, but nonetheless I found myself busy enough in the theatre. William was at first his usual ebullient self, but it didn't take long for my bleaker mood to rub off on him.

'There'll be many a man sorry to see him go,' he remarked, when I told him of Brunel's death. 'You'll be going to the funeral then?'

'I suppose so,' I replied, having thought of nothing else for the entire day.

Brunel's request weighed heavily upon my mind, not so much because of its peculiar character, for nothing in my life these days could really be described as normal, but because I did not want to see the device wasted in such a way. Despite my misgivings about the practicality of replacing a human heart with a mechanical counterpart, I had come to see some merit in the proposition. As Brunel had said, there might come a time when the device would be looked back upon as the foundation stone of a medical revolution, but not if it were buried with its inventor, never to be seen or heard of again. But on the other hand I thoroughly understood Brunel's motives, as the act would remove the device forever from the grasp of those who had done so little to deserve it, and indeed intended to put it to so nefarious a use.

At first I successfully avoided the issue by keeping busy, but it wasn't going to be that easy.

'Someone's left a note for you,' said William. Recognizing Brunel's hand on the envelope, I opened it straight away, the blood on my hands staining the paper and giving me all the more excuse to destroy it immediately upon reading. The note must have been written not long after I had left his bedside the night before. The hand was erratic, and obviously the work of a very sick man.

My Dear Phillips,

My eternal gratitude for agreeing to do me one final service. I write this letter while I am still able to do so but when it reaches you I will be dead. In order to fulfil your promise I have made arrangements for you to have access to my mortal remains prior to burial. Your window of opportunity will obviously be short, so please come to Duke Street at your earliest possible convenience. The man who delivered this note, already known to you as my driver, is a most trusted servant and has been briefed, though he does not know the true motive for your 'visit', and will ensure that you are unmolested while you carry out the task in hand. Mary too will be expecting you and knows better than to ask questions. That is all that is to be said, and anyway my hand can write no more. My eternal thanks for your companionship and assistance on numerous occasions.

Your friend,

Isambard Kingdom Brunel (deceased)

Crumpling the page in my fist, I imagined Brunel smiling to himself as he signed himself off as deceased, and dropped the ball of paper into the top of the stove, where it was engulfed in flame. 'William, where is the man who delivered this?'

He shrugged his shoulders. 'Dunno, sir, he left it at the front, probably couldn't find you to deliver it personal like.'

'Ah well,' I sighed. 'It can't be helped. Let us get back to work.'

With the last of the day's students departed and William left to clean up in the theatre, I slipped into the specimen room, where I had first demonstrated the functions of the heart to Brunel almost three years previously. Pushing aside a jar on a high shelf, which caused the foetus within to bob from side to side as if trying to free itself from a crystal womb, I pulled down the jar concealed behind it. The red fleshy object in this vessel did not float, but like a stone in a lake sat motionless on the bottom. Placing it carefully on the bench, I removed the lid and after rolling up my sleeve and putting on a thick glove slowly immersed my hand in the fluid.

The lung was bloated, as if infected by some terrible growth, the walls distended and thinned by the presence of the solid mass within. It lay on the bench in a spreading puddle of alcohol. Slipping the fingers of my gloved hand into a broad incision in the wall of the sac, I took hold of the tumescent mass and pulled it out through the breach. Glove removed, I untied the string around the bundle and peeled it open. Brunel's mechanical heart sat amidst the dark folds of the oilskin wrapper, its metallic surfaces entirely untarnished by its immersion. Thus the heart was revealed for the first time since I had concealed it in the lung weeks before. What better place to hide it than in a room full of human organs.

I brushed my hand over the surface of the casing and turned the fly-wheel. A flick of the latch and the two halves popped apart, revealing the valves and chambers. A more perfect tool for teaching the workings of the heart I could not envisage, though to display the thing in public would undoubtedly be to risk life and limb. In any case, I had made a promise to a friend: it had been no less than his dying wish that he be buried with this inside him. I surely had no option but to comply. But then, I told myself, there was more at stake here: there was the future of medical science, and indeed Brunel's role within it to consider. As guardian of the heart, a role which had been thrust upon me by Brunel himself, it was surely my responsibility to ensure that the heart was looked after, protected and made available to others for further study. And so, I kept the heart instead of making sure it was buried with Brunel.

With my conscience in turmoil, I once again packed up the heart, wrapping it in the oilcloth and then stuffing it into the preserved lung before lowering it carefully back into the jar. You are doing the right thing, I told myself, and Brunel, had he been of sounder mind before his death, would, I was sure, have been in full agreement. Little did I know how much I would come to regret my decision to ignore his request in the days and weeks that followed.

After failing to find me at the hospital I further sought to avoid Brunel's man Samuel by visiting my club for supper and then spending the night seeking solace between Clare's welcoming thighs.

On my way to the hospital the next morning I picked up a copy of *The Times*, where I found an obituary to the deceased engineer.

Saturday 17 September 1859

DEATH OF MR BRUNEL, CE – We regret to announce the demise of Mr Brunel, the eminent civil engineer, who died on Thursday night at his residence, Duke Street, Westminster. The lamented gentleman was brought home from the *Great Eastern* steamship at midday on the 5TH inst., in a very alarming condition, having been seized with paralysis, induced, it is believed, by mental anxiety. Mr Brunel, in spite of the most skilful medical treatment, continued to sink, and at half-past 10 on Thursday night he expired at the comparatively early age of 54 years. The deceased was the only son of the late Sir Marc Brunel, who for his many public works at Portsmouth, Woolwich, and Chatham, and more particularly the Thames Tunnel, received the honour of knighthood from Her Majesty in 1841. The late Mr Brunel was the engineer of the Great Western Railway from the formation of the company, and all the great works on that line were completed from his designs and supervision. The magnificent bridge at Saltash is another example of his engineering ability; and as most of our readers are aware, the leviathan steamship, the *Great Eastern*, was the last and greatest of his undertakings, and with which his name will ever be associated. Mr Brunel was born in England, but his father was a native of Normandy, and a gentleman by birth. Owing to the troubles of the first French Revolution, he was compelled to emigrate to the United States, whence he came to England in 1799, and was employed at Portsmouth Dockyard to complete the block machinery. Sir M. I. Brunel was educated for the church, but his love of scientific pursuits

led to his embracing the profession of which he ultimately
became one of the leading members.


It was depressing to think that one's life, no matter how fulfilled,
could be crammed into so few words – which in any case said as
much about his father as him. But the obituary served to bolster
my conviction that I was doing right by retaining what would
otherwise be lost.

The day passed without incident and nobody arrived to find out
why I had not appeared at Duke Street. I could only assume that
Brunel, having no reason to doubt I would carry out his instructions,
had left no provision for me to be pursued if I did not. The funeral
was scheduled for the following Tuesday, which meant that the
window of opportunity to which Brunel had referred was fast
disappearing. It promised to be a grand affair at Kensal Green, and
with Brunel safely out of my reach in his coffin I had every intention
of being there to pay my last respects.

If the stature of a man can be gauged by the number of people
attending his funeral, then Brunel, for all he lacked in physical
height, was truly a giant among men. Not since the sea trial had I
seen so many people gathered together in one place. Unable to
proceed any further in the cab, I disembarked and continued on
foot, joining those mourners of like mind in the funeral cortege.
Up ahead, the hearse, pulled by horses decked out with black
plumes, made its slow progress, the crowd parting like a human
wave in front of it. Even on foot it was almost impossible to move
along the streets bordering the cemetery for the crowds waiting to
catch a glimpse of the coffin. Most of these people were railway
workers, some of them still in their work clothes but all displaying
a black armband. Hats were removed as the hearse passed slowly
by and bared heads lowered in silent prayer.

Passage became a little easier when I reached the cemetery gates
where the Yeomanry, decked out in all their scarlet finery, provided
a guard of honour and kept the masses at a respectable distance.

Leaving the crowd behind, the cortege made its way down the tree-lined avenue, the ornate tombs on either side giving the thoroughfare the appearance of a street inhabited only by the dead.

'Quite a turn-out, don't you think?' said Ockham, who had fallen in beside me. It was the first time I had laid eyes on him since returning from the ship, and his immaculate funeral attire bore all the signs of being purchased specially for the occasion.

'I thought I was never going to get here.'

'Have you seen anyone else?' he asked, craning his neck so as to see over the heads of those to our front.

'I thought I caught a glimpse of Hawes back there, but he's the only one thus far.'

'There's Russell, standing head and shoulders above the others,' he observed, by now almost walking on tiptoes.

'So he came back from Weymouth for the funeral.'

'And I think he's with someone,' said Ockham, raising himself a fraction higher by placing a hand on my shoulder. 'Yes, it's Perry.'

'Perry!' I exclaimed too loudly, causing a lady to turn and glower disapprovingly. What with all the upheaval caused by Brunel's death, I hadn't given him much thought since my return from the ship. But now, here he was, the man responsible for Wilkie's murder. His hands may not have committed the crime but they were no less blood-soaked for that.

'Without a doubt,' confirmed Ockham, now returned to his normal height and seeming a little startled as I tugged on his sleeve and dragged him sideways out of the column of mourners.

Leaving the cortege, I ushered him between a pair of stone angels and came to a halt behind a miniature version of a Greek temple, where the sound of feet crunching on gravel could no longer be heard.

'Listen, there's something I've got to tell you, something I learned on the ship.'

'I know all about that. It was Russell after all, wasn't it?'

'How do you know that?'

'Brunel told me. Not exactly a surprise. I knew it was him all along.'

'When did he tell you?'

'I visited him not long after you on the night of his death. Brodie didn't want to let me in but the old man insisted. He told me that you had confirmed Russell's involvement.'

'Yes, but . . .'

Ockham seemed untroubled by the affair. 'Why look so worried? Remember, as from today the heart really does cease to exist.'

'Cease to exist?'

He glanced back at the funeral procession. 'Well, as good as, once it's been buried along with Brunel. If only Russell knew he was saying goodbye to his precious engine.'

'Yes, of course,' I said, playing along. 'I suppose Brunel told you about that as well?'

Ockham nodded. 'That you had promised to carry out the operation, yes.'

'It was the least I could do,' I lied. My chance to come clean, to admit that I had broken my promise had passed. This was after all no time to be creating a scene.

'I had meant to seek you out and offer assistance but . . .' Ockham's countenance suddenly darkened and for a moment words seemed to fail him. 'Well, things got in the way.' It was only then that I realized how deeply Brunel's death had affected him. These past days had no doubt been spent dulling his emotions in an opium den, just as I knew he had done after his mother's death – well, at least her second death. Perhaps aware that he was now betraying those emotions, he stiffened his back.

'Well, then, don't you think we had better see them both off – Brunel and his mechanical heart?'

As we walked between memorials my sense of guilt began to grow like some dreadful tumour. I had spent much time of late convincing myself that going back on my word and disregarding Brunel's request had been the right thing to do. But in truth, I had let down both the living and the dead. No matter how I dressed up my actions, or lack of them, there could be no getting away from the fact that my motives were selfish.

With Ockham still convinced that Russell was the cause of all our troubles, we rejoined the mourners to see the coffin carried from the hearse and placed above the grave, the casket covered by a flag I had last seen fluttering from the mast of the *Great Eastern*.

The coffin sank behind the wall of closely packed shoulders in front of us, between the sombre bonnets and bowed heads. 'Ashes to ashes, dust to dust,' proclaimed the disjointed voice of the presiding clergyman. With the formalities over, the mourners slowly drifted away, but Perry didn't move; he stood as steady as a monument, watching me through stone-cold eyes.

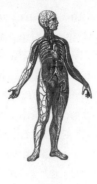

# 31

I am in the heart of Isambard's kingdom, where steam shrieks from open valves and blurs everything before me. Crawling through these narrow spaces I seek a way to the outside world.

The iron panels close around me, leaving no option but to crawl through the narrow, choking spaces. Here, serpents of steam atomize into vapour and hang in the air like a heavy London fog. There, coal fires throw out a patchwork of flickering light, casting my broken shadow across a weave of copper pipes. Everywhere, kettle-hot walls and floors blister fingers wrapped in strips of shirt-torn fabric. Eventually, an opening gives way to a great vaulted hall, where rising and falling pistons send heavy cranks knifing through the air, punching oil to the back of my throat.

That, in a nutshell, was the dream as it appeared to me the night after Brunel's funeral. It recurred every night thereafter, leaving me soaked in a sea of sweat only when it finally sailed across the horizon of morning. It drained my strength with a voracity equal to that displayed by any of the parasitical worms I have ever encountered, lodged, fattened and gorged in the intestines of their victims. Like the parasite, it grew as it weakened me, forcing itself with ever-increasing vitality into the front of my mind and routing any semblance of reality. I was alone that first time, a solitary prisoner in a metal maze, but on other occasions there was someone else – a spectre lurking behind me.

Where this nightmare hid itself during the daylight hours I do not know, perhaps somewhere in the dark recesses of my mind, refuelling itself in the shadows of morbidity. For even in my mind, which I have always considered to be open and enlightened, there must exist dusty nooks and crannies in which the more primitive sensations still hold sway. Although at first Brunel seemed to be the engineer of my nightmare it soon emerged to be of my own making, constructed as it was from the annealed heart of a broken promise.

Sleep brought no rest, and fatigue began to affect my work – so much so that one day my unsteady hand strayed through an exposed artery, causing the patient on the table to bleed to death. I had lost patients before, the suicidal Fisher's wife being among them, but they had been outside my control. This time I had only myself to blame; I had once told Ockham that there were bad doctors, but now with this terrible mistake, it appeared that I had joined their ranks. Once more burdened with guilt, I resolved to take action.

While unknowingly sowing the seeds of my entrapment, Brunel had also provided me with enough rope to pull myself out of that hole but, equally, if I put a foot wrong the same rope would hang me.

At our very first meeting the inquisitive engineer had asked me if the hospital obtained its cadavers from grave robbers. I told him then that practice had ceased with the passing of the Anatomy Act in the 1830s.

Back then I had been a small boy, but William had been in his prime. And what's more, it was common knowledge within the hospital that he had been active in the procurement of anatomical subjects – in short, he had been a grave robber. It was said that in days gone by he had been the leader of one of the many gangs of resurrection men that plundered hundreds of graves in and around London. The story was that, with the passing of the act, one of my predecessors – who may or may not have been Brodie himself – rewarded him for services rendered with a secure position as a porter in the hospital, though there was uncertainty as to whether this was an act of kindness or a bribe to secure his silence on the matter.

William remained cagey when I questioned him about the past, but whatever had happened back then he certainly displayed no compunction when it came to selling bodies misappropriated from the hospital – not quite grave robbing perhaps but not too far removed. Hoping that he felt beholden to me for not reporting his actions – he didn't need to know that my reasons had nothing to do with saving his skin – I arranged to meet him in his local tavern in order to discuss what I described as a small business matter.

William was in a snug, where I found him not only less than sober but also in company. He was laughing and drinking with a man I had never seen before. With my arrival their banter ceased and William introduced his companion, who from the lines on his face and the gaps in his blackened teeth seemed a near-contemporary.

'Don't worry about Bittern, sir, he's an old mate,' he said, nudging the man's arm conspiratorially. 'An' if I'm right about the nature of the business you have in mind then he's just the man you're after. We were partners, see, back in the good old days.'

I began to wonder what sort of mess I was getting myself into and so to calm my nerves took a pull from the dirty glass into which the landlord had poured a large measure of evil-smelling brandy. The raw spirit took my breath away and for some moments denied me the ability of speech. 'They don't serve your posh Napoleon brandy in 'ere, doc,' said William gleefully.

As I struggled to regain my composure Bittern chipped in with what he may have thought was reassurance. 'Don't worry, guv, you'll get used to it. After a couple of glasses you won't know no difference.'

With the crisis passed I turned to business, having no desire to patronize this establishment any longer than was strictly necessary. 'You seem to have gauged my intentions, William?'

'It don't exactly need a Pinkerton man to tell you're after raising the dead. You've talked of nothing but resurrections for days on end. Now tell me you don't want a liftin' done.'

'Yes, William, I'm afraid so,' I admitted, shamed that my efforts at subtlety had been so entirely inept. 'Unsavoury as the idea is, I find myself in a situation where I have to call on your particular expertise.'

Despite guessing my intentions the old porter looked somewhat puzzled. 'But, sir, surely you get enough legal stiffs at the hospital. We're up to our armpits in 'em.' Then he checked himself. 'Well, at least that is since . . . since the late unpleasantness.'

'You mean, since you stopped stealing them?'

He just nodded. 'But why take the chance of robbin' a grave? It would cause one 'ell of a scandal if you was found with a nobbled corpse.'

I took a cautious sip of my drink, this time with only the slightest ill effect – Bittern had been right.

'I can barely believe it myself, but my situation permits no other course of action. But you don't need to know the details – not yet.' I glanced dubiously at Bittern, and although he looked entirely disreputable decided that I had little choice but to bring him in on the job. 'I can't afford to pay you much. Let's say five guineas apiece for the work, but only on the guarantee that you'll both keep your mouths shut.'

'You don't 'ave to worry about paying me, sir,' said William. 'Let's just say I owe you one. And as for keeping our mouths shut – you needn't worry on that score either, sir; it'd go just as badly if not worse for us if we were caught returned to our old trade. We were lucky to escape the gallows last time around. As for Bittern's five guineas – it's fair, generous even.' He turned to his old friend, 'What do you say, Bit?'

'For six guineas I'd provide me own mother's mortals, so for five they'd better be someone else's.'

William laughed. 'Then let's drink to it, shall we?' He raised his glass to make a toast, but finding it empty he held it out to me in feigned surprise. I took both their glasses and fought my way to the bar through the stand of boisterous street-hawkers, labourers, dockers, cabbies and sundry other labouring types drinking to the end of another long day. The floor was covered in sawdust caked with spillage and sputum, which congealed on my shoes and brought to mind the dissection theatre, as did the jaundiced, near-cadaverous faces of some among the crowd.

The landlord refilled my companions' glasses with rum and mine with another brandy – I had one more request to make of the resurrection men and my nerves were still in need of a little bolstering.

William raised his refilled glass. 'Here's to it then, gentlemen, partners in crime.'

This time I drained half my glass. 'I have one more stipulation about our activities.'

'What's that then?' asked William.

'I want to be there when you . . . when you do the job.'

Bittern laughed, 'Well I never. The good doctor wants to go a-grave robbin'.'

William was equally taken aback. 'You been out with me once of a night-time but that was different. No, sir, that's not possible. We work as a team, me and Bittern. There's a skill to it. Someone who doesn't know what they're about would bring the Peelers down on us before we were halfway through.'

His argument was a good one. I was no veteran at finding my way around burial grounds in the dead of night and the last thing I wanted was to become reacquainted with the police. But for what I had in mind there was no other option and I was going to insist when Bittern, having a keen eye for the main chance, saw opportunity in my predicament. 'Well, sir, I'm afraid if you want to increase the risk of us getting caught by taking you along, then the price goes up two guineas. Let's call it danger money.'

William looked at his colleague with some incredulity but said nothing.

Bittern had me over a barrel and knew it. Having told them as much as I had, there was no going back and I could hardly seek out a cheaper alternative – grave robbing wasn't exactly a straightforward service to acquire. 'Very well, seven guineas, three now and the remainder when the job's done. Agreed?'

'Agreed,' said William, on Bittern's behalf.

'Good,' I said without enthusiasm. 'When can it be done?'

'There's no moon and we need all the cover we can get. How about tomorrow night, round eleven o'clock?'

'Eleven o'clock exactly,' I stipulated. As far as I was concerned, the sooner it was done, the better. The dreams were turning me into a wreck and it could only be a matter of time before my degenerating mental and physical condition was recognized by others.

'Where's it to be, this job?' asked Bittern, by now displaying neither a hint of his earlier good humour nor the effects of drink.

'Kensal Green cemetery,' I replied, hoping this information wouldn't bring on another increase in price.

'Kensal Green, eh?' mused William. 'Some rich people in that ground – after a toff, are we?'

'No, I wouldn't say that, and in any case, I had always thought death was regarded as the great leveller. What does the subject's standing in life matter to you?'

William sniffed. 'No matter to us, just better-quality corpses than we're used to, that's all. But there's a lot of posh family vaults and tombs in that place. Your corpse ain't locked away in one of them, is it? If it is we might as well try breaking into the Bank of England, what with all the gates, locks and then a lead coffin at the end of it all.'

I had visited the cemetery more than once of late and had seen for myself the elaborately built tombs and vaults which were all the rage among the rich and famous, some of them even borrowing architectural details from Brunel's beloved Ancient Egyptians. 'No, not in a fancy vault – just a coffin six feet under.'

'Eleven it is then. Meet us on the canal towpath behind the cemetery, opposite the gasometer. We'll go in over the wall.'

I surrendered the down payment and left my new partners to what remained of their drinks. Back at my rooms, I lay on my bed pondering my fate. Which was it to be? Loss of position; struck off as a doctor; public disgrace; thrown into prison or even lynched by the mob – the possibilities seemed endless. I slept for only a short time and while I did so returned to the now all too familiar surroundings of the engine room.

★

There was a cold wind blowing across the cut and, standing on the towpath with my back to the cemetery wall, I checked my watch to find myself at the agreed meeting place a little earlier than planned. Even in the dark, I could make out the skeletal silhouette of the gasometer's girders on the other side of the canal, its telescopic turret almost entirely depressed by the absence of gas inside. Putting down my sack, I blew into cupped hands to keep my circulation going.

Not long after, William and Bittern approached along the path, their arrival heralded by the sound of a chain rattling and the creak of metal against wood. Pushing an old two-wheeled market barrow before them, they drew up alongside me.

William's face was almost entirely covered by a woollen balaclava while Bittern's eyes were shielded beneath the peak of a bonnet pulled low over his head. A canvas sheet sat atop the barrow, partially covering a pair of shovels, a length of rope and some other hardware. An unlit storm lamp was suspended from a nail on the front of the contraption.

We nodded in greeting and William manœuvred the barrow into position with one side sitting flush against the wall. Bittern climbed up on to it and then pulled himself on to the top of the wall. William handed up the shovels, which Bittern dropped over the other side, and then the lamp, which he gently lowered down on the rope. Then, after gesturing for me to follow, Bittern watched with some amusement as I scrambled up. In the meantime William took the barrow and pushed it around the corner of the wall, hiding it from anyone who happened along the path. I was the first to drop down over the side, while Bittern assisted William, who had to climb without the benefit of the barrow. It was even darker beyond the wall, and it took some time for my eyes to readjust before the tombs and gravestones began to appear out of the gloom. The cemetery seemed very different at night but I hoped that once we arrived at the main thoroughfare it would be an easy enough task to find our way.

It felt better to be over the wall, sheltered from the wind and away from the path, which had seemed dangerously exposed.

William bent and lit the lamp, covering it with a shroud to restrict the light to a beam just wide enough to illuminate our progress. Dividing the equipment, which included a strange hook-like device, we set off into the city of the dead.

William handed me the lamp. 'Off you go,' he whispered. 'We'll follow.' The two old men moved with a stealth of which I would never have thought them capable, dispelling my previous concerns about them arriving drunk.

Small, quite modest gravestones and plinth-like memorials inhabited this part of the cemetery, some of them topped by stone urns or carved angels. But as we approached the carriageway, along which the funeral processions travelled, the monuments took on a much grander character, with tall obelisks sitting alongside large family vaults and ornate tombs. Rather than step on to the noisy gravel we kept to the grass and followed the edge of the path, heading away from the main gates and the sexton's office, towards the far end of the cemetery. We continued in this fashion until a yew tree much in need of a prune barred our advance. As I had hoped, a narrower path turned off to the right just behind the tree.

Like sleep-walking mourners we gathered around a low mound of freshly turned earth. The naked soil was hidden beneath a litter of decaying wreaths and withered flowers. 'This is it,' I said, casting the beam from the lamp over a small wooden cross at the head of the mound. This simple marker was just a temporary measure, to be replaced by a grander stone memorial when the earth had settled. A metal plaque was attached to the cross and after taking the lamp from me William bent forward to read the inscription out loud.

ISAMBARD KINGDOM BRUNEL,
9th April 1806 – 15th September 1859

'Well I never, it's your engineer friend. Why in heaven's name do you want to dig him up?'

This was neither the time nor place for me to explain my motives – who would believe me anyway?

'I have my reasons. Let's leave it at that, shall we?'

'Well, it's your funeral,' said William. 'Lord knows what sort of a state he's going to be in now – must have been buried for the best part of a month. Our previous clients always preferred their subjects a little fresher.'

'That's not going to be a problem,' I replied curtly, impatient to get started.

'Not goin' to be a problem!' exclaimed William. 'It's not a barrow that's needed to take 'im away, it's a bloody barrel!'

'We're not taking him anywhere,' I insisted, trying hard to keep my voice down. 'I just need to get into the coffin, that's all. Five minutes' access and then we can close the lid, backfill the grave and get out of here. But before we can do that we've got a hole to dig.'

'I get it,' said Bittern, pushing the old wreaths aside with his foot. 'There's something in there that you want.' Having spread out the canvas sheet, he set to work with the shovel, digging into the mound and dumping the spoil on the sheet. 'What is it? Jewellery, rings maybe, gold? What's down there?'

'There's nothing in there. I'm not taking anything out. If you must know, I'm putting something in. Now can we get on with it? Surely we shouldn't be making so much noise?'

'Don't fret about the noise,' said William, picking up the other shovel and taking position at the far end of the mound. 'There's not been a grave robbed here for nearly thirty years; like as not the gatehouse isn't even manned at night these days. But let's get weaving. This is going to be a much longer job than we planned for.'

'What do you mean longer?' I asked, somewhat vexed to discover that Bittern had previously exaggerated the dangers involved so as to secure a bigger fee.

'When we were resurrecting we had a real quick way of doin' it,' he said, without breaking from his labour. 'We didn't bother diggin' out the entire grave. We just dug down to the coffin from the foot end of the grave. Then we dropped that hook and rope under the end of the casket and pulled it up through the shaft we'd dug. The soil left in the grave acted as a counterweight. Easy peasy, nice an' easy. But now that you want to open the coffin and put something in it' – he cast a curious eye over my sack – 'then you want to seal it back up. All that means emptying the entire grave to expose the lid then throwin' all the dirt back in again when we're done. I'd say it's goin' to take us three maybe four hours longer than normal.'

'Well, gentlemen, it looks as though you're going to have to earn your money after all.'

'The good news is that we won't be taking a corpse out over that bloody wall,' said William, determined to get the final word on the subject. 'Always the most dangerous part of the operation, gettin' the stiff back up the road without being rumbled. Just as well, given it'll be dawn by the time we're done.'

I let the matter drop, and if anything was quietly relieved at William's positive appraisal of the situation. After all was said and done, I wasn't just paying for the job, I was buying peace of mind, and what had to be done had to be done.

The cold was beginning to bite again and made me wish they'd brought three shovels instead of two. For want of anything else to do I shone the lamp down into the hole that was beginning to grow at my feet. Root fibres matted the sides of the deepening trench and here and there an old bone poked out like an ivory hat-peg. I picked a yellowing femur from the heap of freshly deposited spoil and pondered the identity of this long-term resident. While I was distracted Bittern stopped digging and made a grab for the sack, which I had carelessly left unattended at his end of the trench.

'Pretty thing, ain't it?' he said menacingly.

I flashed the lamp to catch him peering into the sack. 'Put that down, Bittern.'

'Bet it's worth a bob or two, eh?'

I took a step towards him, but William interjected before I got close enough to act. 'You heard the man: put it down. Whatever is in there, it ain't got nothin' to do with you.'

'Come on, Will, you're as curious as I am.'

'We're here to do a job, Bit. Put the bloody bag down and get back to work.'

'What's got into you these days, Will? The straight and narrow made you soft or what?'

William was not to be goaded. 'I won't tell you again, Bit. If I have to come over there . . .'

Bittern at last complied, though there was a definite belligerence about him as he took up his shovel again. I retrieved the bag and, seating myself on a grave slab, watched them work, the confidence which William had begun to inspire shrunk to nought. The hole grew deeper, both men now visible only from the waist up. I couldn't stand it any longer and rushed back to the edge of the trench.

'Here, one of you hand me your shovel.'

Bittern looked up, still smarting from his reprimand. 'This isn't work for a gentleman like you, sir, you'll only get calluses on those fine surgeon's hands.'

'Give 'im your shovel, Bit, take a break,' barked William.

Once again Bittern did as he was told and slapped the shaft of the shovel into my hand before vaulting out of the hole. I dropped into his place, careful to take the sack with me. Bittern sat down on his haunches, his back resting against a nearby gravestone. I could feel his resentment growing with every shovelful of earth. The work got harder the deeper we went and my arms soon began to ache.

Noticing that we were in danger of creating two separate shafts, William began to remove the baulk of earth between us. With this done he left me to clean up the remaining loose earth and returned to digging away the trench floor from where not long after came the clatter of iron against timber. The lid of the coffin creaked beneath our feet like a rickety wooden floor. I bent down and swept the surface with my hand, feeling along the edge for the screw heads.

For just an instant I was aware of a commotion coming from above me, from outside the grave, but there was no way of telling what, for rising before me was a now dreadfully familiar iron stairway. Reaching forward with a rag-bound hand, I took a grip on the rail and pulled myself on to the next step. Brunel had taken me to his heart once more.

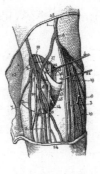

# 32

William stooped over me, the sides of the trench rising around him like tall cliffs. 'Thought I'd lost you there, sir. Take it easy, don't try and move too fast.'

My legs were stretched out along the lid of the coffin, my head resting against the side of the grave. Ignoring William's advice, I attempted to regain my feet. A spasm of pain jumped like a spark from the back of my head down into my shoulder.

'Steady, lad, steady,' said William, gently pulling me forward.

Only then did I notice the stream of blood trickling from his left arm, just above the elbow. Putting a hand behind my head, I found more blood, sticking against a gash nestling in the lee of my ear. 'What the hell happened, William?'

'Bittern clouted you with the hook and then told me I'd get some of the same unless I passed your bag up to him. I did as I was told but made a grab for his legs and sent him sprawling. I tried to climb out to get at him, but I'd forgotten about the pocket pistol he used to carry about. Never did see him use it, not once in all the time we worked together. But he used it tonight all right – the bastard shot me in the arm.'

With the return of my senses, I began to panic. 'The bag – where's the bag, William?'

'Don't overexcite yourself, doctor. It's no use. He took the bag and whatever was in it.'

I staggered to my feet. 'We have to get it back, William, we have to.'

'Can't worry about that now. Got to get out of here,' he replied, eyes squinting against the dirt in his lashes. 'Sexton heard the shot and came on, flashing a lamp after Bittern left. Didn't see us, or the unholy mess we've made. But the sun'll be up soon.'

'We can't leave, not until we've filled this hole back in.'

'Are you mad? If you ain't noticed I've been shot in the arm and you've had what few brains you appear to 'ave left bashed in. Just who do you think is to do the shovelling?'

'We are. Now come on. Pass up the shovels and give me your hand.'

After pulling him from the grave I tied a length of the rope around his arm and stemmed the flow of blood. Smarting, he offered further remonstration, but seeing that I would not leave without putting the grave back as we had found it, he reluctantly agreed to pitch in. With great difficulty we pushed, shoved and coaxed the soil back into the hole as best we could manage. I had to stop at regular intervals to allow spells of dizziness to pass, while William skilfully worked his shovel with one hand and a foot.

By the time we had stamped the earth down and replaced the wreaths, which went some way to disguise our less than perfect restoration, the dawn was well advanced.

William took a last hearty swig from his flask and lay back on the examination table with the wooden gag in his mouth. I could swear he thought the wound a fair exchange for the privilege of openly drinking alcohol in the hospital. At a nod from me he bit down hard and I began to probe the wound in his arm. The bullet had been deflected by the bone and was lodged in the muscle. My vision was blurred after the blow to the head and I was clearly in no condition to be operating on a wounded man. The trip back to the hospital had also taken its toll.

The barrow, which William had brought along to transport the corpse, might have served a useful purpose in carrying one of us away from the cemetery. That was if either of us had been in any fit state to push it. I was all for leaving it where it was but William, quite sensibly, was concerned that it would arouse suspicion if found next to the cemetery wall – especially so as Bittern's gunshot had already been heard. And so, under his direction, I manhandled it to the edge of the path and tipped it into the canal.

Using one another as crutches, we hobbled away from the cemetery, leaving the heavy barrow to slip slowly beneath the surface of the water. Houses round about were beginning to show lights as people rose and readied themselves for the day. As soon as a safe distance lay between us and the cemetery we crossed from the path to a road where, unable to continue on foot, I hailed a cab. Only when the vehicle began to make its way through the early morning traffic did William point out I would have difficulty paying the cabbie. I patted my clothes and discovered my wallet was missing.

'Bittern lifted it when you were out cold.'

We may have been reduced to the status of vagrants but I was determined our journey would continue uninterrupted as William was in immediate need of medical attention. Coming to a halt outside the hospital gates, I ordered him to stay put and, after reassuring the cabman I would return momentarily, popped into the porter's box.

'Been in the wars, sir?' asked the chap on duty at the sight of my clothes caked in dirt and my collar soaked with the blood from my wound. Fortunately, though, the man was familiar to me and after listening to a cock-and-bull story about being waylaid by footpads he agreed to lend me the cab fare.

William was now in more danger from me than the lead ball in his arm and, frustrated in my efforts to locate the projectile, I withdrew the probe. My brow was slicked with perspiration and I was just about to lapse into unconsciousness when a gloved hand took a firm hold of my wrist.

'What on earth has been happening here?' asked Florence.

'He's shot,' I rasped. 'I'm trying to remove the bullet.'

She let go of my wrist and, taking hold of William's arm, gently straightened it out before scrutinizing the hole now enlarged and distorted by my clumsy attempt to locate the bullet.

'I've seen a few gunshot wounds in my time,' she said, tutting at the poor quality of my work. 'Why not let me take a turn?' Grateful to be relieved of the responsibility and feeling decidedly nauseous, I stepped away from the table.

Divesting herself of coat and gloves and then tying on an apron, I expected the nurse to attend to William, but instead she guided me into a chair and began to examine my head, pushing it forward until my chin came to rest on my chest. My nausea began to subside but was replaced by a stabbing pain as Florence prised apart the flesh on either side of the gash behind my ear. Realizing the hopelessness of my situation, I surrendered any pretence at being a doctor and with this capitulation once again accepted the role of patient to her nurse.

'This is down to the bone,' she said, rushing back to the table to snatch up one of the few strips of cloth not yet soaked with William's blood before pouring half a bottle of alcohol over it. I braced myself but still gasped with pain as she applied it to my open wound. 'It looks as though someone came very close to dashing your brains out.'

Guiding my hand to the cloth, she ordered me to keep it in place. 'You will need stitching up, and William is in serious need of attention. I will get help.'

'No!' I gasped, still smarting from the needling pain. 'Please don't do that, Florence. I'll be fine. Please attend to him. There'll be trouble if we are found in this state.'

The bullet rattled around the sides of a metal dish like a ball in a roulette wheel before it slowly came to rest. With the slug removed Florence stitched the wound. It could only be hoped the old man was strong enough to fight off the almost inevitable infection – for him the wheel of chance was still spinning.

Leaving William to rest, Florence returned her attentions to my head and only when satisfied that no dirt remained inside the wound did she begin to stitch me back together. Her needlework was assured and rapid, and for the latter especially I was exceedingly grateful as it hurt like hell.

'What on earth happened to you?' she asked while tying off the thread.

'We were robbed,' I replied, which was at least the truth.

But this did not satisfy her. 'Robbed? What were you doing to get yourself robbed? Surely the neighbourhood is not that dangerous.'

As she had left me no option but to spin another tale I went on to explain that we had been out for a drink the night before and ended up in a disreputable part of town where we were waylaid by a gang of thieves, who proceeded to beat me and shoot William.

'You must go to the police,' insisted Florence, clearly horrified at my portrayal of London's cruel underbelly.

'Can you imagine how Sir Benjamin would react if he were to get wind of the affair? His opinion of me is low enough as it is. And, besides, William can ill afford to be involved with the police.'

'And why is that?'

'Let us just say his past record is less than unblemished. Sir Benjamin would dismiss him for sure.'

'Oh dear,' said Florence, who had become rather fond of the old fraud. 'It would be terrible to see him lose his job.'

William was breathing deeply but regularly; in fact, he was snoring. We agreed that he would be taken to my rooms to recover. All the hospital needed to know was that he was ill. I rubbed my hand over the stitches, which were small and regular – she was indeed an accomplished seamstress.

# 33

'I can forgive most things,' said William, five days after being shot, 'but betrayal ain't one of 'em.'

I had just finished tying fresh bandages around his arm, strapping the limb across his chest. The effect was to make him look a little like one of Brunel's Egyptian mummies. 'I can understand that,' I replied, speaking as one not unfamiliar with the concept.

The mended man tested my handiwork, twisting his torso one way and then the other. I was pleased to see the motion caused no obvious sign of pain.

'So we're going after 'im, right?'

'I am going after him,' I said, having no choice in the matter, as the failure of my mission had served only to intensify my nightmares. 'But I'm going alone: you are in no condition to take part in such an enterprise.'

William grumbled and slipped off the table, bending his knees like a fencer limbering up. 'I only need one arm to fire a gun,' he replied with uncharacteristic determination. 'And anyway, you'll never find the weasel without my help.' He walked over to where his coat was hanging and jerked a bottle from a pocket. Pulling the cork with his teeth, he spat it into a bucket but instead of taking a swig proceeded to empty the entire contents into the drain. 'And there'll be no drinking until the job's done.'

This was all very odd. 'I never thought I would see the day when you poured drink away.'

'Well, it wouldn't do to go into this business half-cut. I want to be stone-cold sober when I kill that bastard – that way I'll remember it.'

William's rate of recovery had been most impressive. His fever had passed after a couple of days, and it was all I could do to keep him resting after that – his thirst for revenge seemed to be driving him like an engine.

He was right of course: I stood little chance of finding Bittern among the maze of wharfs, warehouses, drinking dens and alleys that he and his kind inhabited. William and I both had our own reasons for wanting the man, and so with another night approaching, there seemed little reason to delay the hunt.

'As I can see there will be no stopping you, I suggest we make a start.'

William grinned. 'First off, we're in need of some weaponry. I got a knife but we should be fightin' fire with fire. I know you got that nice little pocket revolver, but what about me?'

'How do you know about the pistol?'

'Oh well now,' he said, realizing his error. 'You know, your coat fell on the floor one day and I just, well, came across the pistol in one of the pockets. Nice little piece she is.'

'You mean you were going through my pockets!' William's light fingers were well known, and I had more than once turned a blind eye to him pocketing a ring or other trifle that occasionally made it as far as the mortuary on a corpse. Though I liked to think he would never lift from me he was clearly not above a little window-shopping.

'I am sorry to hear you suggest such a thing,' he replied indignantly.

'Never mind that now. We should be grateful that Bittern didn't check my coat last night, and I do have another pistol. I'll fetch it from home. Where shall we meet?'

'The Three Barrels,' he said, naming the public house where our meeting with Bittern had taken place.

Agreeing to see him there in little over an hour, I stopped off at the office to collect my hat and coat. Florence caught me in the corridor just as I was about to leave the building.

'You are in a hurry,' she said.

Her arms were full of blankets. 'Don't you have nurses to do that sort of thing?'

'I want an excuse to see what they're doing in the laundry; things are not being cleaned as well as they could be.'

She studied me for a while. 'You look terrible, George.'

'Nice of you to say so,' I shot back, knowing all too well how gaunt I had become.

'How's your head?'

I put a hand to the stitches, which were just about ready to come out. 'Fine, thanks to you.'

She took a step closer as if to check for herself. 'I am really worried about you. Get some sleep, for pity's sake.'

I fumbled with my coat, tugging a sleeve over my arm. 'Easier said than done, I'm afraid. Now, if you'll excuse me, Florence, I really must dash.'

She nodded, but then as I was making my way towards the door, called after me. 'How is William?'

I turned but didn't stop, pushing the door open with my shoulder. 'He'll live. The devil always looks after his own.'

The Three Barrels was just as desperate a dive as I remembered it, and yet again full almost to bursting. William had already made himself at home in the snug, a glass sitting in front of him.

I squeezed in beside him, placing my hat on the table. 'Thought you weren't drinking?'

'I'm not,' he replied, with an unmistakable tinge of regret. 'But it would seem a little odd for me to come in 'ere and not order a glass of the usual.'

'True,' I said, impressed. 'Any ideas yet?'

'Spoke to a couple of likely lads a moment ago. Sometime muckers of our friend. Told me where we might find 'im. Rooms with a lady friend down near the river.'

'Good, very good. Shall we go?' Without waiting for his reply I stood up, only to have him grab my arm.

'It ain't all good news.'

I sank down again.

'Appears Bittern's been throwin' money about. Buyin' drinks and showin' off. Even got a new pair of shoes they tell me.'

'Then he's already sold it.'

'Looks that way.'

'Then we need to know who bought it.'

'And I need to repay my little debt,' said William, grimacing as he tried to adjust his bandaged arm against his chest.

'Is it causing you pain?'

'Only when I laugh.'

'I had better take a look at it.'

'It can wait, sir. Let's find Bittern first.'

'Look after it, William,' I ordered, handing over the pistol. 'It's a family heirloom.'

'If you don't mind me saying so, it bloody looks it. When did it last see service, the battle of Waterloo?'

'Not a bad guess.' I smiled. 'I trust you know how to work it?'

'Don't worry about me, and as for this,' he said, weighing the pistol in his hand, 'we're two old-timers together. I'm sure it'll kill just as well as your new revolver when the time comes.'

William stuffed the gun into his belt and led the way out of the alley into which we had slipped after leaving the pub. We turned a corner and entered a narrow street where the lights were dimmer, a claustrophobic rat run of a lane where people lived out their lives and played out their deaths literally within spitting distance of their neighbours. The open drains were a breeding ground for cholera and all other manner of disease. But like anywhere else people made the best of it they could.

The sound of a fiddle and drunken laughter drifted out from a window above our heads. On the other side of the street a giggling woman walked arm in arm with her beau, though more than likely he was just another customer. Further along we encountered a group of men huddled around a lamp post sharing a bottle and complaining about their wives. 'Evenin' Will,' called out one of them. 'Join us for a tipple.'

William raised his good hand in salute. 'Another time, Tam, got business tonight.'

'And I'm sure we all know what that might be!' laughed Tam.

'I wish!' called back William.

The laughter followed us to the next corner. Lights flickered through blackened windows. Two men stood outside an open doorway, talking in hushed tones and showing no interest in us as we walked by. Further down the street a knife grinder's wheel sent a shower of sparks into the dark, while an old woman waited for the return of her carving knife.

We walked for half an hour or more, the residents of the labyrinth appearing less and less reputable with each turn of a corner. If this were Ancient Greece then a golden thread might have guided our return, but here such a lifeline would be cut into farthing-sized lengths faster than you could say 'Ariadne'.

'Here we are,' announced William, just as I was beginning to fear he had as little idea of our whereabouts as myself. 'The third door on the left there, that's the place we're after.'

'How are we going to do this?'

'Don't know about you, but when I want to get into someone's house I usually knock at the door.'

Unable to think of a less direct approach, I placed myself in his service. 'Very well, William, I'll follow your lead.'

'You do that, sir. I'll go first and knock. Stay out of sight 'til I give the signal, then get inside fast as you can. Better have that revolver ready. I doubt Bittern's expectin' us but he's got a woman in there and they're always trouble.'

We walked across the street where William signalled me to stand to one side of the door. I took out the handgun and with a shaking hand held it by my side. William looked to see if I was ready and after an exchange of nods rapped on the door before pulling the pistol from his belt and holding it behind his back. Presently, there was the sound of movement, the drawing back of a latch and the creak of hinges as the door was pulled open.

'Evenin',' said William. 'I'm lookin' for Bittern, an old friend of mine.'

Although my position denied me a view of anything but Bittern's profile it was apparent from the crack of light cutting across his face that the door had not been fully opened.

'Ain't 'ere,' replied a woman's voice. 'An' if it's money you want you can forget it, the sod's spent the lot.'

'Would you know where I could find him then?'

'Bastard's down the pub.'

'Which one?'

'How should I bleedin' know?'

'Then perhaps you wouldn't mind if I waited inside for his return?'

'Do I look as though I was born yesterday?'

From my vantage point this was not a question I was able to answer, though from her voice alone I strongly suspected that the answer was no.

'I'll pay to wait,' offered William, a hint of frustration entering his voice.

'Piss off, I ain't no slag.'

'I will pay you two shillings to sit in your parlour and wait for him.'

William's face was flooded with light as the door was opened before him. Signalling for me to follow, he slipped the still-concealed pistol into the back of his waistband and stepped across the threshold.

My uninvited appearance was greeted with predictable objection. 'You never said there was two of you!' she hissed, but her surprise soon gave way to opportunism. 'It'll be four shillings for the two of you.'

William, his patience now clearly at an end, produced the gun and brandished it in front of the woman's face. She was a severe-looking sort – grey hair pulled tight behind her head to reveal a sharp nose underlined by a narrow mouth and flanked by yellow eyes. She took a step back. 'Bastards! Ain't nuffin' worth nickin', you know.'

'Sit down,' ordered William, gesturing towards a primitive-looking chair next to the fireplace.

'I think you should do as he says,' I added. 'We're not here to steal anything. As my friend said, our business is with Mr Bittern, not with you. Sit quietly and you'll get your money.'

She appeared to relax a little and backed into the chair. 'What's that old fool done now?'

'This for one thing!' snapped William, pointing the pistol towards his wounded arm.

The woman looked him up and down, her hands pressed to her lap. 'Well, I'm sure you was askin' for it.'

The pistol clicked as William pulled back the hammer. This was not going well. I stepped forward, but not so far as to stand in front of the gun. 'Steady, man, that thing might go off. Let's sit down, shall we?'

William looked around the small parlour. 'And where do you suggest?' he asked, observing only one unoccupied chair.

'You're the wounded man – you take the chair, I'll sit on my coat.'

'I'm going to take a look round first, just to make sure Bittern's not hiding in a closet. Watch her.'

I listened as William climbed the stairs, his feet then stamping against the boards above my head. The woman shifted position as though she were about to stand, but then she saw the pistol in my hand and settled back down into the chair.

'You're a gentleman, ain't you?' she asked, her voice quieter than before. And then when I offered no reply: 'What you doin' breakin' into people's 'omes and pointin' guns at 'em?'

To my relief William returned before her interrogation could proceed any further. 'Nothing,' he said, sitting down on the other chair.

I took off my coat and, rolling it into a cushion, sat down with my back propped against a wall. It was warm in the room, the fire in the grate giving the place a soporific air. It did not take long for my lack of sleep to catch up with me.

I don't know how long I had been in the engine room, struggling from one chamber to the next, when a scream woke me.

'Get away. Run!' cried the woman. William was standing over her, the pistol raised as though to strike. 'No!' I shouted, struggling to my feet. The front door was standing ajar. 'Get after him!' yelled William, resisting the temptation to dash the woman's brains out. 'We should have gagged the bitch.'

Snatching up my coat and pressing it against my chest, I bolted into the street, the metallic echoes of my dream now replaced by the crash of feet pounding along the stone pavement. Bittern was well ahead of me, disappearing into the dark as fast as his legs could carry him. William was close behind me, cursing our clumsiness at letting the prey slip through our fingers. Up ahead, the fugitive ran beneath a gas lamp and dodged around a corner only to reappear almost immediately with his arm raised. There was a flash of light followed by a punch-like thud against my solar plexus, which almost knocked me off my feet. I had been shot.

I stopped in my tracks and looked down for the blood. William wheezed past me but realizing my peril stopped to offer assistance. 'Where did he get you?'

'I don't know,' I cried, dropping the still-wrapped coat to the ground and patting my chest in search of a wound.

William holstered his pistol and picked up the coat, gripping it by the collar and shaking out the folds. The lead ball fell free and rolled across the pavement. I put my finger through a hole in the lapel and wiggled it.

'Looks like this coat just saved your life,' said William.

Anxious to retain its life-preserving properties I put on the coat and dropped the revolver into a pocket. 'We should get after him,' I said, with as much conviction as I could muster.

William looked forlornly down the street at the smoke-filled space recently occupied by my assailant. 'We'll not catch him tonight,' he said, shaking his head.

With further pursuit pointless we walked back towards the door.

'Sorry, William,' I said, aware that I hadn't covered myself with glory. 'I shouldn't have dozed off like that.'

'Don't fret, sir,' said William, with the cheeriness of a hunter enjoying the chase. 'We'll get another chance.'

Just as we were about to re-enter the house our ears were assailed by a sharp crack, which echoed off the walls lining the street. 'Bittern's pistol!' I yelled, spinning around and running back towards the corner. 'Come on, William, he's still close.'

The shot had not been fired at us and so, throwing caution to the wind, I charged around the corner. Once again, William brought up the rear and we sprinted along for fifty yards or so. Not a soul was to be seen as we hammered along the cobbles, the distance between us all the while increasing. But then, out of the darkness to our right and just up ahead of me, someone erupted from the mouth of an alley. There was something vaguely familiar about the shadowy figure as he accelerated away from us.

'It's not Bittern!' I cried, slowing my pace and coming to a stop as I lost sight of the spectre. 'The alley, he's in the alley.'

William crossed the road and we approached the mouth of the alley from either side. We drew our pistols and looked at one another across the dark opening. Eager to make up for my earlier mistake I signalled for him to stay where he was while I stepped into the alley, keeping as close to the wall as I could so as not to provide another easy target for Bittern's wretched pistol. It looked as though he had given us the slip once again, but then, just as I was about to rejoin William in the street, I spotted something, a bundle or coat lying on the floor of the alley.

I approached at a crouch, the pistol held out before me. Reaching forward with my free hand, I patted the bundle, to find that the coat contained a man.

Calling William forward, I waited while he lit a match, its sulphurous flame momentarily illuminating the alley's mouldy walls. Taking it from him I bent down again and held the fragile light over the recumbent man's head. Bittern's dead eyes stared up at me, his face a picture of surprise and his throat cut from ear to ear. Realizing that I was now standing in a sticky and still-growing pool of blood, I stepped back, shaking out the match before William had time to take a look.

But there was no hiding the obvious from him. 'It's Bittern, ain't it?' he said, his disappointment palpable.

'Yes, William, I'm afraid it is.'

'What the 'ell?'

'Ockham's razor,' I said.

William said something in reply but I wasn't listening. I thought back to the figure running down the street before me.

'Got to this sack of shit before I could!' said William angrily, kicking the corpse in his frustration. 'I'll kill the bastard!' he snarled, presumably meaning the assailant rather than the man who barely shifted after contact with his boot. Striking another match he leant over the body, grumbling to himself as he went through the pockets and pulled out one or two coins. Then he commenced to untie the laces of the dead man's shoes. 'Not even broken in,' he said, and then, satisfied that he had taken everything of worth, he snatched up the pistol that lay by Bittern's side and strode back towards the street.

Presently I joined him, but only after wiping the soles of my own shoes clean on the frock of Bittern's coat. William was pacing up and down, and for once I wished he had his bottle with him. 'We've still got to get the heart back.'

'The what?' asked my companion, instantly picking up on this slip of the tongue.

There seemed little point in keeping him in the dark any longer. 'The object in the bag, the thing that Bittern took – it's a mechanical heart.'

If my reply surprised him he chose not to show it. 'But how are we going to get it back? We needed the bastard to tell us who the buyer was.'

'It's all right, William, I know who it is.'

'Not this Ockham bloke?'

'No, forget Ockham, he's done us both a favour,' I said confidently of the empty handed man who had run from the alley, though in truth his appearance had greatly shaken me.

'Who is this mystery buyer then?'

'A man called Perry. He works out of Blyth's shipyard in Limehouse.'

'If you knew that, then why waste your time looking for Bittern?'

'Because I wanted to make sure; there was always a chance Bittern still had it. And anyway, you wanted him.'

'You did that for me?' said William, sounding somewhat abashed. 'Well, er . . . thank you, sir, Dr Phillips.'

'Don't mention it, but will you return the favour now that Bittern's gone?'

'The least I can do.'

# 34

Bittern may have died without surrendering the heart or any information as to its whereabouts but, as I had told William, that was of little concern for I was certain that Perry had the device. His intention was no doubt to sell it and Russell's torpedo to whichever foreign power it was that had employed him and his mercenary company. If I was to have any chance of recovering it I needed to act quickly. But first, there was Ockham to deal with. If he knew that Bittern had been in possession of the heart, for which he must surely have killed him, then he must have realized that Brunel had been let down, which was unfortunate, as I needed as many friends as I could muster. Finding him, however, was going to be no easy matter, as he had long since stopped living on the ship and I did not relish the prospect of trawling the city's opium dens, which since his mother's 'death' were probably providing more succor than ever.

But, as fortune would have it, I didn't need to look for him. It was the day after Bittern's murder and William and I had returned to our duties in the hospital, where we put on our best pretence of business as usual. I carried out a dissection and attended a brief meeting with Brodie and Florence, after which she caught up with me in the corridor.

'What is going on, George? You were very distracted in there and you look worse than ever. Have you considered medication to help you sleep?'

'No I have not,' I snapped but, immediately regretting my tone, added: 'I know you have my welfare at heart, but I can't talk about this now. There are a few problems which only I can resolve.'

But she was not going to let the matter rest. 'This has something to do with William being shot, doesn't it? Oh, George, what have you got yourself involved in?'

It would have been a great relief to unburden myself, to tell her everything, but the last thing I wanted to do was to get her involved. 'I'm sorry, Florence, I need to go.'

William was in the operating theatre, finishing off his duties, while I gathered together anything that might be of use in our forthcoming quest. From my surgical kit I pulled some basic medical equipment, a scalpel and some bandages, while into a bottle I decanted a good quantity of spirit. Crawling under the bench in the preparation room, I opened the toolbox and took from it a heavy carpenter's chisel, a hammer and a small crowbar, putting them all in the carpet bag to which I had already transferred the medical equipment.

Someone shifted behind me. Assuming it to be William, I remained on my knees and continued sorting through the box.

'Good evening, Dr Phillips,' said Ockham, his free hand resting firmly on my shoulder. 'Please don't bother to get up on my account.'

The razor now pressing against my Adam's apple was pulled away just enough to allow me to speak. 'I was about to come and look for you.'

'Hence the heavy weaponry,' he said, looking down into the open bag at my side.

'I can explain. I know where the heart is. I need you to help me get it back.'

His voice hardened. 'Bittern stole it from you but for him to have done that you must have betrayed Brunel. You told me that you had carried out his wishes when we were at the funeral but you had kept the heart for yourself.'

'All I did was acknowledge that I had made Brunel a promise.'

The razor brushed my flesh again. 'A promise you then broke. Don't split hairs with me, doctor, you know I'm quite capable of using this.'

'Yes, I saw Bittern last night. A neat piece of surgery.'

'I gave him every chance to tell me where the heart was, then he pulled a gun on me.'

'He told you nothing?'

'Said he'd sold it but couldn't tell me the name of the buyer.'

'How did you know he had it in the first place?'

'Your man William had been making enquiries in drinking dens I sometimes have cause to visit and he wasn't too subtle about it. But I didn't need an informer to tell me you'd taken the heart in the first place.'

'I can't see how that's possible.'

'Come now, doctor, of course you can – you're just too much of a rationalist to realize it.'

'What are you talking about?'

Ockham let out a mocking laugh. 'The dreams, the nightmares, of course! Whatever it is you want to call them. Why else would you and I be trapped in that infernal engine room?'

At last the pieces fell into place. 'You have the dreams as well!' I exclaimed, forgetting for a moment that there was a razor at my throat. That was why the shadowy figure I had seen running out of the alley the night before had looked so familiar. I hadn't just recognized Ockham, but also my fellow inmate.

'And you know what the strange thing about it is?'

'Stranger than you and I appearing in one another's dreams?'

'That I can never quite catch up with you in there. We catch glimpses, but that's all. Around and around we go, a pair of mad dogs chasing our tails.'

The knowledge that Ockham shared my dreams made a sound explanation for them seem further away than ever. He came from poetic stock and at least had an overindulgence of opiates to explain his delusions. Were Ockham's eccentricities simply rubbing off or can a man become so racked with guilt that he loses control of his mind? Ockham was right: I had made a promise to Brunel, but I had also promised young Nate that I would bring his father's murderers to book. Could one promise outweigh another? Was there a set of balances like those used by the Ancient Egyptians to weigh the heart and the sin carried within it? That would perhaps begin to make sense if I were a devout Catholic, brought up to take sinning seriously, but as it was I wasn't even a churchgoing Protestant. I was a doctor, a surgeon and a pillar of rationality, for God's sake!

But it wasn't just the nightmares. I was kneeling with a blade at my throat because of my own obsession with that accursed device, the mechanical heart which for so long I had written off as impractical but now valued as an important contribution to medical science, even if it had come a hundred years before its time. Perhaps it was all down to Brunel, the engineer who was so uncomfortably at one with his machines, enjoying the plaudits they earned him, yes, but also suffering and perhaps even dying because of them; to use a term I had seen in the newspaper, he truly was the Man of Iron. And then, if all this weren't enough, my emotions also seemed heightened, for the feelings which Florence imbued in me were entirely unlike the more base desires I had previously experienced. Among all of these uncertainties, though, one thing was certain – like Ockham, I was now mad, bad and dangerous to know.

Crouching for so long was beginning to get to me. 'Can I stand up? I'm getting cramps in my legs.'

'Careful.'

Mindful of this advice, I rose slowly to my feet. 'Believe me, I didn't mean to betray Brunel. I thought I was doing the right thing by him. It seemed such a waste to consign the heart to his grave.'

The blade pinched my neck again. 'All with his best interests at heart, I am sure.'

'All right, all right. My own best interests,' I conceded. 'But there is something else.'

'Go on.'

'If we removed the heart from the equation, made it cease to exist, as you put it, then we would take away the motivation for our enemy's actions. Sure, making them think the heart was unfinished kept them off our backs for a while, but the last thing we wanted to do is remove motivation entirely.' It was a fair point, I told myself, even if it did postdate my decision to retain the heart. 'Put it like this, if you want to see a lurcher run you have to set a hare before it.'

He was plainly unconvinced. 'I've heard enough.'

'Who do you think has the heart then?'

'Russell, of course.'

'That's where you are wrong.'

The pressure from Ockham's razor increased. 'I don't think so,' he snarled. 'Brunel told me all about your little escapade on the ship before he died.'

'I told him what he wanted to know – what else do you say to a dying man? The truth is that Russell is involved but he's not the man behind all this, and he doesn't have the heart!'

'Then who is and who does?'

'Perry.'

'Perry!'

'Put down the blade,' said William, cocking his pistol, 'or I'll put a bullet in your brain.'

After a brief pause the razor dropped to the floor and I turned around. William's good arm was at full stretch, the muzzle of the pistol resting against the young man's temple. Ockham's face was a picture of agitation. I stooped to pick up the razor and folded the long blade back into the handle.

It was time to put my impetuous young friend in the picture. 'Perry was behind Wilkie's death and the explosion on the ship. His firm has sold the torpedo, along with the heart, to God knows whom. Russell was just a stooge in need of money.' While he was taking all this in I turned to William and, slipping the razor into Ockham's coat pocket, told him to put down the gun.

'He just had that razor at your throat!'

I rubbed a hand against my neck. 'I'll grant you, he is beginning to make a habit of that, but I think we can count on him as a friend.'

William made no sign of movement so I looked to Ockham. 'Can't we?'

He obliged with a single nod and William begrudgingly pulled the gun away before allowing the muzzle to drop entirely. I waited to see how Ockham was going to respond, but all he did was stand there, his momentum lost. I invited him to take a seat.

'Let's get this straight once and for all. I did not keep the heart to sell it. I am not in business with Russell, Perry or anybody else. I made a mistake but, as you know, I'm paying for it.'

'We are both paying for it,' Ockham corrected.

'That may be, but I was only trying to fulfil my promise to Brunel, belatedly I know, when Bittern took the heart.'

'That was my fault,' said William.

I put a hand on his shoulder. 'No, William. You trusted Bittern just as Brunel trusted me, that's all.'

Ockham sat with his head in his hands, unblinking eyes fixed on me. 'That may be, but how do you intend to make things right?'

My answer required no thought. 'First, we've got to get the heart back, then finish the job I started before Bittern interrupted things. Now are you with us or against us?'

Ockham slapped a hand on to the table. 'All I know is I can't take another night of dreams shut in that place. But cross me and you know what to expect.'

'And why would I do that? We appear to be sharing the same fate, so it's as much in my interest as yours to see things put right. I have nothing to gain by keeping the heart for myself, or allowing anyone else to have it.'

Ockham nodded wearily.

'Now that is settled, I would like to introduce William, who I have to say is not your greatest admirer at the moment.'

'And why is that?'

'You killed Bittern, a privilege he had reserved for himself.'

'The turncoat put a ball through my arm,' said William.

'My apologies,' replied Ockham, rising to his feet and holding out his hand.

William responded by uncocking the pistol and placing it on

the table before shaking hands with the man who five minutes before he would gladly have killed. 'I just hope you made him suffer.'

'Not nearly enough, I fear,' replied Ockham with a cruel smile.

A lot of dirty water had flowed under the bridge since Ockham and I last travelled on the river together in a small boat. As before, he was working the oars, while I peered into the darkness looking for our objective. Then, like an apparition, a ship emerged from the gloom to our right. The hull of the part-built paddle steamer was cradled within a dock cut into the bank of the river. The vessel, an as yet unarmed gunboat, was destined for service in a foreign navy and was being built in the yard of J. A. Blyth, the company for which Perry worked, though in what capacity I was never sure.

The yard was located beside the dry dock, and like Russell's much larger facility at Millwall, which sat a mile or so downstream, included several large buildings. It was a place I had come to know fairly well, having observed it on several occasions over the past few days, both from the streets near by, from the other side of the Thames, and even from the river itself, from where I achieved the most useful views from the bow of a boat which regularly took passengers from the city down to Greenwich. Knowing that Perry's henchmen would be alert to unwanted prying, I went to great lengths to disguise my actions, at one point even hiding my face behind a bandage before walking past the open gates. These observations informed a series of sketches and plans of the place, each surreptitious visit adding a new fragment of information. These had been laid before Ockham earlier in the evening, not long after his recruitment to the mission on which we were now fully engaged.

Getting into Russell's office had been one thing, guarded as it was by just a single watchman, but Blyth's yard was like a fortress in comparison, the defences of which, in the form of a high fence, came down not only to the river on two sides, but also ran along its bank, entirely enclosing the place. But my reconnaissance had revealed a possible weak spot, which if all went well would allow entry not only into the yard but also into one of the buildings, which given its role as a workshop seemed as likely a place as any to find the heart.

Not far away from the dry dock there was an aperture, like a small doorway, in the fence, around seven or eight foot up, through which passed a jetty raised up on piles. It sloped down at a gentle angle all the way to the water, where it carried on over the river until coming to rest just above the surface, around twenty feet away from the shore.

Ockham moved the boat as close into shore as possible, and carefully pulled us towards the jetty, its sloping aspect giving the impression that it was slowly sinking into the mud. With boat hook in hand I prepared to grapple one of the supporting piles, hoping to bring the boat to a stop before we collided. The point of the hook made contact and our movement slowed, the stern swinging round as I grabbed hold of the timber pile and threaded the bow line around it. Meanwhile, Ockham stood up and with outstretched arms buffered the stern against contact as the hull came neatly to rest alongside the jetty. The boat, now partly obscured, would hopefully go unnoticed from the shore.

The stern was to be our point of disembarkation. Ockham went first, clambering up into a kneeling position, while I made my way behind him.

'Damn it,' he said, his foot kicking out as he struggled to gain a hold. 'This thing's covered in grease.'

Now standing, with my hands on an iron rail, I had just discovered the fact for myself. 'Careful, if one of us falls in the game's over.'

Handing over the bag, I scrambled up behind him. Fortunately, the space between what I could now see was a pair of greased rails was occupied by wooden slats, which like the rungs on a ladder would allow relative ease of movement. Ockham had already discovered this and with bag slung over his shoulder was making rapid progress up the incline. This was all well and good until we reached the solid fence, where a locked hatchway blocked further progress. Ockham started prising away with the crowbar, but it soon became apparent that the well-fitting timber was not going to be as easily forced as the flimsy frame of Russell's office window.

Easing the sharp tip of the bar against the edge of the obstruction, Ockham struggled to get a purchase, and when he failed to do so reverted to using a mallet to drive it home. The wood creaked and began to splinter but still gave no sign of capitulation. Looking at my watch, I was concerned to see that our carefully planned timetable was already behind schedule. We needed to try a new approach.

Still crouching behind Ockham, I looked up to the top of the fence, which must have been a good ten feet above us.

'We need a ladder,' whispered Ockham.

'Keep at it. I'll be back in a minute.'

Reversing down the ramp, I retraced our steps and dropped back into the boat. Coiled in the bow was a spare length of rope. Wrapping it quickly around my forearm, I slipped it over my shoulder and rejoined Ockham, who had made little progress with the hatchway.

'Give me the crowbar,' I said, emptying the contents of the carpet bag into his lap. Ockham watched as I placed the bar in the bag and then bound it around the middle with the end of the rope.

After twirling it around my head, the bag flew upward, taking the rope along with it, and, disappearing over the top of the fence, gave a subdued thud as it hit the other side, the fabric bag having served to muffle its impact. Pulling on the end of the rope, I dragged the bag up the other side of the fence. Then, hoping that it would hold fast, I gave the rope a tug, only to pull it over the top and have it land at Ockham's feet.

Undaunted, I repeated the operation. This time the bag landed on the ramp on the other side before slipping into the gap between two of the rungs. A jerk on the rope jammed the bag between the rungs, the bar holding it fast.

'Clever,' said Ockham.

I yanked again on the rope. 'Kneel down and let me stand on your shoulders.'

'What did your last slave die of?'

'A cut throat. Now come on, we're running out of time.'

Ockham knelt down and I took off my shoes. They were covered in grease, and I was going to need a firm grip.

Taking up the slack, I put my right foot up against the wall, where it was sure to accrue splinters but the grip was good. Pushing up against Ockham's shoulders, I pulled hand over hand on the rope. My experience on the roof of Russell's building and then the cemetery wall had put me in good stead and, gaining a good couple of feet, I let go of the rope with my right hand and reached up to grab the top of the fence. From there it was just a matter of hauling myself up, first swinging a knee up to give me a firm perch on the summit. With the strain on the rope released, the bag fell back under the weight of the crowbar, pulling the rope over the wall after it. Now, dangling in the dark, I lowered myself as far as my arms would allow, and to my relief found a ledge in the form of the hatch sill.

Fumbling in the dark, I eventually found a latch and after tugging at it the hatch flipped forward, almost knocking Ockham off the ramp in the process. 'Well done,' he said, crawling through to meet me.

My shoes replaced and the bag refilled, we continued on our way for at least another twenty feet, before reaching our next objective, the hatchway in the wall of the building.

Once again, the hatch refused to give, our efforts limited by our not being able to use the mallet for fear of creating too much of a din inside the yard. Our only option appeared to be to climb down and look for a window, but this would mean prowling around in unknown territory and deny us any route of escape should we be waylaid by a watchman. Nonetheless, I was just about to tap Ockham on the shoulder to signal that we should descend when the flap gave way, again swinging outward like the gun port on a ship of the line. I held it open while Ockham crawled through into the total darkness beyond then, passing the bag through, I followed him.

The match flashed into life before passing its flame on to the lamp. Ockham turned the lamp around the room. The windows were shuttered, which removed any danger of the light being observed from outside, which was just as well as Ockham made like a lighthouse.

Crates of all sizes were stacked everywhere, and one of them, looking like a large coffin, was positioned on the end of the ramp before us.

I hopped down and took the lamp while Ockham did the same before lighting the second one. We stood for a while, looking at the boxes – row after row, pile after pile of them.

Ockham gave out an exasperated whistle. 'Tell me you gave some thought to the exact whereabouts of the heart.'

'It's in here somewhere, I'm sure of it.'

'Well, that shortens our options. I'll take that side and meet you in the middle in two weeks' time.'

All manner of machines lined the walls, giving the place a somewhat similar appearance to Wilkie's workshop, only writ much larger. Passing down an alleyway of crates stacked almost to the roof, I entered into an open space to find Ockham holding his lamp over a bench draped with a canvas sheet. The fabric traced a tell-tale curve, the sight of which was enough to quicken my pulse.

Taking hold of the covering I pulled it towards me, while Ockham pushed the mass of heavy canvas away from him. With the sailcloth piled like a soft mountain range on the floor, we stood and stared at the exposed object, the light from our lamps reflecting off its riveted flanks.

The torpedo looked just as it had in Russell's drawings, cigar-shaped and stranded like a beached porpoise. The thing was either incomplete or undergoing dissection, as most of the upper half lay open, with only the nose and tail represented by complete, enclosed sections. Inside the belly of the beast lengths of copper pipe twisted and turned like intestines, while chambers and tanks nested comfortably like polished organs. But there was no sign of the heart: the thing was obviously incomplete, the most vital component yet to be added.

'Beautiful, isn't it?' said a voice that was not Ockham's.

Perry stepped out of the shadows, a pistol in his hand. 'Good evening, gentlemen. I was hoping you would grace us with your presence.' He smiled with the confidence of one who knows he has the upper hand. Ockham lowered his lamp, his other hand moving towards his coat.

'I wouldn't do that, if I were you,' suggested Perry, gently waving his pistol. 'Strickland, take their weapons. It would not do to have our baby damaged by a stray bullet.'

To my right, the chair man stepped forward from behind a wall of crates. At the same time we were bathed in light shining down from above. Looking up, I saw a third man standing on top of the crates, with his gun covering us from on high.

Strickland, also brandishing a gun, patted his free hand against Ockham's side, grinning as he pulled out the pistol William had liberated from Bittern the night before.

'I would rather surrender mine than have him come anywhere near me,' I said, doing nothing to disguise my revulsion for the man.

Perry nodded. 'Very well, but be careful.'

Putting the lamp on the bench, I reached inside my coat and pulled out the revolver, clutching the butt with thumb and forefinger.

'Now put it on the bench next to the lamp,' ordered Perry. 'Strickland, take the doctor's gun.'

'How did you know to expect us?' I asked. 'We didn't exactly announce our arrival.'

Satisfied that we no longer posed a threat, Perry leant casually against a box. 'Expect you? Who do you think opened the hatch for you? You didn't seriously think your clumsy attempts at breaking and entering were enough to get you in here, did you?'

'And there was me thinking I'd found my true vocation,' said Ockham.

But Perry was not finished. 'The fact that you killed that terrible little man Bittern was calling card enough.'

'Good news travels fast,' threw in Ockham, apparently unperturbed by our rapidly worsening situation.

Perry was clearly getting a little annoyed by Ockham's quips. 'Tell them, Strickland,' he barked.

Strickland needed no second bidding. 'There was no travelling involved. I saw you do it, simple as that. I had just taken delivery of the heart and was on my way back here when I heard the shot.

I dipped into an alley and saw you run past.' He gestured to Ockham with his gun.

'That reminds me,' said Perry. 'We'll have the razor as well, Mr Ockham, or should I say Lord Ockham?'

Ockham reached into his boot and pulled out the folded razor, handing it across to Perry's waiting hand.

He opened the blade and studied it for a moment. 'A primitive weapon, and certainly not that of a gentleman, but apparently effective enough.'

Strickland's version of events had taken me a little by surprise. 'We thought you'd had the heart for a while. Bittern had been seen spending large amounts of money.'

'Your intelligence was not at fault, just your interpretation,' replied Perry arrogantly. 'The money he had been spending was merely a down payment, to guarantee delivery. Strickland paid him the balance on receipt.'

I almost blurted out that we hadn't found any money but then the penny dropped, or at least the couple that William had closed his fist around. I just hoped that William had a few more sur- prises up the same sleeve in which he had hidden the bundle of banknotes.

'Tell me about Bittern,' I asked. 'Did he steal the heart just on the off chance that he could sell it, or was he in your employ all along?'

Perry looked like the cat who had caught the canary. 'Why, the latter, of course. I came by the heart through careful planning, not via good fortune. I trust nothing to chance, doctor.'

I was more confused than ever. 'But what about his friendship with William – are you telling me that he was also part of your plan?'

Perry laughed. 'No, you fool. I employed Bittern after your colleague had drawn him into your desperate scheme to bury the heart with Brunel.'

'But how did you know about that?'

'Let's just say you would have done well to limit your minute- taking to the meetings of the Lazarus Club. One of these days that journal of yours will get you into trouble.' Then he grinned: 'Oh, I forgot: it already has!'

'You found the journal? I thought it was well hidden.'

'It may be,' he shrugged, 'but all we needed to do was get to your ash pan before the dustman.'

'I don't understand,' I said, encouraging him to continue with his irritatingly smug exposition.

'Remember our little visit? Well, while we were looking around your place we came across some charred notes in the grate of your fire, and a few more in the waste bin. Not much, just blackened fragments, but enough to make it worthwhile for us to pay regular visits to the dust heap behind your building. Most of the time there was nothing, but every now and then a singed scrap of information would turn up. One of them was a rather disparaging remark about a drunken old resurrectionist called Bittern, and then the rest was straightforward – find the man and ply him with drink. He told us about your plan to *visit* a grave. He didn't know whose grave, of course, but given that Brunel had not been long dead it seemed reasonable to make the connection. All we had to do then was offer him more money than you had.'

'Clumsy of me,' I said, now feeling quite the fool. I had gone to great trouble to hide my journal from prying eyes but had obviously been a little slapdash with my disposal of the notes I sometimes used as *aides-mémoire* when writing it.

'I wouldn't take it too much to heart, old chap. In truth, that note was a real stroke of luck. Until then we were convinced that Brunel had abandoned the project, that the device didn't exist.'

'Glad to know we did something right.'

'I must say, even I was rather surprised by the extreme lengths to which you were prepared to go to keep the thing away from us.'

'I had my reasons.'

'Alas, we don't have time to go into them just now – but there is one question you could answer for me. How did you tie me into the affair? You didn't get the information from Bittern. He only had contact with Strickland.'

'Russell,' I said, seeing no need to keep his name out of matters.

'Ah yes, our Scottish friend. I had hoped that our intervention on the ship would keep him in his place.'

'And there I was thinking you'd blown up the ship just to get back at him for letting you down on his side of the deal. But perhaps you misjudged him. The man still has a conscience, at least enough of one for him to unburden himself.'

'Quite the confessor, aren't we, doctor? Mr Russell has been nothing but a thorn in the side from the very start. If ever there was a man in the wrong job, then it is he. A talented marine engineer, I am sure, but an absolute disaster as a businessman. I don't know how Brunel put up with him for so long. But that was all to our benefit. His need for additional funds to support that ridiculous ship project put him right where we wanted him.'

'And that would be in your pocket.'

'Exactly. But then, when he couldn't get Brunel to donate his little contraption to the cause we had a problem. And so we find ourselves here tonight.'

Perry was clearly enjoying himself, but the delivery of so much information could only mean one thing and, as if to dispel any doubt as to what that might be, Strickland cocked his pistol.

'You don't even know whether the thing works yet,' I pointed out, rather desperately. 'Perhaps you'd better keep your options open until you do?'

'By keeping you alive, you mean?' He shook his head. 'The surgeon doctor who can't settle to his work and the opium-smoking aristo? I don't think so. We've already delivered the first of them. It's still a prototype, but our client is very pleased with progress.' He stepped forward and slapped his hand against the nose of the torpedo as if he were patting a prize bull. 'And for good reason: what we have here is the most sophisticated anti-shipping weapon ever devised.'

A door clattered back on its hinges. 'Mr Perry, sir!' came a shout. 'Mr Perry!'

'What is it, for God's sake? I told you to watch the gate!'

The owner of the agitated voice appeared from behind Perry. 'Fire, sir, there's a fire over at the lumber store!'

Perry let out a curse, his face twisted with rage. 'Get the pumps working, man! If that gets to the ammunition store we'll all go up!'

'They already are, sir, Gilks and Saunders are on it, but it looks pretty bad – one of the sheds has already caught.'

'Well, get back out there and lend a hand. Get a hose on the store, and more men. Go on, move!'

Perry assisted the underling on his way with his boot. 'Watch them, Strickland,' he ordered, leaving his position by the crate and rushing over to a window. He threw back the shutters to reveal flames licking against a building at the far side of the yard.

'My God!' he yelled. 'We'll never put that out.'

His cool evaporated, he rushed to a cupboard and, unlocking it, pulled out a small box. Apparently oblivious of our presence, he ran to the coffin-like crate on the back of the ramp and taking hold pushed it up so that it fell back on to the floor on the other side. Underneath was another torpedo, its nose pointing down the ramp.

I turned to Ockham. 'That's not a jetty, it's a launch ramp. They've built a shore battery!'

Meanwhile the flames rose even higher, their intensity increasing as they engulfed more sheds. They were getting closer.

'What shall we do with them?' called out Strickland, who had also noticed that the fire was fast approaching.

'Kill them of course,' shouted Perry, without looking up from his task. He had by now removed the heart from the box and was placing it in the torpedo, dropping it in through a small hatch in the top.

It was then I saw Ockham make as if to scratch the back of his neck, his hand creeping behind his ear. Something flashed through the air as his arm shot forward. A razor, released from its hiding-place somewhere in his collar, skated across Strickland's cheek, opening a deep gash in the side of his face. Letting out a dreadful yell, the bleeding man opened fire, sending bullet after bullet in the general direction of Ockham and myself.

I dived to the floor and scrambled for cover behind the far end of the bench. There was the sound of a tussle and between the legs of the table I saw Ockham and Strickland engaged in a deadly hand-to-hand struggle, the latter's gun held at bay as the other tried to force him to the ground. A bullet thumped into the wooden surface of the bench just an inch or so away from ear; my hiding-place provided no cover from the man standing on the crates.

There was another pistol shot, but this time from behind me. I looked to see whether Perry had now joined the fray, but he was still there tinkering with the torpedo. The man up on the crates doubled forward, his pistol clattering to the ground, before he too fell with a sickening crash on to the stone floor. His fall had also dislodged one of the crates, and it slowly tilted over before joining the cascade. The lid splintered open and its cargo of rifles spilled out on to the floor. All of a sudden I had an entire arsenal at my fingertips but, doubting that any of them were loaded, I made a dash for the pistol, which unlike its owner had hopefully survived the fall.

'All right, sir?' asked William.

'I thought you'd never get here,' I cried.

'Well, that fire-starting business ain't as straightforward as it looks, you know!'

William was reloading his pistol – or should I say my pistol, as he had drawn the short straw and once again been issued with the most primitive of the firearms available to us. It was the second time in twenty-four hours that the old man had saved my skin.

'Help Ockham, I'm going to stop Perry.'

Another shot rang out, this time from Ockham's direction. Strickland had fought his way free but not before Ockham had recovered his pistol from the other man's pocket. An exchange of fire was now taking place between the two of them.

'Ockham, William's here!' I yelled, not wishing the old man to be mistaken for one of our foes.

Knowing that Perry too had a revolver in his possession, I approached him cautiously, using the crates as cover and moving at a stoop. He was still hunched over the torpedo, working away with a spanner with all the concentration of a surgeon performing a tricky operation. Only when I was in a position to get a clear shot did I feel confident enough to remind him of my presence.

'Perry!' I yelled. 'Step back from the torpedo – it's too late. The yard is lost.'

His response was to send two bullets in my direction, both of which smashed into the crate behind which I was crouching. Shifting position slightly, I caught another glimpse of him and was horrified to see him bolting closed the access hatch on the torpedo.

'That may be!' he shouted back. 'But I'll be damned if you're going to get what you're after before it goes. Do you know what this is, doctor? Of course you do. It's *the* heart, the one we took from Bittern. The father of many more, perhaps, but still your one and only, and now you're about to lose it for good!'

I pointed the pistol and fired. The bullet ricocheted with a piercing whine off the side of the torpedo, having missed him by only a fraction. The near-miss did nothing to distract him from his task, which now had him furiously pumping backwards and for-wards on a lever attached to a barrel-like contraption beside the torpedo. I guessed he was priming it, compressing the gas which would cycle like blood through its copper veins and arteries. Like a baby wakened from sleep, the thing began to cry and a metallic whine settled into a pulsing, whirring sound as the propeller's revolutions increased in speed. It was now or never.

Ignoring the sound of gunfire from behind me, I once again took aim, imagining that the back of his head was one of those many bottles I had shattered in my father's yard.

I squeezed the trigger, but the resulting explosion was more than I had bargained for. Boxes and crates flew through the air as though they were paper kites. A window shutter fluttered by, turning end over end in a hailstorm of glass shards. Thrown to the ground, I was plunged into darkness as a crate tumbled across my head but, fortunately, it came to rest on another before it crushed me to a pulp. The fire had at last overwhelmed the ammunition store and the explosion had blown in an entire side of the torpedo shed.

Pulling myself out from underneath the crate, I staggered to my feet. The room was full of dust and smoke, and the heat coming through the ragged gap in the wall made the place feel like the hell of my nightmares.

I looked back across to the ramp, which to my dismay appeared entirely unscathed by the blast; the only thing that was missing was the torpedo, and Perry of course. Running across to check, I yelled out for my companions. 'Ockham! William! Are you all right!' There was no answer.

As I had feared, the ramp was entirely undamaged, the hatchway lay open and what looked like an umbilical cord hung loosely from the lever-sprouting barrel I had seen Perry pumping at. He had succeeded in launching the torpedo. Desperately in need of some consolation, I looked for his battered corpse and had high hopes for a sack-like pile lying beneath an upturned trolley, but it was just that: a sack.

'We had better get out of here,' said Ockham, limping out from behind a mountain of debris, still carrying his handgun, his face streaked with blood – only then did I notice that my fingers seemed to be glued around the grip of my own revolver.

'Where's William?' I asked through dry lips.

'I don't know.'

'And Strickland?'

'Dead.'

'Good. You?'

Ockham nodded grimly.

Then, to my relief, I saw William standing at the far end of the hall. Cast into silhouette by the sun-like inferno behind him, he seemed to have grown in stature and girth. He also appeared to have two functioning arms, one of which was holding a pistol to his own temple.

Perry was standing behind him, his own head now coming into view as he checked on our position.

Ockham levelled his pistol at the two-headed man but lowered it when I gestured for him to do so.

'Shoot the bastard,' cried William. 'Don't worry about me – I had my time.'

'Let him go, Perry, you have nothing to gain by harming him.'

Perry hit his hostage with the pistol. 'Don't discount the pleasure of killing the man who burnt down my future.'

385

'He was only following my instructions. Take me instead.'

'Very noble, I am sure, but I intend to see you all dead. You will notice the fire around the boxes.' He gestured with his free hand, giving William the appearance of a man with three arms. 'Any moment now it will ignite the explosive charge in the nose of the unfinished torpedo. I doubt you will clear the building in time to escape the blast. Goodbye, gentlemen.'

'Be good enough to answer me one question before we go. Who's your client? Which foreign power is paying you for the torpedo?'

'Foreign power!' Perry cried, before letting out a cruel laugh. 'You really have no idea, do you, doctor? You should have stayed in the hospital where you belong.'

*At last*, I thought, we are going to learn what lies behind all this, albeit just before dying; but instead of continuing with his exposition Perry seemed to take stock and checked himself. It was possible that even here, where dispensing such information couldn't possibly harm his cause, he could not shake off the cloak of secrecy, or perhaps it was just that the advancing fire was making him nervous.

'Please go on, sir,' I yelled at him, my lips tightening in response to the heat. 'We are keen to hear who pulls your strings.'

Perry's reply came not from his mouth but the muzzle of his gun, which gave out a flash of light followed by a report as sharp as a cracked whip. In response, William's head dropped to one side and, as if falling through heavy air, he slipped slowly to his knees before slumping forwards on to his face.

Letting out a yell, Ockham and I raised our pistols as one and let fly with every bullet we had left. But Perry was gone, darting through a void in the wall just moments before it was filled by a curtain of flame. Bullets crackled like fireworks as an ammunition box succumbed to the wave of intense heat.

'Where to now?' asked Ockham, without a hint of desperation in his voice.

'I don't know' was the only response I could muster. In truth my mind was reeling from the shock of seeing William killed in such a cold and deliberate fashion. The old boy had sailed close to the wind on many an occasion, but he did not deserve the treatment meted out by that monster.

Ockham dropped his pistol and shrugged. 'Perhaps it's better this way. We've lost the heart and I for one don't fancy living with the nightmares for the rest of my days.'

Perhaps he was right, but almost against my will, as if by one of Darwin's theories, my survival instinct at last stirred me into action. Pushing the pistol into my waistband I reached for the trolley. 'Here, help me with this. Grab an end.'

Together we lifted the trolley on to the ramp, its small iron wheels fitting snugly against the rails like those on a miniature train. We climbed aboard, lying side by side on our bellies, and as though it were a toboggan, gripped on to the front edge while trailing our legs behind. I kicked off just as a fresh sheet of flame engulfed the boxes behind us. The trolley rumbled forwards, slowly at first, but by the time it reached the first hatch we were really travelling, the wheels barrelling along the greased tracks. Then, when I thought we could go no faster, a great force, like an invisible hand, pushed us from behind and, as if we had been fired from a cannon, threw us down the ramp at breakneck speed. 'Keep your mouth closed!' I yelled, ducking my head to clear the hatch in the fence, though I doubt very much whether Ockham could hear me over the sound of the explosion, because I couldn't.

The trolley left the end of the ramp and into the river we plunged. The water took us in its cold embrace, pulling us down into its muddy depths. But Old Father Thames seemed to have no need for us tonight, for we emerged from the foul water gasping for air. Burning lengths of timber were still falling into the river all around us, the building now nothing more than a charred husk, belching out smoke and sparks into the brightening sky. We clambered into the boat and, lacking the strength to row, simply lay back and let the river carry us downstream.

My lesson already learned the hard way, after a soaking on the river had almost proved the death of me, I had taken care to stow a couple of heavy blankets on the boat, and these were put to good use. We drifted along the water and in and out of consciousness, each of us now aware that we inhabited the same place when the dream engulfed us. It seemed to be that we only encountered one another, however fleetingly, in the engine room when both of us were asleep, for when I was asleep and Ockham remained awake I could not recall seeing any sign of him there. But even now I tried to retain a doctor's rational view of things, seeing this as nothing more than a symptom of a deteriorating state of mind.

William's loss had only added to these woes, coming as a heavy blow, and a tragedy for which I had to carry full responsibility. It had been my idea that he ignite the cloth stuffed into the bottle of medical spirit and throw it over the fence into the wood store. The aim had been to create a diversion, nothing more than a distraction for the watchmen while Ockham and I went about our search, but as it happened the results were disastrous. My reconnaissance had wrongly led me to believe that the wood store was isolated enough for the conflagration to be contained. Never did I envisage that the ensuing inferno would engulf the entire yard and cause an explosion of the like not seen in London since the Great Fire. How was I to know that large quantities of explosives and munitions were stored nearby, or that we were walking into a trap! But enough of excuses; William had died for an action that I set in motion and I would have to live with that fact.

Such were my thoughts as the little boat bobbed lazily along, its two inhabitants sprawled and parched like survivors cast adrift from a terrible shipwreck. It was as well it was night, for during the day we would most definitely have been mown down by any of the larger vessels that ply their trade up and down the river but, with our passage uninterrupted, we finally came to rest against the south side of the bank near Greenwich.

The sky over Limehouse was still blackened with the smoke from the blaze, though it looked as if the fire had not spread outside the yard. Ockham even suggested that the explosion may have blown the fire out.

Lord only knows what impression we made as we hobbled through the hospital corridor to my office, our tattered clothes hanging from our frames and blood seeping from wounds. But I was past caring, and after giving up trying to apply bandages in the boat due to debilitating fatigue was in urgent need of fresh stock. Leaving Ockham in my office, where he took a reviving draught from my brandy bottle, I headed off to the preparation room.

It was on my return, by now clothed in my soiled operating coat and with a bundle of fresh dressings under my arm, that I encountered Florence. Immediately seeing that something serious was amiss, she dismissed the two nurses in her company and, taking me by the arm, led me into a nearby linen store.

'Now, George, you are going to tell me what's going on.' I made to leave but she closed the door in front of me. 'First I have to pull a ball from William's arm and now you arrive looking as though you have spent the last two months in the Crimean trenches.'

I was too weak to prevaricate. Letting her know anything about recent events, and indeed those preceding them, had never been my intention, but with William's death there seemed no point in shrugging things off or trying to invent a yarn. And so, satisfied that Ockham wasn't going to bleed to death in my absence, I proceeded to tell her the whole fantastical story, albeit in a much condensed form, all the way from Brunel's first appearance in the operating theatre to the taking back of the heart. Florence insisted on dressing my wounds as I described the confrontation at Blyth's yard but could barely hold her hand steady when it came to the telling of William's fate. I used a bandage to wipe a tear from her cheek but she pulled her head away.

Turning her back and drawing a sleeve over her face, she stifled a sob. 'Who killed him?'

'A man called Perry – he was an agent for the yard. They went up in flames together.'

Florence faced me again, her eyes still moist. 'Perry! Francis Perry?'

I nodded. 'Yes, that's his name. Why do you ask?'

She almost spat her answer. 'I know that man.'

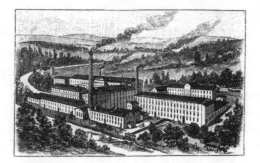

## 35

Ockham had complained bitterly about being abandoned in the office and was now trailing bandages as we hurried into the street. 'What do you mean, you know who it is?'

'It was Miss Nightingale – she knew Perry,' I replied, rushing on ahead to wave down a cab.

'But we know about Perry,' he insisted, taking his seat beside me.

'Yes, yes, but listen to me. Miss Nightingale's father owns a mill in Derbyshire. Some years ago Perry showed up, and after introducing himself as the agent for an unnamed speculator offered to buy him out. He refused but the man wouldn't give up, and then accidents started to happen, machinery broken and workers injured.' Ockham looked none the wiser; his exhaustion was clearly getting the better of him. 'Don't you see? A mill in the north of England? An aggressive takeover bid with Perry acting as the agent? It's got to be our friend the cotton baron. It's Catchpole!'

It took a moment or two for the reality to sink in, but as it did the fatigue seemed to lift from Ockham's face. 'And if it is he will know where the other torpedo is. Can I assume we are on our way to the House of Lords?'

I nodded.

Ockham curled his lip. 'Well, don't expect my title to do us any favours, for while my father lives it is merely that.'

I had learned from Babbage that in some way he blamed his

father for his mother's tragic decline and so refrained from pressing the issue. 'One thing is for sure though. We won't get in dressed like this.'

After stopping off at my rooms and changing our clothes we disembarked from the cab at St Stephen's entrance to the House of Lords. The time, according to the vast clock high up on the new tower, was quarter past eleven. In our hurry we had given no thought as to how we might gain entrance to the building, let alone Catchpole's office, so it was a relief to get through the door on nothing other than a flimsy explanation that we were there to meet Gurney, who some weeks before had been good enough to give me a guided tour of the ventilation system he was installing. He had been grateful for my favourable comments, which, he said, had helped to allay fears that the vents and ducts would encourage rather than prevent the spread of the cholera.

The place was a veritable warren of passages, corridors, debating chambers, offices and stairways. Although no more than thirty years old the building already looked to have been here for centuries, and that had of course been the intention of the architect. Not for the first time Ockham and myself were to find ourselves lost in a maze, only this time it was of stone and wood panelling rather than iron and steel. I had hoped my previous experience of the place would assist in getting our bearings, but as Catchpole's office had not been on my itinerary it was proving of little help. But then, just as we were about to ask one of the smartly attired gentlemen who strode meaningfully up and down the corridors for directions, we turned a corner and spotted a familiar figure.

'Christ, it's Perry!' whispered Ockham as we ducked as one into the recess of a doorway.

'So he did make it out alive,' I hissed, and without a second thought stepped back into the corridor, only to be pulled back by a level-headed Ockham.

'He can lead us to Catchpole.'

He was right, and so with my hunger for revenge suppressed, we waited for him to round the next corner before stepping out and hurrying along the carpeted corridor in pursuit. He had entered on to a stairwell, which we arrived at just in time to see his head disappear out of sight as he descended. One flight down and he set off along another corridor with us at an unobserved distance behind. Not far in front of us now, he turned another corner, where we drew to a halt to observe his progress. It was just as well, for he had reached his journey's end. Halfway along the corridor he halted and turned into one of the many doorways. He had led us to Catchpole's office.

Having seen enough, we dropped back around the corner and stood with our backs pressed against the wall.

'Damn it,' I said, after seeing the two sentinels standing either side of the door. A mere gesture from Perry had been enough to secure his entry but the same casual wave was unlikely to serve as passport for us.

Ockham turned his head away from the corner. 'What do we do now?'

'Listening at the keyhole's obviously not an option, nor is breaking our way in. Even if we get past the doormen, who's to say how many he has in there with him?' I glanced back up the corridor and told myself there was something familiar about the stairwell. 'I'm not sure that's what we want to do anyway.'

Ockham followed me back to the stairwell, where after descending another flight we stepped into a dark, stone, vaulted chamber. 'I've been here before with Gurney,' I said, once again setting eyes on a series of busts sitting on plinths around the walls. 'They're all lords who served as Prime Minister. The one over there with the big nose is of course Wellington; he managed it twice.'

Ockham was unimpressed. 'Very interesting, I'm sure, but we're not exactly here on a guided tour.'

'Yes, but you never know when such a thing will come in handy.' Stepping across the chamber, I tried the handle on a heavy panelled door. 'In here,' I whispered after finding it unlocked. The room was still being worked on by Gurney's men, though fortunately none of them were in it. There was a stack of ornate stone mouldings waiting to be used and one wall was obscured by scaffolding.

The floor was covered by a tarpaulin which bore the dusty impressions of workmen's hobnailed boots.

'Gurney brought me in here. As you can see, they're still working on the ventilation system.' I opened another door. 'Now, if you'd like to step inside.'

'It's a toilet,' remarked Ockham after taking in the design on the blue and white porcelain bowl set into a polished mahogany bench.

'It's the Queen's toilet,' I corrected him.

'You mean Her Majesty sits on that?' he asked, sounding impressed at last.

'When she's in the House, yes – one of her many throne rooms, you might say.' Ockham raised his first smile for some time and I pointed to a metal grille on the wall. 'That's the vent which keeps her private little place nicely aired.' Stepping on to the bench, I pulled the grille free to reveal the duct beyond. 'The system goes all the way through the building, with vents in the floors or the walls of every room. Now, if one of us were to crawl through here to the vent in Catchpole's office, they should be able to hear whatever passes between him and Perry.'

'We'll both go.'

'Don't you think we spend long enough following one another through tight spaces like this without doing so out of choice? No, I will go alone. In any case, I am smaller than you.'

Ockham confirmed this when he stretched out an arm only to have the tight cuff of my jacket come to rest halfway up his forearm. The same was true of his trousers, the legs of which were floating a half-inch or so above his shoes. He watched as I pulled myself up into the duct and on hands and knees began an uncomfortable but familiar crawl. After around ten feet the tunnel branched to right and left. Hoping that I had judged the relative positions of the Queen's water closet and Catchpole's office correctly, I turned to the right, into almost total darkness. A few minutes' more hard crawling and the duct branched again; only this time it went straight up. Bracing my knees and arms against the side of the shaft, I inched my way upward. To my relief the shaft levelled out again after no more than ten or twelve feet, at which point the horizontal duct stretched out for an interminable distance. The passage was illuminated at regular intervals by light shafting down through the vents in its roof, each of them set into the floor of the room above. I guessed that Catchpole's office should be the third or fourth vent along.

I wasted no time in passing beneath the first and second vents, from which the sound of disjointed voices could be heard, but paused under the third. Silence – it was the wrong room. For a moment I was gripped by panic: what if my calculations were wrong, and what if I couldn't find my way back out? But the fear passed and I continued on my way. After recent events I never thought I'd be glad to hear Perry's voice again, but there it was, clearly audible even a good few feet away from the next vent. There was good reason for this. He was shouting.

'. . . because the plans were destroyed in the fire! My office was one of the first places to be engulfed. I need the remaining torpedo to make a new set. Without it we have nothing!'

By now I was directly below the vent and, lying on my back, could make out vague shadows as someone, presumably Perry, paced about the room not far away from the grille. His outburst continued: 'If you had let me kill Ockham and that blasted doctor once we'd got hold of the engine then we wouldn't have lost the yard or the rest of the torpedoes.'

Then it was Catchpole's voice I could hear, further away but still clear enough.

'Irritating as they were I wanted them alive for the same reason I didn't let you kill that fool Russell. As the engine has proved, the Lazarus Club has the potential to throw up all sorts of innovations, some of which I may have the opportunity to procure before they are snapped up by outsiders. So what if most of the discussions revolve around crackpot scientific notions like evolution? Killing off the club's members is not really going to be conducive to creative thought, is it? However, I grant you that, since Brunel's death, the future of the club has seemed a little doubtful and in retrospect it seems we would have been better off with them out of the way. But there is no use crying over spilt milk. As you say, we still have a fully functioning torpedo and from it we can grow many more.'

'Well, Ockham and Phillips are gone now anyway,' added Perry.

'You are certain they perished in the explosion?'

'I killed the old man myself and then the place went up. There was no way out for them.'

This seemed to satisfy Catchpole. 'I want you to load the torpedo on to the *Shearwater* and take her up the west coast. We will establish a new base of manufacture in one of my warehouses at Liverpool. It makes much more sense to build them there.'

'You still haven't explained to me what you intend to use these machines for?'

Catchpole answered the question with a question, albeit in a patronizing tone. 'What business am I in, Perry?'

'Cotton, of course, but I don't understand the connection with the torpedo.'

That made two of us.

'As you full well know,' replied Catchpole, 'the British cotton cloth industry is worth millions, and as you are also aware I happen to own a good proportion of the mills producing it. Most of our raw material is imported from overseas. Some of it comes from India but most of it is shipped into Liverpool from the southern United States.'

'I am aware of that,' said Perry, rather sharply.

'Well, it is my belief,' continued Catchpole, 'that within the next few years this supply, of which myself and my business partners are presently the chief recipients, will be threatened by a civil war between the northern and southern states of America. Buchanan, their fool of a president, refuses to accept the fact, but all the signs are there for anyone who cares to sit up and take notice. The anti-slavery movement in the north is fomenting unrest in the south, where the cotton production depends on slave labour.

'If it comes to war then the north is by far the stronger of the two powers. The coalmines, ironworks, arsenals – most of them are north of the Potomac. The south will undoubtedly be heavily dependent on overseas trade, and one of the few commodities she has to offer in return will be raw cotton. It logically follows that the north will use its navy to choke off this transatlantic trade by blockading southern ports and preventing any maritime traffic either in or out. That, sir, will be bad news for the British cotton industry and most importantly very bad news for me.'

'So you intend to supply the south with the torpedo?'

'Whoever owns that weapon will at a stroke have the upper hand in the war at sea. The sea lanes will remain open and, with her trade secure, the south may stand a chance of winning the war on land.'

'So it's all about your damned cotton mills.'

'No, Mr Perry. Like most people, you fail to see the broader picture. If things are allowed to continue unchecked then the United States of America will very soon represent a dangerous threat to British overseas interests. But if the south wins autonomy in a civil war then a humbled USA will have an overtly pro-British neighbour to contend with. Of course, I expect the new Confederate States of America to be very grateful for my contribution to the war effort – the least they could do in the circumstances would be to offer me a monopoly on the cotton trade. And there you have it: business continues to thrive and the nation benefits as a result. Very satisfactory, wouldn't you say?'

What little light there was in the duct disappeared as an eclipsing Catchpole, whose voice had suddenly grown in volume, stepped on to the grate. I was terrified that if he looked down he would see my face staring up at him. Instead, a blizzard of glowing embers fell into the space above my head. The devil had knocked the ash from a cigar into the grate. I turned my face away and stifled a cough but fortunately he moved on almost immediately. Suspecting he might return to do the same again, I shifted position slightly so that my face was no longer located directly beneath the grate.

My new location did not affect my ability to hear Catchpole. 'Now, Mr Perry, don't you think it time you were on your way? It is vital that you get the remaining torpedo out of harm's way.'

I had heard enough.

*

Returning to my point of entry, I looked down to find Ockham seated on the Queen's throne, his head tipped to one side in sleep. A gentle application of a foot to his shoulder was enough to bring him round.

'Good of you to warm Her Majesty's seat for her,' I said, as he looked up at me through bleary eyes.

I gave him a few moments to stand and pull himself together, knowing full well that I was not the only one just returned from a dreadfully confined space. For a moment or two he bore the haunted expression that I knew must hang like a grey mask from my own face at every waking. But this was no time for self-reflection.

The detail of what I had overheard could wait and so I got straight to the point. 'Perry's taking the torpedo out of the river up to Liverpool on a boat. Have you heard of the *Shearwater*?'

Ockham was now fully awake. 'The *Shearwater*? She's a small screw-driven steamer, usually moored in the Pool. She was built by our old friends Blyth's a year or so back. Don't know who owns her now, but given she's of the latest design it wouldn't surprise me if his name was Catchpole.'

We arrived at the exit just in time to see Perry leaving through the gate, accompanied by the two men we had earlier seen standing outside Catchpole's office. 'He must be on his way to the boat,' said Ockham. 'If the torpedo is already on board then we have little chance of stopping him before they cast off.'

'There has to be a way,' I said, without having a clue what it might be. One thing was certain, though: we needed help.

Dodging back into the building, I asked for the use of pen and paper at the reception desk and then, handing the folded note to Ockham, instructed him to give it to one of the policemen hovering around the entrance. 'Tell him that it must get to Inspector Tarlow immediately. If he shows any lack of urgency then let him know that the security of the nation is at stake.' I could only hope that the terrier Tarlow would appreciate me throwing him a bone for once.

While he was delivering the message I dashed across to the House of Lords telegram office which was tucked away on the other side of the foyer.

When we were reunited outside the gates, I asked Ockham, who now appeared entirely reinvigorated, if he had access to a boat. He shook his head but then told me he had been using an old steam barge for work over at Millwall. 'It's a wreck and won't stand a chance of outrunning the *Shearwater*,' he said, guessing what I had in mind, 'but if Perry is sailing from as far west as the Pool of London we may be able to get a headstart overland and then intercept him on the water as he heads downriver.'

During our hurried cab ride I told Ockham a little more of what I'd overheard while in the air duct, and only then did the full implication of Catchpole's ambitions begin to dawn. 'Whoever controls the sea lanes has the power to control the fate of nations. If he uses the torpedo to draw us into another war with America, he could bring Britain to her knees. The United States is far more powerful than it was back in 1812, and we didn't do so well then either.'

'And all to protect his damned business interests!' exclaimed an exasperated Ockham. 'Businessman be damned, he's nothing but a bloody warmonger. He sat there in our midst feeding off all those ideas with the one clear aim of putting them to the worst possible use.'

By the time we arrived at Millwall our blood was well and truly boiling and we were doubly determined to see Catchpole's plans foiled. There certainly seemed no better way to extract revenge for Wilkie's and William's deaths. The only problem was that neither of us had any idea of how we were going to achieve that beyond getting on to the river ourselves.

Some effort had clearly gone into removing the blackened remains of Ockham's windmill, and after we crossed over the river wall it became apparent that the barge we were about to commandeer was to be used to carry the debris away. The flat deck was covered in carefully stacked piles of timber, much of it at least partially charred by the fire. Most conspicuous, though, was the dreadful iron casket which had once contained the body of Ada Lovelace.

'The boilers are stone-cold,' reported a grave-looking Ockham on his return from the engine room. He looked upriver and seemed only slightly relieved not to see the *Shearwater* approaching. 'We can only hope he didn't cast off straight away.'

It took us the best part of an hour to light the boilers and get up anything like enough steam to power the vessel. It was difficult to concentrate on the task, as every few minutes one or both of us would take a break from shovelling coal and watching pressure gauges to step up on deck and check the river. Vessels large and small regularly passed by, but all of these were propelled by either sails or paddles and as yet, thank God, there was no sign of a screw-driven vessel. Half an hour later and I was casting off and Ockham steering the vessel out into the Channel. If the *Shearwater* wasn't going to come to us, we had decided, then we would go and look for her.

We were saved the trouble, however, as just as we pulled away from the jetty she hove into view, coming around the bend. Her stack belched smoke but her sides and stern were clearly bereft of paddles. Ockham had already proven himself to be a proficient river man and so I had no reason to doubt him when he said she must be doing at least fifteen knots. Whatever rate she was travelling, it was fast, because even to my landsman's eye there could be no doubt that she was approaching at unnerving speed. 'All we can hope is that we can block her course and drive her into the shore.' Ockham turned full on the wheel to take us out into the Channel, our rear-mounted paddle wheel turning faster now as he opened the valves.

'He won't be expecting us,' he shouted over the noise of the engine. 'I'm going to head upstream on a parallel course to his and then try and ram him before he realizes what's happening. If I can hole her he'll have no option but to make for the shore!'

Pulling out my pistol, I checked that each of the chambers contained a bullet, hoping against hope that last night's submersion in the river had done it no harm. There was little time for preparations, however, as Ockham ordered me to throw more coal into the hungry fire.

'Careful you're not seen!' yelled Ockham when I made to climb out of the engine well on to the deck. His meaning was immediately obvious, as there was no more than a hundred feet between the two vessels and being recognized was a real possibility. Making as if to wipe oil from my face with a handkerchief, I walked as casually as possible across the deck until concealed from view by a pile of timber. By my reckoning our present course would take us along the port side of the *Shearwater* with a clearance of around thirty feet. But already I could feel us inching to starboard. The closer we got the more obvious our change of course became. Men had appeared on the prow of the *Shearwater*, and Perry was among them. Our intent had been understood and there was much shouting and waving as the *Shearwater* lurched away from us.

'Brace yourself!' cried Ockham, giving a sharp pull on the wheel. There was a dreadful crash on impact, followed by an ear-splitting squeal as the blunt prow of the barge scraped its way along the entire length of the other vessel.

Splinters of wood lanced into the air as bullets peppered the deck around me, and I looked up to see the *Shearwater* pulling away from us, her keel almost exposed as she pitched heavily to starboard. She had been scarred but not obviously punctured by our contact. The gunfire was being delivered by two men positioned on her stern. One of them was Perry, who by now could not have failed to recognize me. I replied with two bullets from the pistol, to no apparent effect.

Seeing that we had merely grazed the *Shearwater*, Ockham was taking out his frustration on the wheel, hammering it with his fist and cursing his failure. To the surprise of both of us however the *Shearwater* was not taking advantage of her close shave and speeding off downriver but was coming about in a wide circle.

'They're coming after us!' I yelled.

Our course had steadied and was now taking us upstream. I ran up to the wheelhouse, hopping over the timbers now littering the deck. 'Downstream, Ockham, we need to go downstream!'

Without question he put a spin on the wheel to bring us about, paying little heed to other vessels, which were forced to change course to avoid collision. By the time we straightened up, the *Shearwater* was close behind us. The riflemen were now shooting from her prow, bullets thumping into the timber blades of the paddle wheel.

'Can we stay ahead of them?'

Ockham shook his head and pressed himself into the wheel as though trying to urge our lumbering vessel on. 'But something's not right,' he added, glancing back over his shoulder. 'They should come alongside and shoot us to pieces from a safe distance. What are they doing back there?'

'Trying to shoot off our paddle wheel?' I suggested as another plume of wood chips puffed from our stern.

'I hope not,' he said with a tired smile. 'They'll be chasing us all the way to France. We need *more* steam. Let's see what this tub's got left.'

I dropped down into the well again and shovelled more coal, finding it hard to believe that after spending all that time down in the engine room of my nightmares, here I was, humping the black stuff into the fires for real. After another half-dozen shovelfuls the needle on the pressure gauge shivered and then crept on. Returning to Ockham's side, I reported that she would do no more. Nonetheless, the skipper seemed satisfied. 'She's picked up a fraction,' he said, checking again over his shoulder, 'we've pulled away a little. Look, we've widened the gap.'

'What does it mean?' I asked, now as puzzled as he about our pursuer's behaviour.

'It means we've hurt them. The collision must have ruptured a pipe or cracked a boiler. She can't go any faster!'

When viewed on a map the bends and curves of the Thames resemble a great intestinal tract folded into the body of the city – an especially fitting analogy given the amount of raw sewage transported by the river. Now, for the first time since coming about, I took note of our position and looked out over our bow to see one of the most dramatic of these folds, at the tip of the Isle of Dogs, approaching. And there, across the island, on the other side of the marsh, was the sight I had been waiting for.

Rounding the promontory, with the grand Georgian façade of Greenwich naval academy on our starboard side, the massive hull of the *Great Eastern* hove into view. Brunel's ship was not long returned from Weymouth, where she had successfully completed a fresh sea trial following her repairs and now, like a salmon returned home, was swimming again in the river of her birth. Even across half a mile of water and over the sound of our own engine we could hear the dull growl of the three engines buried deep within her. Though the paddle wheels were stationary the waves from their fresh backwash lapped at our hull. Having just minutes before cast off from her berth, she was now idling just outside the middle of the Channel with her bow pointing towards us.

'My God,' said Ockham. 'She's picked her time to go for a cruise.'

'No, my friend,' I replied, 'we picked her time.'

He threw me a puzzled look and then ducked as a bullet slammed into the frame of the wheelhouse. The noise from the ship's engines increased and the two great paddle wheels began to turn, each in opposition to the other. The river boiled as the ship slowly began to rotate on her central axis, and like the needle on a compass the bow swept across our front to point north, while the stern came round towards the southern shore.

'What the hell is she doing!' exclaimed Ockham.

I recalled that Brunel had once told me he was building a ship and not a bridge. 'It's Russell. He's closing the gate.' We both watched aghast as the 685-foot-long ship manœuvred in a channel which at high tide could be no more than 1,000 feet wide. But the tide was low and mudflats extended out from the south shore, leaving precious little room for manœuvre and ultimately the narrowest of gaps at the bow and stern – so little in fact that it looked almost possible to cross the river dryshod across her deck.

'I sent Russell a telegram from the House of Lords,' I said in answer to Ockham's unspoken question. 'I didn't know how he could help but, given that Perry tried to blow up his ship, I guessed he would try something.'

Movement of the paddle wheels had almost ceased, but every now and again a partial rotation of the starboard wheel, which sat before us, was accompanied by the violent frothing of water to the stern as the screw worked in opposition to keep the vessel in position and prevent her from colliding with the shore. The *Shearwater* had come to a dead stop behind us and Ockham was careful to keep as much distance as possible between her and us and the newly created river wall to our front.

Perry was clearly not intending to sit forever trapped like a ship in a bottle, and as the *Shearwater*'s engine started up again I fully expected her to turn and head back upriver. There was also an increase of activity on her foredeck, where the removal of wooden panels from the sides of a cabin-like structure quickly revealed the boat's true intent. There sat the torpedo, atop a ramp which sloped gently down towards the bow.

Ockham put the paddle wheel back into gear. 'Damn it! He's going to use the torpedo against us.'

'No,' I said. 'He's going to launch it against the ship . . . finish her off once and for all.'

'If that torpedo goes up, that'll be our last chance gone.'

'That can't be helped, but if he sinks the ship here the Thames will be blocked for years.' As if to illustrate the point the channel to the stern of the *Shearwater* was already becoming choked with river traffic.

Ockham needed only the briefest of moments to come to terms with our latest circumstance. 'You're right. We've got to stop him. Can you keep the barge between the *Shearwater* and the ship?'

'That won't work. She has a flat bottom. If the device swims at anything deeper than a foot it will pass harmlessly beneath us.'

Shallow beam or no, Perry wasn't taking any chances and had begun to manœuvre the *Shearwater* clear of our stern, lining her up with a point on the ship just to the rear of the paddle wheel. To one side of the torpedo someone was pumping away at the box attached to the device by an umbilical, just as we had seen the night before at the yard.

'They're building up the compression. We don't have long,' I yelled, leaving the wheelhouse and dashing across the deck. 'Try and put her in the torpedo's path.' Ockham turned on the wheel and watched as the torpedo slid down the ramp and sent up a column of water as it hit the river. 'It's in!' he shouted. 'The cigar fish is swimming!'

Working as fast as tired limbs would allow, I tied the rope hanging from the steam-powered crane around the iron casket but, lacking the knowledge to operate it, had to call on Ockham to do so. 'We've got to get the casket in the water!'

With the vessel positioned astride the torpedo's estimated course, Ockham joined me. At first he seemed unwilling, as though he were unsettled by the idea of sacrificing an object so closely associated with his mother.

'We're going to lose the heart whatever we do. But if the *Great Eastern* goes down then Liverpool will at a stroke become Britain's first port. Are you going to stand by and let Catchpole benefit from that?'

It was enough to galvanize him into action and within moments the casket was in the air with my hand guiding it towards the side of the boat. The torpedo was fast approaching, its course now marked by a slight disturbance on the surface of the water.

'A little more to the left . . .' I gave the box a last push. 'That's it. Let her go!'

Ockham released the brake and, as the rope ran freely through the pulleys, the casket dropped like a stone before jerking to a halt like a hanged man at the end of his drop. With the casket suspended beneath the surface we both ran as fast as we could towards the stern.

There was an almighty crash as the torpedo hit the perfectly positioned casket. The force of the explosion sent up a huge spume of water and lifted the front of the barge clear of the river. Caught by the blast before I could leap over the side, I was thrown to the deck where, with hands covering my head, I expected death at any instant as flying timbers and pieces of metal landed all around. Miraculously, though, the storm passed me by and the crash and thud of falling debris gave way to the hiss of escaping steam and then a dreadful watery sigh as the broken hulk began to sink by the bow. Timbers slid past me and soon I too was slipping down towards the brown water now rushing up the tilted deck. For all their frantic workings, neither hands nor feet could find a purchase firm enough to break my descent. But then, just as the water looked likely to swallow me along with the barge, something caught my wrist. I looked up to see Ockham crouching above me, left hand locked on to my arm and the other clutching the rail behind him. Lord knows where he found the strength, but after he had swung me from side to side like a weighted rope I caught a hold on the railing. 'Our carriage awaits,' he said before dropping over the side, with me following immediately behind. Once in the water we dragged ourselves on to a raft of charred planks that had once been part of the windmill's floor.

For the second time we were cast adrift on the river, only this time we really had been shipwrecked. The timber was doing only a partial job of keeping us afloat and we would be lucky to reach shore without having to swim. Lying on my belly, I watched as the barge's paddle wheel sank out of view, leaving behind it a gently rotating whirlpool and a scatter of floating timbers, amongst which we were just one more piece of flotsam. I had almost forgotten about the *Shearwater*, but the slap of a bullet landing in the water close by served as an effective reminder of her presence.

Visible on the stern of his vessel and no doubt enraged at our success, Perry was making one last desperate attempt to dispatch us. Reloading the rifle, he took aim once again and put a bullet through the wood not three inches away from my head. Had his shooting platform been stationary then I would have been dead in the water. But the *Shearwater* was on the move again. To my surprise, though, she was not turning tail but making towards the stern of the *Great Eastern*, where the gap between the ship and the shore was wider than at her bow. Ockham took a pause from paddling with a plank. 'He's going to try and squeeze through!'

We watched transfixed as the *Shearwater* drew parallel with the northern shore and picking up a little more speed made a straight course for the only part of the channel promising any hope of escape. Dwarfed by the towering bulk of the ship, Perry's vessel approached the overhanging stern where he would throw everything into gaining passage between the ship and the shore.

But Perry had not counted on Russell's next order, which carried with it the *Shearwater*'s fate as it travelled along the ship's telegraph from bridge to engine room. On its arrival the ship's chief engineer ordered his minions to make the giant paddle wheels rotate again, only this time in an anti-clockwise direction. He had put the ship into reverse! The stern propeller, one blade of which protruded like a shark's fin from the river, also began to turn, churning up as much mud as it did water this close to the shore. In a move that in normal circumstances would have been the height of folly, the ship travelled backwards before crashing into the bank, scattering the small crowd of bystanders freshly gathered to watch the bizarre proceedings. The force of the impact pushed the ship's rudder aside and, like the fluke of a huge whale, it slammed against the port bow of the *Shearwater*, forcing her into the path of the propeller as though she were nothing more than a length of timber being pushed on to a band saw.

New sounds of destruction rent the air as the massive propeller made contact with the smaller vessel. All efforts to manœuvre the boat out of harm's way were fruitless and the knife-edged blades ate into her hull, shredding timber and metal with equal ease. The screams of men accompanied the evisceration of flesh and bone. Severed limbs flew through the air and landed in the water like so much bait thrown to flesh-eating fish. Blood and gore mixed with the mud churned up by the propeller and spattered up against the ship's underside, to cling there like the plaster on the ceiling of the devil's own house. Two crewmen leapt over the side, only to be drawn into the propeller on the strong current swept up by its revolution. Within moments they too were turned to splinters and pulped flesh.

Inch by inch the *Shearwater* was being devoured by the revolving iron teeth, and what destruction the blades did not wreak the exploding boilers did. Only when the great ship was itself in danger of injury did Russell give the order for the engines to be stopped, by which time the *Shearwater* had been reduced to nothing more than an oil slick in which were suspended the remains of both man and machine.

I picked up a length of timber and tried to keep in time with Ockham as we paddled back to the shore. We had not made much progress when a man in a rowing boat pulled alongside and took us on board. He introduced himself as the waterman responsible for this stretch of the river. Far from being upset about the destruction we had wrought on his territory he seemed quite delighted at the prospect of so much debris floating on the water.

'I'll drop you off just opposite,' he said, making as much speed as he could manage towards the shore. 'I'll need to get to work before this stuff drifts off my beat.'

Ockham looked over to where the *Shearwater* had gone down. 'You may find more than you bargain for out there.'

The waterman just laughed. 'That won't worry me none, sir. I've pulled dozens of bodies from the river in my time. Why, over the past year and more there must have been eight or nine.' He paused, not seeming so chipper all of a sudden. 'A strange business it's been, real strange.'

I looked over at an uncomfortable-looking Ockham but said nothing.

# 36

The waterman dropped us on to the muddy shore, and we watched as he began his frantic collection of floating objects.

'He's de – de – dead, isn't he?' I wondered out loud through chattering teeth.

'Perry?' replied Ockham, who knew full well who I meant. 'Oh yes, he's dead all right. No one came out of that mincing machine alive.' His voice was flat, without any hint of satisfaction, and I knew why.

'If it makes you feel any better, that wasn't the original heart blown to kingdom come in the torpedo.'

'What the blazes are you talking about?' replied Ockham as he paused to watch the great ship turn once again, stirring up water cluttered with floating wreckage as she went. Russell was reopening the gate.

'The heart, or should I say the engine, in that torpedo wasn't the original, the one Bittern stole from us. They used ours as a template to build others at the yard, probably after taking it apart and drawing up a full set of plans. One of the copies was driving that torpedo.'

Ockham shot me a piercing glance, his bloodshot eyes boiling within the cauldrons of their sockets. 'My God, man, why didn't you say so before? I hadn't given any thought to that. Do you think there would have been any gain from recovering a copy, a counterfeit of the original?'

'I don't know.'

'My guess is not. And if that is so then where the hell is the original?'

'Perry put it in the torpedo he launched from the yard.'

'Are you sure of that?'

'He told me so as he was doing it!'

Impassioned again, Ockham pulled off his one remaining shoe and in stockinged feet strode off along the shore. 'Then we have one more chance! Come on, man. What are you waiting for – pneumonia?'

By the time we arrived back in town, in a carriage laid on by a Russell relieved to have at least in part redeemed himself, it was too late to take any further action. And so after returning to my rooms to dry off and take what rest our dreams would allow we made for Rotherhithe the following morning.

We were on the south side of the river, directly across the water from Perry's yard and close to the entrance to Brunel's tunnel under the Thames. Thin traces of smoke were still shifting in the breeze and black feathers of ash drifted across the cobbles even on this side of the river.

The tide had just turned, and close to the bank below us the receding water revealed a growing expanse of thick black mud. Ockham handed me his telescope, which took some time to focus. The yard was a wasteland, nothing more than a smouldering heap of charred timbers, some of them still upstanding but now nothing more than blackened and broken teeth arranged around the mouth of a huge crater. People moved across the debris, like maggots wriggling over a corpse, picking up a likely object here or discarding something too far gone there. Despite this devastation, the fire seemed to have limited itself to within the perimeter of the yard, for even the paddle ship in the dry dock had survived unscathed.

'Take a look at the ramp,' said Ockham, guiding the telescope towards the river in front of the yard.

The rear of the ramp, the part that had been inside the building, was now nothing more than a knot of twisted iron, but the front portion, where it extended out over the river, seemed to be entirely undamaged. 'It's still there.'

'Now take a straight line out from the front – where does it bring you?'

Dropping the glass from my eye, I drew an imaginary line back across the water. 'Right here,' I said, realizing it terminated on the bank just below us.

'Now, if we assume the torpedo travelled on a straight trajectory, it should have hit the bank just in front of us.'

'And exploded?'

'I don't think so,' said Ockham, moving closer to the edge, where the piled bank dropped down on to the black mud freshly exposed by the falling tide. 'That may have been his intention, to remove it from our grasp, that or save it from destruction. Whatever the case, if it had exploded there would be some trace, a destroyed vessel or damage to the bank this side of the river.'

'You mean –' I cried, rushing forward to join him on the edge – 'it's down there, in the mud? We can get the heart back, and the original one to boot? But how?'

'Someone has to go and find it.'

'You mean go down there? Into that foul, stinking mud?'

Ockham looked a little dismayed at my lack of enthusiasm. 'You want the heart back, don't you?'

'Of course I do but . . .'

He picked up a stone and tossed it into the mud, where it quickly sank out of sight. 'Don't worry,' he said, his face breaking into a smile, 'I made an arrangement. Look behind you.'

I turned to see walking towards us the most bedraggled-looking band of men, women and children I had ever laid eyes upon. Their tattered clothes were caked with mud and their unshod feet blackened through prolonged exposure to the same. Each of them carried a stick and several of the adults had sacks slung over their shoulders.

'Mudlarks,' I said, seeing at once what Ockham had in mind.

One of the men stepped forward from the pack, his eyes shielded beneath the peak of his leather cap. 'Right, mister, 'ere we is. Where do you want us?'

'Down there,' said Ockham, pointing to where the stone had landed.

'There's rich pickin's on the other side after that fire. For us to stay on this side'll cost yer two bob now and another two when we're done.'

Ockham reached into his pocket and pulled out a purse. Handing over a small clutch of coins, he issued instructions. 'You are looking for a large metal object. I will keep you right from up here. Check as close to the water as you can and all the way up the bank.'

'Right you are, guv, but anything else we find is ours,' said the chief lark, closing his dirty fingers around the coins and turning to the others. 'You 'eard the gentleman. Let's be at it. The quicker we finish 'ere the quicker we can get over the other side.'

The motley crew trooped down a nearby flight of steps and ventured out on to the flats, where only the flat planks of wood now strapped to their feet prevented them from sinking to the waist, while the smallest of the children barely made an impression in the mud. When feet were pulled free of the clawing quagmire the holes left behind immediately filled with water. Following Ockham's directions from the bank, the larks began to probe with their sticks, wiggling them before pulling them out to move to a new spot. The children were sent out closest to the water, where the mud was softest. Every now and again someone would bend over and pull an object from the morass, give it a quick wipe and then drop it into a sack.

We watched from above like medieval lords supervising peasant labourers.

'What a way to make a living,' said Ockham.

It was quite fascinating watching them, entirely at ease in an environment where most of us would fear to tread. 'They seem cheery enough though.' And indeed they did, laughing and joking among themselves as they picked their way across the slime.

They had been working for about an hour, their progress marked by the watery pockmarks left by their feet. 'They should have found it by now,' admitted Ockham.

'Perhaps it's buried deeper?'

'No. If it's there it shouldn't be too far under the surface, at least not yet.'

The implication was obvious. 'It didn't make it this far, did it?'

Ockham made no reply.

I looked towards the deep water in the middle of the river. 'Then it's out there somewhere. It's sunk, and so are we.'

The tide was beginning to turn again, the water slowly creeping back across the mud. Unable to stave off the inevitable, the larks retreated to the shore. Ockham handed over the balance of their fee and, not seeming too downcast at having missed low water on the other side of the river, they went on their way, leaving behind them a trail of muddy footprints.

The water grew closer and closer until at last it drew level with the iron lip of the hole at my feet, from where it threatened to continue upward and drown us like kittens in a barrel. But there it stopped, and as the bell was lowered beneath the surface it looked as though the river had been reduced to nothing more than a circular puddle. Ockham was shouting into a funnel attached to a tube, our only link with the men on the barge above us.

'Steady as she goes. Levelling out now.' I could already feel the change of pressure inside my ears but reassured myself that this was keeping the water at bay.

After failing to find the torpedo trapped in the mud we had returned to our lodgings, once more disappointed. There was, it appeared, to be no getting round the fact that the heart was lost, and with it all our hopes of escaping the nightmare. The next day, still tired after another exhausting sleep, I returned to the hospital, where I spent half of the morning pondering which poison would make the swiftest end.

I glanced up from the apothecary's manual to see Ockham standing there, looking as though he had been dragged through a bush backwards. 'Ah, the man of my dreams,' I quipped wearily.

'Come on, I have a cab outside,' was all he said, already making for the door. I folded down the corner of the page and followed him – stopping just short of calling William to let him know I was leaving.

And so we returned to Rotherhithe and there boarded a waiting steam barge not unlike the hulk we had lost two days before, but this time she was crewed and carried a diving bell. It was the same bell I had first seen in operation on the *Great Eastern*, perched on a platform which enabled access through the hole in the flat bottom.

Ockham slapped the side of the device. 'The torpedo may be on the bottom of the river, but thanks to this we should still be able to reach it.'

'But isn't it a bit like looking for a needle in a haystack?' I asked, the barge now pulling away from the shore.

'Not at all,' was his confident reply. 'The torpedo sits somewhere on that line between the ramp and the place we searched yesterday. All we have to do is drop the bell and scour the riverbed along that line. We'll start at the ramp and work our way across until we find the point where it hit the bottom.'

The barge cast off and with her stern-mounted paddle wheel stirring the water set out for the ramp on the opposite side of the river. Looking back beyond the wheel, I noticed that the place from where we had watched the mudlarks was marked by a red flag, which, Ockham told me, would provide an aiming point once we began our sweep.

And so here we were, descending through the dark waters of the Thames, not far from the end of the ramp down which the torpedo had been launched. Although my dreams should have prepared me for such an experience I had to try hard not to think about the tiny space in which we were enclosed, but it wasn't long before the water in the hole turned to the foul-smelling mud that was the riverbed. Mimicking the actions of the mudlarks, Ockham took up an iron rod and began to probe the silt. Meeting no resistance on the first insertion, he pulled the rod free, an act that served only to release even more of the terrible odour locked inside, and immediately drove it back in again a few inches away.

This process was repeated perhaps half a dozen times, each with the same result, before he was satisfied that the torpedo did not lie beneath us. Setting the muddy pole aside, he took up the speaking tube and bellowed into it. 'Lift and take us forward five yards.'

There was a jerk as the bell was pulled free from the sucking mud, and a slight lurch as we were dragged through the water. We were left dangling for a while as the bell, like a stone on a rope, steadied itself. Plonked into the mire again, Ockham worked away with the rod, standing astride the hole and using both hands to drop it down and then draw it back out. Again instruction was sent to the surface and the bell shifted location.

'Here, let me take a turn,' I said, holding out my hand. If the rod itself were not heavy enough, the effort involved in drawing it back out of the sucking mud was almost backbreaking. In and out went the rod, each time returning with nothing but a fresh coating of slime.

Four submersions later and we still had nothing to show for our efforts, unless you count an old anchor, three bottles, half a dozen links from an old chain and a chamber pot. We were beginning to run out of riverbed. 'You don't think there's a chance we missed it? We are searching a very narrow corridor, an inch or two to the left or right and we would pass right by without knowing it.'

The bell shifted location and, by now feeling utterly exhausted, I stirred the mud half-heartedly. The tip of the rod clinked against something hard and unmoving. I shifted its position by at least a foot, handling it more carefully this time. Again it came into contact with the buried object, which I was now sure was metal. I withdrew the rod and glanced across to my companion, who had his eyes fixed on the hole at his feet. Rolling up his sleeves, he stooped down and thrust an arm into the mud, all the way up to the elbow.

'This is it!' he cried, stroking the unseen object. 'It carries on in both directions and is aligned just as it should be.' He looked up, his eyes pricked with tears of relief. 'By God, Phillips, we've found it.'

With some difficulty he looped the end of a rope beneath the body of the torpedo and pulled up the other side before tying it tightly. I picked up the speaking tube and he nodded at me. I yelled into the cone, 'Bring us up; we've found it!'

For the last time the bell reluctantly rose clear of the mud. Ockham stood astride the hole, feeding out the rope as we climbed back to the surface. The dripping bell broke free from the water. Ockham dropped down through the hole before we came to rest on the platform.

I joined Ockham at the rail. 'Will it hold?' I asked, following his gaze to the rope where it joined with the water.

'We are about to find out,' he replied, turning to the gantry from which the rope dangled. He waved his arm as a signal to the crane operator. Lever thrown, the idling engine belched into life. The rope snapped tight and, like a dog fresh from swimming, shook out a mist of water. Taking up the strain, the jib shuddered while the torpedo was tugged free of the mud, then after what seemed no time at all it was swinging and spinning in the air, screw-tipped tail pointing skyward.

The cigar fish had at last been caught and now all we had to do was land it. Unarmed it may have been, but not taking any chances, we cradled the nose in our arms, cushioning its gentle descent on to the deck. At Ockham's instruction one of the crew threw a pail of water over the muddy flanks of the thing, flushing the filth on to the deck, exposing afresh the fastening rivets and bolts. He crouched beside it and released the access plate with a dozen or so quick turns of the spanner. With the innards exposed he picked his way through the tool box and, selecting a pair of smaller tools, went to work on the inside, loosening nuts and bolts and disconnecting pipes. Then, as was sometimes the case with a difficult patient, it was down to brute force, and with both hands he pulled at the reluctant organ, rocking it against the mounting until at last it gave.

'Here, take the damn thing,' he said, passing me the heart and wiping a wet sleeve across his forehead. 'And whatever you do, don't let go of it again.'

Scarcely able to believe that the heart was once again in my possession, I wrapped it in a rag before dropping it into a smelly old sack; demeaning apparel for such a finely wrought object perhaps but less likely to draw attention than the polished mahogany boxes that had at one time or other been its home. Meanwhile, Ockham continued to direct his attentions towards the torpedo, replacing the plate he had removed to extract the device.

Then, task complete, he stood up and said to no one in particular, 'Let's do mankind a favour, shall we?' and without further ado issued rapid instructions as crewmen gathered around the stranded beast.

At the count of three a gang of crewmen pushed the device forward, giving out a communal groan as the torpedo made a half-roll. The men steadied themselves, another count was delivered and another push exerted. The process was repeated several times until the torpedo teetered on the very edge of the deck. Then, with a last shove, it dropped over the side, tumbling into the water close to where it lapped against the barge's hull. The impact sent up a wall of water, causing us all to take a step back. Amidst this momentary tempest the great metal cylinder disappeared beneath the surface, returning forever to its watery grave. Ockham brushed his hands together to signify a job well done.

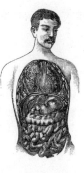

## 37

I shouldn't have come back to the hospital but nonetheless had made it my first port of call after the successful conclusion of our unusual fishing trip, the cab dropping Ockham off along the way. From his willingness for me to retain custody of the heart I could only assume that any lingering doubts about my trustworthiness had finally dissipated.

Closing the office door behind me, I took the device out of the sack and began to polish it as though it were a silver teapot freshly lifted from the dresser. But within minutes there I was, back in that cursed engine room, playing cat and mouse with Ockham, who was obviously lying somewhere asleep himself. That was when Florence found me, collapsed across the desk and entirely unaware of her entrance.

'What did you mean when you said you are going to put it where it belongs?' she asked at last, her narrowed eyes fixed on the metalwork. She was referring back to our conversation in the linen cupboard some days before.

'Fulfilling his last wish,' I replied, closing the heart as though it were a book I had finished reading.

'George! They buried the man two months ago!'

'Nearer three,' I corrected.

'Please tell me that you are not planning to . . .'

I nodded. 'To dig him up again.'

'And when do you propose to carry out this . . . this macabre operation?'

'Tonight, after dark.'

'But you are in no condition.'

'I'll be in worse condition tomorrow and even more so the day after that. I need to do this now, Florence.'

'On your own?'

'With Ockham.'

She raised her hands, exasperated. 'From what you tell me he is in no more a fit state than you. This is madness. You do realize what will happen if you are caught? It will mean the end of your career, if not imprisonment.'

I stood up and put the heart in a drawer before locking it. 'All I know is that if I don't do it, I will never escape from my nightmares.'

Now she too was on her feet, making for the door. Not knowing whether to feel pity or anger, she settled for an uneasy marriage of the two. 'Then I wish you all good fortune, George, but if you will excuse me I have a ward to check on.'

Listening to her stamp down the corridor, I decided that anger had definitely outweighed sympathy, which was good because it meant that I had only one thing to worry about: getting that damn heart to the place where it belonged.

I spent the little that was left of the day giving what impression of normality I could, making sure that my face was seen about the place by all but Brodie, who would of course by now be after my blood. That way, if he asked about my whereabouts, my colleagues would be able to report that I had been busy about the hospital. But covering my tracks was by now a fairly low priority, as things had come to such a pass that my present position and future prospects in the hospital were of little concern to me.

In truth, though, I also hoped that my perambulations around the building, all the while with one ear constantly cocked for the sound of Brodie's voice, would bring me into contact with Florence again, for it concerned me still that my actions had caused her unnecessary upset. But alas, she was nowhere to be found, and so with the time for my second rendezvous of the day with Ockham approaching, I left the wards and made for the hospital yard. Outside, in the cold air of evening, dusk was already giving way to darkness, and out in the street, beyond the hospital railings, the lamp lighter had begun his rounds.

As previously arranged, a horse, albeit an old nag, had been harnessed to the gig usually used to transport staff or provisions about the town. The stablehand greeted me and without any question as to my destination or intent was pleased to hand over the reins.

'I'll be a few minutes yet,' I told him. 'I have to get some things together, just wanted to check that everything was all right.'

'Don't you worry, sir,' said the lad, fondly patting the horse's neck. 'Old Sally here's as happy standing still as she is moving.'

Now we were on first-name terms I felt a little guilty for harbouring disparaging thoughts about the horse's appearance, and patted her myself by way of apology. Sally snorted in gruff response, breath billowing like steam from her flared nostrils.

Satisfied that our transport was ready, I returned to the office, though only after avoiding bumping into a vexed Brodie, who came marching down the stairs with one of my colleagues in tow. 'If he's not in his office then where is he?' he growled at the doctor. 'I am sure I don't know, Sir Benjamin, but he was on the ward this afternoon.'

'He drifts in and out as he pleases and never keeps appointments – a disgrace to the profession. I'll have him before the commissioners, I swear it.'

I waited beneath the stairs as they passed by, pressing myself into the shadows and praying they wouldn't see me. Once they were safely around the corner I dashed to my office, which logic would dictate to be the best place to hide as they'd already looked for me there. I locked the door and removed the heart from the drawer. Setting it on the desk, I opened it up and took another look inside.

There was a rap on the door, and then a whispered plea. 'Phillips, it's me, Ockham. Let me in, man.'

I opened the door just a crack and peered out.

'Come on, let's get going.'

Thrusting my head into the corridor and seeing the coast was clear, I grabbed Ockham by the lapel and pulled him in.

'Your boss is still after you then?' he asked.

'Never mind him,' I insisted. 'Take a look at this.'

'Glad to see you've managed to keep hold of it.'

I ignored the remark. 'Look at this chamber wall.'

Ockham bent forward, straining in the dim light to see the distorted copper shell. 'It's bent.'

'It's been pushed in by pressure exerted through the valve. It worked for a while and then folded under the strain. The torpedo died of a heart attack.'

Ockham straightened. 'Just like Brunel.'

'You could say that.' I reached forward and snapped the two halves together. 'But as I've said before, I'm a doctor not an engineer. If I'd taken more care to keep the two things separate then we wouldn't be in the mess we're in now.'

I wrapped the heart in the cloth, returned it to the sack and, taking up my hat, made for the door.

Back in the yard, Sally was still waiting, her knock-knees all but touching and her greying snout buried deep in a feedbag. 'Take these,' I said to Ockham, passing him a pair of shovels.

With the gig loaded and the feedbag removed we climbed aboard. I took up the reins and lifted the switch from its rest. 'You are sure you can drive this thing?' asked Ockham nervously.

His question made me smile. 'I'm a country boy. I was driving horses while most boys were putting a stick between their legs and saying giddy up.'

I flicked the switch and Sally moved off, pulling us at a leisurely pace towards the open gates. But then, just as we were about to pass into the street a figure dashed out in front of us, blocking our exit. He was a slight fellow, dressed like a son in his father's clothes, head covered with a cloth cap at least one size too big.

'Out of the way, boy,' demanded Ockham, waving his arm from side to side in reinforcement of the command.

The boy paid no heed and so I had little choice but to pull Sally to a halt, dropping the switch back into its holder. I called down to the stubborn young man: 'You are likely to get yourself run over if you go on like that.'

'And you are likely to end up in prison if you go on as you are.'

'Florence! What in God's name . . .'

With hands on trousered hips she threw back her head and announced, 'I'm coming with you.'

Ockham rose to his feet and bellowed: 'Florence? That's your beloved Florence Nightingale?' Already he'd said too much and I shifted with embarrassment, regretting I had ever mentioned her name. 'What the hell is the woman thinking? Coming with us? Not a chance!'

I pulled Ockham back down into his seat and jumped to the ground. 'Florence, what are you doing? This is our problem, not yours.' I took her cap by the peak to reveal her hair mounded up on the top of her head. 'And these clothes – what are you playing at?'

'Well, I'm guessing that my usual attire isn't really going to be very appropriate for what we're going to be doing. And in any case, you may not mind being exposed as a surgeon turned grave-robber but I have a reputation to consider.'

'No, Florence, I will not permit it. You must leave us to do what we have to do.'

She snatched the cap back from me and pulled it down over her head. 'You are two fools together and I am sure you deserve one another. But I happen to care about you, George – you are a fine surgeon and I would hate to stand by and see that talent wasted. I may be just a woman, but neither of you are in any condition to do this, and I can help.' She took a step closer to me. 'Now, either I come along or I raise the hue and cry right here and now and nobody goes anywhere.'

'She can't possibly be serious,' chipped in Ockham.

'*She* is the cat's mother,' snarled Florence. 'And *she* is deadly serious. Now are you going to take me aboard or do I call for a policeman?'

I looked back up to Ockham, who capitulated with a shrug of his silhouetted shoulders. 'What choice do we have?'

I stepped aside to let Florence by and then followed her back through the gate. Just as she was about to climb aboard she turned to me: 'What's this about your beloved Florence?'

I hoped she couldn't see my reddening cheeks in the dark.

Sally may not have been the fastest horse in the world but long experience had given her a steady confidence. It took only the slightest tug on the reins to make her turn or a snap of them to encourage her forward. The redundant switch soon found its way back into the holder, where it spent the rest of the journey. Not surprisingly, the traffic at this time of night was much lighter than during the day, just the odd trolley bus on its way back to the depot and the ubiquitous hackneys, carrying their passengers to whatever night-time pursuits had drawn them out of doors. From Southwark we crossed London Bridge and then struck out west, eventually reaching Paddington, where we turned on to the Harrow Road, which took us to the cemetery.

Seeing the cemetery up ahead, I turned Sally on to a part of the green not yet given over to it, at a place conveniently close to the canal and the towpath which would once again provide our point of access. After coming to a halt beneath a stand of trees Ockham offloaded the tools and I hobbled the horse before placing the feed-bag around her neck. Despite Ockham's objections Florence pitched in and from her seat in the back dropped the shovels down on to the grass.

'Let's hope no one steals her while we are away,' I said to Ockham as we shared out the equipment for carrying.

Florence picked up my bag and stepped down from the gig. 'I trust you are not referring to me.'

'No, Florence, I mean the horse, the carriage.'

'Why would they?' asked Ockham, looking disdainfully back at Sally. 'I doubt prices at the glue factory would make it worthwhile.'

Walking in the lee of a thorny hedgerow on the edge of the green I took the lead with Florence just a few steps behind, and Ockham, the shovels in a sack slung over his shoulder, bringing up the rear. Reaching the end of the hedge, I briefly halted our column before stepping out on to the towpath. All was still, aside, that is, from the distant chuffing and clanking of a coal train as it shunted into the siding of the gasworks on the opposite side of the canal. In order to limit our time in the open we covered the fifty yards or so between the hedge and the cover of the cemetery wall at a more accelerated rate.

'This is the place,' I said, taking my bearing from the position of the gasometer across the water.

'You mean we go over the wall,' said Ockham, casting a doubtful glance at Florence.

'Well, I would suggest going in through the gate but given the circumstances . . .'

'You need not worry about me, Lord Ockham,' said Florence. 'I am sure the wall will not prove an insurmountable obstacle, even for a woman, especially with two strong gents to help me over.'

'I'll go first,' said Ockham, who was learning at last that Florence was not a woman easily daunted.

With my back to the wall and hands cupped to provide a stirrup, I gave out a grunt as he pushed off and narrowly avoided being kicked in the eye as he pulled himself up. Removing the shovels from the sack, I passed them up so he could drop them down on to the grass on the other side. He then placed the other bags on the wall behind him. Next up was Florence, who was pushed upwards by me while Ockham took hold of her wrists and pulled from above. Thankfully, though, what she lacked in height she also lacked in weight and so with the minimum of fuss, and no small amount of dexterity on her own part, she too was soon sitting on the wall, though rather than straddle it like Ockham, she opted for a more ladylike side-saddle approach. Bringing up the rear, I offered a hand up to Ockham, who almost jerked my wrist out of my arm.

He was the first into the cemetery, standing by to offer help should it be needed as I let Florence down. His interjection was not required, and he took the bags from me before I too dropped down once again into the city of the dead.

'Which way now?' asked Ockham as I pulled out a couple of lamps.

I pointed between the two trees ahead of us. 'Through there and to the left if I remember rightly.'

'I hope you do,' said Ockham, as he surveyed the various tomb-stones and grave slabs, only just visible in the murk. 'Christ, you could really get lost in this place – it's bad enough in the bloody daylight.' He checked himself and apologized to Florence for his profanity.

'Lord Ockham, I served in a military hospital for two years. I am no stranger to a little colourful language. Now, shall we move on?'

I smiled as I handed one of the lamps to Ockham, its flame now sputtering into life. 'Ladies, please. We have a job to do – shall we get on with it?'

'Lead the bloody way,' said Florence, straightening her cap and taking up the bag again.

Ockham let out a stifled laugh and followed, his lamp providing illumination for Florence's footfalls.

My navigation was spot on and within a very few minutes we were standing beside Brunel's grave. The earth had still not fully settled, the turf bowing upwards to form a slight mound, while here and there irregularities in the divots provided lingering evidence of my last visit to the site.

Ockham sat his lamp on a nearby table-top tomb. 'Nice to see they haven't yet got round to building one of these monstrous great tombstones over it. That wouldn't make for easy digging.'

'I think Brunel had something a little more modest in mind, but yes, we couldn't have left this much longer.'

'I'll say,' vouchsafed Ockham, 'I feel dead on my feet. It's going to be a long night.'

'Can we be certain of proceeding undisturbed?' asked Florence, taking in the nature of her new surroundings.

'We'll be fine,' I said confidently, as much to reassure myself as her. 'The gatehouse, even if the watchman isn't in the tavern, is about half a mile away, and nobody expects grave robbers in this day and age.' No sooner were the words out of my mouth than I realized they were almost exactly those spoken to me by William during our first nocturnal visit to the grave. The memory of him made me pause for a moment: how I wished he were with us now.

In contrast, Ockham found our situation rather amusing. 'We're the only grave robbers in history to try and put something in a grave rather than take something out.'

A good point, I thought, imagining those very words being spoken as our defence in a court of law. Eager to proceed, I took up a shovel. 'I'll cut the turf. You two can stack it over there. Try and keep the sods together, we need to leave this place as tidy as possible.'

I separated the turfs and eased them out on the point of the shovel, from where Ockham and Florence removed them by turn, carrying them the short distance to stack them. With the turf removed Ockham and I started digging, throwing the soil down on to a canvas sheet. We worked at opposite ends of the trench, pushing our shovels through soil that was thankfully still very loose in comparison with the surrounding earth. But despite these favourable conditions our task was handicapped by our fatigue. It wasn't long before our progress slowed considerably, even to the point where Florence, who until then had been holding a lamp to illuminate our labours, offered to take a turn. Ockham knew better than to argue, and so handed her the shovel while he took a short break. Florence took to the work as though she had been digging graves her entire life, her secret being not to overload the shovel, which I realized was exactly what I had been doing. After five minutes' break Ockham took my shovel and let me step from the hole which, alas, was still possible without too much effort.

Working up a sweat now, despite a slight chill in the air, Ockham asked if I'd brought any water. I had remembered to pack a small flask, and each of us took a gentle swig, knowing full well that we would have more need for it before we were done. Having already divested myself of my coat, I stripped off both my jacket and waistcoat, Ockham following suit. Florence, perhaps at last finding a limit to her pretence at being male, chose to go no further than her waistcoat, which like the rest of her clothes hung loosely from her slender frame. It took us little short of an hour to make the hole knee-deep, but digging in brief shifts was definitely the best way to proceed, and I was now sure that the additional effort provided by Florence was going to make all the difference between success and failure.

I knew we were really beginning to make progress when the pit became too deep for Florence to shovel spoil on to the surface. Eager to remain useful, she returned to holding a lamp over the trench, from where it cast our workspace into stark relief. One of us worked while the other took a break at their end of the trench, the stale air in the hole being far from conducive to heavy labour. I was beginning to have doubts about our ability to get all this soil back in the hole once the deed was done. Then the tip of my shovel struck the lid of the casket.

'My God, that's it. We've done it!' cried Ockham.

I proceeded to scrape the excess earth from the lid and throw it back up towards his feet. 'I've been here before,' I reminded him. 'Let's save the celebrations until we're patting down the turf.'

'Wise words indeed,' said a dreadfully familiar voice as the light suddenly dimmed.

I looked up to see someone standing behind Florence, her warning cries reduced to a whimper behind a hand held over her mouth.

'Perry!'

'Good evening, gentlemen. Surprised to see me?'

'I have to admit yes,' said Ockham coolly. 'We thought the *Great Eastern*'s propeller had done for you.'

Perry pressed his arm into the small of Florence's back, forcing her to take a step forward. The fact that we were entirely unarmed seemed to have escaped his notice, as he continued to shield himself as best he could behind her slight frame. 'I jumped into the river just before Brunel's hulk turned the boat to matchwood. It could be said that you can't keep a good man down – but then I thought the same about you after the yard fire.'

'More like the devil looking after his own,' I added bitterly. 'You're a damned coward, Perry, hiding behind others as usual.'

He pointed his pistol down towards me. 'Well, as I appear to have you at such disadvantage I suppose I can let the lady go.' Then into Florence's ear he hissed: 'Make so much as a whisper and your friends are dead men. Understand?'

She nodded her head as much as she was able.

'Very well. Stand over there and don't move.'

Still clutching the lamp, Florence backed away to the end of the trench, coming to a halt just above Ockham.

'Now, where is the device, Phillips? I know you haven't put it in there yet.' He directed the pistol towards the coffin beneath me.

'You mean you've been here all along?'

'Long enough.'

'And you let us dig this bloody great hole before making your move.'

'It seemed the sensible thing to do – after all, this hole may yet prove a very worthwhile investment of labour. At least from my point of view.'

'You're going to kill us regardless of whether you get the device or not, aren't you?'

'I am considering it. Now, where is it, in the bag?'

I nodded.

Crouching down, he opened the bag without taking his eyes or the pistol off me and pulled out the cloth-wrapped heart.

'Now all we need to do is retrieve the plans for the torpedo from Russell and we're back in business. Or should I say all *I* need to do; thanks to your actions it looks like Lord Catchpole will be dancing on the end of the rope before long. The Crown seems to take a dim view of what they are calling high treason.'

Perry unwrapped the device. 'Beautiful, isn't it?'

'It's cost enough, that's for sure.'

'Cheap at twice the price.'

'You heartless piece of shit.'

'Not any more,' scoffed Perry, as he waved the device before me. 'You call me heartless, but what are you doing, endangering a woman like this?'

'Don't hurt her, that's Florence Nightingale, for God's sake.'

He looked at her anew and grinned. 'I didn't recognize you in your fancy dress. So you're William Nightingale's little girl? Your father is a very stubborn man. He would have saved himself a lot of trouble if he'd sold that mill for the fair price offered. He must have been delighted when you ran off to the wars.'

'Yes, I am William Nightingale's daughter,' said Florence, matter-of-factly. 'But some people know me better as the Lady with the Lamp.'

With that she twisted from the waist and let go of the lamp from an outstretched arm. Like a shooting star the missile flashed across the sky above my head. Perry tried to dodge out of the way but it struck him in the left shoulder, where it shattered and fell to the ground. Kerosene flooded from the shattered reservoir and ignited against the wick, sending up a sheet of flame. The momentary conflagration drove him closer to the grave and so I grabbed him by the ankle and tried to pull him in, but he fell backwards, out of my reach. Opportunity lost, Ockham and I scrambled against the earth walls, desperately trying to get out of the hole, but given our fatigue, it wasn't easy. Florence got to Perry first, before he could regain his feet. Straining on my elbows and with one leg drawn up on to the trench edge, I watched helplessly as she tried to pull the gun from his grasp. He struck her with his free hand and she too fell to the ground.

His shoulder still smoking, Perry got to his feet just as I struggled to my own. He levelled the pistol at me and pulled back the hammer. 'I'm going to enjoy this,' he said.

I closed my eyes and waited for the impact. A shot rang out and when I looked again Perry was lurching towards me, his pistol falling to the ground and a hand clutched to his chest. He fell to his knees as if in prayer and then toppled backwards, his legs folded beneath him.

I rushed over to Florence, who was shaken but otherwise unhurt and crouched down to cradle her head as she came round. 'That was quite a thing you just did.'

'How dare he underestimate me just because I'm a woman!'

I looked across to Perry, his body bent back like a folded knife. 'I don't think he's going to be underestimating anything from now on.'

The light from the second lamp, which was still perched where Ockham had left it, was momentarily dulled by someone walking in front of it.

'Who the hell is that?' asked Ockham, now standing beside me.

I could barely believe my eyes as the figure revealed itself in the lamp's light. 'That, my friend, is Nathaniel Wilkie.'

I didn't know whether to laugh or cry. 'I thought you were in America, Nate?'

He walked towards me and then stopped beside Perry. 'Was this the man who killed my father?'

'As good as,' I said.

He looked down at me, his boyish features now settled into the handsome face of a young man. 'I never got on the boat. I couldn't just run away like that and let them get away with it.'

Ockham handed me a jacket, which I rolled up and placed under Florence's head. 'You mean you've been in London all this time?'

He nodded. 'On and off. Been keeping an eye on you. I knew you'd lead me to them eventually.'

Standing up, I realized he was much taller than when I'd last seen him. The foal had grown into his skin. 'So you're the one who has been following me round London!'

He nodded. 'And a merry dance it's been, sir. I'm only sorry I wasn't better at it. Perhaps if I'd been here during your first visit things might have come to a quicker end.'

I put a hand on the young man's shoulder. 'Nonsense, Nate, we owe you our lives, and for that I will be eternally grateful.'

Not quite able to muster a smile, he looked over to Perry once again. 'He got his just desserts, that's all.' Then he held out his hand. 'You can have this back now.'

I took the pistol from my guardian angel and traced a hand over the inscription on its barrel. My father would have been proud to see it put to such good use. But this was no time for sentiment. 'We still have work to do. I hope to God nobody heard the shot.'

Florence tried to regain her feet. 'No, stay there and rest. You've done more than enough, and we have another to help us now.'

I dropped back down into the trench, taking care not to land too heavily on the coffin. Ockham offered to hold the lamp on the end of a rope, but I assured him he wouldn't want to be anywhere near the edge of the grave, so following my instructions he suspended it from the shaft of a shovel lying across the trench. Taking the crowbar, I then set about prising the lid of the casket open. It was a two-part lid and so I directed my attentions to the half that would give access to the incumbent's torso. The timber cracked and splintered, the nails eventually giving away and releasing their bond. Before pulling open the lid I took a handkerchief from my pocket and tied it tightly around my nose and mouth. Giving the embedded lever a final jerk, I took hold of the edge and pulled, the hinges on the other side squealing in protest as the lid gave way.

I might as well have been opening the gates of hell, so terrible was the stench that was released. Despite my rudimentary precautions the noxiousness of the miasma almost knocked me backwards, and it took a few moments to bring my retching under control. Only just managing not to vomit, I stood up, banging my head on the lamp in the process, and signalled for Ockham to give me the bag, taking the opportunity to hold up my mask to take a precious few gulps of fresh air. But even outside the hole the smell was bad, and Ockham pinched his nose as he reached down to me.

It took some time to find a viable position that would not send me tumbling face first into the open coffin. I settled on my knees, upper body stretched over the opening and supported by a gloved hand resting against the splintered edge. To my relief, the shroud, which was blackened with decay, covered Brunel's face, and I had no intention of looking beneath it, though the depressions created by his eye sockets left little to the imagination. I concentrated on the torso, and taking up a scalpel from the bag set about making an incision, cutting down through the sternum and ripping up through the weakened ribs.

Exposure of the partially liquefied organs assailed my senses with a far from fresh assault, again forcing me back to the surface, where I sucked in more air. I was no stranger to the corruption which takes hold of the human body after death, but this was entirely different. I was operating at the very limits of my constitution.

'Give me the heart,' I gasped at Ockham, whose hand was firmly fixed over his nose and mouth.

Returning to work, the cause of all of this trouble resting between my knees, and unable to think of a more appropriate instrument, I picked up the crowbar and wedged it into the chest cavity. Using a similar action to that which had opened the coffin, I pushed the lever first to one side and then the other, creating a considerable gap between the severed ribs and the sternum. Relieved to discover that removal of the organs would be impossible as well as unnecessary, I shook the heart loose from its wrapping and without pausing pushed it through the gap. Withdrawal of the crowbar reduced the size of the gap, but I had to press against the ribs with my hand to close it entirely. A little uncertain about how to finish off, I covered the wound by resting the cloth, napkin-like, over the chest.

A few words may have been in order before I closed the coffin, but things being as they were I simply touched Brunel's forehead, closing my eyes for a moment before gently lowering the lid. After removing my soiled gloves and dropping them on to the casket, I passed the bag up to Ockham. Then he and Nate, taking an arm each, pulled me from the hole.

'Get the soil back in there' was all I was able to croak as I staggered away from the grave. It was good to see that Florence was back on her feet, and now it was she who expressed concern for my well-being while I sat on the edge of a grave slab and slowly regained my composure.

Ockham and Nate went to work with the shovels, throwing the spoil back into the hole. Our new recruit entered into the task with all the vigour of youth, immediately finding a natural rhythm and shovelling in at least three loads for every one of Ockham's, and any doubts I may have had about our ability to backfill quickly evaporated. Then I remembered Perry.

'Stop,' I cried, a little taken aback at how quickly the pile of earth was disappearing. Rushing over to his body, I put my fingers against his neck, checking for a pulse. 'Nate, take his legs.'

Nate wrapped his arms beneath Perry's bent knees and I took hold under the arms, his head lolling back into my lap. Walking backwards, I led the way to the grave. As soon as Nate was in position we tossed the body in, where it landed with a thud on the layer of earth now covering the coffin. Snatching the shovel from Ockham, I threw in a hefty load of soil.

'Ashes to ashes,' said Ockham with a grin.

Nate joined me and very soon another foot of earth lay in the trench.

Ockham sidled up to the grave and looked in. 'I trust the man was dead.'

'Well if he wasn't, he is now.'

Ockham looked aghast. 'Good God, doctor, remind me never to come to you if I'm feeling poorly!' Then he laughed and snatched the shovel back.

Just half an hour later and the hole had all but disappeared, the only problem being that a considerable volume of spoil still remained on the sheet, the addition of Perry's body having reduced the amount of space available by quite a degree.

I leant against the shovel and stated what was fast becoming the obvious: 'We're not going to get all of that in, but we've got to get rid of it somehow.'

Nate dropped his shovel. 'I'll be back in a minute,' he said before striding off. Very soon after we heard a squeaking noise, which quickly grew nearer. The lad reappeared with a wheelbarrow, albeit one in need of a drop or two of oil. 'There's a dug grave awaiting a coffin back there; nearly fell in it on my way here. No one's going to notice if the great mound of soil next to it is a bit higher come morning.'

'This boy's a godsend,' said Ockham, with whom I had to agree.

While we replaced the turf, Nate, still as energetic as when we began the task, filled the barrow and then trotted off into the dark behind it. Florence folded the sheet and, just as I was about to order our retreat, insisted that we congregate at the graveside and bow our heads. Finding the words that had evaded me while in the grave, she spoke a brief prayer, which included a heartfelt reference to William, who had been denied both funeral and grave.

Our business at last well and truly done, we hastened back over the wall and breathed a sigh of relief to find Sally still waiting for us.

# 38

If I had expected a dream-free sleep that night I was to be disappointed. Dropping off as soon as my head touched the pillow, I immediately found myself in that old familiar place, scrabbling around in never-ending pursuit of my fellow inmate. Everything was as before: the boilers, the burning metal and the scalding air. But there was no sense of disappointment – things were just as they always had been and would always be.

Or so it seemed. For, after I don't know how long, there was a change, and a new part of the metal maze opened itself before me. Crawling through a narrow tunnel, itself familiar enough, I happened upon a hatchway in the wall, the existence of which I had not before been aware of. I turned the handle and pushed the little door open, the hinges carrying it away from me into whatever space lay on the other side.

Squeezing myself through the aperture, I entered into a much larger compartment and, standing, which itself was a great relief, I looked up to see a shaft, square-walled and laddered, rise up above my head. So high was the thing that it was impossible to see all the way to the top, the iron ladder simply disappearing into a gloom that settled like low cloud at an indeterminate altitude.

Finding little merit in returning to the dreadfully confined space I had lately left behind, there seemed no option but to climb the ladder. As was always the case, the metal was uncomfortably warm to the touch.

Up I went, hand over hand, foot following foot. At one point I rested and looking down saw that the floor of the shaft had shrunk to a tiny illuminated square, the open hatchway just visible where it protruded into the space. Then the ascent continued into the gloom, from where it was impossible to see the hands in front of my face, let alone the floor so far below me.

Falling from the ladder never once entered my mind, even when my arms and legs began to ache almost beyond endurance. With still no end to my climb in sight I paused once again, holding on with just one hand then the other as I tried to shake its partner back into life. It was then that a slight vibration coming up through the ladder was joined by the sound of someone climbing up behind me. I doubled my effort and continued upward.

For the first time I could recall the metal did not feel hot, or even warm to the touch. Pausing momentarily to take stock of this sensation, I once again heard the sound of feet striking against the rungs below me. Reinvigorated by the drop in temperature, which was far from uncomfortable, I carried on upwards.

Another twenty feet or so and my hand, raised to pull me on to the next rung, came in contact with an obstruction. There, just above my head, a hatchway signalled the top of the ladder. Finding the handle, I took a step down, just in case it opened downward rather than up, and pulled the latch to one side. Nothing happened. So, stepping back up a rung, I put my shoulder against the hatch and, straightening my knees, applied all the upward pressure of which I was capable. Begrudgingly, the hatch gave and began to open upwards.

Light flooded through a crack, which quickly became a gap and then a skylight as the door of the hatch fell back on its hinges. The cool breeze ruffled my hair and began to soothe the stinging sensation in my eyes. Advancing upward just one more rung was enough to put my head and shoulders out through the hatch, from where I saw the deck stretching out before me. Freeing my arms,

I pulled myself out, and lay there on my back, looking up at the masts and beyond them to the clear blue sky.

On shaking legs I hobbled over to the railing and from there looked out over the sea, as blue and calm as the sky above. Tears trickled down my cheeks and I turned to see Ockham pulling himself from the hatchway. I stepped back and looked down to see the whites of his eyes shining out from a face blackened with coal dust. He took my outstretched hand and with one last effort was also free, standing beside me on the deck of Brunel's great ship. He too was on the verge of full collapse and so I guided him to the rail, where he could find support, and there we stood, side by side, watching the gulls as they traced low arcs over the water.

# Postscript

For the first time in months, I woke feeling refreshed and ready to face the day. To my everlasting relief the dream was never again to haunt my sleep, though at times I did find myself on the deck of the great ship, taking the sea air and stretching my legs on its expansive promenade.

I should perhaps regard this as a happy ending to my story, but not everything worked out the way I would have liked. It would be nice to say that my love for Florence blossomed but, alas, I knew all along that this could never be. Though I do not doubt that she loved me also, and perhaps loves me still, her devotion to her work was marriage enough for her. A year on from its opening, her nursing school is a great success and she is mother in kind to all of her students.

I did see Tarlow once more. The dog was indeed grateful for his bone and he sought me out to thank me for the tip-off about Catchpole and to tell me he'd been made a chief inspector for his part in the affair. After our brief conversation I remained none the wiser as to how much he really knew about my role in the 'River Angels' case, though it was undoubtedly more than the newspaper which had coined the term when the story of the bodies in the Thames finally broke. Of course he took the credit for solving that one as well, the sly dog.

My own career did not weather the storm so well. There was no question of my return to the hospital, not after all that had happened. Perhaps if I had thrown myself on Brodie's mercy he would have accepted me, like the prodigal son, back into the fold, but the place carried with it too many associations, too many ghosts.

And so I returned to my father's house and took over his practice, staying long enough to deliver my sister's child, whom she named after me. But the pace of life was far too slow and I soon found myself yearning for pastures new. At first I tried to ignore these urges but in time they overwhelmed me.

To Lily's great distress, but eventually with her blessing, I sailed for this country aboard the *Great Eastern*, leaving Liverpool docks and arriving in New York ten days later. There were times during the crossing when I would catch a glimpse of Ockham, taking a break from the engine room, where his role as a ship's engineer kept him voluntarily confined for much of the time. On these rare occasions words for some reason seemed superfluous and so we would simply exchange a nod before going about our business.

Not much more than a year has passed since my arrival in the New World and my skills have ensured that making a living has not been a problem. Quickly tiring of a metropolis which perhaps reminded me too much of London, I took to travel, dispensing my services in small towns which at times made my native village seem like a city in comparison.

Then, not long after, the war that Catchpole had predicted broke out and turned the nation against itself. Soldiers dressed in grey fought those dressed in blue; neighbours called one another enemy and the storm of battle swallowed all in its path.

Although Catchpole wasn't around to see it, having committed suicide just days before his trial, the North did impose a naval blockade on Confederate ports and, despite the stubborn efforts of blockade runners, some of them sailing out of Liverpool, the export of cotton has all but ceased. Whether Russell's torpedo, powered by Brunel's device, would have made any difference is a matter of speculation and perhaps best left to future historians, but what is certain is that there will be a lot more suffering before this war is over.

For a time I tried to avoid the war, but I am my father's son and so here I am, dressed in the uniform of a Union army surgeon, operating on yet another poor victim of the dreadful slaughter which yesterday took place on the banks of the Bull Run, near a small railway junction called Manassas. The battle went badly for us and the army, along with those civilians foolish enough to think battle a spectator sport, were chased most of the way back to Washington, DC.

But this is not just anyone lying before me, with a bullet lodged in his side. His is a face I know. His fellows-in-arms tell me that Nate had been among the first to enlist in their rifle company, his thirst for adventure entirely unquenched by his experiences back in England.

Removal of the ball should not be too much of a problem, but whether he survives the infection, which takes away so many of these young men, and makes it to the end of the week, will be entirely in the lap of the gods. Taking a respite from my labours, I take up a week-old copy of the *New York Times*, which in the absence of its longer-established namesake I have taken to reading whenever I can get hold of it. Among the war news, which bears little resemblance to the terrible reality, another story has caught my eye: 'Body of woman pulled from Hudson.' I probably wouldn't give it a second thought were it not for the next line: 'Organs removed – police hunt lunatic.'

Meanwhile, thousands of miles to the east, Brunel's great ship plies her course, straight and true, with all her engines pounding. I know – I can feel them in my heart.